A Mad Passion

Heart's Temptation Book One

By
Scarlett Scott

A Mad Passion
Heart's Temptation Book One

All rights reserved.
Copyright © 2016 by Scarlett Scott
Published by Happily Ever After Books, LLC
Print Edition

ISBN: 978-1523896103

Cover Design by Wicked Smart Designs

This book or any portion thereof may not be reproduced or used in any manner whatsoever without the express written permission of the publisher except for the use of brief quotations in a book review.

The unauthorized reproduction or distribution of this copyrighted work is illegal. No part of this book may be scanned, uploaded, or distributed via the Internet or any other means, electronic or print, without the publisher's permission. Criminal copyright infringement, including infringement without monetary gain, is punishable by law.

This book is a work of fiction and any resemblance to persons, living or dead, or places, events, or locales, is purely coincidental. The characters are productions of the author's imagination and used fictitiously.

For more information, contact author Scarlett Scott.
www.scarlettscottauthor.com

A lost love
Seven years ago, the Marquis of Thornton broke Cleo's heart, and she hasn't forgotten or forgiven him. But when she finds him standing before her at a country house party, as devastatingly handsome as ever, old temptations prove difficult to resist. One stolen kiss is all it takes.

A proper gentleman
Thornton buried his past and his feelings for Cleo long ago. He's worked diligently to become a respected politician with a reputation above reproach. The only trouble in his otherwise perfect life is that he can't resist the maddening beauty he never stopped wanting, no matter how devastating the cost.

A mad passion
Cleo is hopelessly trapped in a loveless marriage, and Thornton is on the cusp of making an advantageous match to further his political ambitions. The more time they spend in each other's arms, the more they court scandal and ruin. Theirs is a love that was never meant to be. Or is it?

Dedication

For A and S, my beautiful little miracles. And for my husband, who has taught me everything that love should be.

Chapter One

"A beautiful woman risking everything for a mad passion."
– Oscar Wilde

Wilton House, September 1880

CLEO, COUNTESS SCARBROUGH, decided there had never been a more ideal moment to feign illness. The very last thing she wanted to do was traipse through wet grass at a country house party while her dress improver threatened to crush her. Not to mention the disagreeable prospect of being forced to endure the man before her. What had her hostess been thinking to pair them together? Did she not know of their history? A treasure hunt indeed.

Seven years and the Marquis of Thornton hadn't changed a whit, damn him. Tall and commanding, he was arrogance personified standing amidst the other glittering lords and ladies. Oh, perhaps his shoulders had broadened and she noted fine lines 'round his intelligent gray eyes. But not even a kiss of silver strands earned from his demanding career in politics marred the glorious black hair. It was most disappointing.

After all, there had been whispers following the Prime Minister's successful Midlothian Campaign that a worn-out Thornton would retire from politics and his unofficial position as Gladstone's personal aid altogether. But as far as she could discern, the man staring down upon her was the same insufferably handsome man who had betrayed her. Was it so much to ask that he'd at least become plump about the middle?

Truly. A treasure hunt? Gads and to think this was the most anticipated house party of the year. "I'm afraid I must retire to my chamber," she announced to him. "I have a megrim."

Just as she began to breathe easier, Thornton ruined her reprieve. His sullen mouth quirked into a disengaged smile. "I'll escort you."

"You needn't trouble yourself." She hadn't meant for him to play the role of gentleman. She just wanted to be rid of him.

Thornton's face was an impenetrable mask. "It's no trouble."

"Indeed." Dismay sank through her like a stone. There was no way to extricate herself without being quite obvious he still set her at sixes and sevens. "Lead the way."

He offered his arm and she took it, aware that in her eagerness to escape him, she had just entrapped herself more fully. Instead of staying in the safe, boring company of the other revelers, she was leaving them at her back. Perhaps a treasure hunt would not have been so terrible a fate.

An uncomfortable silence fell between them, with Cleo aware the young man who had dizzied her with stolen kisses had aged into a cool, imperturbable stranger. For all the passion he showed now, she could have been a buttered parsnip on his plate.

She told herself she didn't give a straw for him, that walking a short distance just this once would have no effect on her. Even if he did smell somehow delectable and not at all as some gentlemen did of tobacco and horse. No. His was a masculine, alluring scent of sandalwood and spice. And his arm beneath her hand felt as strongly corded with muscle as it looked under his coat.

"You have changed little, Lady Scarbrough," Thornton offered at last when they were well away from the others, en route to Wilton House's imposing façade. "Lovely as ever."

"You are remarkably civil, my lord," she returned, not patient enough for a meaningless, pleasant exchange. She didn't wish to cry friends with him. There was too much between them.

His jaw stiffened and she knew she'd finally irked him. "Did you think to find me otherwise?"

"Our last parting was an ugly one." Perverse, perhaps, but she wanted to remind him, couldn't bridle her tongue. She longed to grab handfuls of his fine coat and shake him. What right did he have to appear so smug, so handsome? To be so self-assured, refined, magnetic?

"I had forgotten." Thornton's tone, like the sky above them, remained light, nonchalant.

"Forgotten?" The nerve of the man! He had acted the part of lovelorn suitor well enough back then.

"It was, what, all of ten years past, no?"

"Seven," she corrected before she could think better of it.

He smiled down at her as if he were a kindly uncle regarding a pitiable orphaned niece. "Remarkable memory, Lady Scarbrough."

"One would think your memory too would recall such an occasion, even given your advanced age."

"How so?" He sounded bored, deliberately overlooking her jibe at his age which was, if she were honest, only thirty to her five and twenty. "We never would have suited." His gray eyes melted into hers, his grim mouth tipping upward in what would have been a grin on any other man. Thornton didn't grin. He smoldered.

Drat her stays. Too tight, too tight. She couldn't catch a breath. Did he mean to be cruel? Cleo knew a great deal about not suiting. She and Scarbrough had been at it nearly since the first night they'd spent as man and wife. He had crushed her, hurt her, grunted over her and gone to his mistress.

"Of course we wouldn't suit," she agreed. Still, inwardly she had to admit there had been many nights in her early marriage where she had lain awake, listening for Scarbrough's footfalls, wondering if she hadn't chosen a Sisyphean fate.

They entered Wilton House and began the lengthy tromp to its Tudor revival styled wing where many of the guests had been situated. Thornton placed a warm hand over hers. He gazed down at her with a solemn expression, some of the arrogance gone from his features. "I had not realized you would be in attendance, Lady Scarbrough."

"Nor I you." She was uncertain of what, if any, portent hid in his words. Was he suggesting he was not as immune as he pretended? She wished he had not insisted upon escorting her.

As they drew near the main hall, a great commotion arose. Previously invisible servants sprang forth, bustling with activity. A new guest had arrived and Cleo recognized the strident voice calling out orders. Thornton's hand stiffened over hers and his strides increased. She swore she overheard him mumble something like 'not yet, damn it', but couldn't be sure. To test him, she stopped. Her heavy skirts swished front then back, pulling her so she swayed into him.

Cleo cast him a sidelong glance. "My lord, I do believe your mother is about to grace us with her rarified presence."

He growled, losing some of his polish like a candlestick too long overlooked by the rag. "Nonsense. We mustn't tarry. You've the headache." He punctuated his words with a sharp, insolent yank on her arm to get her moving.

She beamed. "I find it begins to dissipate."

The dowager Marchioness of Thornton had a certain reputation. She was a lioness with an iron spine, an undeterred sense of her own importance and enough consequence to cut anyone she liked. Cleo knew the dowager despised her. She wouldn't dare linger to incur her wrath were it not so painfully obvious the good woman's own son was desperate to avoid her. And deuce it, she wanted to see Thornton squirm.

"Truly, I would not importune you by forcing you to wait in the hall amidst the chill air," he said, quite stuffy now, no longer bothering to tug her but pulling her down the hall as if he were a mule and she his plow.

The shrill voice of her ladyship could be heard admonishing the staff for their posture. Thornton's pace increased, directing them into the wrong wing. She was about to protest when the dowager called after him. It seemed the saint still feared his mother.

"Goddamn." Without a moment of hesitation, he opened the nearest door, stepped inside and pulled her through with him.

Cleo let out a disgruntled 'oof' as she sank into the confines of whatever chamber Thornton had chosen as their hiding place. The door clicked closed and darkness descended in the cramped quarters.

"Thornton," trilled the marchioness, her voice growing closer.

"Your—" Cleo began speaking, but Thornton's hand over her mouth muffled the remainder of her words. She inhaled, startled by the solid presence of his large body so close behind her. Her bustle crushed against him.

"Hush, please. I haven't the patience for my mother today."

He meant to avoid the dragon for the entire day? Did he really think it possible? She shifted, discomfited by his nearness. Goodness, the little room was stifling. Her stays pinched her again. Did he need to smell so divine?

"Argnnnthhwt," she replied.

She needed air. The cramped quarters dizzied her. Certainly it wasn't the proximity of her person to Thornton that played mayhem with her senses. Absolutely not. The ridiculous man simply had to take his hand from her mouth.

Why, he was nearly cutting off her air. She could scarcely breathe.

Thornton didn't seem likely to oblige her, so she resorted to tactics learned from growing up with a handful of sisters who were each more than a handful themselves. She decided not to play fair and licked his palm. It was a mistake, a terrible one and not just because it was unladylike but because he tasted salty and sweet. He tasted rather like something she might want to nibble. So she did the unpardonable. She licked him again.

"Christ." To her mingled relief and disappointment, he removed his hand. "Say a word and I'll throttle you."

Footsteps sounded in the hall just beyond the closed door. If Cleo had been tempted to end their ruse before, her sudden reaction to Thornton rattled her too much to do so now. She kept mum.

"Perhaps you are mistaken?" Thornton's sister, Lady Bella ventured, sounding meek.

"Don't be an idiot, Bella," the dowager snapped. "I know my own son when I see him. All your novels are making you addle-pated. How many times must I implore you to assert yourself at more improving endeavors like needlepoint? Women should not be burdened by knowledge. Our constitutions are too delicate."

Cleo couldn't quite stifle a snicker. The situation had all the elements of a comedy. All that yet remained was for the dowager to yank open the door so Cleo and Thornton would come tumbling out.

"You smell of lavender," he muttered in her ear, an accusation.

So what if she did? It was a lovely, heady scent blended specifically for her. Lavender and rose geranium, to be precise. "Hold your breath," she retorted, "if you find it so objectionable."

"I don't."

"Then what is the problem, Thornton?"

"I find it delicious."

Delicious. It was a word of possibility, of improbability, improper and yet somehow...seductive. Enticing. Yes, dear heaven, the man enticed her. She leaned into his solid presence, her neck seeking. Even better, her neck's sensitive skin found his hungry mouth.

He tasted her, licking her skin, nipping in gentle bites, trying, it would seem, to consume her like a fine dessert. His hands anchored her waist. Thornton pulled her back against him, all semblance of hauteur gone. Her dress improver cut viciously into her sides.

She didn't care. She forgot about his mother. Their quarrel and complicated past flitted from her mind. Cleo reached behind her with her right arm and sank her fingers into his hair. He stilled, then tore his lips from her neck. Neither of them moved. Their breaths blended. Thornton's hands splayed over her bodice, possessive and firm.

"This is very likely a mistake," he murmured.

"Very likely so," she agreed and then pressed her mouth to his.

He kissed her as she hadn't been kissed in years. Strike that. He kissed her as she hadn't been kissed in her lifetime, deep and hard and consuming. He kissed her like he wanted to claim her, mark her. And she kissed him back with all the passion she hadn't realized she possessed. Dear heavens, this was not the political saint who took her mouth with such force but the sinner she'd once known. Had she thought him cold?

Thornton twisted her until her back slammed against the door with a thud. His tongue swept into her mouth. Her hands gripped his strong shoulders, pulling him closer. An answering ache blossomed within her. Somehow, he found his way under her skirts, grasping her left leg at the knee and hooking it around his lean hip. Deliberate fingers trailed up her thigh beneath three layers of fabric, finding bare skin. He skimmed over lacy drawers, dipping inside to tease her.

When he sank two fingers inside her, she gasped, yanking back into the door again. It rattled. Voices murmured from far away in the hall. "Thornton," she whispered. "We should stop."

He dropped a hot kiss on her neck, then another. "Absolutely. This is folly."

Then he belied his words by shifting her so her body pressed against his instead of the door. She no longer cared why they should stop. Her good intentions dissipated. Her bodice suddenly seemed less snug and she realized he had undone a few buttons. Heavens. The icy man of moments ago bore no resemblance to the man setting her body aflame. Scarbrough had never touched her this way, had never made her feel giddy and tingly, as if she might fly up into the clouds.

Scarbrough. Just the thought of her husband stiffened her spine. Hadn't she always sworn to herself she would not be like him? Here she was, nearly making love in who knew what manner of chamber with Thornton, a man she didn't even find pleasant. The man, to be specific, who had betrayed and abandoned her. How could she be so wanton and foolish to forget what he'd done for a few moments of pleasure?

She pushed him away, breathing heavy, heart heavy. "We must stop."

"Why must we?" He caressed her arms, wanting to seduce her again.

"My husband."

"I don't hear him outside the door."

"Nor do I, but I am not a society wife even if my conduct with you suggests otherwise. I do not make love with men in closets at country house parties. I don't fall to his level."

"Madam, your husband is a louse. You could not fall to his level were you to roll in the hay with every groom in our hostess' stable and then run naked through the drawing room."

She stiffened. "What do you know of him?"

"Plenty."

"I doubt you do." The inescapable urge to defend her wastrel, blackguard husband rose within her. How dare Thornton be so arrogant, so condescending when he himself had committed the same sins against her? And had he not just been on the verge of making love to a married woman in a darkened room? He was no better.

He sighed. "Scarbrough's got scads of women on the wrong side of the Park in St. John's Wood. It's common knowledge."

Of course it was, but that didn't make it any easier to hear. Especially not coming from Thornton, the man she'd jilted in favor of Scarbrough. "I'm aware Scarbrough is indiscreet, but that has little bearing on you and me in this moment. This moment should never have happened."

"We are once again in agreement, Cleo." His voice regained some of its arrogance. "However, it did happen."

Her name on his lips startled her, but she didn't bother taking him to task for it. After the intimacies she had just allowed, it would be hypocritical. She wished she could see him. The darkness became unbearable.

"How could you so easily forget your own sins? You had your pretty little actress all the while you claimed to love me."

He said nothing. Silence extended between them. It was obstinate of her, but she wanted him to deny it. Thornton did not.

"Aren't there orphans about somewhere you should be saving?" She lashed out, then regretted her angry words. That was badly done of her. But this, being in Thornton's arms after what he'd done…it went against the grain.

"I think you should go," she added.

"I would if I could fight my way past your bloody skirts.

There's no help for it. Either you go first or we go together."

"We can't go together! Your insufferable mother may be lurking out there somewhere."

"Then you must go first."

"I shall precede you," she informed him.

"I already suggested as much. Twice, if you had but listened." He sounded peeved.

The urge to stamp her foot hit her with fierce persistence. "You are a vexing man."

"And you, my love, are a shrew unless your mouth is otherwise occupied."

She gasped. "How dare you?"

"Oh, I dare lots of things. Some of them, you may even like." His voice had gone sinful and dark.

The dreadful man. She drew herself up in full countess armor. "I'm leaving now."

Then he ruined her consequence by saying, "Lovely. Though you might want to fasten up your bodice before you go. I should think it terribly difficult to convince my mother we were talking about the weather when your finer bits are on display."

Her finer bits? It was the outside of enough. She slapped his arm. "Has the Prime Minister any idea what a coarse scoundrel you are? None of my…person would be on display if you hadn't pulled me into the room and accosted me."

"You were well pleased for a woman being accosted," he pointed out, smug.

She hated him again, which was really for the best. He was too much of a temptation, too delicious, to borrow his word, and she was ever a fool for him. "You're insufferable."

"So I've been told."

Cleo gave him her back and attempted to fasten her buttons. Drat. She pulled. She held her breath. She tugged her bodice's stiff fabric again. The buttons wouldn't meet their moorings. "Did you undo my lacings?" she demanded, realization dawning on her.

"Perhaps." Thornton's voice had gone wistful. Sheepish, almost.

Good heavens. How did he know his way around a woman's undergarments so well he could get her undone and partially unlaced all while kissing her passionately? Beneath his haughty exterior still lay a womanizer's heart.

There was no help for it now. She couldn't tight-lace herself. "I require some assistance," she mumbled.

"What was that?"

Cleo gritted her teeth. "I can't lace myself."

"Would a 'please' be in order?"

"You're the one who did the damage. It seems reasonable that you should repair it."

"Perhaps I can slip past your voluminous skirts after all," he mused.

"Please help me," she blurted.

"Turn around," he ordered.

Cleo spun, reluctant to face him again. She could barely see him in the murkiness, a tall, imposing figure. His hands slipped inside her bodice, expertly finding the lacings he had loosened.

"Breathe in," he told her.

She did and he pulled tightly, cinching her waist to a painful wasp silhouette once more. "Thank you. I can manage the buttons."

He spun her about and brushed aside her fingers. "I'll get them." She swore she heard a smile in his voice. "After all, it only seems reasonable I repair the damage I've done."

"Fine then." His breath fanned her lips and she could feel his intense gaze on her. She tilted her head to the side to ease her disquiet at his nearness. Was it just her imagination, or did his fingers linger at the buttons nearest her bosom?

"There you are." Thornton fastened the last one, brushing the hollow of her throat as he did so.

She closed her eyes and willed away the desire that assaulted her. This man was not for her. He ran the backs of his fingers along her neck, stopping when he cupped her jaw.

"Thank you," she whispered again.

"You're most welcome," he said, voice low.

The magnetism between them was inexorable, just as it had been before. Despite the intervening years, despite all, she still recalled the way he had made her feel—weightless and enchanted, as though she had happened upon Shakespeare's moonlit forest in *A Midsummer Night's Dream*.

His thumb brushed over her bottom lip. "If you don't go, I'll undo all the repairing I've just done."

She knew he warned himself as much as he warned her. Sadness pulsed between them, a mutual acknowledgment their lives could have turned up differently. So many unspoken words, so much confusion lingered.

"I must go," she said unnecessarily. She was reluctant to leave him and that was the plain truth of it. "I find my megrim has returned."

With that, she left, returning to the hall, to sunlight streaming in cathedral windows. More importantly, she hoped, she returned to sanity.

Chapter Two

THE MISSIVE WAITING in each guest's chamber that night was an invitation to a dinner *en plein air*. Lady Cosgrove, their hostess, had transformed her Middle Ages inspired banquet hall into an outdoor seascape. The effect was masterful. Great curtains painted to appear as ocean waves and sand had been hung over the walls, pooling in ethereal beauty to the floor. Candles gave a soft yellow glow from a table littered with seashells, fresh flowers and long mirrors to reflect light as if it were water. The gas lights on the walls hadn't been lit on account of the billowing curtains and an otherworldly sheen enveloped the entire room.

Cleo had been seated next to Thornton, much to her dismay. The man's presence was distracting enough without his divine scent making its way to her nose each time he shifted. No man had a right to smell that heavenly.

The Earl of Ravenscroft sat across from her, with her younger sister Tia to her left. The Duke of Claridge and her older sister Helen sat to Ravenscroft's right. Cleo wondered at Lady Cosgrove's placement. Thankfully, at least, the draconian dowager Lady Thornton was seated far away with her daughter in what may have been another kingdom for the distance between them. It suited Cleo fine. The last thing she needed was the interference of the dowager to increase her discomfort. The woman's son was punishment enough.

"I missed you during our hostess's games this afternoon, Lady Scarbrough," Claridge said, giving her a conspiratorial glance.

Her face flamed. She took a healthy sip of her wine to compose herself before answering. "Indeed. I'm sorry to have missed the festivities. I regret to say I was indisposed."

"Are you feeling much improved, my lady?" Thornton asked, solicitous. To the casual observer, he probably appeared unconcerned, even cool.

"Yes, though I had quite a harrowing afternoon," she replied, unable to keep a tart edge from her voice.

"Do tell." Thornton affected boredom like no other could.

She yearned to kick him beneath the table. "A terrible attack of the megrims."

"I hope all is well." Claridge put himself back into the conversation.

Cleo smiled at him with too much warmth. He was handsome in a thoroughly English way and had been making polite overtures to her for over a season. "I'm much improved indeed."

The company remained silent but for the clattering of silverware on plates and some murmurings down the table. Thornton bumped her foot with his. When she shot him an annoyed glance, however, he ignored her, eating his roast pheasant as though nothing untoward had occurred.

"I say, where were you this afternoon, Thornton?" Claridge asked.

Cleo hurried to answer before Thornton could. "He was kind enough to escort me back to the main hall. After that, I expect he headed for the library as he said he would. Did you find the volume of Chaucer you were seeking, my lord?" She aimed an inquiring glance at him.

"I certainly found what I was looking for," he responded, his tone mild but the undercurrent obvious to her.

"I'm delighted to hear it." Her smile felt pained. She truly hated him. This time, she did land a fairly solid kick in his shin. "The Parliament of Fowls, was it?"

A barely audible *oof* could be heard.

"Did you sneeze, my lord?" she asked him in feigned sweetness. "Perhaps you caught a chill."

"I daresay he wears the countenance of a man who has been kicked," Ravenscroft interceded.

"Kicked?" Claridge perked up. "By whom?"

"Fate?" Tia suggested in a honeyed voice. Bless her sister, always championing Cleo. She and Helen had been Cleo's sole friends during the darkest days of Thornton's betrayal and her marriage to Scarbrough.

"How so?" An intriguing smile flitted at the corners of Thornton's mouth.

Cleo wanted to kiss him. Oh dear. This wasn't good. How could she want him after what he had done to her? Was she a dullwit? A wanton? Perhaps both?

"Fate has kicked you into realizing you should cease being a hermit and rejoin society," Tia invented nicely. "Sometimes a sound proverbial kick is just the thing, I've discovered."

"Perhaps," Thornton said, all noncommittal perfection.

"Or you've been kicked by love," Ravenscroft added.

Cleo shot him a suspicious look. Why did she get the feeling the man knew more than he could or should? Had he seen them together? Had he spied her subtle kick beneath the table?

Ravenscroft returned her gaze, appearing somehow innocent and fallen at the same time. He was a gorgeous creature, raven haired and blue eyed and bad to the core if his reputation was to be believed. Whispers abounded that he lived as a kept man.

"Have you never been kicked by love, my lady?" He spoke softly, his brilliant gaze upon her.

She swallowed. Not only had she been kicked—she had been run over like a lamb by a locomotive, first by Thornton, then by Scarbrough. "Yes. Have you?"

He gave her a crooked grin. "Half a dozen times or more, I'm afraid."

"Do speak up so we can all hear you, Ravenscroft," Thornton demanded.

Cleo turned back to him. "Churl," she muttered under her breath.

"Shrew," came his equally quiet invective.

She glared at him openly, no longer caring for propriety. He stared back with maddening calm. How could he be so imperturbable, the blighter?

"The scenery is lovely," she said, determined to ignore him for the duration of the evening and, very possibly, the next fortnight.

"Lady C. has outdone herself," Claridge agreed with a jovial air.

She turned her attention back to him. The duke was tall and slim, with golden hair, blue eyes and patrician features. In her experience, he was always polite and always at the best of society events. He neither smoked nor caroused with opera singers or actresses and was not addicted to cards or horseflesh. But he was not Thornton, a traitorous voice whispered. Heavens, what was she thinking? How could he make her want to forget?

She graced Claridge with her most becoming smile, determined to cast Thornton from her mind. "Do tell me about the renovations you've undertaken on your ancestral home, Your Grace," she implored.

"Christ," she heard Thornton grumble.

"I'd be happy to," Claridge began. "I've employed the architect Giles Courtenay and he's assured me we can restore the manor to its former glory…"

Cleo turned her attention to her meal and the soothing drone of the duke's voice. She very nearly forgot Thornton's presence altogether. But not quite.

LATER THAT EVENING found Cleo and her sisters in Helen's chamber, catching up on everything from the ancient Lord Gull's horrid Georgian era wig to Lady Smithton falling asleep during the soup course. Helen sprawled over the high poster bed with its elaborate carvings, Tia draped herself stylishly over a patterned chaise and Cleo had been stuck with a rather uncomfortable *Louis Quatorze* chair.

"I have decided," Tia announced like a monarchal decree, "that Cleo shall have an *affaire* this fortnight."

"Scandalous." Helen grinned. "And far too fast for our dear Cleo. She's not really the sort."

"Nor are you," Cleo pointed out in a tart tone. "I'll thank the both of you to keep your pointed noses from my business. I haven't the slightest desire to share a bed with anyone."

Tia raised a brow. Helen rolled her eyes.

"Well it isn't as if you even know what married love is like, Helen," Cleo shot back. "I'm not missing anything other than copious sweating, petting and noise-making. A lot of fuss for nothing, if you ask me." Making love had not been horrid before John, a wicked inner voice argued. It wasn't as if Thornton's advances earlier had failed to produce a heated response in her blood. But no, she would not entertain that thought now. There was happiness in loneliness.

"Scarbrough must be deadly dull." Tia waved her hand in a dismissive gesture. "It's a wonder he curries the favors of all those actresses the way he does. But they're after his coffers, I suppose and not his prowess."

Cleo reddened. She did not prefer to speak so plainly about John, married life, or his indiscretions. The topic was tired, a dead horse that didn't need to be kicked, least of all dragged through the middle of the village.

"Let's not talk about the blighter." Helen gave Cleo a sympathetic look. "He's not worth the breath. Though I still don't think Cleo is the sort to have an *inamorato*, Tia."

Cleo straightened her posture. "Why not?" She could be brazen when the need arose. Hadn't she flirted madly with Mr. Carey-Harthwaite last season? He'd been attractive and dashing in his own way. That had to count for something, even if their relationship had never been consummated.

"There was Mr. Carey-Addlepate," Tia pointed out, sounding a bit nasty.

"Harthwaite." Cleo was compelled to correct. "He wasn't that much of a dullard." True, he had been very interested in the cut of his coat and had often been boring and self-important. Not to mention overly fond of his hair, even if it was a glorious flaxen and prettier than her own.

"He was stupid," Tia said with her typical bluntness.

"A bore," Helen added.

"An original," Cleo argued.

"Originals are female, never male. Tell her, Helen."

Helen appeared aggrieved. "Original is a title appropriate to women only, I'm afraid. I love you, Cleo, but truly. Addlepate earned his diminutive the hard way and he outreached himself with you. His grandfather was in trade."

"Moreover," Tia sounded triumphant, "Carey-Babblethwaite does not an *affaire* make."

"Leave poor Mr. Carey-Harthwaite out of it." Cleo rose from her chair. "I shan't stay here if the two of you insist on mucking about in my personal matters. There is a warm bed waiting for me only two doors down the hall and it would certainly trump sitting here in a blasted uncomfortable chair listening to the two of you plot."

Tia pooh-poohed. "Nonsense."

"I don't have the slightest desire to take up a lover. My life is fulfilling just as it is."

"Yes, of course it is," Tia drawled.

"That's harsh, Hypatia." Helen took her turn again. Then she ruined her admonishment by shimmying closer to the end of the bed. "Who do you think it should be?"

"No one." Cleo despaired. Must her sisters always be so vexing, so determined, so wrong-headed in their pursuit of happiness for her? "Tia, you've been widowed for two years. Why don't you find yourself a lover instead?"

Tia ignored Cleo's protest. "The Duke of Claridge is a handsome fellow. Then there's Ravenscroft, who's deliciously inappropriate and who else, Helen?"

Helen tapped her chin. "Who else indeed? I suppose we shall have to wait, as they say, and see."

"What you will see is an awful lot of puffed up society fellows who smell of tobacco and wear too much hair grease," Cleo sniffed.

"I have a feeling, dear sister, that you may be wrong," Helen said.

"Very wrong," Tia added, sounding smug. "I think I have just the man in mind."

Cleo rose from the chair, determined to put an end to the sisterly machinations for good. "Men are the last thing I want on my mind ever again. Now if you will excuse me? I must retire."

She left her sisters to their plotting and their gossip and escaped to the privacy of her chamber. Seeing Thornton, falling so easily into his power once more, shook her more than she cared to admit. Still, she had changed so much since those naïve days. It was difficult almost to reconcile herself with the painfully foolish girl she'd been. The awful, aching possession, the agony, all juxtaposed with the wonders of being touched and kissed and held by him…seemed distant and improbable as years had intervened. She'd begun to wonder if her grand love had been a fancy of youth.

Not so, she now found. Oh, it wasn't that she still loved Thornton. Not at all. Indeed, what she felt for him was rather sinful and altogether impure. She had mostly forgiven him, somewhere along the years, for leaving her to an empty life with John. She'd accepted responsibility for her own part in the debacle. She was not even certain the betrayal she thought he'd committed occurred entirely as John had then suggested.

Truly, they should have been able to meet here as impartial adults, perhaps even as two strangers. But it remained obvious neither of them could manage it. For her part, upon seeing Thornton, the old hurt lingered, a wound which had never healed.

Her hand crept to her midriff, empty beneath her rigid stays. Cleo scarcely allowed herself to think of the babe she'd lost so soon after her hasty marriage to John. Those had been dark days as her world came undone. Thornton, she recalled sternly, had been long gone, enjoying a holiday in America when it happened. He had never known, had never suffered over the loss.

John had been at his club as she miscarried. When he returned at half past nine in the morning from an entire night of gambling and drinking, he tapped her on the shoulder as she wept and informed her it was best she not have someone else's get anyway. Then he passed out on the bedroom floor. Losing the babe had been the worst and lowest moment of her life.

She extracted a handkerchief from her reticule and blew her nose. Being disrupted like this wouldn't do. She'd thought she had moved beyond painful memories. The fates had played a cruel game with her, bringing Thornton here and opening old doors long kept locked. Cleo was now in a different position, no longer blinded by her husband's facile tongue.

John, who had accused Thornton of the very same sin, had married her for her money. His grandfather withheld funds from John, knowing him for the wastrel he was. John enjoyed cards, loose women and drink, all of which required a fat purse. Cleo's large inheritance had been necessary, she'd learned, for him to uphold the lifestyle of a sporting gentleman about town.

Seven years ago John had been very adept at persuading her to believe in him. He no longer bothered to make the effort. He corresponded with her through the odd missive she thought likely scrawled by his tarts now that his secretary had quit. They always smelled of appalling perfume and contained excessive misspellings. She had not even seen him for at least a year. John kept a separate residence in London in addition to the house or two he kept for his paramours.

Given all, how was it, she demanded of herself with a burning inner rage, that her attraction to Thornton could be as potent as ever? Perhaps it was that she had become a rusty matron and so longed for the touch of a man it did not matter that Thornton did the touching.

No. It would not be prudent to prevaricate. There had been men in her past, Carey-Addlepate, for instance—drat her sisters for the name—but certainly none had stuffed her inside a dark closet and nearly made love to her. None had dared. She wouldn't have stood for it. Yet Thornton set her aflame and she didn't care if he acted a dog in the manger. She should be horrified by her conduct.

In a sense she was, of course. But in another sense she was…intrigued. He was infuriating and arrogant and altogether wrong for her. He had broken her heart seven years ago and skimmed a hand over her knickers as if no time had passed between them. She had allowed his conduct, enjoyed it even.

It was utter folly to let him back into her life again. This she knew. But she was altogether afraid she would not be able to keep him out. And that was the crux of the thing.

Chapter Three

CASTING MEN—PARTICULARLY THORNTON—FROM her mind would not prove easy when their hostess once more threw them together the very next day. Because they had both missed Lady Cosgrove's dubious treasure hunt, Thornton and Cleo had been partnered yet again in a Shakespeare recitation. The bad news officially arrived the next morning at breakfast.

"The scene shall be wonderful, I know," Lady C. confided to Cleo. Excitement flushed her cheeks. "You are to be Rosaline and Thornton is Biron."

She choked on the sip of chocolate she'd just taken. *Love's Labours Lost?* How could Lady Cosgrove not know of their past? There had been so much talk at the time, almost a scandal after the haste with which she'd married Scarbrough. Surely Lady C. must have heard the whispering. To ask Thornton to play the part of lovesick swain was exceedingly bold.

Cleo replaced her cup in its saucer with care and chose her words with equal intention. Her sisters, she knew, had been partnered with Ravenscroft and Claridge respectively, which left only two other late arrivals, Thornton's mother and sister. "I thought Lady Bella and I would make a splendid team."

"Just so, my dear, but…" Lady C. paused with dramatic verve and lowered her voice. "I'm afraid the dowager has requested she and Lady Bella be excused from the festivities. Apparently, the girl has stage fright."

"How horrible for her," Cleo murmured, glancing down

at her plate. How horrible for Cleo, too, to have to endure Thornton's company for the next two days.

"I dare say it must be debilitating and the poor girl is too timid to admit it."

"Oh?" Cleo looked back up at her hostess, who eyed her back with an unsettling expression.

Lady C.'s face cleared. "The dowager asked me not to mention it to Lady Bella on account of it distressing her."

"It is kind of the dowager to be so concerned for her daughter's welfare," she offered. It was bad of her, but she wished the dowager had not been as solicitous. How was she to bear being partnered with the marquis?

"Isn't it?" Her ladyship beamed. "I expect you and Lord Thornton will want to familiarize yourselves with the dialogue when he returns from his morning ride."

He was out riding, was he? Perversely, she thought he must still sit a horse like a true sportsman. He had the lean grace and muscular build that gave a man an excellent seat. She pictured him dressed in riding clothes, leaning over a black stallion, wind in his hair. In their furtive courtship, they had ridden together but a few times and yet she recalled so well how handsome he'd looked on his hunter.

She shook herself from the vision. "I'm sure there's no hurry."

"Don't be silly. You must have enough time to rehearse or I'll consider myself a failure as a hostess." Lady C. caught the attention of one of the servants stationed by the buffet. "Jones, run and fetch the copies of the script I set aside for Lady Scarbrough and Lord Thornton if you please."

With a bow, the young man left, taking with him any chance Cleo might have had to regain her sanity in the next two days. Lady Bella and the dowager entered the morning room then, with Tia and Helen close on their heels. Cleo had ever been the early riser in the family, with all the rest of the Harrington girls quite the slugabeds.

"Here are your sisters and Lady Bella herself," Lady C. announced, ignoring the dowager for a moment. "Oh yes and the marchioness, we mustn't forget. Good morning to you lot. I trust you found your chambers to your liking?"

"Indeed." The dowager sent Lady C. a frigid smile as she was seated at the table. "Although I dare say I missed my own dear bed at Marleigh Manor. Nothing quite like the comforts of one's home, as they say."

Lady C.'s gaze narrowed on the dowager. "Yes, I suppose they do say a great deal these days."

Cleo shifted uncomfortably in her chair. "The weather is lovely this morning, is it not?"

"I wouldn't know," the dowager clipped. "I haven't been outside as of yet."

"The sun does appear to be shining in the loveliest manner," Lady Bella chimed in with false brightness.

"It will be a good day for all manner of sport," Tia declared with a wicked glance at Cleo. "Wouldn't you say, dear sister?"

With great difficulty, Cleo swallowed her chocolate and schooled her features into a polite façade. "What sport did you have in mind, Tia dearest?"

"Why, hunting I should think." Tia turned to Helen and gave her an arch look. "What do you say, Helen?"

With a perfectly serious expression, Helen murmured, "Ideal weather for hunting, it seems."

Cleo knew her sisters. And she knew the hunting they suggested was for men and not the fox or the hare. If she could have reached them beneath the table, she would have delivered a sound kick to each of their saucy shins.

"I do so love the hunt," Lady C. declared, spearing a bit of kipper on her fork. "Don't you, Lady Thornton?"

"I've never had the constitution for it myself," the dowager replied in icy tones. "I find women engaging in male pastimes to be altogether vulgar and, one might even venture to say, *American*." She announced the last with great disgust.

"Why am I not surprised?" Lady C. quipped in low tones meant for Cleo's ears alone.

Cleo suppressed a smile and kept her eyes trained on her plate.

"I have heard, however," the dowager continued, "that you are quite the huntress, Lady Scarbrough."

Startled that Lady Thornton had even deigned to address her directly, Cleo glanced up. The elder woman watched her as if she were a smelly, dirty street urchin come to fleece her purse. "I am only passably fair, I should think," she answered with care, "having had little practice."

The dowager sniffed, her expression hardening. "Tut. That is not what I heard at all."

Cleo did not misunderstand the dowager's implication. "I believe you must have heard wrong, my lady." Her voice had acquired a touch of steel. She was not about to allow this woman to trample roughshod all over her. "You do know what they say about the dangers of believing common fame. I find in this polite society of ours, one rarely hears truth unless one hears it from the source herself."

"Indeed." Lady Thornton inclined her head, her countenance glacial.

Lady Bella cleared her throat. "I've been admiring your dress, Lady Scarbrough."

"Thank you, my dear." Cleo eyed her with sympathy. It was clear the dear girl felt the need to make amends for her mother's ill manners. She may as well give up on that lost cause, however. As far as she could discern, nothing would improve Lady Thornton's temperament save a needle and thread to sew her mouth closed. At least that way, one wouldn't be forced to listen to her dreadful remarks.

"I am of the opinion of Mrs. Haweis," the dowager interjected, dropping the name of the well-known arbiter of taste and ladies' fashion, "that pale green has a propensity to make fair ladies look like corpses. However, I'm sure you do it suitable justice, Lady Scarbrough."

Cleo fought the urge to sigh. Between company like the dowager, the matchmaking of her sisters and the too-clever hands of a certain marquis she could not quite bring herself to hate as she ought, it was going to be a long fortnight. A terribly long fortnight.

CLEO STOOD BEFORE Thornton in a sitting room off the library, a quiet, less opulent chamber meant for family rather than guests. He hadn't changed from his riding clothes and he smelled of the outdoors, the fresh scent of moss, woods and clean air. Mud specked his boots, his black hair carelessly wind tossed. He was, in two words, sinfully tempting.

At the moment, however, he appeared immune to her presence. A peeved expression marred his face. Lady Cosgrove had arranged their rehearsal, offering up the private room and making certain a footman directed Thornton to Cleo immediately upon his return. It had perhaps been an unwise decision, but she had not wanted to affront the gracious lady.

She decided to strive to be pleasant. "Good morning, my lord."

"Good morning, my lady." He gave her an abbreviated bow and then spoiled the effect by opening his mouth again. "Is there a reason I'm brought to your heels like a mongrel?"

Cleo sucked in a breath. "I'm sure you smell of one, having been roaming about the countryside for the better part of the morning. As for why you should feel like a mongrel, I can't say, unless you've been dallying with other female guests in darkened rooms recently."

Thornton gritted his teeth. "I think we both agree our mutual enmity makes the task Lady C. has set upon us impossible."

"Enmity? I adore you, my lord," she drawled, determined to meet him, verbal stride for verbal stride. He would not win a match of rapier wits with her.

"What, do tell, has her esteemed ladyship selected for our farce?" he demanded, crossing his arms over his chest.

It was a delightfully broad chest, she noted against her will, and strong too. After all, she had been intimately pressed against it just yesterday. Probably, she should be sent to the asylum at Broadmoor. Her body was betraying her mind.

"I do not like this any more than you." She felt compelled to remind him. He was not the only suffering party in their hostess's madcap plans.

He eyed her with an unconvinced glare. "For a woman professing to be in vehement disagreement, you certainly capitulated with alarming rapidity."

Cleo narrowed her gaze. "That is merely because I do not wish to be rude to our hostess."

"We waste time," he decreed, imperious as ever. His lips thinned with impatience. Gone was the passionate lover of yesterday.

Indeed, she began to wonder if her heated imagination had not dreamt the entire episode. It infuriated and yet somehow intrigued her that he could be so warm and then so cold, so remote.

"Act two, scene one," she said. "Happily, it is a scene in which Rosaline delivers a most deserving setdown to Biron." In that moment, she praised Lady C. for her choice. Really, it could not be more suited to reality.

She handed him his lines. "If you don't wish to make a fool of yourself, you ought to practice."

"I dare say I've already done that," he muttered, taking the papers from her.

Cleo pretended she hadn't heard him. "Would you prefer to study on your own first?"

"No, damn it, I wouldn't." Thornton ran a hand through

his already mussed hair.

Cleo moved to the window, a safe and respectable distance from him. She trained her gaze on the scene Lady C. had provided them. Not looking at him, she knew, would make the effort more pleasant. "Very well. Your lines are first, Thornton."

He muttered something that sounded like 'damned meddlesome biddy', then cleared his throat before beginning. "'Hear me, dear lady. I have sworn an oath.'"

She sighed and was forced by habit to glance up at him. "No, you've the wrong lines. You are not the king, even if your ego suggests otherwise."

"Tut." He gave her a sullen expression. "You needn't be a shrew over it."

"Your mother says 'tut', you know," she pointed out in her most amenable tone. "It quite makes you sound like a doughty old matron, which is, one may suppose, a status very near to that of political saint. You are without the dress and heaving bosom, of course."

Thornton's nostrils actually flared. "As I said before, your tongue is far more appreciated when it is engaged in an activity other than speech, Countess."

A gentleman, a true gentleman, would never dare utter such vulgarity to a lady. Oh, he was a most vexing man, rigid and haughty at one turn and bawdy at another. And thoroughly appealing. She wanted to cross the room and kiss him or slap him. She wasn't certain which. This wouldn't do.

"Look to the star Lady C. marked for you," she directed him. "It will tell you where to begin."

"Can I not be the king?" He grinned. "I rather fancy the line 'your ladyship is ignorant.'"

"Tut," Cleo repeated in her most mocking tone.

"*Touché.*" His gray eyes warmed as they raked over her.

"Let us begin again." She smoothed a palm over her tiered skirt to calm herself.

"At this house party, or at the dialogue?"

Well, both really. How much simpler her life would currently be had she not feigned a megrim? Likely, she would have been partnered with the always elegant, always agreeable, always above reproach Duke of Claridge. Certainly, she would not be all odds and ends, her stomach tossed as a ship, her heart too fast, her flesh too warm, her dratted dress improver once again too cinched.

"The dialogue," she clarified, at last recalling his question. The man had the most unsettling, undesirable effect on her. "Let us begin the scene anew."

"Yes. Very well." He glanced down at the play. "'Did not I dance with you in Brabant once?' Brabant? You know, I've never been there. Where the devil is it?"

"Thornton!" She threw up a hand in frustration. "You've muddled the lines."

"Who gives a damn? We haven't an audience."

True, she mused. All the more reason for her to cleave to the window. "Yes, but one doesn't make interjections while one rehearses for a play."

"Perhaps one doesn't," he growled, "but I do. And you haven't answered my question. Where the devil is Brabant?"

"It was a duchy in Belgium," she answered, exasperated. "But now we must begin again."

"Are we to recite our lines from opposite ends of the room?"

"Perhaps I wish to retain a safe distance from your odious presence."

He stalked toward her, a knowing smile dawning on his mouth. "Or perhaps you don't trust yourself to be close to me."

"You are presumptuous." And too perceptive. She held the scene out before her like a shield. "You needn't stand so near. I hardly think Biron and Rosaline were atop one another."

"No, I should think that came a bit later."

Cleo bit her lip, meeting his gaze. "You are beyond the pale."

"Go on," he said lazily. "I enjoy hearing my many faults cataloged. It brings my ego to earth. I'm sure it distracts you from your inconvenient attraction to me."

"There is no attraction, inconvenient or otherwise." Though she tried to keep her voice cool and unaffected, she feared she sounded anything but. Her hands trembled as they clutched the play. She lowered them so he wouldn't see. "Are you ready to continue?"

"Of course." Thornton stepped closer. Her hem dragged across the tip of his boot.

Her dress improver tightened yet again.

He didn't bother to examine the script, just kept his stare trained on her with an intensity she found most disconcerting. "'Did not I dance with you in Brabant once?'"

His gaze caught her, sent her tumbling headlong into memories she had no wish to relive. Dancing with him, laughing with him, riding with him. Kissing him. His crushing betrayal, the days and nights of heartache, the loss. She could not forget, would not forget, what loving him had cost her.

"Cleo?" Thornton's voice, gently prodding, brought her back to the present. "Are you well?"

"No." She swallowed, then exhaled. "No, I am not well. If you don't mind, I think I shall go and lie down."

As she moved to pass him, he stayed her with a hand on her shoulder. "Wait."

She stilled, watching him, terrified she would make a cake of herself by pitching into his arms or worse, by sobbing. "What is it?"

"It is…" He faltered, seeming as much at a loss as she. His free hand captured her other shoulder and he pushed her until her back pressed against the cool windowpane. Her full skirt sprang forward into his legs, but he stepped closer, the descent inevitable. "It is this, I'm afraid."

His lips claimed hers. The effect on her was almost violent. She felt as though gunpowder had been lit and then tossed into her body. As though she would explode with wanting him. Cleo tossed the script to the floor and reached for him, her hands grappling with his broad shoulders. Her fingers sank into his hair.

Thornton's tongue slid into her mouth, his hand covering her breast as if it belonged there. She was overcome. She pulled her mouth from his and pressed her heated cheek to the cool glass. His lips feasted on her neck. "Thornton, this is madness."

"It is always thus between us." He snagged the décolletage of her gown and dragged it down, exposing her breasts. "It will always be so until we have had our fills of one another."

She was not so convinced it would easily disappear. Cleo didn't think she could ever have her fill, as he had so crudely phrased it, of Alexander de Vere. "Then let us have it now," she pleaded, heedless of the consequences.

"Yes," the word hissed from him, agonized. He sucked a nipple into his hot mouth and tugged.

Liquid heat pooled instantly in her core. "Thornton," she begged, her pride cast off like an evening mantle.

She wanted to be wicked with him. It had been so many years, but she had never forgotten the thrill of making love with him. She yearned to taste every inch of the muscular man he'd become.

"Say my name," he commanded.

"Alex," she whispered. Her hands scrambled down his back, resting on his firm derriere. She squeezed.

"Cleo, what you do to me, woman." He raised his head to stare down at her, his gaze sweltering and laden with promise.

"Alex?"

The sweet, questioning voice interrupted their interlude

abruptly. It was as if a pail of cold water had been tossed upon them. Embarrassment surged through her. "Thornton, 'tis your sister," she murmured.

"Hell." He tore his mouth from her breast and stilled. "Tell me she isn't in this room."

Dreading the answer, Cleo raised on tiptoes to peer over his shoulder. Bella stared back at her from the threshold of the library, eyes wide, a pale hand clasped to her heart. "I can't," she said lamely.

"Jesus." He tugged her bodice back into place with a rough hand. "Jesus Christ."

"Yes." She squirmed. Her dress improver was still beneath her breasts, digging into her rib cage with uncomfortable tenacity. Oh well, no hope for it now. They would have to do their best to convince young Lady Bella that she and Thornton had merely been practicing their lines. "Say something to her."

"Bollocks."

Seeing that she would clearly have to attempt to set the matter to rights, she pressed her palms to his shoulders and shoved. Thornton staggered backward. Cleo swept away from the window. "No, Thornton. You've got the words all wrong again." She sank to pick up the script she'd dropped. "It says right here that the line is 'Did not I dance with you in Brabant once.'"

"I am not a bloody actor," he said, taking her cue.

"Lady Bella," Cleo chirped, pretending to have just espied his still gobsmacked-looking sister. "Welcome, my dear. Do come in. You have caught us unawares in a most disastrous moment."

Bella entered the room, wisely closing the door at her back. She lingered on the periphery of the room, hesitant. Cleo could almost hear her thoughts churning. She would be wondering what she had witnessed. Had it been a rehearsal, or had it been something wicked?

"Good morning again, Lady Scarbrough," Bella offered, along with a hasty curtsy. "I see you are practicing for Lady Cosgrove's great affair on the morrow."

"Indeed." Cleo sent her a bright, conspiratorial smile. "I look forward to the event, but I am afraid I must despair of your brother."

"Oh dear." Bella's smooth brow knitted. "How so?"

A glance at Thornton revealed he had restored himself. He was once more all icy hauteur. "He is terribly vexing, forever confusing his lines."

"But Alex always has been possessed of a most formidable memory," his sister protested demurely.

"I've never had a head for drama, I fear," Thornton offered, sounding almost unaffected by their brief but melting interlude.

"My megrims have returned." Cleo turned to Bella. "If you will excuse me, my dear? I am off to my chamber. I find a bit of rest to be just the thing for them."

"Of course, my lady." Bella dipped into a curtsy again. "I wish you speedy recovery. It must be terrible to suffer from the headache so often."

Cleo chose to ignore the subtle jibe, startled nonetheless at the girl's surprising temerity. Self-preservation sounded the urge to evacuate the scene of her crime.

"Forgive me my ill manners and averse memory," Thornton added.

Cleo scarcely chanced a peek at him before she fled. Her clothing was askew, her breath cut short by both her unsettled undergarments and the aftereffects of Thornton. She was sure she blushed madly and that she looked a guilty fright. Worse, she was sure she had quite lost her mind, acting as impetuously as she had just done with him. Had anyone other than Lady Bella intruded on them, there would have been an uglier scene accompanied by a hailstorm of vicious gossip.

There would be no more rehearsals, she decided as she

made her way to her chamber and narrowly avoided a collision with a clumsy footman. He mumbled an apology and disappeared after knocking into a painting and nearly overturning a vase brimming with red roses. She didn't figure the unfortunate fellow would last long in his position.

An awkward footman was as auspicious as a wife who was fast renewing a *grande* passion for a man other than her husband. Even for the society ladies with well-orchestrated arrangements between lover and husband, the situation was far from ideal. Cleo had no wish to destroy her life for a fortnight of pleasure.

Chapter Four

$\mathcal{H}$E HAD NO wish to destroy his life for a fortnight of pleasure and yet he seemed somehow determined to do just that by mucking up all he'd been working toward ever since he'd mucked up his life the first time seven years before. His world had been utterly perfect before this cursed house party. He'd been about to announce his engagement, to settle down and wed a suitable, biddable girl from the right family.

His career in parliament had never been better, his three pamphlets on reform well-received, his work on Gladstone's campaign highly regarded. His party and his Prime Minister depended on him.

But he closeted himself with Cleopatra Harrington for ten minutes and nearly ravaged her and destroyed his carefully wrought reputation in the process. He wanted to start a family, beget the proverbial heir and spare, live out his life in boring and respectable fashion while leaving his duty-bound mark upon good old England, damn it.

Thornton had never had more cause to fear he'd lost his bloody mind than the moment his sister walked in as he was about to push up Cleo's skirts and do what they both wanted so desperately right up against the cold window. It hadn't been his finest hour, but perhaps that was owed to the fact he'd been hard as a hunk of coal since first kissing Cleo yesterday afternoon. No relief in sight. Yes, he was depraved.

He leaned his back against the window Cleo had just vacated and eyed his sister. She was lovely in an understated way, rigged out in ridiculous fashion by his mother in a frothy gown with tiers of pale pink and too much lace. Bella seemed small and ornate, like a new doll yet to be removed from its box. Innocent was the word for her. She was the picture of fresh, rosy-cheeked English country girl innocence. He felt doubly the cad.

Bella gazed at him with an inscrutable expression. He wondered if she had the town bronze to even realize what she'd witnessed. But he didn't need to wonder for long.

"What manner of folly is this, dear brother?" Her voice soft but still nettling, accusatory even.

"Shakespeare." He adopted a casual air, hoping to avoid confrontation. Damn, but one didn't want to be upbraided by one's virginal younger sister.

"Lady Scarbrough does not look in the slightest like the bard to me," she said shrewdly. "Pray don't be obtuse. We haven't been close these last few years, but I am not so naïve nor so ignorant of your past history with her ladyship that I can be swindled by you."

Shite. "Very well. Clearly, I would appreciate your discretion."

Bella crossed the room to him, her face pale and earnest. She reached for his hands and clasped them loosely in hers, fine-boned and fragile. "Brother, you have my discretion without asking. However, I must ask you if you think it wise to…behave as you have done with the countess."

"Christ, Bella."

"Your language, Alex. You haven't answered the question."

"Very well." He paused. "Of course not. But wisdom has little to do with anything that is worthwhile."

Her brow creased. "Are you not nearly engaged to Miss Cuthbert?"

"Yes," he gritted. This interview grew more uncomfortable by the moment. "Bella, we were rehearsing and lost ourselves in the scene. That is all. It shan't be repeated."

"But Alex, I saw you with the countess yesterday when *Maman* and I arrived," she protested with gentle insistence.

Well, yes, there had been yesterday as well. Curse it, his innocent sister was treading on territory where her dainty slippers decidedly did not belong. "This is not your affair, sister."

"Alex," she implored, "it's not my intention to interfere in your personal matters. Indeed, I know it's not my place to do so. However, I care for you and while I was but a girl in the nursery seven years ago when Lady Scarbrough jilted you, I know all too well the effect it had upon you. Suddenly, you were mad for the races and cards and fast women. You kept three different ladybirds on the wrong side of the park, actresses with painted faces and colored hair. Until politics had an improving effect, that is."

"Bella," he interrupted, scandalized by her knowledge of his misspent youth. "Where have you heard all this?"

"Oh." She flushed and glanced away. "I eavesdrop upon *Maman*'s conversations with Aunt Julia. It is reprehensible I know, but the only way I ever get to hear gossip. You would be surprised at how able our mother is to hide every interesting book, scandal sheet and newspaper from me. I'm rarely even allowed to go amongst my own crowd, she is so protective. But that's neither here nor there." She gave his hands another emphatic squeeze. "What does matter is that it cannot be wise to carry on an affair with Lady Scarbrough. Now or ever again."

Had he thought her spoiled? No, a nuisance was a more apt description. Meddlesome. His-mother-with-claws.

He smiled grimly. "You're right of course, little one. With age, you'll realize that not all life's choices are as simple as you would have them. I did care for Cleo as a foolish young man, yes. What I feel for her now, however, is a great deal less valorous. That is all I can or will divulge to you. This conversation is not fit."

He tugged his hands from hers and brushed past her, stalking across the room. The urge to take another ride, feel the wind slapping against his face and the fury of a well-muscled stallion beneath him, was strong. He needed distance. Escape. Good Christ, after first Cleo's searing reaction to him and now his sister's awkward prying, he needed a brandy and soda-water. Perhaps three.

"Alex, don't be angry with me, please," she called after him.

"I'm not angry, Bella." He stopped and turned. "But don't meddle in my affairs. What I choose to do with Cleo or any other woman here is no one's concern but mine."

"Why do you call her by her Christian name?"

"Because she is Cleo to me," he said, the admission torn from him against his will. "She will always be Cleo." Cursing and aware he had revealed too much both to his sister and to himself, he spun on his heel and quit the room.

"WHO IS THAT man?" Tia murmured in her sauciest voice later that day as the company gathered formally for another of Lady C.'s entertainments. A group of London players was set to perform *Romeo & Juliet*. Chairs and an impressive, if slightly rustic in appearance, set had been erected in the ballroom where all gathered awaiting the curtain's rise.

Cleo followed her sister's gaze to a corner of the room where Thornton sat. "It is the marquis, as you must know," she replied, irritated. He was debonair, arrogant and perfect as ever. It wasn't possible, but she swore she still felt his kiss on her mouth.

"Not him, ninny." Tia made an impatient sound. "The gentleman seated to his right, the fellow with the blond hair and arresting profile."

Dismay surged through her. She hadn't even noticed the man at first look. He was rather striking, though not nearly as attractive as Thornton. "I haven't the slightest," she drawled in contrived boredom.

"Mr. Jesse Whitney," Helen added. "An American."

"Great lot of those circling amongst our ranks these days," Cleo commented, trying desperately to ignore Thornton's presence. Drat it, her eyes kept straying to him. They had twice caught one another's stares already.

"Yes indeed," Tia said from behind her fan, "and with a face like that, one wishes for more."

"Are you not taken with Viscount Darlington any longer?" Helen fanned herself.

"Darlington who?" Tia asked sweetly, even though she had been spending time in that handsome fellow's company earlier in the day.

"Marrying an American is quite the rage these days," Helen added. "They are invading our shores and marrying our crusty old titles."

"It's a shame one of them didn't snap up Scarbrough's crusty old title before Cleo could," Tia lamented too loudly for propriety's sake.

Cleo was compelled to admonish her, even if she wholeheartedly echoed the sentiment. "Hypatia."

Tia sniffed. "Cleopatra."

"How was your rehearsal earlier today, dearest?" Helen asked, attempted, in her familiar way, to defuse the tension between her sisters.

"It would have gone swimmingly had it not been for Thornton's abysmal ability to read the proper lines." Cleo's voice sounded tight as a well-tuned string, even to her ears.

"It's just as well that Tia and I are partners." Helen drew her fan across her face and leaned toward Cleo. "Sisters may be a bother, but they certainly do not cause the distraction of a man."

"Helen, I'm shocked." Cleo summoned outrage, which would have been a deal easier to find had Thornton not been a distraction. And more.

"Do you think Mr. Whitney might care to distract me?" Tia whispered.

Her eyes strayed across the ballroom and meshed with Thornton's once more. She jerked them away, her gaze landing on the back of Margot Chilton's ridiculously complicated hair. No more rehearsals with him, she reminded herself. Avoid Thornton at all costs. Yes, if she could only listen to her conscience, she could pass the remainder of the house party in relative peace.

"Have you seen Margot Chilton's hair?" She kept her voice low, addressing her sisters.

"That silly cow." Tia tsked. "How much false hair do you think her lady's maid put inside that monstrosity?"

"It's larger than her actual head," Helen breathed.

Good heavens, it was. Cleo was saved from making further conversation, however, by the appearance of Lady C. at the front of the rustling curtain. She beamed, lovely in her sea foam colored, French Revolution inspired gown complete with small false panniers. It was a fashion only Lady Cosgrove could wear without appearing excessively ostentatious. "Sans further soliloquy," she announced to the group at large, "I give you *Romeo & Juliet*."

The assemblage applauded politely and Lady C. clapped her hands at the pair of liveried footmen who were to raise the curtain. And so the play began. If the actors misquoted the odd line or the women's faces bore too much powder and paint, no one spoke of it. Not until the intercession, at least.

Cleo, Helen and Tia were sipping champagne near an alarmingly realistic bust of Eros when Lady C. joined their trio. "I'm sure Juliet is five and thirty if she's a day," she grumbled without preamble, much to the delight of Tia, who had just pointed out as much to her sisters. She nearly spat her champagne upon Cleo, who had the misfortune to be standing directly across from her and was thus in grave peril.

"It is a marvelous evening, however," Cleo hastened to assure their hostess. "Truly, your house party will be, as always, the talk of polite society."

"Yes, but we do need some matchmaking for it to be a true success." Lady C. drained her champagne flute. "I have just the thing. My dear Lady Helen, have you met the dashing Mr. Whitney?"

"The American," Tia added with an unladylike smirk that would have set their mother on her ear.

"I can't say that I have, my lady," Helen answered, her voice neutral.

"I shall bring him to heel for you." Lady C. wandered away before any of the sisters could offer protest.

"Oh dear," Cleo ventured aloud. Likely, with Mr. Whitney would come the dratted Thornton, whom she had vowed to avoid and ignore for the remainder of the fortnight.

"What is the matter, sister dear?" Tia looked and sounded like the proverbial cat gotten into the cream.

"Lord Ravenscroft is traveling in our direction," she answered, seizing upon the excuse. After all, he was heading their way in a determined saunter, even if she had only just now taken notice.

Helen sighed. "He is a rather fascinating man for all that he has a dubious reputation."

"Dubious! The man is notorious," Tia corrected.

"No one cares with a face that handsome," Helen offered.

"True," Cleo agreed, watching the object of their conversation. No doubt about it, Ravenscroft was beautiful in a rare, masculine sense of the word. If only she had been partnered with him instead of Thornton. If only he made her pulse pound and her breath catch.

Ravenscroft reached them and bowed. He smelled of decadent French cologne. "Ladies, I trust you are enjoying our hostess's fine display of theater."

"Indeed we are," Cleo answered, proffering her hand. The earl placed a lingering kiss upon it before turning to Tia and Helen. "What of you, my lord?"

"Other than the fact Juliet is old enough to be my mother, the play is delightful." He gave her a wicked grin.

Tia gave him a playful tap on the arm with her fan. "You do the lady grave insult, my lord. She is not so ancient, as you, I think."

"You think me ancient, dear lady? I'm wounded." He held a hand over his heart. "Truly, Juliet is old enough to be my dam."

His assessment earned a shocked laugh from the sisters. "You compare yourself to a dog, Ravenscroft?" Helen interposed, sounding amused.

"Fitting, don't you think?" he returned.

"The more salient question," Cleo couldn't help adding, "is why you are so certain of Juliet's age."

"Ah." His grin deepened. "While it is a subject not fit for the ears of ladies, I confess to having had a certain association with the lovely Juliet some years back."

"Lord Ravenscroft, you are scandalous," Helen pronounced, but far from shocked, her tone was delighted. She even sent the notorious lord a coy smile.

Oh dear. The formidable Lady Helen Harrington was never coy. She didn't play at romantic games with men. Indeed, she was too busy being formidable to manage the effort. She suffered fools most ungraciously.

"I should think scandalous preferable to boring any day, Lady Helen," Ravenscroft parried with a wink before making an impolite gesture to impending company. "Speaking of boring…"

Thornton and the American appeared then, within earshot for Ravenscroft's cheeky introduction. Thornton's face was set in grim lines. He made no secret of his dislike for

Ravenscroft. The American, on the other hand, seemed utterly at ease in that insufferable way only a people hailing from such a vast continent have.

Thornton bowed to Cleo, his gaze impersonal. "Countess, good evening. Lady Stokey, Lady Helen. May I present to each of you my good friend, Mr. Jesse Whitney?"

Introductions went around, with an awkward pause as Thornton attempted to ignore Ravenscroft. The earl appeared unaffected as, with a mild tone, he performed his own. Which in turn only nettled Thornton more.

Cleo decided it would be terribly fun to ignore Thornton herself. She offered Mr. Whitney a smile that was a trifle too warm for an initial meeting and gave him her hand. "Mr. Whitney, we've heard such a great deal about you. It's my greatest pleasure to at last make your acquaintance."

Mr. Whitney inclined his head, dropping a respectful kiss on her hand. "The pleasure is mine, Lady Scarbrough."

He was dashing, the American. Perfectly polite as well, which was rare in her experience. Quite a few American heiresses had made their tittering way across the Atlantic in hopes of marrying into the peerage, without much to recommend them save their fortunes.

"Tell me, what brings you to our glorious shores?" she asked, moving a bit closer to Mr. Whitney and forcing Tia to take a step away from him.

Mr. Whitney grinned, producing an appealing dimple in his right cheek. "Business interests primarily."

"Business," she repeated. Americans adored industry. The English found it appalling. Truly, she knew very little of business matters, being possessed of one of the last remaining English fortunes. Of course, John was doing his best to run the coffers dry. By the time she reached her dotage, she'd likely have to hire herself out as a charwoman.

His grin deepened. "Have I lost my charm already?"

"Naturally not," she said in a teasing tone. "Your charm is

too great to be so easily tarnished by a tawdry involvement in business."

That earned her an appreciative laugh from Mr. Whitney and a scowl from Thornton. How delicious. She adjusted her stance to turn her body more fully toward her quarry.

"You are the first woman I've met here with a sense of humor," Mr. Whitney confided. "While your women are lovely as magnolias, they tend to be just as fragile."

"That's our Cleo," Tia interrupted, never one to be brushed aside for long, "sturdy as a carriage horse. Why, there isn't a single thing about our dear girl that is fragile, is there Helen?"

Cleo shot darts at Tia with her eyes. In wisdom, Helen chose to change the subject and after just a few sentences, Cleo's attempt at seducing Mr. Whitney was dashed. Drat. Needling Thornton brought her such satisfaction. Even if she did have to admit that it wasn't Mr. Whitney she wanted to spend hours kissing but rather his insufferable friend Thornton. Their conversation grew tepid and polite to do penance for Ravenscroft's inappropriate comments, Thornton's animosity and Cleo's blatant but brief flirting.

In short order, the intercession was at an end and Lady C. was loudly directing her milling guests back to their seats for the remainder of the play. Tia grabbed Mr. Whitney's arm nearly before he offered it, Helen partnered with Lord Ravenscroft and Cleo was left with Thornton. She took his arm.

"If I didn't know better, I'd suspect you had a *tendre* for Jesse," he murmured for her ears alone.

She cast him an arch look. "Do you know better?"

"Of course." A smile tugged at the corners of his lips for the first time that evening. His charming, dratted dimple made a rare appearance.

"And how would you know better, my lord, when you know so very little about me in the first place?"

"If you will but think on it, you shall realize I know quite a lot about you these days."

"You're an arrogant cad, my lord," she admonished him, not entirely meaning it, much to her chagrin. She still yearned for his touch anyway.

"So you have told me before, Countess."

"So I will tell you again before this fortnight is through, I predict."

"Are you a fortune teller, my dear?" He sounded unconcerned, blithe almost.

"No, merely cursed by Fortune's wheel to be continually plagued by you."

"Pray, don't work yourself into a temper on my account, Lady Scarbrough." Thornton clucked his tongue. "It makes your nostrils flare."

She huffed. Now he stooped to examining her as if she were a prize mare? "I wouldn't work myself into anything on your account, Lord Thornton. Indeed, I rarely think of you at all."

"Indeed." He chuckled and it was apparent from his tone he didn't believe her.

Cleo sought to discomfit him. "Have you learned your lines yet?"

The left corner of his sensual lips curved upward in a half-smile. "No. I've been at it all afternoon and can't recall a word after Bruges."

"Brabant," she corrected.

"Er, yes. Just so." He leaned into her closer than propriety dictated. She caught his masculine scent, so much richer and earthier than Ravenscroft's cologne. "Perhaps you would like to practice later this evening?"

The man knew no bounds. She should be outraged at his improper suggestion. In truth, it piqued her interest. She was fast turning into a Messalina, in thought if not in deed. Thank heavens unlike that infamous historical figure, Cleo didn't have a husband such as Emperor Claudius to have her executed.

"I'm shocked at your insolence," she lied in her haughtiest tones, knowing it for the best that she not encourage him. There could be no future in such an *affaire*, only the risk of too much heartache. She had already lived through more than enough of that at his hands, thank you.

"But I rather think you like it," he said lowly, before bowing and leaving her safe—and dejected—at her seat.

Cleo didn't hear a word spoken by either the lovelorn Juliet or her beau Romeo for the remainder of the play. Her mind was quite preoccupied with unsettling possibilities. Delicious possibilities. Oh dear. There was that naughty word of Thornton's again, a perfect adjective for her current predicament. *Delicious.*

Chapter Five

WHEN THORNTON RETIRED that evening after some late *fine-champagne* and cigarettes with Jesse and a few others in the company, he discovered a curious note. It had been placed on the writing desk by the window and caught his eye at once. The flowery script on the envelope appeared unnaturally large, as though the writer had taken great pains to seem impressive with monstrous letters. As he picked it up, the scent of lavender reached him.

Cleo. No, she was not the naïve, sweet-tempered girl he remembered. But in her place was a fiery goddess with the tongue of a shrew. Closeting himself with her had been a mistake. Touching her had been tantamount to eating the forbidden apple. Already, he wanted her like mad, as he had never wanted another before or since her.

Pursuing her would be folly indeed at a house party where everyone knew everyone's business and his mother haunted the drawing room. An *affaire* could well have negative implications for his political ambitions. There was his betrothed-to-be, Miss Cuthbert, to consider as well. Untoward gossip would almost certainly reach her ears.

And yet, he tore open the envelope anyway.

"My dearest Thornton," he read aloud. "We've much to discuss. Perhaps a private audience, away from the ever-open ears of our company is in order? If you should call, my door will be open. Midnight. Yours, C."

Oh hell. He was as hard as he'd been yesterday with his

hand up her luscious leg. What did she want from him? He started undoing his necktie but then thought better of it. If he went to Cleo's chamber, he couldn't very well appear in a robe only. That would be presumptuous, an insult. Not that he intended to go, mind you.

Thornton raked a finger under his collar and studied the letter. No, he wouldn't take her offer. As a reckless youth led by his prick and little else, he would have gone. Whatever strangeness attracted them—the pull of the unattainable or the dark thrill of discovery—it had passed. It surely would pass after this godforsaken fortnight of temptation.

God, he regretted their damnable past. If he could but forget, perhaps he could focus on the important aspects of his life once more. His fist closed on the pretty note, crumpling it until it was unrecognizable. Still, the words remained sealed within his hand as surely as his mind, taunting him. With a grunt, he tossed the wad into the grate. A low fire begun by a servant before his arrival licked the note with flame. In less than half a minute, all traces of it dissipated to fine ash.

Lavender lingered in the air, mingling with the scent of tobacco. Cursing, he shrugged out of his jacket and tossed it to the nearest chair. He had no wish for the company of his manservant and decided not to ring for him. No doubt Oliver would read his foul mood like a book.

Thornton shucked off his shirt. This had all the makings of a long, sleepless night. Stupid though it was, he wished to hell Cleo hadn't stopped him yesterday and that his sister hadn't interrupted them earlier. Damn Scarbrough for popping up in Cleo's conscience and ruining their interlude. If she had waited but fifteen minutes more, her scruples would have been too bloody late and his shaft wouldn't now be such a painful reminder of what could have been. Of course, he couldn't truly blame the innocent Bella for her interruption. She may have an inkling of the nature of his feelings for Cleo, but she hardly knew how he would be demonstrating them up against the damn window. Still, as Oliver would say, that didn't mean he wasn't hard enough to hang a coal bucket from his knob. It had always been the way of things between them, he recalled with a rueful grimace, from the first.

THE FIRST TIME Thornton saw Lady Cleopatra Harrington, he was sipping flat champagne at a dreadful country dance his mother had forced him to attend. "You must take the place of your father," she'd urged, "now our mourning is over. It is your duty to assert your presence even in the country."

His mother had been correct so he'd done the pretty. He was fresh out of Oxford, new in his position as the head of his family only a year after his father's death and—well he knew—a green lad. But even he knew his father's Buckinghamshire estate was in a shambles. The old marquis had been the worst sort of gambler, a poor one. As a result, Thornton, his mother and his younger sister bordered dangerously on utter penury. It was his duty to see them and Marleigh Manor through it and part of that duty was keeping up appearances.

He was considerably bored with toadying country squires and puffed-up baronets and their daughters eager to secure the title of marchioness. After a discreet consultation of his watch, he reckoned he would remain for only another quarter hour before escorting his mother home. It was as he tucked his timepiece back into his waistcoat that he saw her.

She stood with another young lady as fair as she was dark, laughing on the outskirts of the dancers, so lovely he wondered for a moment if he'd drunk too much bad champagne. Glossy black curls framed her round face, woven through with a bit of gold chain. Her dress was unremarkable save for the way its pale yellow silk hugged her luscious figure.

Determined to win himself an introduction, he turned to the awkward and, if he were honest, dull squire at his side.

"Squire Dunston, are you familiar with the exquisite ladies just over there?"

Dunston followed his gaze, keen to assist. "That would be Lady Helen in the blue dress and Lady Cleopatra in yellow, daughters to the Earl of Northcote."

What luck. Northcote's lands bordered Thornton's own. He vaguely recalled visiting the family as a boy and had a fleeting impression of girls with braids and dolls and a fat black cat.

"Perhaps you might introduce me?" he suggested, eyes still on her. Cleopatra. The name suited her. She possessed the kind of dangerous beauty that could eat a man alive.

"Of course, my lord." Dunston led the short distance to the still chatting sisters. "Please accept my most humble apologies for the intrusion, my ladies," he intoned with a formal air. "May I introduce the Marquis of Thornton? Lord Thornton, the Lady Helen and the Lady Cleopatra."

Lady Helen shook his hand, taking him by surprise. She was a handsome woman rather than classically beautiful, taller than her sister, with freckles dotting her nose. She made no attempt to powder them, unlike most ladies of his acquaintance.

"My lady." He bowed.

She offered him a genuine smile. "It is a pleasure."

"Lady Cleopatra." He bowed again, noting that her eyes were a most unusual, bewitching shade of green.

She extended her dainty hand, watching him with a frank gaze. "Lord Thornton." Her lips were pink and full, meant to be kissed. Even the upturned tip of her nose charmed him.

If he held her hand longer than necessary or forgot about the presence of Dunston and Lady Helen, it could hardly be helped. She was more than lovely, he realized. Lady Cleopatra was perhaps more alluring than her namesake. She quite took his breath.

"We are neighbors, I believe." He knew it was inane conversation, but he'd found his tongue at last.

"Indeed, are we?" A lovely smile curved her mouth. "I had not realized. That is to say, I knew, of course, that an estate bordered father's and that estate was held by the Marquis of Thornton. I merely didn't realize it belonged to you."

He found her fluster endearing. "That is interesting, my lady, since I recall a number of visits to your holdings in my younger years."

"Your younger years? Are you so very old, then?" Her face flushed. "I didn't mean to imply that you look ancient, only that you don't appear…old." She bit her lip.

Thornton grinned. "Do you doubt me?"

"No." She sputtered, flushed, foundered for words.

He took pity on her then. "There was a remarkably fat black cat, girls with braids and dolls and I feel quite secure in the recollection that I tossed one of those dolls into the Poseidon fountain. It was the god of the sea, was it not?"

"Clementine was not fat," she huffed, adorably indignant. "She was merely plump in a delightfully feline way. She made an extraordinary pillow, though I dare say waking up with cat fur in one's mouth isn't always the thing. It was Helen's doll you tossed into the fountain, so I shall forgive you that and yes to Poseidon, a frightfully angry looking guardian of the family fountain if you ask me."

He laughed, couldn't help himself—the girl was infectious—and she giggled with him. A waltz struck up in the background. "Would you care to dance, Lady Cleopatra?"

Her green eyes lit. "Yes. Oh, yes."

And just like that, he was thoroughly, hopelessly, smitten.

TO HELL WITH it. Jolted back to the present, he stalked across the chamber and yanked open the wardrobe. There was something between them. There had been something between them seven years before and it was still there, simmering beneath the surface of every innocuous gaze and polite word. It had been prodding him in the gut the previous evening as she showered her coquette's charms on Claridge. It was kicking him in the arse now.

He slapped on a fresh shirt. It would definitely kick him in the arse on the morrow. His good sense had fled him. There was no earthly reason why he should be buttoning up a fresh shirt at a quarter 'til midnight with the intent of seeking out Cleopatra. Thornton snapped up a new coat and shrugged into it. No earthly reason at all save one.

CLEO WAS WASHING away her troubles, the hazard of her run-ins with Thornton. Bridget had drawn a hot bath for her in the chamber's luxurious contemporary bathroom. Lavender floated on the sweet-scented water. The tub itself was no hip bath as most country homes still had, but full-sized and deep, with running water ready at the tap. Wilton House had only the best of modern conveniences. Cleo, accustomed to the dank, gas light-less country seat of Scarbrough, was always impressed with the amenities when here. Of course, John spent money on women, not houses.

With a sigh of genuine satisfaction, she reached for her bar of French soap. The *savon* too was lavender, direct from a quaint little shop she'd found in Paris during her last stay there. It usually calmed her.

Not tonight. Tonight her mind swirled with questions and worry knots. It was growing impossible to convince herself that her attraction to Thornton was an aberration, particularly since she'd wound up in his arms once again that afternoon.

Her reaction to him took her by force, had always done. Lulled by the warmth of the water, she allowed her mind to consider simpler times between them.

"No, that shan't do at all." Cleo tilted her head to study the landscape she'd been sketching from another angle.

"Won't it?"

The masculine voice startled a gasp from her. Clutching her charcoals and sketch book to the bodice of her dress, she spun to find the voice's owner. Seated as she was on the grass—indecorous yes, but most importantly, comfortable—she had to tip her head back so far her hat fell. She saw his boots first, then his riding trousers, fitted lovingly to lean calves and narrow hips. Good heavens, his trousers fit him exceedingly well. Blushing, she hurried her gaze to his face. He grinned with a boyish ease and her breath caught again, but this time not because she'd taken a fright.

He was glorious. Sun haloed his ruffled black hair. His eyes were gray, crinkled at the corners, lively too. His slashing nose was perhaps a bit long, but his mouth was a wonder, firm and, well, almost pretty, she dared say. After all, she'd seen it on a few occasions already and had deemed it imminently kissable to her sisters.

It was Lord Thornton, her charming dancing partner of the other evening. Oh dear. Her delight at his unexpected interruption dissipated as she realized the picture she presented. Curls escaped from her simple chignon. Her hat was lost, her walking dress a castoff of Helen's and as she glanced down at herself, she realized she'd quite mussed the silk bodice with charcoal streaks.

Embarrassed to be caught at such a disadvantage, she raised a hand to her hair in an effort to subdue it. "My lord. Have I made my way onto your lands by accident? If so, I apologize. I do have the most appalling sense of direction. Ask my sisters and they'll concur. But they fare no better, the affliction being a family trait, I fear."

His grin deepened and he sank down on his haunches,

bringing them eye to eye. He smelled of a distracting combination of sandalwood and man. "You needn't worry that you trespass, Lady Cleopatra. Visitors as lovely as yourself are always a welcome addition."

Her face heated again, not from the sun's late summer rays. "Thank you, Lord Thornton. I wouldn't have imposed, however, had I realized I'd be disrupting your ride." She gestured weakly to the horse he'd abandoned some ways away, its reins slack, nibbling at the grass. "Goodness, you haven't tied your mount. You may want to go and retrieve the poor fellow, else you'll be forced to walk back like me. I dare say I forgot to wear the proper shoes for walking but I do love August as it's certainly the loveliest month of the year and everything is at its zenith. I'm afraid I lose my head when I'm in search of the proper sketch."

Lord, she was babbling. Babbling like a simpleton and she couldn't keep herself from speaking and making a cake of herself. If only he didn't stare at her so intently with those striking gray eyes. If only he weren't so handsome and so close and smiling with that charming dimple in his left cheek. Double oh dear.

"My mount will remain. Don't worry yourself." He leaned closer to her as if he were about to impart a secret. "But I do think you may upset her if you go about referring to her as a fellow."

"Oh yes." She swallowed, vastly discomfited. "I wouldn't wish to upset your horse. Bilious horses are so difficult to ride, don't you find?"

"Of course. Nothing worse than a bilious horse."

They stared at one another in a charged silence. His eyes dropped to her mouth, but he did not kiss her as she suddenly wished he would. Instead, he reached out with a gloveless hand. With great care, as if it were formed of finest china, he tucked a stray curl behind her ear. She held her breath as his fingers lingered close to her cheek before retreating. Disappointment surged.

"Thank you," she whispered, biting her lip.

His grin faded. "You never answered my question, Lady Cleopatra."

"Your question?" She'd forgotten it.

"When I approached, you were lost in a most vehement conversation with yourself," he drawled, "saying something shan't do. What shan't do?"

He'd overheard her talking to herself. How lowering. "My sketch." She proffered it to him with reluctance, aware that it was hopelessly smudged.

He took her small notebook from her hands and examined it. "An excellent likeness."

"Pooh. That tree resembles my old governess."

"Truly?" He laughed.

Cleo smiled at him, unable to help it. "Sadly for Miss Hullyhew, yes. She was, as my father once commented, sturdy as a chimney. Not a compliment, as you can imagine."

"No, I should think not. But the unfortunate, sylvan Miss Hullyhew aside, the sketch is rather fine."

There was sincerity in both his expression and his voice. A strange sensation blossomed in her chest. "It is kind of you to say so."

"Nonsense." He winked. "Now I shall banish my charm by telling you that your dress is hopelessly ruined."

"I know." She attempted to take the sketch from him, but her fingers brushed his. A spark frissoned over her skin.

"Lady Cleopatra?" He caught her hands, leaned even closer until his breath was a soft caress on her cheek.

"Yes?"

"I should like to kiss you," he informed her with a gravity that would have been amusing had not she been dying inside for him to do precisely that.

"Then I wish you would, my lord." She swayed forward.

"Call me Alex," he murmured and that quickly, his

mouth was hungry and demanding on hers.

Cleo kissed him back, opening to his seeking tongue and somehow, they fell to the grass. Her sketch was forgotten. A long time later, they discovered her crumpled hat and the charcoal dust staining his white shirt.

SHAKING HER HEAD to clear the foggy remnants of memories she'd do well to forget forever, Cleo soaped her arms with ginger care. The plain truth of it was she found herself in the same hopeless position as all too many society ladies married to a blighter, longing for another. She knew she ought not even entertain thoughts of Thornton, but her heart's old wound seemed suddenly sore again. How could she not?

The floor creaked behind her. "This is an interesting place for an audience," drawled a deep voice laden with bad intentions and sinful promise.

She swirled around in her bath, flinging her arms over her chest and pulling her knees up. Thornton leaned in the open doorway, the soft light from her bed chamber glowing behind him so that he looked other worldly. Like a fallen angel come to tempt the wicked wife. How had she thought him a saint?

He was sin personified, wearing a white, un-tucked shirt with an improper amount of buttons open, a black jacket and no shoes. His bare feet drew her notice, strong and disturbingly attractive. It occurred to her she'd never in her life seen a man's bare feet, neither Thornton's nor John's. It shocked her to think he had walked the hall sans shoes, in a state of half dress. And he'd entered her chamber. Had anyone seen him? Was he mad?

"What are you doing here?" she demanded, keeping her voice stern. It wouldn't do to let her eyes slip to the enticing expanse of chest visible beneath his shirt's gaping vee. Even if it was strongly muscled and lightly bronzed. Did he work out of doors without a shirt? How uncivilized, yet how thrilling.

Thornton continued to rest his hip against the doorjamb with the negligence of a conqueror. His gaze traveled to her bathwater and then back up to her face. "You sent me a letter."

"I sent you no letter."

He grinned. "No need to be coy, love."

"I'm not being coy, you lackwit." She glowered at him. What was he about? "I didn't send you a letter!"

"Of course you did, requesting a private audience here in your chamber."

"While I'm at my bath?"

"How was I to know what you had in mind?"

"You must leave at once."

He stroked his chin in mock thought. "Not yet, I don't think."

"I'm completely unclothed in this bath. Leave now."

"All the more reason for me to stay."

"You're horrid!"

"You didn't seem to mind earlier today."

"Does the Prime Minister know of your penchant for assaulting innocent ladies in closets, libraries and bathrooms?"

A grin worked his sullen mouth. "I wouldn't call you innocent, darling."

Cleo glared at him, at a loss. The man was insufferable. Despicable. Insolent. Seductive. Oh, drat. She had to get him out of here before he made her do something regrettable. Something daringly foolish. Seeing no other alternative, she splashed a great handful of water toward him. It slapped him in the chest with a comical thwack. His expression was brilliant.

"You just threw water at me like a child." Surprise colored his voice.

"You're interrupting my very private bath," she countered. "You've fabricated a letter to barge your way in here and now you refuse to leave. Water is my only ammunition."

He raised a brow. "Send enough of it my way and you won't be able to hide in it."

"Did you really walk down the hall half-dressed and looking like some sort of Visigoth?" she asked, ignoring him.

"Of course I did." He glanced down at himself, then back to her, his gaze smoldering. "Do I shock you, my lady?"

She disregarded that as well. "Did anyone see you entering my chamber?" The last thing either of them needed was a scandal.

"Only my mother and seven or eight servants. Why do you ask?"

That earned him another splash. It was surreal to see him standing over her bath, disheveled, bare-footed and wet. He no longer appeared aloof or forbidding or even particularly unfamiliar. Odd though it was, no time might have passed between them. Their banter, their easy attraction—all remained, a fire she hadn't known still burned.

They played at a dangerous game. Something told her she could love this man again, perhaps had never stopped. It was her greatest fear that the match she'd convinced herself was a childish infatuation gone wrong was all too real.

Cleo grew serious. "You cannot be here like this."

Thornton stilled, the grin leaving his eyes. "I know."

She swallowed. "Then why did you come?"

"Your note."

Why did he insist on subterfuge? "I sent you no note," she told him again, only to have a sudden suspicion edge its way into her mind. "Unless…no, they wouldn't." Yes, they would, she realized. "My lord, I believe you and I have been the recipients of malicious interference."

Growing understanding dawned on his handsome face. "You mean to say someone else wrote me a note pretending to be you? Who would do such a thing?"

"My sisters," she said matter-of-factly.

"Your sisters. Ah." Thornton passed a hand through his hair. "I hadn't thought of that. It was signed in your name. I assumed…"

"Yes." It occurred to her that he had truly thought she'd asked him to bed. And he had come.

Oh, it was common enough practice at country house parties. Bored husbands and wives found new lovers beneath the auspices of many a generous hostess. Proprieties were observed. The guilty parties returned to their own beds before dawn and all was well. The country house liaison was nothing exceptional.

But knowing Alexander de Vere, the haughty, saintly politician Thornton, had come to her thrilled Cleo just the same. He stared at her now as if he wanted to pull her from the bath and devour her. Yes, this game was dangerous indeed, fraught with perils and best not played. If she went through with an *affaire*, Claridge was the far safer choice.

"You must go," she said again.

He sketched an ironic bow. "It seems I owe you an apology. I've thrust myself into your company quite unwanted."

Not unwanted, she yearned to say but could not. "You've been making a habit of it all day."

A self-mocking smile curled his sensuous lips. "You have my apologies, my lady. I'll leave you to your bath."

"No." The denial left her before she could think better of it.

He paused, watching her. Those eyes burned her skin worse than any flame.

"Could you help me with my hair?" she queried on impulse. "Bridget always assists me, but I sent her to her chamber for the night because the poor dear has a terrible cold." It was true that her hair was an unwieldy mass difficult to wash on her own. But true also that she wanted him to linger, to touch her again, possibly to kiss her. Possibly to do far more.

"You sent your woman away because she has a cold?"

"Of course." She knew many ladies did their best to pretend that servants didn't have feelings, or that as social inferiors they were not entitled to them, but Cleo was not one of them. Bridget was valued, loyal and extremely talented.

"That was kind of you." Thornton was staring at her with a strange, indecipherable expression.

"You seem surprised." She studied him. "Would you have not done the same? In your pamphlet on the working class, you urged that they be treated with the same kindness and respect we favor to members of our own set."

"You've read my work?" His voice was shaded with surprise.

Oh dear. She hadn't meant to reveal as much. Her fish was fried, as it were. "I did." Her chin went up in defiance, daring him.

"I'm honored," he said at last, "but as to your question, I can't say I've ever known Oliver to take sick."

"Perhaps he has but you haven't noticed." She doubted this, but was feeling cross enough with him to suggest it.

Thornton hadn't budged from the threshold. "I'm quite observant, you realize."

Oh, she had realized. At the moment, he was being rather observant of each bit of her skin bared to his gaze. Asking him to wash her hair had been foolhardy. If he touched her, she would slide to the bottom of the tub like a boneless lump and drown. How sobering.

He sauntered into the room, his feet making an intimate sound on the floor. It did not seem possible that years had passed and yet in two days, the careful architecture of her world had been disassembled as though never there. She had not lived with a man, had not been truly drawn to a man since she and John took separate residences a few months after their marriage. Somehow, Thornton turned her into a heroine torn from the pages of an old gothic romance, swooning over him.

The spirit of the house party had driven her to madness, she was convinced of it.

"I'm sure this is ill-advised," she murmured, watching him warily.

A knowing smile curved his wicked lips. "I'm sure everything that's ever been worthwhile throughout history has been ill-advised."

She sank lower in the water until her chin grazed its warm surface. "Do you swear on your honor to touch my hair and my hair alone?"

Her request wrung a chuckle from him. Cleo liked the deep rumble of his laughter, rich and contagious. His gray eyes glinted into hers. When he smiled he looked less arrogant and more reminiscent of the young man she'd known.

"I swear on my honor," he promised.

"I don't know if I trust you." Or if she trusted herself.

His grin deepened. "I assure you that, apart from the occasional indiscretion, I am quite the decent fellow."

"The occasional indiscretion?" she repeated. "Is that what yesterday and this afternoon were to you?"

Thornton drew closer to the tub and rolled his shirt sleeves to his elbows. His forearms, she noted, were dark and strong. She wondered again if he went about Buckinghamshire shirtless when he was up from town. Cleo never would have guessed him for a barbarian. But she fairly savored the thought of it now.

"Shampoo?" he requested.

"On the chair just over there." He had not answered her question. Was she a mere indiscretion to him? A careless dalliance? Why did the thought bother her? She should be pleased. "Ridiculous creature," she scoffed beneath her breath. "Ninny. Hen-wit."

"Have you just called me a hen-wit?" he asked from very close to her ear.

She started at his proximity and turned. Her lips nearly touched his. "I rather thought you hadn't heard."

"It isn't done to berate the man about to wash your hair, you know. I could pull it, or some such." Thornton's strong hands sank into her hair, turning her face away from him. He began dismantling her complicated chignon.

Pins slid one by one from her scalp. A soft sigh escaped her lips. The only sensation better than her hair being released from its styling was the laces on her corset going slack. It occurred to her that he was unusually handy with hair pins.

She couldn't keep herself from commenting on it. "You know your way around a lady's tresses, Thornton."

"Is that jealousy I hear curdling your sweet voice, my love?"

"Aren't you a wit?" She paused for a moment, nettled by his attempt at humor. "For a gentleman who claims to be quite the decent fellow, you are remarkably well skilled, is all."

Her hair was almost completely down around her shoulders now. "I should like to think so."

He pulled the last pin from her hair before gently massaging her scalp. Bridget never did that. Cleo sighed with pleasure and leaned her head back into his capable hands. If she wasn't careful, the man would seduce her without as much as a kiss.

"Lean your head back into the water," he ordered.

She obeyed, keeping her arms over her breasts and sliding forward in the tub. Thornton's face hovered over her, impossibly handsome even upside down in the low light of the gas jets. Their eyes met, his fingers caressing her scalp, and somehow there had never been a more intimate moment in her life. She experienced the sudden, foreign urge to yank him into the tub and make love with him.

"You would make an exceptional lady's maid," she said instead.

"So I've been told."

She caught her bottom lip between her teeth. "Do you make a habit of accosting women while they're at their baths and then washing their hair?"

Cleo was prying and she knew it was none of her affair what Alexander de Vere chose to do. She had jilted him long ago. She was a married woman. Trapped, it was true, by society's refusal to allow a woman escape from a loathsome union. He could bed every woman in the house party if he wished. She had no claim on him, no reason to harbor the sudden, irrational longing for his touch.

"Up."

Wondering if he would ignore this question as he had the last, she scooted backward, pulling her hair from the water. Silken strands clung to her back. His mere presence heightened her every sense.

She heard him lathering her shampoo in his hands before his fingers once more descended to her head. "You well know I'm only here because of your meddling sisters."

His words stung a bit. "If it was such a hardship, why did you come?"

"I never said it was a hardship." He chuckled again. "I merely pointed out that I ordinarily grace a lady's chambers when I have been invited."

Which she supposed happened with alarming frequency. No denying it, the thought galled her. She remained silent, listening to the sounds of shampoo and hands and wet hair. Perhaps he had not changed at all despite his sterling reputation.

"Lavender," he murmured.

Her shampoo, like her soap, was of the finest French lavender. Her signature scent. He had noticed. A smile curved her lips. Cleo was feeling naughty.

She pursed her lips. "Do you like it?"

Thornton cleared his throat. "Indeed, yes, your hair is lovely. Longer than most ladies' locks and singularly soft."

A laugh escaped her. "I meant the lavender, though I do appreciate your commentary on my hair."

"Of course." Thornton's voice was gruff, slightly pained. "Generally speaking, I find lavender to be an agreeable scent."

"I am relieved."

That earned her a sound dunking. She re-emerged from the water sputtering and dashing suds from her eyes. "Thornton!"

THE OBJECT OF her ire was having a difficult time producing ire of his own. In fact, he was currently preoccupied with the buoyant quality her breasts seemed to have taken on. Truly, she had no idea that he had an excellent view of her perfect pink nipples. Thornton knew he should be ashamed of himself, but he couldn't summon up an inner admonishment.

"Well?" she demanded, magnificent in her anger. Her long dark hair was slung across her back and she had turned to face him—all the better to berate him, he supposed. Her green eyes spat fire and her ordinarily pale cheeks flushed with becoming color.

"How would you have me rinse your hair?" he asked, careful to keep his inwardly roiling emotions from his voice.

"A trifle more delicately than attempting to drown me."

"Your nostrils are flaring again," he pointed out because he knew it would peeve her. In truth, he found it adorable. Christ, he wanted to shed his clothes and hop into the bath with her. She shifted into a more decorous position and her breasts bobbed as if to tease him.

"I'll splash you again," she warned.

"If you do so, I shall be compelled to think you wish for me to join you in the bath." God knew he certainly wished to do so. Could think of little else, in truth, other than the gleaming beauty of her bare skin in the low gas light.

"Insufferable man."

"I fear we are back at the beginning of our conversation, and that you've run out of insults for me."

"You are quite wrong." Her chin went up a notch. "I called you horrid earlier, not insufferable."

Hell. What was he doing here in her chamber where he didn't belong, trading banter with her as if they stood in a drawing room, both fully and respectably clothed? He wanted her. But taking her…

Taking her would be folly.

"I think I must go," he said softly, his gaze tangling in the lush mossy depths of hers.

"Do you?" He swore it was the closest she'd come to requesting him to stay.

"Yes." He leaned across the tub and dropped a kiss on her damp cheek. She even tasted of lavender, sweet and seductive. "You and I are playing at a game that could be ruinous. Though we squabble like children, our desires are not infantile in the least. I overstepped my bounds in coming here tonight."

She reached for him then, her wet hands snagging in his hair. Water droplets fell to his shoulders. Locking gazes, she pulled him to her, her mouth seeking and open. He allowed her to kiss him, groaning when it deepened and her tongue entered his mouth. He wanted desperately to sink into the warm water with her, test the silky weight of her breasts in his palms, make love in the tub with suds splashing across the floor. To wake up every last guest with their ruckus.

The guests. Damn. It took every last reserve of strength he had, but he somehow managed to tear his lips from hers. "Good night, sweet Cleo," he whispered, wondering if *Romeo & Juliet* had made him maudlin. His conscience getting the better of him, he straightened, rolled down his sleeves and stalked from the room and her chamber before he could change his mind.

He was in such a tumult he stepped right into the corridor without bothering to check first and he could have bloody well kicked himself in the arse when he saw Hollins, his mother's steel-haired maid, whisking around a corner. There would be hell to pay with the dowager if she had an inkling of this and he was afraid that Hollins had seen exactly which room he'd emerged from, half-naked, wet, and guilty as sin.

Chapter Six

𝒜 BITTER TASTE pervaded the dowager marchioness's mouth. Something was afoot between her son and Lady Scarbrough. She had it on good authority this very morning that Thornton had been seen exiting the countess's chamber last night. Most unacceptable. As far as the dowager was concerned, the woman could take after her namesake and hold an asp to her bosom.

"Bella, do sit up straight," she snapped at her only daughter, who was hunkered on a divan in the library like a washerwoman. "Slouching is common. Next you'll be selling oranges in the street."

Bella obliged, holding herself as a proper woman ought at last. The dowager despaired of ever finding a good match for the chit. She was too bookish, too prone toward frumpiness with her skirts always crushed to wrinkles and her wavy black hair forever coming undone. The dowager herself had been an ethereal blonde in her day, but both her children had inherited the dark looks of her husband. She still held it against him.

"Bella, put down the book. A man doesn't seek a wife who hides in the pages of tawdry literature all day long. I shall have it destroyed."

Her daughter blinked, making the dowager wonder if her excessive book reading was making her eyes go bad. "*Maman*, it is Lady Cosgrove's book and it is merely an edition of Shakespeare."

"Pooh, nobody reads Shakespeare these days. He was vulgar. Isn't he the fellow who championed the eating of babies? Put it down."

"This gathering revolves around a Shakespearean Theater, *Maman*. Besides, it was not Mr. Shakespeare who wrote about the babies but Jonathan Swift. It was satire."

"Satire," she harrumphed, "is more vulgar than a French novel."

Thank heavens she'd convinced Lady Cosgrove to exempt herself and her daughter from those ninny plays. The dowager was of the same mind as her grandmother Hammond who had once decried dramas as coarse and common self-indulgences better suited to children and the poor than anyone of consequence. Moreover, Shakespeare's ribaldry was far too fast for the tongues of innocent young ladies. Lady Cosgrove was a peacock who fluffed and preened and didn't have a sensible thought in her head. If her house parties weren't so famed, her balls not regal crushes, the dowager would never have consorted with a woman of her ilk. She had the look of trade about her.

Bella opened her mouth as if to argue.

The dowager smoothed her skirts and fixed her with a stern gaze. "Being argumentative is a most unbecoming trait in a lady."

"I don't wish to be a lady," her hopeless daughter grumbled.

"Grumbling beneath one's breath is only effective when it can't be heard," she said pointedly. "Do behave, Bella. We've important matters to discuss."

"Oh?" Bella did not appear suitably impressed with the gravity of the situation.

"There is a catastrophe in our midst. I'm afraid that Scarbrough woman has set her cap after your brother." Ordinarily, the dowager would not have lowered herself to discuss such unacceptable behavior with her daughter, but she did not underestimate Lady Scarbrough's appeal for her son. She saw the looks they shared. She knew of his past infatuation. She knew too that indiscreet actions here would have dire recriminations elsewhere.

Miss Cuthbert would cry off, the dowager was certain of it, and ruin Thornton's chances of acquiring the perfect wife to accompany him in his future career as the perfect statesman. Moreover, a scandal could well ruin him. While she frequently bemoaned his inattentiveness, the dowager was endlessly proud of her son. She expected him to one day become Prime Minister and lowering himself with a married woman of loose morals did not fit into that plan any more than his marrying a Covent Garden flower girl would.

Bella's nose was still buried in her Shakespeare drivel. "How can she set her cap, *Maman*? Her cap has already been thrown away on that no-account Lord Scarbrough."

"Pre-cise-ly!" She stretched out each syllable for emphasis. The dowager would have given her knuckles a stern rap on the mahogany arm of her chair as well but for the fact it was so dreadfully unladylike and would smart for a time afterward. She disliked pain of all sorts—her constitution was delicate as was only fitting for a lady of her circumstance—so much so she had barred the marquis from her chamber after Bella's birth. An heir and no spare but she hadn't cared.

Abruptly, she recalled what she had been about to say. "Precisely, my dear. However, some women, you will discover, do not allow matrimony to curb their...activities. You appear shocked, my innocent daughter. It is true, filthy but true, I assure you. I shudder to expose you to such a world as ours, but I must warn you in advance—"

"*Maman*," Bella interrupted in a rude manner, "Do you think that Lady Scarbrough is Alex's paramour?"

The dowager was certain her mouth was agape. "I'm sure I don't know where you learned that vile word, Arabella de Vere." She thought for a moment. "I can only surmise it must have been from that dreadful Beaumont chit. She is disgraceful and common. I forbid you from any contact with her from this moment forward. Yes, I can believe she would well know a word such as para…para… Well, you know, because she will end up wearing the dubious title one day soon if she continues to comport herself as a trollop."

"*Maman*, I read it in a novel."

"Your filthy novels!" She was having heart palpitations. This daughter would put her in an early grave. "Smelling salts?"

"I have none, mother," Bella said calmly.

"A fan?" Was it too much for which to hope?

"Sadly not." Her daughter's eyes dropped to her book once more.

"Disrespectful girl," she admonished in her sternest tone. "Have you no heart for your ailing mother?"

"Yes, of course, *Maman*." Bella's voice did not sound contrite in the least.

"Hollins witnessed your brother leaving the countess's chamber last evening," she snapped, frustrated beyond propriety.

"Oh dear." Bella raised a hand to her throat. "I had not thought they would go so far."

The dowager was instantly suspicious. "You had not thought? What do you speak of?"

Her daughter looked away, cheeks flushed with a telling cherry stain. "It is nothing."

She snapped to attention, her favorite whalebone corset giving a creak. Though some ladies favored the modern steel dress improver, she knew it would only damage a lady's inner being. "It is not nothing, Arabella. You must tell me at once."

Bella squirmed on the divan and the dowager fought the urge to remind her to adjust her posture. "It is only that I wandered into the room off the library yesterday whilst Alex and the countess were practicing and I felt strongly that something untoward had happened."

"Oh." The dowager pulled a handkerchief from her pocket and gave it a dainty press to her forehead. "It is as I feared. She nearly ruined Thornton seven years ago and now she will do it again."

Bella was sweetly concerned. "Do you think it so?"

"Of course. Of course it is so, daughter." She fanned herself with the perfumed scrap of lace. "If Miss Cuthbert hears of Thornton's indiscretions, she may well cry off. You know what a great match this is for him. Miss Cuthbert is the epitome of lovely womanhood and with her father's connections in parliament, the alliance is perfection. It shall cement your brother's good standing in the political realm."

"I had not thought of it in those terms. He assured me that nothing untoward would occur."

"Pish." The dowager scoffed. "He is a man, Bella. But we are very fortunate in that we, as women, know how to fix man's every foible. There's no hope for it. We must confront that woman at the nearest opportunity."

"But *maman*, do you not think it hard of you to—"

"Silence. You will confront the countess, my daughter, and convince her to cast her wiles elsewhere."

"Me?"

"Don't play the meek mouse now, girl." The dowager smiled cat-style. "Yes, it shall be you."

AT ROUGHLY THE same time that morning, Cleo was, she acknowledged it, hiding from Thornton in the library after his mortifying rejection of her the previous night. She didn't know what mad passion had come over her, but suddenly she wanted him despite all the impossibilities having him inevitably entailed. She wanted him, certainly not her rotten husband, not any other man. She wanted Thornton. And he had simply kissed her and then left her.

Three days and her life was in utter shambles. Every last shred of sanity she may have possessed had been tossed from the window like rancid water from a vase. She was attempting to distract herself with a volume of Tennyson, a poet she had never particularly cared for but had chosen for precisely that reason. If she was vexed with his form, perhaps she would not be stewing over Thornton. As it happened, her plan had yet to work.

And then, she found her solitude disrupted by the all too handsome Earl of Ravenscroft. He—unwisely, she thought—closed the library door at his back as he sauntered into the monstrous chamber. Though buffeted by a storm of unwanted emotions for Thornton, she nonetheless did not remain immune to the cagey sensuality and athletic grace of the man she'd grown to know a little and like quite a bit. He was a cipher, a clever wit and a dangerous Lothario. She should take her Tennyson volume and go.

She stayed put and watched him as brashly as he perused her, wishing herself more worldly. Truly, her life would be so much simpler if she were the average bored society wife willing to take pleasure where she could without losing her heart or her conscience. Thornton reentered her mind and she frowned.

Ravenscroft reached her, smiled with enough practiced seduction to melt a woman's resistance and tipped up her chin. "A frown does not belong on so fair a face, my lady."

His finger lingered on her skin and she drew away to break contact. "Trite flattery does not belong on the tongue of so clever a man," she returned.

"*Touché.*" He drew her hand to his mouth and pressed a kiss to her bare skin. "What does belong on this tongue is the sweet taste of your flesh, if I may be so bold."

Cleo withdrew her hand. At times she wondered if he merely played a role society expected of him. "You may not.

Please, Lord Ravenscroft, if it is dalliance you seek, I am not the woman for you."

"You wound me." He retreated and sank with leonine ease into a chair opposite her. "Perhaps I misunderstood our blossoming friendship?"

"You did not."

"Then let us dispense with formalities." His full mouth thinned and his features grew taut with uncharacteristic harshness. "As you are undoubtedly aware thanks to the gossips and the scandal rags, I whore myself for married ladies of a certain circumstance."

His unvarnished words, free of the veneer polite society imposed upon speech, scandalized her. "I find your daring most distressing, Lord Ranvenscroft. Pray, let us steer the ship of our conversation into safer waters."

Cleo couldn't be certain who she wished to save from embarrassment more, herself or Lord Ravenscroft. Never before had a man uttered the word 'whore' in her presence and she felt her face heat.

"I prefer honesty and plain speaking, Lady Scarbrough. It is not my intention to offend, merely to elucidate. I am a kept man. A whore, by nature and definition. There can be little shame in truth, no?"

She swallowed, choosing her words with care. "I too prefer forthrightness to humbuggery. However, I cannot help but to think you do yourself a great disservice."

"Humbuggery." He laughed, appearing, if possible, even more handsome. "What an original you are. I haven't heard that word since my governess, Miss Fitzhiggins, years and years ago."

Cleo raised a brow, comfortable now that it seemed the word 'whore' would no longer lurk between them. "I shall take it as a compliment to be compared to a woman as estimable as a governess."

"Oh, I would never compare the two of you." Lord Ravenscroft grinned rakishly. "As my brother was wont to say, she had the look of a hag who had fallen from the ugly tree, hitting each branch on her way down. The thickest ankles you can possibly imagine were stuffed into musty old kid boots and she made a swishing noise whenever she walked. She always smelled of an attic trunk no one had bothered to open for a decade or so. Not to mention her penchant for beating us with old broomsticks."

"Such categorization was unkind of your brother, but I suspect I would feel the same had my governess abused me in such an appalling fashion."

His expression turned wry. "It only lasted until we were both of us old enough to head off to Eton and besides, it was immeasurably preferable to fists."

"Fists?" She hadn't imagined public school lads could be that vicious.

"The dead earl," he clarified, "may his rotten hide swelter in hell for the next several hundred years at least." The current earl cursed his father without the slightest hint of anguish. It occurred to her that the man before her was an illusion, an elaborate act. He may have been speaking of a game of croquet if not for the slight glint in his eye.

For a moment, as she locked gazed with him, Cleo realized this was what a man who was jaded beyond his years, utterly soulless, and terribly scarred looked like. Discomfited by the revelation, she glanced down at Tennyson still open in her lap. She wondered how she must appear to others. Cool and complacent? Heartless and arrogant? Pathetic and sad?

"You need not avoid my gaze, Lady S. I know speaking ill of the dead and airing one's ugly family secrets is not done. But when a man has sunk to my level, platitudes and pretty rules cease to matter."

Cleo considered him again, strong and handsome, immaculately dressed in first fashion. Presumably, it had been provided by his last rumored conquest, Lady Hampton, whose elderly husband was deaf, daft, and sinfully rich.

"I do not mean to be callous, my lord, but it seems to me that your level, as you say, has been a place of refuge. Perhaps if you were to—"

"What?" He interrupted her suggestion. "Marry myself off to some plump little heiress with a father to keep me tethered to her heels? I'd sooner keep my freedom for as long as I'm able. As for trade, it would ruin my sisters' marriage hopes. I haven't the head for business. I've been raised a proper, useless Englishman, good at sport, skirt chasing, and looking down my nose."

"You underrate yourself, I think."

"You flatter me, my dear." He rose and bowed elegantly before her. "It is a pity your head's been turned by that turnip-faced Thornton. I like you."

Cleo took to her feet and extended her hand to him, their actions together as formal as if they had been engaged in proper conversation rather than propositions and thwarted seductions. "Thornton is not turnip-faced." She paused. "You do not like your other lady friends?"

His lips twitched, his blue eyes deepening to the purest navy of an early night sky. Truly, that gaze could trap a woman if she were so inclined. "Like is not apt. We have our mutual uses for one another and that is a different beast altogether. You, Lady S., are a rare treasure. Scarbrough ought to be hung by his toes."

"Preferably by the neck," she quipped before she could stop herself. When he appeared startled by her bluntness, she gave him an innocent shrug. "I know it is not done to speak ill of one's husband, but we've already established that like you, I prefer plain speaking."

"A woman after my own black heart." Lord Ravenscroft bestowed a lingering kiss upon her hand again. "Can I not persuade you to look upon me with favor and abandon that snout-nosed Thornton?"

Cleo laughed, charmed despite herself. "Lord Thornton is not snout-nosed either, nor do I look upon him with favor."

"Call me not a fool though you may call me many things, sweetheart. I've seen the way you two look at one another when you think no one is watching."

"You are mistaken, sir. Thornton and I do not look at one another with anything more than mutual enmity."

"As you say." He sounded as unconvinced as he appeared unconcerned. "Your past together is well-known and whilst I would not ordinarily be so blunt after such a short acquaintance—unless we were in bed, that is—I assumed you and Thornton were exercising your regrets in amorous pursuits."

"You assumed incorrectly," Cleo informed him, her voice tart. Need the man be so perceptive? "Thornton and I are old friends. Do not believe idle gossip, my lord. It so often lies."

In her distress at the direction of his unerring probes, Cleo dropped the Tennyson. It landed with an ominous thud near her hem, but she feared her dress improver, painfully tight-laced as it was for her form-hugging morning gown, prohibited her from retrieving the runaway volume. Thankfully, Ravenscroft was more gentleman than he pretended and fetched it for her.

He sank to his knees like her loyal vassal and offered the leather-bound book to her. As she grasped it, their fingers brushed. The library door opened at that exact instant and Thornton stalked inside.

"Ravenscroft, you bastard," he remarked in a deceptively casual tone, "have you become so depraved you've taken to peering beneath ladies' skirts in the library?"

Not even Cleo was immune to the dig. She winced on behalf of the earl, who, while of questionable moral fortitude, really was a pleasant man after all. Ravenscroft released the Tennyson but seized her free hand, bringing it to his mouth for a protracted kiss. Good heavens, was that his tongue she felt on her wrist?

"Thornton," he said after removing his lips from her shocked skin. He never took his eyes from Cleo or allowed her hand to stray too far from his ready mouth. "Have a care with your language in the presence of a lady."

"All the more reason for my presence here," Thornton returned, smooth as the cut of his trousers. "Have a care for the countess's reputation. Surely you realize the ramifications of time spent alone in your dubious presence?"

Ravenscroft rose and spun on his heel to face his opponent. Cleo imagined herself quite like the proverbial bone watching two dogs square off over her.

"What would you have me do, my lord?" the earl demanded. "Leave her to *your* dubious presence?"

Her skin tingled with the heat of a revealing flush. She met Thornton's steel eyes, both of them knowing Ravenscroft's words too true. She also knew, as did all three of them, that one of the great—if scarce—freedoms of a married lady was her ability to consort with men of her choosing in private. This occurred particularly at house parties and especially, though by no means exclusively, when the husband in question gracefully ignored his wife's peccadilloes. Since Scarbrough had not even seen Cleo in over a year, his acquiescence was a given. In other words, Cleo was quite safe in either man's company, despite Ravenscroft's sooty reputation, and she informed the two men before her of as much.

"Sooty?" Thornton was disdain personified, the born in the purple aristocrat he was. Then, true to form, his words utterly ruined the brilliant display. "You make him sound like a chimney sweep. His reputation is mired in pig shit, is more like."

"Pig shit, is it?" The earl laughed as though he discussed nothing more benign than a lover's sonnet. "Thornton, you silly lad. It isn't pig shit I so often find myself in."

She pressed her lips together to stifle a gasp of shock.

Good heavens, the man knew how to string a proper crude sentence. Thornton went livid. He advanced on Ravenscroft, a gothic hero intent on restoring the honor of his heroine. Oh, she supposed she read too many old novels and ought to be reading more of Helen's aesthetic books instead. But she couldn't help herself, just as she couldn't tamp down a primeval excitement at the thought that these two solid, roguish men might come to blows over her. It was rather delicious, she thought, only to frown when she realized she'd once again borrowed Thornton's word. Drat him.

He grabbed a fistful of Ravenscroft's shirt, but the earl stopped him with a steady hand and a mocking drawl. "Oh dear. I hope I haven't overset you. I merely meant to clarify that, while you had mistaken me for a country gentleman such as yourself, I do not find myself in pig shit often. Quite the opposite. I find myself in only the best of everything."

"As a result of your whoring."

"Thornton!" This time, Cleo leapt to her feet. She knew not where Tennyson plopped, nor cared.

She watched the scene before her, a spectator to two grown men losing possession of their wits. This time, Ravenscroft acted first, launching himself at Thornton. She sidestepped a *Louis Quinze* table and said a hasty prayer before inserting herself into the skirmish. She placed a staying hand on each man's arm, attempting but unable to separate them.

"You cannot come to blows like this." She tried for reason and logic, supposedly the fountainheads of manhood. "It will be said you fought over me."

"We are fighting over you," they said in unison, locked in a death glare with one another.

She yearned to level a sound kick to each of their shins to gain their attention. Or, better yet, pull their ears like a stout governess. Though they claimed to be fighting in her name, they more likely sought to assuage their mutually damaged pride. What an insufferable lot men were! She had all the painful dramatics of an *amour* and yet reaped none of the benefits.

"Blessed angels' sakes! Why would you fight over me?"

"Because you're a beautiful woman," Ravenscroft announced through gritted teeth at the same moment Thornton muttered, "Damned if I know."

Affronted in spite of her best efforts to remain the restorer of order, she released the earl to better berate Thornton. An error in judgment, that. Ravenscroft took the opportunity to land a painful-sounding punch to Thornton's jaw.

Thornton's head snapped back. He recovered with haste, rubbing his jaw before taking up a pugilist's stance. The earl followed suit, holding his large fists before him, swinging, feinting to the left then right. Thornton delivered a swift blow to his chin.

"Stop!" Cleo swatted at them, as ineffectual as a butterfly attempting to halt a marching brigade. Her erstwhile suitors were determined to ruin the very reputation they'd just argued over by beating one another senseless in Lady C.'s library.

"Stand aside, Cleo," Thornton ordered her, swinging again.

"I will not! This is madness. Childishness," she continued, savoring the harangue on her tongue.

The earl gave her a gentle shove and she lost her balance, her moment of triumph ended in rudest fashion. Cleo landed in a chair some few feet from the impending melee. Pandemonium ensued. Thornton pounced on Ravenscroft, slamming the earl's body against the wall of books. Several tomes fell to the floor in a jumbled heap. An upholstered chair tipped next, followed by a crystal decanter shattering on the floor. Ravenscroft tackled Thornton onto the *Louis Quinze* table and its legs gave out.

Catching onto the commotion, guests and servants milled into the library. Naturally, the first woman through the door was the gossipy Margot Chilton and the second, the equally free-lipped and possibly more odious Lady Grimsby. Cleo's horror mounted as she spied the dowager marchioness, Lady Bella, Lady C. herself and Tia and Helen's wide eyes. Not even the servants were immune. The butler lost his composure and gaped from the threshold along with the housekeeper.

"Fight!" hollered an impudent young footman as he rushed past them and into the library, his wig askew.

Cleo fought the urge to shield her face. Thornton and Ravenscroft pummeled on, either oblivious to or uncaring of their growing audience. This was the end of her reputation as a respectable woman. They'd truly made a muck of things now.

Tia gesticulated in a less than subtle manner, indicating that Cleo should cross to the other side of the room to lessen the obviousness of her involvement. Taking the cue from her younger sister, she began a slow retreat from the spectacle. She feared, however, the damage had been done. Between Lady Grimsby and Margot Chilton, all the Quality would know in short order that the notorious Ravenscroft and the ordinarily respectable Thornton had beat one another to bits over the Countess of Scarbrough. Before Cleo could reach the haven of her sisters, Lord Cosgrove made his way through the crowd.

"What is the meaning of this?" he boomed, apparently having been summoned from his smoking room and customary bottle of port for this very purpose.

Predictably, neither Thornton nor Ravenscroft appeared to notice. Unfortunately for Lord C., enraged by the insult to his authority as one half of the hosting duo of the best country house party in England, he stumbled into the fracas.

Cleo winced. Ravenscroft landed a sound punch to Lord C.'s arm before he realized what he was about. To his credit, Lord C. answered with a respectable cuff to the earl's head. She was quite certain she'd never witnessed the like. Their host's interference in the scrap appeared to have a sobering effect on Ravenscroft and Thornton. She could discern the precise moment Thornton realized he had an audience. To the impartial observer, his demeanor would remain as impassive and arrogant as ever. But Cleo recognized the quirk of his brow, the slight intake of breath. She knew when he caught sight of his forbidding mother from the way he stiffened. He met her gaze and smirked. There went that dratted dimple.

The air fled from Cleo's lungs. Like a hare, she had been caught in a snare. Keenly, she recognized a kinship with the doomed creature of a hunt. Helpless. Thornton was her fate. Perhaps Shakespeare had rotted her brain and rendered her maudlin and terribly romantic. Perhaps she'd been reading too much poetry. Whatever the reason, she was his. He was hers. The shocked ladies and lords around them mattered naught. His gray eyes gleamed in triumph. She was his.

Chapter Seven

THAT EVENING, DINNER was yet again a grand affair, this time in Elizabethan style. Lady C.'s guests—minus two since Thornton and Ravenscroft had been politely exiled from company following their fisticuffs—supped on borage salad, a trio of rich game stews, porret soup, codlings, pheasant and medlar fruit tarts. Cleo ate without gusto, bearing the scrutiny of at least a dozen eyes with as much grace as she could summon.

Thanks to the ruckus, the Shakespeare scenes Lady C. had taken great care in preparing had been postponed until the following afternoon. Cleo was spared from having to perform in a play, yet was forced to remain an actress for the evening.

She was heartily glad the two sources of her current predicament were lying in their chambers tippling whiskey and applying poultices to their blackened eyes. Their absence, however, did little to appease the blatant curiosity of the men and women at table.

Much to her dismay, Lady Grimsby was seated two chairs away, ignoring the contents of her plate. "Miss Chilton mentioned you were the only other person in the library when she entered, Lady Scarbrough. Do tell us what could have sparked such an inglorious display betwixt the earl and marquis."

Finally, the question she'd dreaded all day arrived. She had carefully formulated her response, had even practiced alone in her chamber before the mirror to keep her face expressionless. She smiled with benign elegance at the elder gossip. "I dare say you will be surprised to learn it, Lady Grimsby, but it appeared to me upon entering the chamber myself that their lordships were arguing over a volume of Tennyson."

Her ladyship raised a thin blonde brow. "Then you weren't in the library prior to the argument?"

"I'm afraid not." She had decided, while hiding from everyone in her chamber, that prevarication would be her best hope of avoiding scandal.

"Miss Chilton was so certain you were there," Lady Grimsby insisted.

"She must have entered at my heels. With the commotion, she likely failed to notice me." Cleo took a delicate sip of her wine, pleased with herself. That Miss Chilton was seated too far down the table to be solicited on the matter was fortuitous indeed.

"Coming to blows over a volume of Tennyson?" the Duke of Claridge intoned, slicing liberally at his roasted pheasant. "I didn't realize Thornton and Ravenscroft were such bookish men."

Tia coughed. Helen kept her wine goblet pressed to her lips. Cleo gritted her teeth. Sisters. Couldn't they at least offer her some support instead of barely concealing their laughter at her expense?

"Apparently, Tennyson stirs the hearts of men," she offered with a lame shrug.

"Something stirs the hearts of men, to be sure," Claridge said.

"Hearts are not all that stir," Tia whispered to Cleo with a saucy chuckle.

Lady Grimsby's eyes sharpened. "What was that, Lady Stokey?"

Tia blinked, appearing innocent as a deb. "I merely said that I shouldn't find it surprising Tennyson had such an effect on our dear earl and marquis. I too feel an angelic stirring in my very soul whenever I chance to read *The Charge of the Light Dragoons*."

"Brigade, my dear," Lady Grimsby corrected with haughty condescension. "The poem is called *The Charge of the Light Brigade*."

Tia was unaffected by the slip. "Just so."

"I've always preferred female poets to their male counterparts," Helen interrupted, challenging the gossip to an unspoken game of wits. "For instance, I find Christina Rossetti's work to be a positively illuminating experience compared with Alfred Tennyson's pretensions. What think you, my lady?"

Having possession of a very limited literary landscape, the lady could only sputter. She looked quite like a hen robbed of her eggs. Cleo narrowed her gaze and turned her head to the right and the similarity was uncanny. Even her nose resembled a pointed beak.

"Men always make for better poets. They have a fount of rational intellect," Lady Grimsby added at last.

"Called arrogance," Helen remarked tartly.

"I say," Claridge broke in with a charming grin, "should I be offended?"

"Not at all, Your Grace," Cleo interjected, gracing him with a flirtatious smile. After all, it wouldn't hurt to make their scandalmonger think it was the duke she preferred. Perhaps that would lessen the sting of her current predicament. "I'm sure that, like me, my sister holds you exempt from her singular opinions."

"I am relieved." He shared a smile with Cleo and she wondered what she would do if she suddenly had three suitors rather than the already unmanageable two.

Oh dear. Apparently given to a similar vein of thought, Tia delivered a subtle kick to her beneath the table. Cleo glared at her sister. Tia began flirting madly with Claridge in response. And it was just as well, she supposed. Although she admired their mild flirtation, she knew it was a mere fancy. The sole man in her thoughts, impossible though it may be, was Alexander de Vere.

When the opulent meal came to an end, Cleo pleaded a headache and slipped away to the sanctity of her chamber. She needed time away from everyone. Time to think about how on earth she could proceed, knowing their troubled history, despite his arrogant sneers, despite his interruption of her otherwise stable life, the fact that he frustrated her at every turn, that she could never truly have him thanks to her ill-chosen husband and despite his irreverent and shockingly improper pugilistic display in the library...

She wanted him.

The realization struck her with such force she nearly stumbled in the hall outside her chamber door. She paused, reaching up to trace the placard that had been neatly inscribed with her name, Countess of Scarbrough. For her entire adult life, it had been a mantle she wore, a title to which she gave little heed. She was five and twenty and she had never felt for her husband the inexplicable draw that pulled her to Thornton. It had been a mere matter of days and already she found it difficult to envision her world without him again, their troubled past be damned. She wanted his touch, his kiss. She wanted to wake up in his bed, in his arms, to wear the scent of him on her skin like her French perfume, to...

What was that rumbling noise emanating from her chamber? Her hand stilled on the placard and she listened to the distinct sound of a man snoring. It couldn't be. Cleo swung open the door and stepped inside, shutting it at her back when she spotted the object of her tortured musings lying in slumber on her bed. He was clothed from head to toe in black, still wearing his boots, ankles crossed, arms resting behind his head. As she entered the room more fully, she discerned a purple bruise marring his jaw and a split in his otherwise perfect lips. The gas lights flickered low, but even in the sparse illumination they threw off, he was beautiful and tempting.

Truly, she should have been shocked to find him there. If she had the slightest bit of sense, she would wake him by boxing his ears, the blighter. He'd delivered more blows than those he'd given Ravenscroft today, yet here he was, blithely snoring away, resting on her bed as if he belonged. Worse, there was no hope for ringing for Bridget now.

Fortunately, she'd worn one of her newly designed gowns that opened down the front bodice. But that hardly solved the matter of what to do with the sleeping giant in her bed. Waking him after she'd disrobed seemed like a poor plan. On the other hand, her dress improver was altogether too tight.

Opting for sensibility, she gave Thornton a gentle shake to wake him. His gray eyes opened and he gave her a slow grin as he stretched. "Is it morning, then?"

"Sadly not." Cleo eyed him sternly, doing her best to fortify her inner defenses. "What are you doing in my chamber besides snoring like a drunken sailor?"

"How many drunken sailors have you heard snoring in your day, my lady?"

"None," she admitted.

"Thought not." His grin deepened to reveal that charming dimple. "Was I snoring?"

"Loudly." She smiled back.

"I had some of Cosgrove's whiskey," he confessed, sheepish. "My head hurts like the devil."

"'Tis what you deserve for rolling about in the library as if you were a common street urchin."

"No mercy, Cleo?"

"You had none for me," she pointed out.

He winced. "I suppose you heard an earful, yes?"

"Of course I did." She swatted him on the arm because he didn't look nearly repentant enough for her taste. "Everyone assumed you had been fighting over me and I was left inventing the miserable excuse that you had come to blows over a volume of Tennyson's poetry."

Thornton scoffed, sitting up suddenly, the picture of affronted manhood. "I don't even like poetry. In fact, the practice is utterly useless unless one takes into consideration the odd sonnet that gets a man under a woman's skirts."

His pronouncement earned him another swat, this time on his ear.

"Ouch." He glared at her, rubbing the side of his head. "I didn't deserve that."

"You most certainly did." She became aware she was shaking her finger at him as her governess had done, but she couldn't seem to upbraid him without a wagging digit, so she continued. "You are a rotten man. All you've done in the last few days is to make trouble for me. First you closeted me inside a darkened room and undid my bodice—"

"You liked that."

"And then you found your way into my bath. But you couldn't leave it at that, oh no. You had to fight with the most notorious man in the realm over me, then throw me to the gossips while you got silly on whiskey. And now you're in my bed talking about using sonnets to seduce ladies—"

"I said nothing about ladies."

"Which is even worse," she huffed, swatting him again for good measure. "You hide beneath a pose of coolness and unimpeachable honor, but you are truly a rogue at heart."

Thornton gave her a smoldering look. "Guilty as charged, I think. Care to kiss me?"

Of course she wanted to kiss him and that was entirely the problem. Did he not realize how difficult she found it to be in his presence without touching him? Even now, she yearned to be wrapped in his arms. Certainly, she wanted to oblige him, God help her. Instead, she ran a light finger over his split lip. "Does it smart?"

Thornton winced, ruining the raffish air he'd created on the bed with his bruised face, slight shadow of a beard and sleep-mussed hair. "The damned earl has an impressive right hook."

"I had Bridget take you a poultice."

"The bloody thing reeked of medicine. I couldn't stomach it." He kissed the finger that had stilled over his gorgeous mouth. "The gesture was most appreciated, however."

Unable to stop herself, Cleo swayed into him, pressing her face into the deliciously scented skin of his neck. His arms caught her to him in a tight embrace and he hauled her onto the bed so that she lay atop him. Neither of them spoke for a few minutes. He nestled his face into her hair. His hands stroked her back. Beneath her lips, his pulse thrummed. She kissed the vital cords of his neck, breathing deeply of him, savoring him. The effect he had on Cleo frightened her.

She tipped her head back to gaze at him. "Thornton, what are we playing at?"

His gaze met hers, a wry smile curving his lips. "The games of men and women."

"I don't think I can do this," she said with bare honesty.

Thornton's hands stilled. "We are both of an age."

He would not be serious with her, then. Men always strove for humor whenever real emotions got into sight. Rather than argue, Cleo opted for a change of subject. "Did you know Lord Cosgrove sacked the poor footman?"

"Footman?"

"The one who began the chant," she explained, recalling it all too well. Thornton, Thornton, Thornton.

"The Cockney lad who wanted me to beat Ravenscroft to a 'bloody frigging pulp', you mean?"

"Just so. I expect he forgot himself in the hubbub."

"He and at least half a dozen others were chanting my name." He had the nerve to grin as if he'd enjoyed himself. Which he probably had, the cad.

"Likely only because of its ease," she scoffed with an unwanted touch of laughter in her voice. "Fewer syllables, you know."

"Or because they knew a victor when they saw one." His grin grew into the same bold smirk he'd worn earlier that day in the library.

Cleo tapped his nose. "You are too much, my lord."

He kissed her finger again, his eyes darkening with a serious intent. "Cleo, I'm sorry to have made you the object of speculation. I assure you it wasn't my aim."

She searched his gaze for meaning. "What was your aim, Thornton?"

"My aim in attending this house party was to please my mother, who requested my distinguished presence here to ease my sister's transition into society." He gave a rueful laugh. "My aim in the library remains questionable, however."

"I have little doubt Scarbrough shall hear of it," she murmured.

"Again, I apologize. I too have little doubt that news of our contretemps will find its way to his ears."

"I don't think I care." She was aware of the implications of her words. Surely it was wrong of her to feel this way for a man of such short acquaintance, their long-ago engagement aside. Surely she should be ashamed of her boldness, of her desire for him. Yet she couldn't summon even a crumb of conscience.

"I know I don't care." He caught her hand and pressed another kiss to her palm, then her wrist, stopping at the pulse there. "Your heart thrums fast, my dear."

She swallowed, inexplicably nervous now that she had taken the inevitable leap. "I should tell you that I have never, save a few misplaced kisses throughout the years, been unfaithful to Scarbrough."

"You cannot be unfaithful to a man who has no faith. Know that."

"Thornton, would you—"

An insistent knock at the door swallowed the words she'd been about to say. Thornton groaned. "Is it your blasted maid with yet another poultice? Hang me if it is."

"Cleo!" The hiss from the corridor was unmistakably Tia's. "Cleo, Helen and I must speak with you at once. Do let us in!"

"It's not my blasted maid, it's my blasted sisters," she whispered.

"Pretend you're sleeping."

"The gas lights are on."

"They can't see that beneath the door."

"They've been known to lower themselves to the floor to peek," she warned.

"The devil. How could they manage it in their corsets?"

"We can see you've your light on," Tia trilled. "Stop trying to avoid us."

"I told you so." She rolled away from him and slid to the floor, frantically straightening her skewed bodice and fluffing her flattened skirts. "Hide somewhere," she ordered him when he remained lounging on her bed.

"Where would you have me?" With a sullen frown on his lips and his black clothing, he appeared disreputable and delicious. Yes, there was his word once more. She found she rather liked it.

"Cleo!" The knocking grew louder.

"A moment," she called to her dratted sisters. "Get in the bathroom," she directed.

"Right," he grumbled, swinging his long legs to the floor. "Going. Don't mind me. I'll just sleep in the bloody tub for the evening whilst you chat away with your sisters."

She glared at him before hurrying across the chamber to the door. With one last cursory smoothing of her hair and skirts, then a glance to be certain he'd truly hidden himself, she pulled it open. Tia's eyes narrowed. Helen looked suspicious.

"What took you so long to answer the door?" Helen demanded.

"I was writing in my journal," she lied.

"You don't keep a journal," Tia countered.

"Of course I do. 'Tis where I keep my innermost thoughts." She took a step back and gestured for her sisters to enter. "Come in, you sorry lot."

Her sisters did as they were bid, Tia scarcely waiting for the door to close before she sniffed the air. "It smells of a man in here. Cleo, are you entertaining without telling us?"

She wondered if her guilt showed on her face. "I'm sure you don't smell anything at all, you odious creature."

"Enough squabbling," Helen interrupted, asserting her august elder sister role. "The real reason we've come," she emphasized, ruining her presentation by poking Tia in the ribs, "is to make certain you have weathered the storm, so to say."

Her annoyance at the intrusion abated as quickly as Lord Cosgrove could quaff a few drams of good Scottish whiskey. "It is sweet of you to check on me. I am as well as can be expected. I dare say Scarbrough has done worse."

"Of course the bastard has." Tia patted her on the shoulder. "It's time you had a scandal of your own."

"A scandal?" Cleo winced. She hadn't thought it that bad. Well, not precisely, anyway.

"You don't expect anyone to truly believe the earl and the marquis fought over a volume of Tennyson, do you, darling?"

"Tia." The admonishment came from Helen, but too late.

"What?" Tia shrugged. "'Tis true."

"Of course not," Cleo admitted with a rueful smile.

"Really," Tia went on, "Tennyson. No man would fight over something as over-valued as poetry, least of all his. Horses, perhaps. Women, naturally. Tennyson? Absolutely not."

Cleo glared at her younger sister. "You needn't overdo it, Tia."

"Well, it was a terribly stupid excuse."

"Tia." Helen poked her in the ribs again.

"Ouch." Tia rubbed her bodice, frowning at Helen. "Your fingers are quite sharp, you know."

"Perhaps if it had been Shakespeare," Helen suggested.

"No, I fear Tia is right in her assessment and not even old Will could help me to extricate myself from this scrape." Cleo sighed.

"Even so, it's rather unheard of." Helen beamed. "Two men coming to blows at Lady Cosgrove's house party! You may be lauded as the epitome of the modern woman."

"But I am not a modern woman. Not at all."

"No one will blame you," Tia agreed, "particularly not with that sordid story circulating about Mrs. Giroux taking tea in your Mayfair house."

"What?" Cleo was properly outraged. How dare Scarbrough install his mistress at Cleo's respectable home? It was unthinkable.

"Oh dear." Tia frowned. "I suppose you hadn't heard that one."

"No."

"These days gossip is passed around more than naughty French novels." Helen patted Cleo's shoulder. "Think nothing of it, dearest. It's probably not true anyway."

It probably was true, which they all knew, but none of them mentioned. Sometimes, truth is best left unspoken.

"Darling, are you certain you're perfectly well?" Tia's countenance grew serious, concern furrowing her light brow.

No. The truth was she quite feared she'd gone mad and the rest of the world had yet to realize it. Was it really she who had brought an infamous rake and the brooding marquis to blows in the library? How was it that Thornton waited for her in her bathroom, that even now she wished to shoo her sisters into the hall so she could be alone with him? How was it that she'd gone from hating him to…well, not loving him. But certainly, the enmity between them had dissipated in favor of a *grande* passion that could be the unraveling of them both. No, she didn't really think it hasty or melodramatic or even terribly gothic of her to deem it such. Not a bit.

In fact, her life was beginning to take on a disturbing similarity to a Shakespearean play. She knew not yet if it was to be comedy or tragedy, but she rather hoped for the former.

"Cleo?" Tia's voice interrupted her reflections.

She sighed. "Actually, my dear, dear sisters, I fear I have the megrims."

Helen's eyes narrowed this time. "You needn't pretend to have the headache for us, you know."

"It is all too real, I swear it," Cleo told her sisters in half-truth.

"Well." Tia examined her with a knowing air. "I suppose we should leave you to your sleep. We wouldn't want your megrim to affect you unjustly. Whenever I have an attack of the megrims, I find that it is best to sleep through them." She made a pretty moue of horror. "Fortunately for you, Cleo, you have no husbandly demands to worry about this evening. Does she, Helen?"

Helen sent Tia a conspiratorial look that Cleo did not miss, nor was she meant to. Her sister smiled. "I should think wifely duties are the last thing on dear Cleo's mind this evening. Are you sure you wish us to leave you, Cleo?"

"It is best, I think," she said weakly, wishing she hadn't been cursed with such clever sisters. She loved them, but they could be more merciless than the most cunning of foxes. Thankfully, in this instance, Helen and Tia were willing to retreat rather than finish their hunt. They exchanged good evenings and she saw them out the door just as the faint rumbling began again.

Snoring. A hasty trip to the bathroom confirmed that

Thornton had once again fallen asleep, this time on the corner chair where Cleo rested her towel while she was in the bath. She called his name, but he didn't stir, so she approached him and gently shook his shoulder. Though none of the gas jets had been lit in the bathroom, light crept in from the chamber, bathing him in a golden glow.

His eyes blinked open. "Mmm?"

"Thornton, they've gone," she murmured, uncertain of how they were to proceed.

"Who?" He appeared genuinely perplexed as he sat up straighter in the chair and stretched his arms above his head. He gave a loud yawn punctuated by a belch. "Do excuse me, my love. That was quite rude of me. Quite—" He hiccupped. "Quite bloody rude."

Oh dear. He'd gone from mildly foxed to thoroughly inebriated in all of ten minutes. Just how much of Cosgrove's whiskey had he consumed?

"My sisters have gone," she supplied, "but it's of little consequence now. I fear you've indulged more than I thought."

"I may have tippled a bit while I was waiting," he admitted with a crooked grin and gestured to a bottle on the floor at his side.

"You duffer!" His confession earned him yet another swat. "How could you?"

"Boredom?" He shrugged.

She made a noise of suffering.

"Was that a growl, my love? How naughty of you."

"Stand up," she commanded, losing her patience with each passing moment. Cleo had been on the brink of giving herself to this man and he'd merely been on the brink of finishing their host's whiskey collection. "We've got to get you to bed. I'm afraid it's the only answer to your particular circumstance."

"Excellent idea." He stood and swayed against her. "Good

Christ. Why is that wall moving about so? It's making me feel ill."

"Oh no." She wrapped her arms around his waist to steady him. "You aren't going to be sick, are you?"

"I'll have you know I can hold my whiskey. Better than Ravenscroft, I'd wager." His mouth found its way to her ear. "I love your ears."

"My ears?" How unromantic of him. She'd never heard the like. Then he kissed the object of his affections and she hurriedly forgot she'd been unimpressed. His tongue caught the whorl, his teeth tugged on the sensitive lobe. Oh my.

"They're perfect." He kissed a path down her neck, sucking on her skin. "And your neck. I love your neck." He tongued the hollow of her throat. "This spot where your pulse beats, I love it too." His mouth found its way to the tops of her breasts, exposed by her décolletage. "And these are absolutely brilliant. I love your breasts." He buried his face between them and inhaled deeply. "Why do you always smell so damn delicious?"

She smiled, feeling wicked. "To torment you."

"You're succeeding." He swayed again.

"Thornton?"

"Yes, my love?" As his face had yet to move away from her bosom, his voice was quite muffled.

"You're stepping on my foot."

He muttered a curse and removed the offending appendage. "Sorry."

She took his hands in hers. "Come, you must try to return to your chamber and get a good night's rest."

"Not my chamber, surely. Can't I remain here in yours?"

"I do not think it a good idea."

"I realize I'm a miserable sot for everything I've done today." Thornton's fingers tightened on hers, his eyes intense. "But I confess I don't think it in me to stagger back to my chamber just now."

How utterly unromantic. It wasn't the wooing she'd expected this evening and it took the wind out of her a bit.

"You may stay for a time," she conceded, for there was really no other option.

Chapter Eight

*D*AWN ARRIVED TOO soon. She slept little, savoring the protection of Thornton's arms around her, the warmth of his big, strong body at her back. He'd fallen asleep almost immediately, but she hadn't minded. She'd been too ensnared in the new, strange emotions assaulting her. Goodness, she had not shared a bed with a man in years. Scarbrough paid her as much attention as the drapery. Even in the first year of their marriage when he had been far more attentive, he had done his business and returned to his own chamber. Never had he wanted to touch her as if she were a person from whom he took comfort. As if she were a person for whom he possessed tender feelings.

With Thornton, everything seemed different.

Until reality, with all its vulgar implications, stole into her chamber as if it were the morning sun. What would they ever have together beyond these fleeting, stolen moments? She wouldn't contemplate it just now.

"Thornton, you must wake."

He rolled over.

"Thornton, 'tis nearly morning. The servants will be about soon and you must not be seen leaving my chamber." Cleo shook him with—she had to admit—unkind force.

He groaned and sat up. Through the meager light of the lone gas light she'd lit, she discerned the hard muscles of his back, each clearly delineated. When she placed a cool hand against his hot skin, he jerked.

"I think the damned devil is dancing a jig inside my skull," he muttered with unprecedented bluntness.

"I will send Bridget to you—"

"I don't want a goddamn poultice." He threw back the bedclothes.

"Very well." She drew herself up with as much dignity as she could manage while abed. "You shan't get a goddamn poultice if you don't want a goddamn poultice."

"Shrew."

"Lout."

"Virago."

"Noddy."

"Noddy? Is that the best insult you can find?"

He fumbled about for his shirt on the chaise. Had she just been thinking of tender feelings? Had she mistaken his hold for something more? Uncertainty swirled about her like cold bathwater. And what was wrong with noddy, anyway? She thought it quite effective.

"Thornton?"

He sighed, the sound ragged. "I'm sorry." He kept his back to her as he shrugged on his shirt first, then his black jacket. "I'm a bit of a bear in the mornings."

"You don't say." She wanted to keep the hurt from her voice, but wasn't certain if she'd succeeded.

"I've the devil of a hangover," he explained, casting her a bleary-eyed look.

"The devil surely seems to be on your thoughts this morning."

"I'm sure you know why," he returned.

Of course she did and suddenly the morning seemed bleaker for it. Yes, the sun was steadily on the rise, casting a few golden strands of light into the room to battle the gas lamp. Mere heartbeats before her world had bloomed bright with meaning. Now it appeared like the autumn day it would be after all, ashen gray and cool. An awful sensation of portent crept over her.

"Perhaps we should no longer see one another in private," she whispered, hating herself even for suggesting it. Cleo didn't think she could endure not being able to speak freely with him, to touch him as she liked.

"Impossible," he said, clipped and final. He stalked to the door and swept out. It closed with a snap that was louder than propriety would have preferred.

She flinched. Impossible. In so many senses of the word, he was right.

"RIDICULOUS," THE DOWAGER marchioness boomed to her daughter later that morning from her private chamber. "Your brother has been behaving abominably ever since our arrival and I tell you daughter, I have begun wondering whether he has finally fallen into drink as everyone on your father's side of the family is prone to do. Bless the de Vere women before me for their fortitude. How they must have suffered! And your own dear brother, so young to succumb. Oh! It hurts my mother's heart to think he has become depraved, but I fear that is the case. Next he shall die of delirium tremens in a hospital for the poor. Do you think him in a very bad way, Bella?"

She sniffled and raised a black lace handkerchief to her nose. This morning, of all mornings, she had chosen to wear her most depressing gown. It was severe and muted with horizontal stripes of dove and jet. Still, she thought it turned her out to advantage. At least if Alexander left the family in disgrace, no one could say it happened while she looked a fright.

"*Maman*, I do realize his fight with the earl was ill-advised," Bella began.

"Ill-advised? My child, it was infamous!" She reached for

her fan and began madly waving it about before her face. She needed air. When had she ever supposed her lovely, well-bred daughter would be the death of her? Surely it would be her son, who was following in his father's dubious path with that horrid woman whose name she would not even think. No, she couldn't. Like a man looking Medusa head-on, thinking the woman's name would surely turn her to stone. Or at the very least her heart. Yes, it would turn her poor, aging heart to stone and lead her to an early grave.

"It was not so bad as all that," Bella continued calmly. Even the dowager had to admit her daughter did not seem as bookish today. Her hair was dressed in soft feminine waves around her face and she—as few misses could—wore a pastel pink gown with the natural elegance of an English rose. "Many of the people to whom I spoke yesterday speculated that the earl had insulted Alex. No one spoke of anything untoward between my brother and Lady Scarbrough."

Oh, the wretched name! That wretched woman. The dowager feared she may swoon. "Don't say that name, Bella. My heart is going into palpitations. I shall die of the stress of a broken heart. Why have you not spoken to that woman as I asked you?"

"*Maman*, you are putting Mr. Shakespeare's characters to shame," Bella chided.

The dowager's spine stiffened. "Do not scold me. I am your mother."

"I merely wish you to calm yourself."

"I cannot calm myself." She dismissed her daughter's suggestion with a wave of her handkerchief. "There is no hope for it. We must put ourselves to good use. The countess must be stopped at all costs before she ruins my poor Thornton."

Bella rose from her chair and crossed the room to kneel at the dowager's side. She dabbed gently at her cheeks with a handkerchief, a gesture that nearly brought more tears to the marchioness's eyes.

"*Maman*, you must collect yourself. Mr. Whitney will arrive at any moment to escort us down to breakfast."

"Not that no-account American." She was aghast, truly aghast, that her daughter would ever deem such a lowly person a suitable escort for women of their elevated rank. "It's horrid enough that your brother dabbles in trade with him. I will not tolerate his uncouth presence for one moment longer than absolutely necessary."

"Mother, Mr. Whitney is a perfect gentleman." Her daughter's tone was stern and unless she missed her mark, there was a lingering gleam of admiration in her eyes. Heaven have mercy. Perhaps she had cause to watch closely over Bella after all, lest she take lessons from Thornton's heedless ways.

"He cannot even pronounce the King's English," she felt compelled to protest.

"He is from Virginia."

"Where I have heard there is an inordinate number of rabid kangaroos and wild apes," the dowager informed the hopelessly innocent girl before her. "Really, you must not ever think him your equal, for then he will attempt to win you. That is the way of it with Americans. They are not to be trusted. Think, Bella. Should you like to spend the remainder of your life warding off insects the size of a small child? Do not look so surprised. I have it on good authority that such monstrosities exist in the Americas. Along with poisonous snakes and not to mention the appalling brash characters they all possess, voices so loud, hands as broad as any laborer's and their ears. Did you not take note of the extraordinary size of that Mr. Whittleby fellow's ears, my darling girl? Your children would be equipped to take flight."

Bella stood. "I have it on good authority that Mr. Whitney is a true gentleman. You will be kind to him, mother. Furthermore, you will not ever mention rabid kangaroos or child-sized insects in his presence."

"Of course I wouldn't." The dowager raised her lorgnette

and peered at Bella with as disparaging a glance as she could muster. "To do so would be unpardonably rude."

Lady Scarbrough,

Please forgive me.

Yours,
Thornton

Lord Thornton,

While I do not require a complete soliloquy, a listing of your faults may do a great deal to heal my wounded heart.

Yours,
Cleopatra

Cleopatra,

I am a bear. An Utter bear. I beg you a hundredfold. Forgive me.

Thornton

My lord,

True, your conduct was appalling. Indeed, I should think that if both you and a bear were entered into a comportment and manners competition, the easy winner would be the bear. However, one bear does not a listing of faults make. Do try harder.

Cleopatra, Countess of Scarbrough

Darling Cleopatra,

I have not pages long enough. Though I do think it fortunate that no such competition between man and bear exists.

T.

Most frustrating Marquis,

Nor have you the desire to admit your shortcomings.

C.

Darling Cleo,

Why should I have shortcomings when I possess the great de Vere height? No, I dare say I am rather tall.

T.

Most vexing man,

Your deliberate and unabashed obfuscation leaves me thinking perhaps I should not exchange notes with you at all.

C.

Darling,

I shan't believe a word of your obligatory protestations, so you needn't worry. Meet me as soon as you can near the copse of trees south of here.

Your servant,
Alex

The last missive, carried to her discreetly by Bridget on a silver salver, nearly undid Cleo. Truly, he had not been Alex to her for seven long years, though he demanded she call him by his Christian name their first day here. It quite took her back. He was not the young man he had been then. Neither was she the easily cowed young lady eager to bend to the silver tongue of Scarbrough. Still, how she wished in that moment that she could return to those simpler times when she had been free.

Bridget waited quietly for Cleo's response. She was good at feigning ignorance of her mistress's comings and goings, but this was a new task for her. Never before had Cleo engaged in the intrigues of society men and women. Now it would seem she was hopelessly entangled. Cleo scratched her response, hastily—it needed few words. She would meet him. There was no other choice.

She handed the missive to Bridget. "There will be no answer."

"Yes, mum." Bridget curtseyed and disappeared.

In less than an hour's time, Cleo rode to the edge of the tree copse, Thornton already waiting. He wore high riding boots, fitted brown trousers and a crisp white shirt beneath a tweed overcoat. He had yet to shave, she noted, the shadow of his beard affording him a darker appeal. He appeared more rugged and dangerous.

Without speaking, he helped her to dismount. They tethered her horse to a great oak. Then he crushed her against him, lifting her feet from the ground and spinning her in circles until he dizzied them both. Their mouths fused for a long and lingering kiss. It had only been hours since he left her at dawn, but she had missed him.

She laughed when he set her back on the ground. Their arms remained around one another. "I take it your head has improved, my lord?"

He dropped a chaste kiss on her smiling mouth. "Much improved, thank you."

She rose on her toes to touch her lips to his again. "We should not be meeting here like this."

His strong hands anchored on her waist, drawing her more firmly against him. "You are forever worrying about what we should not do. Look around you, my dear. There is no one to be seen or to see us."

Thornton was correct. A glance in any direction revealed only gently sweeping pastures, a distant stream and the odd grouping of trees. Their meeting location had been carefully chosen for its distance from Wilton House, she well knew.

He stepped back and took her hand. "Come. Let us walk."

Cleo entwined her fingers with his, savoring the simple contact. It was an intimacy they would always be denied in public. Here, in the sylvan privacy of Lord Cosgrove's estate, they could touch one another as they pleased. "I feel very much like a young girl being courted again," she said.

"I seem to recall many country walks during our brief courtship," he returned with studied nonchalance. "Particularly that first country day when I walked upon you whilst you sketched."

Ah, so this was a topic they would broach after all. She didn't want to ask the question that had begun burning within her and yet she could not avoid the asking. "Did you truly care for me then?"

They walked deeper into the woods, his fingers tightening on hers. "I should think it obvious both then and now."

She swallowed. "It was obvious to me then, before I became confused."

"Before Scarbrough's interference, you mean." His voice was hard. He stopped in the shade of a tree and caught her in an intense gaze. "Cleo, what passed between us those seven years ago…I must know. I vowed I would never lower myself to ask it of you, but did you have any tender feelings for me at all?"

"I…" She searched his unfathomable gray eyes. Not so very long ago, she had been convinced that her feelings for him had been a mere infatuation and his for her a sham. But her reaction to him now gave that away for a lie and his reaction to her did the same.

Thornton pressed a finger to her lips before she could reply. "Hush. Spare my pride your answer."

"No." She shook her head and pulled his finger away. "I want to answer you. I must answer you. I was confused then, Thornton. I was but a child, after all, so young and so full of my own importance. What I felt for you then—what I feel for you in this moment—is far stronger than any emotion I have ever experienced toward another and that is the truth of it."

"God." He leaned into her, burying his face in her neck. "Cleo, I'm mad for you. I have been mad for you these seven years and hadn't an inkling of just how lost I was until I saw you in Lady Cosgrove's gardens. It all came back to me as if time had never come between us."

"I feel the same," she whispered, clutching his lapels and breathing deeply of his rich masculine scent, so familiar and dear to her. "I am hopeless."

His hot mouth trailed kisses up the side of her neck, across her jaw, stopping at her mouth. He kissed her then, a swift and claiming possession that took her by force, branding her as his. He knocked her smart hat to the ground, tunneled his fingers through her hair.

Their lips melded, his tongue plunging into her mouth. He pressed her back against the wide trunk of the tree and she felt its abrasion on her back. It mattered naught, for his body trumped all, hard to her soft, tempting and oh so delicious. His word again.

Thornton broke their kiss and caught her wrists, raising them above her head, pinning them to the bark with one strong hand. Her breasts rose full against the bodice of her gown, her hard nipples sensitive to every slight movement of the stiff fabric. She was instantly gratified she had chosen not to wear her dress improver. The decision had been a wise one. Very likely, she would have fainted had she been wearing stays.

Thornton looked into her eyes and a most wicked smile curved his mouth. "Now that I've got you at my mercy, will you call me Alex?"

"Thornton," she began.

"Naughty, naughty," he said in a low voice, pulling her wrists higher. With his free hand, he untied the lacing of her jaunty cape and sent it to the ground. His dark head sank to her exposed décolletage and he kissed his way to the tip of the valley between her breasts. "Do you repent, my lady?"

"Repent what?" she asked, breathless and feeling cheeky. "I have not sinned, my lord."

"Not yet." He caught the edge of her bodice and yanked it down, revealing her breasts entirely. She felt his hand slide to her back, working at the lacings of her habit. "Limited undergarments. Good girl."

"You seem to forever be making free with my...ah." She could not complete the sentence. His demanding mouth had closed over one of her nipples, dragging and sucking. Cleo attempted to tug her wrists free of his grasp, but he was unyielding.

Thornton glanced up at her, flicking a lazy tongue over the aching peak of her breast. "I am making free with your what, darling?" He blew a tantalizing breath of warm, moist air onto her skin. "With your breasts? I do love your breasts, but I've already told you that, haven't I?"

"You said they were brilliant."

"Did I?" He smirked. "And you remembered?"

"It is not a compliment I receive on a daily...oh heavens." He was at work on her other breast now and his incredibly talented hand had undone the fastenings on her dress. With one firm shove, it went spilling to the ground around her feet. She stood before him in nothing but her drawers, not even a shift. Even so, if the autumn air was chill, she could not feel it for the heat of his body on hers.

"No?" He cupped her buttocks, molding her against him so his rigid arousal pressed into her stomach. "You mean to say that during the course of breakfast, it is not *de règle* for the company to compliment the sheer brilliance of your lovely breasts? I am aghast, I confess, at such a travesty."

She laughed, charmed by the combination of his wit and his sensual grace. "Perhaps I have been breaking fast with the wrong crowd?"

"Indeed." Thornton glanced up, meeting her eyes again.

"It hasn't been me."

"But I have it on good authority that you are an utter bear in the mornings," she pointed out with a saucy smirk of her own.

He kissed her neck, nipping the tender flesh. "*Touché*, my love."

"Let me touch you," she begged, both aroused and frustrated at not being able to feel his skin beneath her fingertips. He still wore all his clothing, which was dreadfully unfair.

"Not yet." His mouth met hers for another scorching kiss. "You must want it very badly first."

"I do."

"But not enough." He kissed the corner of her mouth, his lips teasing hers in a gentle, seductive manner that belied the urgency of his words and the haste with which he had divested her of her riding habit. "And I want you naked first."

His words sent shivers of pleasure skittering over her, warming her blood. "Then finish undressing me," she ordered, her voice bold. Never in her life had she been so forward and yet nothing had ever felt so right.

"With pleasure," he growled and in a breath's span, her drawers too were gone.

She stepped out of them, naked save her stockings and her boots. It was a truly glorious sensation to wear nothing other than cool air and Thornton's devouring stare. Cleo shivered.

"And are you cold, my dear?" Though he had asked the question as politely as he would have done had they taken a turn about lady Cosgrove's formal gardens, the wicked slant to his mouth quite spoiled it. His free hand roamed to cup her.

"Yes," she sighed, tipping her head back against the rough tree trunk.

"But you do not feel particularly chilled to me," he whispered, gazing intently into her eyes as he worked her nub.

"No. I meant to say no," she bit out. Pleasure swirled through her, fast and demanding.

"Really? No?" His hand stilled.

He was, possibly, the most sinful man in all of England. And she adored it.

"Do not tease me, Alex," she returned, knowing her capitulation at using his name would affect him. Dare she hope it may earn her a reward?

Chapter Nine

If Cleo had been hoping for a reward, she certainly hadn't anticipated it arriving in the form of fat rain droplets splashing onto first her face, then her bared breasts. They came faster and harder until both she and Thornton had been abruptly ensnared in a deluge that was no longer of the passionate variety. Indeed, it was most distressing if not highly vexing to be in the midst of lovemaking one breath and clamoring to scramble back into one's hastily discarded dress the next.

"My darling, I fear we are once again to be thwarted."

"I'll not have it." Her breath escaped her. She was attempting to regain her garments, but the sodden fabric was proving rather tricky. Devilish tricky, if she were truthful. She had been so heated mere moments before and now the chill autumn storm lashed at her tender skin.

He kissed her, his hands moving over hers to help her restore her bodice to a hint of its former formidable glory. Thornton even had the gall to laugh. "As you fear, I suspect you'll not have it at this particular juncture."

"Dare you laugh?" She stilled, arms trapped inside acres of sodden fabric.

"If I don't, I shall cry, my darling." His eyes sparkled with mirth.

It was unfathomable to her how he could possibly find the situation amusing. The rain was cold and miserable, the lovely updo Bridget had carefully crafted felt as if it were hanging down her neck like a rat, and her dress was in utter shambles. Not to mention that she would have to return to the household in such desperate straits.

"Is my hair utterly ruined?"

A great clap of thunder sounded.

"Your hair is a moister version of its original styling," he told her with politic kindness.

She wanted to smack him. Would have done, maybe, had her dress been more accommodating. "Where is my hat?"

He bent low, retrieved it and held it out to her. A large, muddied footprint marred the brim.

"You've stepped on it, you oaf."

"So I have."

"Well?" Really, the man was infuriating. "Aren't you going to apologize?"

"Cleo, I just nearly took you against that tree, we're in the midst of a thunderstorm, we've a half hour's ride back to the house and I don't find an apology for having trod on your bloody hat—which, to be honest, wasn't the most fetching piece of millinery I've ever seen—necessary at the moment."

"Are you losing your temper with me? Really, Thornton, that is quite inexcusable. This entire mess is your fault, if you will but think on it. And how dare you ridicule my hat? I frequent only the finest milliner in London, I'll have you know."

"The best milliner in London wouldn't have sold you a hat with a brim the size of Buckinghamshire."

"It's a Gainsborough hat!"

"My love, it's an abomination. But your questionable taste in hats aside, I do think it imperative we seek shelter at once. The rain seems to have no appreciation for millinery debates."

Her teeth began to chatter. "Is it truly a half hour's ride back to Wilton House? It seemed so much shorter before."

Another ominous boom of thunder clacked overhead to

punctuate the end of her sentence. Thornton grinned down at her, clearly exhilarated by what she could only presume was a combination of their encounter and the storm. He looked reckless, wild, and even a little dangerous. Her stomach tipped like an upended teacup. Right there, in the midst of the lashing rain and their silly argument over hats and his rude mockery of her millinery taste, with her garments soaked and stiff and her hair a bedraggled ruins, her greatest fear came to fruition.

She fell in love with Alexander de Vere, Marquis of Thornton, her sometime almost betrothed and now a man whose heart she could never truly claim as her own. She had no right, no expectations, no hopes. But there it was, simple and true, depressing as the gloomy cast of the afternoon.

"Cleo, are you well?" Thornton dropped her sodden cloak around her shoulders and his grin dissipated as worry furrowed his brow. "You're pale."

She drew her cloak around herself as if it were a protective shield. "I am..." Drat. What could she say? She fought for the words and could only finish, "I am getting a bit of a megrim, I think."

"Let's get to the horses." He took her hand in his and began to guide her out of the forest with large, ground-eating strides. "I don't want you to take ill."

"What will we tell the others? Surely it will be well-noted when we arrive together."

Thornton gave her cold fingers a reassuring squeeze. "Don't worry. I'll think of something to spare you the scandal."

"MY HORSE WAS spooked by the storm," Cleo related to her enraptured—and mostly female—audience from the safe haven of a warm and dry drawing room. As it happened,

Thornton's explanation was rather self-serving. And as she delivered it to the eager ladies surrounding her at afternoon tea, she had to admit she was a good deal put out with him for it.

"Poor darling," Margot Chilton interjected with a false air of concern. She gave her curls a subtle boost with her hand and glanced around the room in search of her quarry. "You must have been terrified until the marquis rescued you. My lord, you are a hero."

A small round of feminine applause ensued, much to Cleo's dismay. In their effort to blunt the speculations of the gossipy house guests, they had made Thornton into a Gawain. Several young ladies cast him admiring looks just now, each most likely picturing herself being rescued by the dashing marquis.

Having been distracted from his conversation with Mr. Whitney, the Duke of Claridge, and Lord Fordham, Thornton had the grace to appear embarrassed. Well he should for reaping the rewards of a false rescue. If the ladies swooning over him knew he'd been ravishing her in the woods, their hearts wouldn't beat nearly as fast.

"Truly, I cannot claim a hero's status. I was merely gratified that I could assist the countess in her time of need."

Cleo choked on her tea. Tia gave her a curious look and offered her a discreet tap to the back. Her time of need indeed. She would murder him in his bed tonight. Better still, if he happened to appear in hers yet again, she'd kick him in his tempting backside.

"My son is too modest," the dowager broke in with her best *vicar projecting in church* voice. "I'm sure Miss Cuthbert will be pleased to hear he has become the hero of Lady Cosgrove's Shakespearean Theater."

Miss Cuthbert? Cleo's eyes flew to Thornton, who had an angry gaze only for his mother. Who was this person the dowager spoke of as if she had a claim upon the marquis? An ill sensation skittered through her.

"Indeed," Tia chimed in, looking in high dudgeon. "I am equally certain that Miss Humpbert shall be pleased, whomever she may be. She is unfamiliar to me, but is nevertheless a lovely example of English womanhood, I'm sure."

Oh dear. The dowager took on a purple hue and appeared quite apoplectic. Tia could be so very condescending when she chose. It was an admirable, impressive, and simultaneously crushing trait. No one could deliver a setdown like Tia. She was good *ton* and she lived as if all the world should know it or feel the sting of her wrath. One could have easily mistaken her for a younger, much more attractive version of the queen herself.

"The weather is lovely," Cleo interrupted before a petticoat brawl ensued. Besides, she felt partially responsible for the current contretemps. Who needed to celebrate Shakespeare's plays when her own life had all the pitfalls and romps of a modern-day comedy turned tragedy? She sighed to herself and sipped her tea.

"The weather is dreadful," the dowager harrumphed, "unless one enjoys a storm. Since you were so recently trapped in this cruel rain, one would think you less forgiving, Lady Scarbrough."

Double oh dear. She'd quite forgotten about the rain since she wasn't seated near the high arched windows on the opposite end of the drawing room. How could she have recalled it in their current indoor hailstorm? And how dare the dowager imply with such an open, casual air that Cleo had gotten trapped in the storm so she could throw herself at Thornton?

"Storms are aesthetically pleasing for those of us with an artistic temperament," Helen came to her defense. "Although I dare say we prefer not to become drenched by them. Cleo is quite accomplished with charcoal, aren't you my dear?"

"I would not say so," she hedged, though it was true she still often relaxed by sketching the world around her. Cleo hardly fancied herself accomplished, even if her sisters and friends professed to cherish the sketches she bestowed upon them. She did not fool herself. They were not likely to tell her she was horrid.

"My sister is too modest," Helen continued in a tone that, while warm and conversational, disallowed refutation. "The truth is apparent to anyone with a pair of eyes."

"Quite so," the dowager agreed with a sour frown. She glanced from her son to Cleo and her lips compressed until they became nigh invisible.

Cleo and Thornton shared an intimate yet troubled glance. It was too quickly severed for propriety's sake, but even so, they could convey volumes to one another. *What are we to do? I will explain.*

They were words they had shared before, in different scenarios, in different places and times. But they were words that resonated now. She wanted—nay, she needed—to know who Miss Cuthbert was to him. She yearned for the comfort of Tia and Helen's counsel.

Being secretive was not in her nature and she longed to confess all to her dear sisters. They were such champions of her. They did not deserve her artifice. And yet, what could she possibly tell them when she didn't even know what maelstrom had enveloped her? Was she in love? Utterly. Was she frightened? Terribly. Thornton could never be hers, not truly and not as she wanted him to be. The awful reality of it was that he could very well be betrothed to this Miss Cuthbert person and she could not say a word about it. She was helpless to intervene. She had no claim on him save passion. A mad passion, for neither one of them had anything of substance to freely give the other.

She drained the dregs of her teacup in lieu of openly weeping. Never in her life had she felt more miserable. Not even holding her head high amidst Scarbrough's conquests and tawdry scandals compared to being within steps of Thornton after so much had passed between them and yet being unable to touch him. She wondered for a moment's folly if everyone in the room could see so plainly that she loved him, that his mother knew it and disapproved severely, that Bella sat at the edge of her *Louis Quinze* chair as if she expected it may bite her *tournure* at any moment, that Tia and Helen sought to give their sister strength and support, that Thornton tried to stop himself from looking at her and couldn't keep from stealing glances. Their lives had intertwined and she had become as disguised as any actress who trod the boards in a role other than her own.

"Lord Thornton," Margot Chilton interrupted Cleo's dark musings then, "you must tell us about your connection to the incomparable Mr. Whitney. However did the two of you meet up in the first place?"

Before Thornton could manage a reply around the bite of cucumber and watercress sandwich he'd just taken, Lady Cosgrove interrupted their gathering. The dear lady rang her husband's family silver against her teacup with such vigor that the cup broke. White fragments dropped to the carpet like egg shells. Only the handle remained in her grasp.

"Oh bother," Lady C. mumbled as the company grew silent and watched. An efficient servant sprang forward to clean up the pieces. "That was, while suitably dramatic, entirely unintended." She cleared her throat and straightened as she realized her guests waited. "My darlings, what better time and place than now and here in the drawing room to amuse ourselves by reciting the scenes assigned to us during the scavenger hunt?"

Cleo wanted to plead a headache and retire from the room. The very last thing she needed was to enhance their scandalous attraction by playing lovers before the entire assemblage. Besides, she recalled only too well the naughty turn their rehearsal had taken. While Thornton gave it highest praise, she had no wish to bare her bosom to the house party at large.

"That was a damn fine teacup, Lady Cosgrove," grumbled Lord Cosgrove. His bulbous nose was shiny and red even from across the large room. "Does anyone else feel that draft in here? I'm for a draught of whiskey!" He hobbled away from his place at his wife's side, the notorious souse Lord Chilton following closely, no doubt deliriously happy at the mere mentioning of Lord Cosgrove's impressive stores.

"In the spirit of today's dramatic storm and Lord Thornton's equally dramatic and chivalrous rescuing of our delightful Lady Scarbrough," their hostess continued, unperturbed by her husband, "I thought the pair may wish to entertain us first. Lord Thornton? Countess? Will the two of you be so gracious?"

THORNTON GULPED THE last of his dreadful sandwich—really, cucumber and watercress was an appalling culinary combination—and nearly choked on it at his hostess's trilling voice.

Not the benighted scene they were to have memorized. Thornton cursed inwardly. He'd forgotten all about the bloody thing and with good reason. He was too busy being tempted by a beautiful woman to care two pence for committing a scene from…whatever play it had been to memory. He had to confess he'd never been a lover of Old Will's work. Except for the sonnets, of course, which often gave one a great advantage with the fairer sex.

"My lord? What do you say?" Lady C., the damnable meddlesome biddy, persisted.

What choice did he have? He washed his sandwich down with a healthy swig of tepid tea and gave her a smooth smile. "Of course, my lady. Where would you have us perform?"

Though he spoke to Lady Cosgrove, he slanted a glance

back at Cleo, who watched him with the hopeless expression of a woman flailing in a sea, about to be swept under by the tide. In fact, it was the very same expression she often wore before pleading a megrim, which he'd come to discover was her dramatic way of begging out of an indelicate situation. *Oh no,* he told her with his eyes, *you and I are in this together, my dear.*

"In the center of the drawing room, if you please," Lady C. ordered with the air of a queen. "I should tell the company that, of course, the two of you will be portraying a portion of a scene from a play dear to my heart, *Love's Labour's Lost.* The countess is fair Rosaline and the marquis is Biron."

He gave her a half bow, then crossed the room to retrieve his partner in mayhem. As he clapped a hand on Cleo's elbow, he leaned into her and caught the delicious scent of lavender. Christ but he wanted to lick her everywhere. And instead, he had to spout Elizabethan nonsense like a simpering fop.

"Are you mad?" She frowned at him. "You haven't an inkling as to your lines."

Damned if she wasn't right. Still, no need telling her that. It would make her ego insufferable. "Hush. We'll muddle through it together."

"We'll make a spectacle of ourselves."

Yes, very likely they would. But avoiding Lady Cosgrove's offer would be akin to admitting they had never practiced their scene together at all. Since he'd already created a stupid scandal by tumbling with Ravenscroft, he couldn't well cry off. It would instantly make all their time spent together suspect and with good reason. There was no alternative save dashing headlong into it together. Perhaps they'd be fortunate and no one would be familiar with the play. Damn, but he still recalled the soliloquy in *Julius Caesar.* Why couldn't they have been given that scene?

He led Cleo to the center of the drawing room, too aware of the eyes trained on them, the hush that had fallen over the usually loquacious crowd. They smelled blood. Thornton placed Cleo before him, willed her to recall her lines even if he could not, and took a breath. The first line, at least, was easy enough.

"'Did not I dance with you in Brabant once?'" he asked, careful to keep his tone intimate yet allow it enough strength to carry.

A shutter closed over Cleo's green eyes. She sent him a coy smile. "'Did not I dance with you in Brabant once?'"

Thornton stepped closer, the hem of her gown brushing his boot. He smelled lavender again, sweet and teasing in his nose. "'I know you did.'"

Cleo withdrew from him, eyes snapping. "'How needless was it then to ask the question!'"

"You must not be such a shrew," he improvised, having forgotten most of the rest of the scene.

She frowned at him and he knew he'd been caught. "''Tis long of you that spur me with such questions.'"

"Your…" Damn it, his mind was as blank as a new sheet of paper.

"Do you mean to insult my wit?" Cleo asked, prompting him with her eyes and words.

He wanted to kiss her but knew he could not. Their acting could not go so far. "Indeed, dear lady. 'Your wit's too hot, it speeds too fast.'" He paused for effect, then stepped closer to her again. " 'twill tire.'"

Cleo spun away from him, presenting him with an opportunity to appreciate the elegant lines of her back. Her glorious black hair, he noted, had been flawlessly re-pinned even after the havoc he had wreaked upon it. "'Not 'til it leaves the rider in the mire,'" she said archly.

The subtle tension of the scene was not lost on him. If possible, it made him want her more. It somehow mirrored their wordplay when alone and their seductive push away, pull back relationship. He'd never in his life been this overpowered by a woman.

Worse, he even recalled the bloody lines. "'What time o'day?'"

She made a graceful quarter turn and gazed at him over her shoulder. "'The hour that fools should ask.'"

She enjoyed delivering that line, the minx. He could tell. Already he knew her so well. Impossibly well, it seemed. Thornton took the steps forward she had taken in retreat, cupped her elbow and spun her back to face him. He employed more force than necessary, making her cling to his arms to keep her balance. Her lovely features betrayed her discomfiture.

"'Now fair befall your mask,'" he ordered in triumph.

She attempted to extricate herself but he would not let her. "'Fair falls the face it covers.'"

The next line was meant to taunt and sting—he knew it well. "'And send you many lovers.'" Only me, his eyes told her. He would not share Cleo, especially not with her bastard of a husband, even were the man to appear suddenly in Lady C.'s entry hall.

He felt more than heard their audience titter. They adored the slightest hint of scandal, the quality. He could almost hear the whispers already beginning, even if Shakespeare himself had written the words and not Thornton.

"'Amen,'" Cleo said with relish, pulling herself away from him and giving her head a defiant toss, "'so you be none.'"

"'Nay,'" he told her softly, then stopped, losing the rest of his line, the closing words of their blasted scene.

"Then be gone," she directed him in a convincingly august voice.

There was a pregnant moment of silence before the company erupted in applause led by Lady Cosgrove and joined most reluctantly by Margot Chilton. He'd noticed the chit aiming her cap at him and was doing his best to dodge it.

"Well done my brave lambs of sacrifice," their hostess

crowed, bobbing forward, clapping enthusiastically all the while. "Well done indeed."

Thornton met Cleo's eyes, but she looked away. He bowed to her. She curtseyed. In that moment, they may have been utter strangers. The underlying emotion in their scene may not have existed. It was terribly surreal. He yearned to reach out to her. Instead, he turned and strode back to Jesse's side. Let her be aloof now if she wanted. He knew what her ice became in his arms.

THE SCENE LEFT Cleo's emotions in a ferocious muddle. Thornton had been intense and too near to her for her mind to function properly. She found it dreadfully unfair of him to push her so far before an audience, especially after his mother had only just announced the presence of the mysterious Miss Cuthbert in Thornton's life.

Ravenscroft appeared readily available to make her other suitor pay. She deliberately walked past Thornton on her way to the earl, who looked pleased to be her unwitting dupe.

"Fetching display, my lady." Ravenscroft's voice was like warm honey sliding over her skin. "I thoroughly enjoyed your performance."

"You are far too kind, I dare say." Even so, she gave him her best smile. "But I must thank you just the same."

"I am not ordinarily kind." He winked at her. "However, my kindness can be bought."

She laughed—too loudly if the censorious gazes cast in her direction were any indication. Thornton took instant notice. He caught her with a thunderous glare. No man could exude imperious arrogance like Alexander de Vere.

"How do you propose I buy it?" she teased.

"What sort of currency have you in mind?" Ravenscroft's grin was wicked.

"Not the sort you have in mind."

Thornton's dark voice interrupted their *tête-à-tête*. He

grabbed her arm and drew her to him. "Excuse us, Ravenscroft."

Ravenscroft's mouth tightened into a grim line. "Of course."

"I apologize," Cleo murmured. "We can continue our conversation later, I hope?"

Thornton dragged her away without waiting for the earl's response. Lady Cosgrove announced that the next scene would begin after the servants cleared away the tea and sandwiches, but neither Cleo nor Thornton paid her much heed.

He did not release his hold on her until they were well removed from Ravenscroft. Thornton held himself stiffly, jaw working with fierce determination. She knew he would not speak until he had harnessed his temper. The anticipation was worse, Cleo feared, than an outright row. She had been deliberate in her actions and he was now all too deliberate in his response.

"What are you about, madam?" he ground out so lowly it was a wonder she had not misheard.

"I was merely enhancing my acquaintance with the earl." She pinned a sweet smile to her lips as they passed Lady Grimsby whose cunning, fox-like ears were perked and whose sharp nose trembled with repressed malice. "Is not Lady Grimsby looking well this evening?" she asked in a voice designed to carry to that lady herself. "Yellow complements auburn hair in a most lovely manner, I find."

"Do not think to change the subject." He neatly guided her away from Lady Grimsby. "I've seen more attractive lead mules on a farmer's plow. No amount of yellow can alter ugliness."

"You're harsh." She sniffed and turned her head away from him so that he had no recourse but to stare at her Bridget-repaired coif.

"Have I not reason to be?"

"I think not, my lord." She stopped near a potted palm

and made the mistake of glancing back at him. "I fear I have yet another megrim."

His eyes burned into hers. He gripped her elbow, his fingers punishing. "My lady, I fear you are a damn liar. I dare say you've never had a megrim in your life, though you claim them often enough."

How dare he be rude enough to call attention to her artful avoidance of conflict? Did he have such few dealings with ladies that he didn't realize feigning megrims was a lady's prerogative? His dexterity with undergarments would certainly suggest otherwise.

"Let me go, you brute. Someone will see." Cleo cast a frantic glance about the room, but its occupants all appeared to be engaged in some manner of gaiety or another in the wake of Lady C.'s announcement. She had quite been forgotten, as had Thornton. Margot Chilton had turned her wiles upon Mr. Whitney, hedging her bets in case of lowered expectations. Wise girl, though Cleo thought the American far too handsome a man for the likes of Margot Chilton. Even the dowager was, for a moment, impossibly allowing the drunkard Lord Chilton, returned with whiskey in hand, to flummox her into a heated debate of some sort.

No one to come to her rescue. Drat. Thornton was glaring at her with an expression that made her insides wilt.

He lowered his head, bringing their faces inappropriately close. "I'll restrain you if need be. God knows that like any good mare, women need a guiding hand."

She gasped. "Your nerve astounds me, sir."

"As does your complete lack of grace after the time we shared together mere hours ago!"

"Who is she?" she demanded, no longer able to pretend the mere mentioning of that woman's name had not shattered the fragile porcelain of her good mood.

Thornton raised a brow, at his most imperious. "What?"

"This Miss Cuthbert person. Who is she?"

He did not answer at once, but took his time working his jaw as if in preparation for the explanation to come. Chagrined was the term she'd apply to his expression. "This is neither the time nor the place for such a discussion."

True, they were in a room filled with many people, but they stood on the back fringes where they could easily affect the appearance of listening without having to do so. No one stood nearby thanks to the accommodating size of Lady Cosgrove's drawing room.

"I find that I do not wish to wait," she informed him coolly. "You'll tell me now."

He struggled with her demand before finally biting out, "Miss Cuthbert is my expected betrothed."

She exhaled. It was as she feared. "Expected?"

"Nothing is certain, Cleopatra."

"Carrying on a dalliance whilst you've an expected betrothed waiting somewhere seems certain enough to me. Would you not characterize it as such?"

"I would not," he began lowly, "call you and I a dalliance, Cleo. Nor, I hope, would you. But neither can I escape that I am a man before you with a past behind him. Clearly, I could not have anticipated what would pass between us. In truth, I did not even know you planned to attend."

"Yet you could have easily avoided what passed between us by being a man of honor and not pursuing me at all," she pointed out.

"And you could have been a woman of honor by remaining true to your husband," he retorted.

"Lower your voice." She kept her eyes trained on the center of the room where Margot Chilton and the Duke of Claridge had taken their places to enact their scene. "That was cruel and you know it."

"Forgive me." His hand gave hers a surreptitious brush for a breath. "I am not the only one deserving of blame. I should not have brought Scarbrough into the matter just as you should not have brought Miss Cuthbert into it."

"If I recall correctly, your mother managed that feat on her own."

"To be fair, my mother dropped Miss Cuthbert's name because she is so intent upon the match and she fears you," he whispered.

She glanced at him. "Why should she fear me? I have no claim on you. This entire argument has only served to prove as much."

Thornton's eyes darkened with intensity. "You have every claim on me, Cleopatra."

"You must not call me that," she said, shaken by his statement. "Everyone calls me Cleo."

A smile twitched at his sulky lips. "You listen better when I use your full name."

Did he think to manage her completely? She sniffed again. "You are an insufferable man."

"You tell me so on a regular basis."

"It's very improving to hear one's faults. Perhaps I will help to tame your ego."

"You have already quashed it mightily, my dear. Trod on it any more and it shall cease to exist."

"I'm not as bad as you imply," she huffed. But perhaps she could be a trifle of an overwhelming personality at times. She could admit it to herself, but never to Thornton. "Margot Chilton is stammering over her lines. Hush now. I wish to listen to her make a fool of herself, as it will make me exceedingly happy."

"You are every bit as bad," he whispered into her ear. He pressed his palm to the flat of her back for just a moment.

"You're worse."

It was an intimate gesture, deceptively casual and fleeting, but she felt it to her core. She had an ill feeling that, like Margot's attempt at being an actress, their *affaire* would end badly. They watched the remainder of the sketches in silence.

Chapter Ten

CLEO AVOIDED HIM for the next two days, which took her safely to the end of the first week of the house party. It was no easy feat, considering how determined Lady Cosgrove was to perpetually entertain the company. She cried off dinner. She allowed Ravenscroft to escort her everywhere. She took tea with him, went riding with him, made certain she was seated next to him for a performance of *The Tempest*. And she also made the vexing discovery that no matter how beautiful a man or how tempting a wit or how divine a flirt he may be, the earl did not make her feel even the smallest shred of passion Thornton aroused within her.

On the morning of the third day, Tia and Helen ambushed her in her chamber before she even rose from bed. Which was entirely anticipated but not wholly appreciated. Indeed, there was nothing like sleeping after tossing about half the night only to have said slumber rudely disrupted by daylight pricking her eyelids and the incessant chatter of her sisters piercing her ears.

"Do wake up, dearest." Tia, already resplendent in a golden morning gown with English daisies embroidered on its impressive skirt, perched herself on the bed. "You can't lie about all morning, you know."

Cleo swatted her. "Of course I can, you ninny. I'm doing it now."

"Helen, you know what this means. Fetch the water."

"No water." Cleo glared at her sisters through bleary eyes.

"Who allowed you lot in here?"

"Bridget of course." Helen, wearing a muted green gown that flattered her taller frame, seated herself on the other side of the bed. "She's worried about you, as are we. You haven't been yourself these past few days."

Tia leaned forward, a wicked grin lighting her expressive face. "What Helen really means to say is that we simply must know whether or not Ravenscroft has ravished you yet."

Cleo groaned. "Tia, you are incorrigible. Of course he hasn't ravished me."

"Precisely right." Helen sent Tia an arch look. "I told you, did I not? Cleo's heart isn't involved with the earl. I have a suspicion it's been reserved for someone else."

"Truly, it is too early in the morning to discuss my personal affairs." She frowned at her two sisters.

Tia grew pensive. "Oh dear. It's as you feared, Helen."

"Just so." Helen nodded, examining Cleo with an intensity that made her want to pull the counterpane over her head. "Thornton has addled her wits."

"I beg your pardon." Cleo shifted into a sitting position. "Did not the two of you demand I engage in an *affaire*?"

"But Ravenscroft would have been a wiser candidate." Tia tsked as she settled the voluminous fabric of her skirt with an artistic hand. "Thornton is not for you. Surely you see that, Cleo."

She pressed a palm to her forehead. "My head understands that but my heart does not."

"What has your heart to do with this?"

"You've gone and fallen in love with him, haven't you?" Helen asked with quiet precision.

Tia blinked. "With Ravenscroft, do you mean? That's terrible."

"It's horrible," Cleo agreed, "but it's not the earl."

"Thornton." Helen and Tia both spoke his name simultaneously, Helen's tone knowing and Tia's incredulous.

"That arrogant, brooding, imperious hawk of a man?" Tia looked aghast now. "Whatever for? You weren't meant to do that."

"Did not the two of you forge a letter to throw us together?"

Tia flushed. They had never spoken of it. "That was before."

Cleo fought her temper. "Before what, precisely?"

"Before I realized that Thornton is altogether unacceptable," Tia explained, giving Cleo's arm a condescending pat.

"He is to be betrothed," Helen added, her voice soft and sympathetic.

"I am aware." Cleo pressed her lips together, choosing her words with care. "But nothing is certain."

"My dear, it is the worst folly to fall in love with your lover if he is engaged to marry another." Helen kept her voice gentle. "It's why we regret our somewhat feeble attempt to bring the two of you together now we've learned of Miss Cuthbert."

"You regret it now?" Cleo laughed without mirth. "Isn't your regret a trifle tardy? After all, without your meddling, Thornton and I may have never…"

"Never what?" Helen looked at her askance. "You didn't?"

"Oh dear." Tia gripped her hand. "You haven't, have you? Cleo, it would be quite ruinous."

Cleo scoffed. "You needn't insult him, you know. Half the ladies in attendance, married and unmarried, have been swooning over him these past few days. He's hardly an ogre."

"Yes, but he's Thornton. While I agree that he cuts a fine figure and can seat a horse better than any man I know, not to mention his prowess at all things physical—really, you should see the man play rounders—he seems such a cold fish."

"When did you see him playing rounders?" Cleo demanded, unnerved.

Tia smiled again. "Earlier this morning. I went for my

walk and spied a few of the gentleman at play. I do love a well-muscled man."

"He isn't a cold fish," Cleo said sternly, "but you are to stay away from him. No more spying on him whilst he plays rounders or otherwise."

Tia pished. "Helen, darling, do ring for Bridget. I can't think of where she is with our chocolate. As late as it is, I fear we are to be relegated to our chambers for breakfast."

"Yes, your majesty." Helen dropped from the bed and made a mock curtsy rival to any court presentation. "Whatever your majesty wishes."

"Don't be a wit," Tia ordered, tipping her nose up in the air with regal grace. She directed her attention to Cleo again. "Cleo, I'm appalled. You were meant to conduct a respectable *affaire* with Ravenscroft."

"Tia, an *affaire* is not respectable," Helen chided from across the room.

"It's a bit like saying 'the nice executioner'." Cleo felt compelled to agree. It was too early for her to be bombarded with such meddlesome sisters. Really, why couldn't the Lord have blessed her with meek, mouse-in-the-hole misses instead? Oh, well enough, she would dearly miss her ferocious sisters if they were plaguing someone else's chamber, but they could be deadly trying at times.

Tia swatted the air as if it contained a swarm of deeply distressing gnats. "You know what I meant to say. Thornton was to have been the one at first, but then when I saw how the earl danced attendance on you, I thought perhaps he was safer. But now you've gone and ruined it."

"What is so terrible about Thornton?" Cleo's protective instincts prickled to the surface of her pride.

"I think what our sister wants to say, in her circuitous way," Helen began as she crossed the room and once more perched herself on the bed, "is that your heart would not have gotten involved with the earl. Whereas the marquis—dearest, it is plain to see, especially after your scene together the other evening, that you have deep feelings for one another yet."

"I already said as much," Tia grumbled, wearing a most aggrieved expression.

Helen raised a brow. "Yes, but I merely translated it into plain English."

Cleo picked at the stitches on her exquisite coverlet. Sisters could be such a bother. Why did they always see and know so much? Did nothing escape their eyes? "I have been avoiding Thornton for just the reasons you both have mentioned. Indeed, I sought out Ravenscroft as a distraction from Thornton."

Bridget entered the chamber just then, bearing a silver tray and pot of hot chocolate. "Good morning, my ladies." She beamed, unaware of the serious nature of the conversation she had only just interrupted. "It's sure to be a fine day today. The sun is shining, not a hint of clouds and the birds sing the sweetest songs."

"Bridget," Cleo began, much aggrieved, "in future, please do refrain from allowing miscreants into my chamber this early in the morning."

Bridget bit her lip to keep, it would appear, from laughing. "Yes, my lady."

"Impertinent," Cleo grumbled, but no one listened. It was well known that she was fond of Bridget and permitted free speaking between her staff and herself. Bridget took all in stride, dear woman that she was, and ignored her mistress.

"Chocolate." Tia rose from the bed, smiling. "Thank you, dearest Bridget. You may leave us."

Bridget set her tray carefully upon a table, curtseyed and hesitated. Cleo knew her maid well enough to know she wished to speak.

She sighed. "Yes, Bridget?"

"My lady, it is only that I wished to inform you of the gossip belowstairs." Bridget's pretty face was earnest. There was no ill will, no malice meant by her in gossip exchanges. Ordinarily, Cleo and Bridget shared a laugh over the latest scandals of the glittering set. This was different.

At the word gossip, her sisters' ears perked up as if they were hounds. Cleo was sure she didn't want to hear the gossip in the servants' wing. Tia and Helen appeared equally sure they did.

"You may most assuredly stay, Bridget." Tia smiled over her chocolate. "Do tell us."

"It's sorry I am, my lady." Bridget frowned, looking distraught. "I know it's not my place to interfere, but I've heard it from Hollins, Lady Thornton's woman, that Lord Thornton is soon to be wed to a girl who's certain to further his politics. Seeing as how I heard Lord Thornton and Lord Ravenscroft fought over you the other day, I thought you may wish to know."

Mortification forced a blush to her cheeks. "They were fighting over a volume of Tennyson," she objected, though even she knew her denial was a lame one. "Lord Thornton and I have had very little conversation since my arrival."

"Of course, my lady." The maid's expression made it plain she did not believe Cleo. "I only wished to pass on gossip to entertain you ladies."

"You have not done wrong," Cleo forced herself to say. Though it embarrassed her to no end to suddenly find herself at the midst of a romantic contretemps and belowstairs tongue wags, she could not punish the loyal Bridget. "I am aware that the marquis is expected to become betrothed to further his political achievements. Undoubtedly, it will be a perfect union." And the thought of it rendered her perfectly dejected.

"Has anything else been said, Bridget?" Helen asked, her tone cautious.

"Not to me." She met Cleo's gaze. "I recall how heartsick you were then, my lady, when the marquis proved a scoundrel."

"That's just it." A faint, mirthless smile curved Cleo's lips. "I'm afraid I cleaved myself to a scoundrel and ran away from a gentleman."

"My lady?"

"You cannot think in this vein," Tia protested. "No good shall come of it."

"Too late," Cleo whispered, shaken to her core.

"Cousin Alex, what is this I hear about you suffering a case of the blue cock?"

Thornton reined in his hunter and glanced sternly at his reprobate cousin, Lord Fordham. Thornton, he and Jesse were indulging in a morning ride. It was the perfect opportunity to escape the scrutiny of the house party, a chance for fresh air and good company. And now the brazen lad was utterly spoiling the fine mood.

"I'll bloody well cut off your cock if I ever hear you talking about mine again," he growled, aware that he'd allowed his temper to get a hold over him. Ordinarily, he did not countenance displays of emotion, but it would seem that being within Cleo's grasp wreaked all manner of deviltry on his controlled life. He couldn't recall when he'd ever attempted to make love to a woman against a tree. Or a window, put to point.

Ford scowled. "You needn't be so sensitive about it. I dare say I've experienced it once in my admittedly short lifetime."

"Can't say as I have," Jesse offered, grinning like a smug bastard.

"Americans," Thornton grumbled.

"You sound like the dowager," Ford pointed out.

"I'm going to fucking kill you," Thornton said with great forced cheer.

His cousin swallowed. "Not a bit like her now that I think

on it."

Good. Give the blighter a bit of fear.

"Better, but I'm still going to cut off your knob if you ever say 'blue cock' in my presence again." He glared at Ford because he knew it was partially true. Cleo had him in an uproar. She had disturbed everything, shredded every last sense of peace he'd ever claimed. She'd ruined him for the second time. And now, she was waltzing about with that whoreson Ravenscroft, ignoring him. Forgetting his existence.

He told himself she was a married woman. He told himself she betrayed him once before, believing Scarbrough over him, marrying another man and tossing their love aside. He told himself he didn't care a straw for her, that she could warm the bed of every man in the house party if she dared and it would not bother him. But it seemed he didn't care about the first two and the third was an utter falsehood.

"Maybe you should visit with the lovely Lady Boniface," Jesse suggested, his tone polite, almost pitying.

"Maybe you should," he bit out. "I don't need a bedmate."

"You needn't be such a bear." Ford winced. "Christ, I only said something because Lucy the chambermaid told me she heard belowstairs gossip that you were courting Lady Scarbrough but she had a *tendre* for Ravenscroft. I thought it a lark."

"And what were you doing with Lucy the chambermaid?"

Ford looked abashed. "Alex, I know you said not to trifle with the servants, but I'm not trifling with Lucy. She's a rum one, knows her way around a man. Beautiful breasts I could suck on all day long…"

"Ford!" Thornton felt like his cousin's father sometimes. The lad needed guidance. Truly, he needed to join a monastery.

"You do have a stick up your arse," Jesse intervened.

Thornton raised a brow. "You aren't supposed to side

with the stripling. You're my friend."

"Let him have his fun," Jesse said quietly. "You were his age once."

Yes and he'd been in love with Cleo. He hadn't been shagging maids, for Christ's sake. Guilt crept into his thoughts then. He had, however, been shagging Cleo like a common country wench, without benefit of marriage. Perhaps her betrayal had not been entirely her fault, he realized. After all, he had not offered for her, but had put the task off as a future certainty. He'd been too busy with Marleigh Manor, too weighed down by his mother's demands and the challenges of refilling his empty family purse to worry about marriage. Cleo had been a young, innocent girl. She had no reason to believe he would make an honest woman of her. She had, in truth, been treated little better than Lucy the chambermaid. He had no right to admonish Ford. He had no right to harbor enmity for Cleo. She had made the decision any sensible young lady would have.

It had only taken him seven years to acknowledge his error. Oh, hell.

"Alex?" Ford interrupted his thoughts. "Please don't be angry. I swear to you that Lucy approached me first."

Thornton clenched his jaw. "I'm not angry about the damned maid. I'm angry at myself for being a hypocrite. Jesse's right."

"You shagged a maid at a Shakespearean whatnot?" Ford gave an unrepentant grin.

"Worse." Thornton grimaced. "I'll spare the details."

"The saint was once a sinner?" Ford appeared to relish the idea.

Jesse caught his gaze. "Go to her," he urged.

It was all the encouragement Thornton needed. He spun his mount around and headed back to Wilton House in a full gallop.

CLEO WAS JUST leaving the breakfast room in Ravenscroft's company when Thornton strode into the entry hall. The expression on his chiseled face hardened as his gaze honed in on her companion. Alex was disheveled, dressed in riding attire and unutterably handsome. Her heart gave a great pang.

"Cleo?" The earl kept his voice low, comforting. She suspected he felt her body tensing at the mere sight of Thornton. Though he was many things, fool was not among his catalog of sins. Julian, as she had begun to call him in private, had proven a reliable and loyal confidante to her in the last few days. He had not even bothered to further his cause with romantic overtures. Naïve though perhaps she was, Cleo believed him sincere in his desire to merely befriend her.

"It is well with me," she murmured. "Please do not resort to brawling like a pair of ruffians on the docks."

"I would not drag you through the mire again for the world," he said softly and she knew he spoke truth. This man—unlikely though it may be—meant to protect her.

Thornton reached them, jaw clenched, eyes dark as obsidian. He managed a curt nod in Julian's direction. "Ravenscroft." He turned abruptly to Cleo. "Lady Scarbrough, a word?"

She intended to deny him, but instead, another word emerged from her traitorous lips. "Where?"

"The library?" he suggested, polite and even urbane. To an impartial observer, he would appear impervious, the collected politician to his blue-blooded nose.

Julian could not resist a jibe. "You wish to return to the scene of my trouncing of you?"

A perfect smile curved Thornton's lips. "Go to hell, Ravenscroft."

"Not yet." Julian grinned.

Cleo released her grip on his arm and accepted the arm

Thornton proffered. She realized too well that if Thornton and Julian remained within the same breathing space for a minute more, they would be at one another's throats physically rather than verbally. "Thank you, Julian," she whispered.

From the rigid bunching of muscles in his arm, she knew Thornton had heard and had not liked the familiarity. Good, she thought with stern defiance. She did not appreciate the phantom appearance of his perfect future wife, either. Let him stew.

They walked the short distance to the library in silence and found its massive environs blessedly empty. Thornton slid the lock home to bar potential interlopers. Wise, given their last interlude in another book-lined haven. She continued walking deeper into the chamber, unable to sit for the nervousness attacking her stomach yet needing to put distance between them. She did not trust herself, nor him.

Cleo approached a set of shelves, running her finger over an unprecedented smattering of dust just beyond a set of Latin treatises and histories. Lady C. would be horrified were she aware of her servants' lapse. She blew lightly, sending it skittering into the air as dancing dust fairies. The motes turned over themselves in anxious discord, much like her own tumultuous emotions.

"What did you wish to discuss?" she asked the question in as light a tone as possible. Then, she made the error of looking back over her shoulder. He watched her like a predator, his lean hips propped against a shelf, his booted feet crossed in a deceptively casual pose. Her dress improver tightened another inch.

"He is Julian to you now?" His voice was equally light, yet fraught with dark undercurrents, like water that appeared to be shallow and yet was capable of drowning a man. Or a woman, as it were.

"We're friends." Wary, she turned to face him completely.

"I don't like you associating yourself with him. It's lowering."

Her chin tipped up. "I'm afraid you haven't the right to object, my lord."

Thornton sauntered across the parquet floor. "He stole it from me."

Instinctively, she backed against the shelves. "Julian?"

"Scarbrough," he ground out.

Cleo found herself genuinely perplexed. "What do you mean to say?"

"Christ, this is coming out all wrong." He ran a hand through his hair, stopped and began to pace. "I've been thinking, Cleo, about a good deal of things. About our past, about what you said to me that day when you broke off with me, about how you said Scarbrough told you this and that. I was so bloody angry at the time, so hurt you'd take his word over mine, that I overlooked the obvious."

"The obvious?" A small sensation blossomed in the depths of her belly as she watched him. She knew, she realized, what he was about to say. Secretly, she had suspected as much.

"Scarbrough needed funds. Scarbrough took on the French Nightingale as his mistress, Cleo, not me as he told you. All along it was him, playing us both like a deck of cards. It was the ultimate game for him, I'm sure of it, and we allowed him to win."

She clasped her hands together, awash in turmoil. "I know he lied to me about many things. For these last few years, it was easier to believe his lies that you had betrayed me than to think I had allowed myself to—"

"You cannot blame yourself," Thornton interrupted, stalking closer to her. "I gave you no reason to believe I would marry you. And Scarbrough, well, he proposed to you while I cooled my heels trying to get Marleigh Manor in order and you…" He stopped before her and took her hands in his. "You were an innocent young woman who had been taken advantage of, out of her elements. I am at fault for this, all of this."

"No." She took a deep breath, her fingers tightening on his reassuring ones, taking comfort from his warmth and strength. Cleo could not allow him to take sole responsibility, nor could she keep the truth from him any longer. "You are not at fault. I made the decisions that led me here, not you. I was naive and scared, and I was with child."

"What?" He inhaled sharply, as if he'd been wounded.

"I was with child and when John told me his lies and I could not reach you…you know, I saw you at the opera with the French Nightingale myself. Why were you with her if it wasn't true?"

Thornton exhaled on an ugly string of curses. "Scarbrough convinced me to take her, said he had to make an appearance for his mother and that the Nightingale would throw him over if she didn't go to the opera on the arm of a gentleman. Jesus. I was so stupid, but we were friends then, he and I, and I thought I was doing a mate a favor. I didn't realize he was escorting you, intending for you to see it all along so that he could steal you for himself. But a babe, Cleo? Why did you never tell me?"

"I miscarried," she confessed. "Shortly after marrying John and you had gone to America by then, already embarking on your great political career."

"I would have returned." His face took on a savage quality that almost frightened her with its intensity. "Damn it, if I had only remained, if I had demanded you listen to me instead of being so wrong-headed and foolish and full of my own pride. Maybe you wouldn't have lost the babe."

"Thornton, no."

"To hell with Thornton. We are Cleo and Alex, nothing more. And we had a child together." He ran his hands down over her flat bodice as if he could feel the slight mound that had once been there. "Cleo, we had a child."

"I know." Tears gathered in her eyes, crystallized on her lashes. "Alex, I'm sorry." A horrible, embarrassing sob emerged from her.

He crushed her against him, burying his face in her neck. She could hear the harshness of his breathing, could feel the small heaves of his powerful chest against her own and knew that he too wept for their child. It was the first time in seven years she had truly been free to mourn the loss.

"I'm sorry, Cleo," he breathed. "I'm sorry I wasn't here for you when you and the babe needed me."

She held onto him as tightly as she could. Their hearts beat against one another, hard hammers she felt into her core. She breathed deeply of his familiar, beloved scent, taking solace in his presence. In his arms, she had never felt more complete or more fully at home. He was her home and she knew it now with devastating certainty. Though they may fall apart once more, go separate ways by the week's end, become strangers once again, he would always be the one who understood her, the one who knew her like no one else could or would again. There would be no other for her. There was only Alex. Her Alex, the handsome, charming young man who had danced with a bumbling country girl and found something in her to love. Something worth cherishing.

"I'm sorry I did not trust in you," she told him, pressing a kiss to his neck, to his ear, to his hairline. "My heart is filled with regrets."

"Let me erase them," he whispered, his mouth finding hers.

Chapter Eleven

"Alex," she whispered against his mouth, clutching at his broad shoulders. She experienced the frightening desire to press herself against him, become a part of him. Her tentative hold on her resistance broke. She kissed him back, raking her tongue against his.

"My love." His hands slid from her waist to her breasts, cupping them possessively through her bodice and the stiffness of her corset.

Cleo moaned, arching her back and falling against the ceiling-to-floor bookshelves. A musty tome fluttered to the floor but they paid it no heed, caught up in one another. His scent, spicy and delicious, filled her senses. She shucked his coat, frantic to have him, desperate for what they had been so long denied.

He ended the drugging kiss, drawing away to deliver tingling, tantalizing kisses to the corner of her lips, her jaw, her cheek, her ear, her neck. "Christ, I'm mad for you," he rasped. "I thought I could go slowly, but I can't wait."

"Nor can I," she whispered, fingers sinking into his soft, thick hair.

"Good." The distinctive sound of fabric rending filled the air between them and then her breasts were bared to his gaze, mouth, and hands.

He had ripped the front bodice in two so both pieces hung open, revealing her completely. He yanked her corset down to free her nipples and she let out a slight yip of pain as her stays bit into her waist. Any discomfort she experienced was dashed away by his wicked mouth suckling her, drawing her taut nipples into his warm, wet mouth until she cried out.

"Yes, love." His hand moved to bunch up her skirts, then disappeared beneath them.

He found the split in her drawers. Deliberate, knowing fingers skimmed over her slick flesh softly at first, then with greater insistence. He found the nub of her sex and worked it until her every breath tore from her in heaving gasps and she feared she would expire from the maddening pleasure of it.

And then he sank a finger slowly into her, followed by another, beginning a strong, wicked rhythm that threatened to undo her entirely. "Put your leg 'round my hip, darling," he cooed, licking the side of her breast.

She did as he asked, hooking her left leg around him, opening herself to him more fully. "Kiss me, Alex," she begged. "I want to feel your mouth on mine."

With a guttural groan, he fused their mouths together. Suddenly, her sex was the center of her body, filled with need, so wet she could hear his fingers slipping in and out of her. He increased his rhythm, using deliberate pressure to bring her to the brink of release.

Then he stilled, abruptly taking them from her. He kissed her, then met her gaze. "I want to make you mine in every way," he said lowly. "I need you, Cleo. God, how I need you."

"Yes." She was helpless, trapped in his thrall. "Make me yours, Alex."

Before she realized what he was about, he lowered himself to his knees. "Hold up your skirts," he ordered.

"Alex?" Cleo was sure she should be scandalized by what he was about to do. He had done it before, long ago and she had been so ashamed she hadn't been able to face him for an entire week. Now, she wanted it.

"Trust me, my love."

"I do," she said, meaning it. She clutched at her voluminous satin and raised it to her waist.

He pressed his mouth to her inner thigh. "Hook your leg over my shoulder."

She did as he asked, hesitant but titillated. When his sinful lips burned a trail over her, his tongue flicking over her most sensitive places, she cried out with the pleasure. "Oh heavens, Alex."

This time, there was no answer. He sank his tongue inside her in a glorious, slippery stroke. He laved her, tasted her as if she were the finest dessert. Just when she thought she'd expire from the decadence of his ministrations, he rubbed his face over her. The abrasion of his stubble nearly drove her mad.

Her skin had never felt more alive. Her nipples tightened, her breasts tingled, and her thighs weakened. She'd never been given to swooning, but she felt quite certain that at any moment she may topple over in an indecorous heap of satin, lace and bustle. The sight of his beautiful dark head at the juncture of her limbs, the exquisite sensations he evoked…the combination was positively delicious. His word again.

"Delicious," she whispered.

In the next moment, he increased his pressure on her nub and dipped his fingers inside her again. She cried out, arching against him, entire body trembling with the power of her release.

"Precisely my sentiments," he rasped as he stood, his gaze never leaving hers.

And then he was unfastening his trousers, his cock springing free. She took him in her hand, admiring the length and satiny heat of him. He was thick and long, perfectly formed, hard and tempting in her palm. He groaned, his ordinarily sullen mouth going slack. Cleo was mad for him, desperate for every inch of his skin she could caress or kiss or lick. She leaned into him, kissing his strong neck, reveling in the divinely spicy scent of him. Unable to behave herself, she licked and nipped as her hand guided him to where she wanted him most.

He lifted her so her sex met his. He was inside her in half a breath and it was deep and good. She exhaled on a moan. "Christ," he muttered, his hands on her breasts. "You feel so bloody sweet."

"Take me," she urged him, scarcely recognizing herself for the wanton she'd become in his arms. "Take me now."

"I've been wanting this from the moment I saw you again, darling," he gritted, his face taut with the strain.

In response, she gripped his firm buttocks, driving him deeper. Her sheath tightened, pulling him inside until she was filled and nearly mindless with sensation. Alex began a fast, driving thrusting that she eagerly met. Once, twice, thrice and she was coming undone again, tears pooling in her eyes at the sweetness of it. She would have screamed had he not swallowed it down with a voracious kiss. Then, he too climaxed as her passage contracted with delightful aftershocks. He surged inside her again and again, his seed a hot spurt within her.

They collapsed as one against the bookshelves, sobbing and laughing, their mouths grazing every bare expanse of skin on one another. Cleo had never been more certain she was desperately in love with him.

"My darling," she whispered against his neck, kissing a path up to his jaw and strong chin before moving on to his wonderful lips.

Their mouths came together in a slow, consuming kiss that spoke more eloquently of their feelings for one another than words. Somehow, the years and delicate deceptions had fallen away and ceased to matter. They were once again Alex and Cleo, man and woman.

Alex's hands framed her face as he broke their kiss, his eyes unfathomable and dark. "Cleo, sweet. That was incredible."

"Incredible," she echoed, a sliver of fear piercing her heart.

What if the emotion she read in his actions was instead mere lust? What if he was simply having an *affaire* before wedding Miss Cuthbert and she was to lose him yet again? After all, there was his career at stake. Rising stars in the Liberal Party could not afford to engage in open seductions of married ladies, particularly ladies who were married to peers.

He must have sensed her thoughts for his arms tightened around her, holding her to him. "Cleo, please don't worry."

"I must worry for us both," she told him, sadness replacing the fear. "You have much to lose."

He pulled back, meeting her gaze once more. "I will not lose you." His tone was vehement, brooking no opposition. She fancied he used it on his political enemies.

"You haven't got me," she reminded him. After all, it would not do for either of them to spin fairy tales. She was married to Scarbrough and Alex was about to become betrothed to another woman. "Our circumstances are inextricable, are they not?"

"Nothing is inextricable." He shifted, withdrawing from her and beginning to rearrange his riding clothes.

"You don't mean to suggest?" Cleo tugged at her bodice only to recall that he had thoroughly ruined it. She pulled the rent seams together and shuffled her skirts back into place.

"Divorce?" He raised a black brow. "It is not entirely unheard of."

"For the scandal and shame it brings," she snapped, irritated to have to face such depressing realities so soon after their transcendent lovemaking. "You know as well as I it is very nearly hopeless for a woman to obtain a divorce. Her husband may beat her, ill use her, spend all her funds and still she cannot escape."

"Women have been legally able to sue for divorce since the fifties, Cleo. True, it's damned complicated if not impossible, but why not consider it? You certainly have grounds on charges of adultery. God knows Scarbrough makes no secret of his paramours. The aggravating circumstance bit would prove more difficult. You'd need to prove cruelty, incest, or bigamy."

"Are you asking me to divorce my husband?" She stilled. No peeress could manage such a feat and well he knew it.

"Are you telling me you do not wish to?"

"Thornton, I—"

"Ah." His features hardened. "I'm back to Thornton now that you've had your fill of my prick."

She gasped, shocked by his almost violent reaction. Visceral rage emanated from his powerful body. "It is not that I do not wish to divorce Scarbrough but that it is, as you say, complicated if not impossible. I cannot prove bigamy or incest, likely not even cruelty though he's an intolerable brute. He hasn't yet beaten me, after all." She gave a bitter laugh. "I fear too for the ramifications of doing so for my family and friends. For you, Alex. Even if I were, by some sheer miracle, able to divorce him, I would not be any more available to you. Do you think that you'll be able to keep your career, as Gladstone's aid, to continue with your good reputation, if you were to become involved with a divorced woman?"

"I'll do as I bloody well please," he bit out. "I won't sit back and allow him to have control over you. Do not ask it of me."

She began to understand. "If your concern is that he will demand his conjugal rights, you need have no fear. We have not shared beds or homes for years."

"It's more than that, Cleo. It's freedom."

Freedom. The word struck her with exceptional force. It was a long abandoned dream for her. There was no escape from unwanted matrimony, from a husband who was an unfeeling scoundrel, who had manipulated her into wedding him in the first place. There was no freedom to love and live as she wished.

"You misunderstand." She clutched at her bodice as if

doing so could make more sense of the jumbled emotions skittering through her. "It's different for women, Alex. We are born without freedom. It's something to which we never grow accustomed, having been fashioned by man to live without it."

He exhaled on a long sigh, closed his eyes and rested his forehead against hers. "Forgive me. Don't let's have a row."

She gave in to her weakness and dropped a lingering kiss on his so-close mouth. "This is a tangled web. At the moment, my greatest concern is how on earth I shall pass discreetly back to my chamber with a ruined bodice." It was a lie. Of course her worry centered on the impossibility of their future together. But she strove for lightness, needing to break up the pall that had settled over them.

It worked. He gave a rare laugh and kissed her in return. "Apologies for the damages."

"It's quite ruined, you know." A smile curved her lips even as she admonished him. Truly, she didn't have a care for the ruined gown. There would always be the convenience of a servants' stair nearby.

"I'll buy you another."

"It was specially designed for me by Worth himself." She frequented the famed couturier, but she wanted to inspire at least a bit of remorse in Alex. "And very dear, too, at a hundred pounds."

"I prefer you naked," he countered, apparently immune to her attempts at goading.

"One hundred pounds too much for your purse, my lord?" She gave him a coquette's pout.

He grinned. "I'm merely partial to your skin, darling."

Cleo couldn't help herself. She leaned forward and kissed him again, stopping only when his hands glided back inside her torn bodice.

"We can't." She stilled his hands even though her body protested. "We've been in here long enough as it is. If someone should discover what we've been about, scandal will erupt."

"This is insupportable." He rubbed his thumbs over her sensitized nipples.

"What are we to do?" She kissed the corner of his mouth.

"Come away with me."

Her heart tripped. He could not be serious, could not mean such an impossibly scandalous suggestion and yet…"To where?"

"The Continent."

"We'd be excommunicated by society," she whispered.

"Would you care?"

"Not terribly. I would miss my sisters, I dare say. What of you? Parliament, the Prime Minister, your betrothed?"

"Christ." He kissed her again. "Leave him."

"Throw your betrothed over."

"I haven't got a damned betrothed," he gritted.

"But you've an understanding," she persisted. "I heard so from my maid, who heard it belowstairs."

It was hardly fair of him, she reasoned, to be so demanding of her when he had a Miss Cuthbert hanging over them like a veritable thundercloud. While divorces were not unheard of as he'd said, making a social recovery from one certainly was. Moreover, the laws rendered it far easier for a man to divorce his wife, and Scarbrough would not be likely to relinquish his hold on her. There was too the sobering Mordaunt case to think of, not five years past. Lady Mordaunt had notoriously carried on affairs with numerous men—the Prince of Wales among them—and her husband had sued her for divorce. In the process, the poor woman had gone mad. She could leave Scarbrough as Thornton requested, but the taint would remain. The freedom for which she yearned would prove elusive.

His mouth thinned. "What do belowstairs gossipmongers know of such things?"

"I am afraid for my heart," she confessed. "It's my greatest fear that this is a mere country house fling to you, that I am no more than a ghost brought back into your path for the moment and that when we part ways in a week, you'll return to London and forget about me. Indeed, I could not fault you if you did so, for it would be the most prudent course for your future."

"Listen to me." He took her hands in his, pulling her against him, his eyes intense once again. "The only obligations I have to Miss Cuthbert are those of a gentleman. She deserves to hear from me that my heart has changed and after this house party, I mean to seek her out and do so. A marriage settlement has not even been broached. I'm free to do as I wish and what I wish is to be with you."

"Cleo?" The less than subtle whisper, accompanied by a rather frantic series of knocks on the library door, interrupted the heavy conversation.

"Not your bloody sister again," he groaned.

Cleo winced. It did sound unmistakably like Tia's dulcet voice. "She is a mother cub," she defended, "with good intentions."

"Terrible timing." He grimaced. "Can we not marry her off again? What of the Duke of Claridge? My young cousin Ford, perhaps?"

"The Duke of Claridge is too boring for Tia and your cousin Ford is too unsuitable, being both impecunious and fond of house maids."

"House maids?" Thornton's dark brow went up.

"Belowstairs gossipmongers," she informed him archly. "Poor Lucy is quite in love with him, telling all the other servants they may run off to Gretna Green."

"Gretna Green marriages have been obsolete for over twenty years," Thornton scoffed.

"Tell that to *le pauvre* Lucy. I don't think the unfortunate girl ever heard."

"Cleo!" Tia was growing impatient with their hesitation.

"Thornton, you utter scoundrel, let my sister be!"

"Tia, do be quiet," Cleo instructed, unable to resist dropping another kiss on his beautiful mouth.

"Let me come to you tonight," he murmured, catching her lower lip between his teeth and giving it a gentle tug.

Their arguments and the weighty cares of the world around them somehow fell away whenever his mouth was on hers. "Yes," she agreed, breathless.

"Cleo!"

"Very well." Cleo tore herself from Thornton and, holding the ragged ends of her once grand morning bodice together, she crossed the library to the door. "Tia, are you alone?"

"Of course, you ninny! Not for long, I dare say. Do let me in. Darling, you don't know what you're about!"

"Do cease being so exclamatory," she returned, popping open the door a bit. Her sister's pretty, worried face stared back at her. "We can avoid scandal if you will only cease drawing attention to us."

"Us?" Tia frowned. "I knew he was in there. Thornton!"

"Hush," Cleo ordered in a low tone. "And find me the nearest servants' stair." She had noted, much to her dismay, that none appeared to be accessible from the library.

Tia's mouth opened in shock. "Cleo? You haven't…"

"Servants' stair." With that, she closed the door in her sister's face.

Chapter Twelve

AS IT HAPPENED, Tia was extraordinarily assiduous in locating a servants' stair and shepherding Cleo into it without being seen. Their covert operation was very nearly thwarted by the dowager marchioness, who Thornton was able to distract at a crucial moment by appearing in the hall and complimenting her dress before she could notice Cleo skulking into obscurity.

Thornton spent the formal luncheon trying to ignore his mother, who was seated between Ford and Jesse and, as such, was thoroughly consternated. The insulting questions she peppered her surrounding company with were legion, chief among them, "Do you know how many Americans are infiltrating our society these days?"

To which Jesse replied, "Not nearly enough by my calculations, ma'am."

Thornton, meanwhile, did his best to ignore her, which didn't require much effort since Cleo was seated next to him. She wore a silver gown with jet bead overlay and she looked fey and gorgeous, like a parcel he dearly longed to unwrap. He thought of how he'd made rude love to her in the library as if she were no better than a Lucy. Damn it all, he should never have spent himself inside her. He should have at least acted with caution in that regard if no other, but he had been so swept up in the moment he hadn't had a care.

And then he thought of how she'd tasted so sweet, of how beautiful and perfect her pale breasts had been in his hands, how delicious and hard her nipples had been in his mouth. Uncomfortable in his trousers, he shifted and in so doing, afforded himself a delectable view down her daring décolletage.

He groaned before he could stifle it, then feigned a cough to cover up his misstep. Christ. Whatever evil she wrought on him, it was thorough and complete. The saint had too quickly become an unrepentant sinner. It shouldn't have been so easy for him to want to discard everything for which he had worked for the last seven years. Asserting himself in the political sphere had been no easy feat. Much of his youth had been spent in politicking, strategizing, speech writing and analyzing his political enemy. He'd been unimpeachable in his integrity, impeccable in his honesty, sterling in reputation. The few affairs he'd conducted had been discreet and civilized. He'd never cared for the dramatics of opera singers or the theatrics of actresses. Instead, he had taken his pleasure with older women, often widows of diplomats or fellow peers. Never had he thought to abandon everything for a woman.

Until today, when the words had spilled from his lips as if from a mewling babe. He was rendered helpless in her presence, hopeless to defend himself against the onslaught of her beauty. He loved her still, loved her more than he had as an untried youth. She had suffered deeply for his defection at a time when he should have stood by her and made right by her. Instead, he had allowed pride to rule. Now he rued the day he had ever allowed Scarbrough to interlope and steal the woman he loved.

Love. The word made him queasy. It made him swallow his trout with difficulty. It made him want to gallop hell for leather back to London and lock himself inside his study to pore over reports from Ireland and from the East End of London and from India.

Cleo laughed, the crystalline sound skittering down his spine like her fingernails raking his back. He hardened even more, then forced himself to recite the Lord's Prayer to tamp down his rampant arousal. It would not do to be sporting an erection at the luncheon table with his hostess and all the company to witness the mortifying event.

"I'm sure it's improving to be in company with your civilized neighbors across the Atlantic," the dowager was condescending to Jesse.

"Mother," Bella objected with quiet dignity, clearly embarrassed. It hadn't escaped Thornton's notice that his sister seemed to turn a suspicious shade of pink and smile more than proper in the company of his older and infinitely unsuitable-for-her friend.

"I hope you don't take umbrage, Mr. Whitney," Thornton's mother said with a startling lack of sincerity. She took a delicate sip of her lemonade. "I only mean to say that it is a wonderful opportunity for Americans to join us here and experience important society. From what I understand, little civility at all exists in your country. Why, are you not still at war with one another or some such?"

Jesse offered a pained smile. "Our war has been at an end for fifteen years, ma'am."

"Just so," the dowager intoned with a great sense of her own importance, "and yet to see a country still struggling after so long. It is a shame, is it not, Your Grace?"

This last question she addressed to the Duke of Claridge, who wore the expression of a man who had swallowed something whole and feared choking. "I'm sure the Americans are well off, my lady, despite whatever ill may have once befallen them. They are a resourceful lot, are you not, Mr. Whitney?"

"We consider ourselves to be so." Jesse smiled at Bella across the table.

Thornton's eyes narrowed. He'd have to keep a closer watch on his sister and his friend, damn it all. Something was afoot.

"Do tell us more about the Wild West, Mr. Whitney," Bella requested.

Thornton scowled at his sister. "I should think that an inappropriate topic for the table, Bella."

Jesse sent him a speculative look. The dowager appeared pleased. She beamed at him. "I'm sure you're right, my lord. Let us talk about something more pleasant, shall we? I had the most delightful epistle from Miss Cuthbert today."

Oh dear Christ. He felt Cleo stiffen at his side and reached beneath the table linens to give her hand a reassuring squeeze. Her fingers tightened on his. Outwardly, her lovely face showed no expression save the slightest drawing at the corners of her rosebud mouth. He longed to escape the stodgy boredom of the luncheon and make love to her again. Being so near to her and yet in the presence of the rest of the company created the worst sort of torture.

"She writes from the Lake District," the dowager continued, "and begs that I remember her to you fondly."

He did not miss or mistake the smug glance she sent in Cleo's direction. That his mother would speak openly of private correspondence was an indication of her dudgeon. She made no secret of her distaste for Cleo or of her desire for him to wed Miss Cuthbert.

"I do adore the Lake District, do you not, dear Bella?" His mother produced a rare smile. "Thornton, Bella and I are on to Windermere following the conclusion of this lovely week. Aren't we, Thornton?"

They had planned no such trip and she well knew it. She merely sought to manipulate him into putting himself in close proximity to Miss Cuthbert and her father. He refused to allow it.

"Unfortunately, I have some pressing interests in London that will take me back up to the city," he told her smoothly.

The dowager's eyes glinted with a panther's keen determination. "I dare say we shall discuss it later." She turned her wrath on Cleo. "Tell us, Lady Scarbrough, how is your husband faring? I'm certain he writes you often with all sorts of *bon mots*."

Cleo tipped her chin up. "I'm afraid his lordship has not written recently, my lady. He has many interests that keep him quite occupied."

Brave girl, he congratulated her silently.

"Indeed?" The dowager was not so easily swayed. "I had no idea, I confess it. What interests, do share?"

Cleo kept a polite smile pinned to her lips. "Hunting, of course. Grouse and snipe."

The pun was not lost on Thornton. He had to cover his mouth to hide his chuckle and noted Claridge and Jesse doing the same. Bella merely frowned at Cleo, ill disguising her dislike. Apparently, his mother did not notice, for she had no retort, merely a soft harrumph at having her attempt at upsetting Cleo so neatly thwarted. Thankfully, she went back to mincing her trout into infinitesimal pieces she only pretended to consume.

"Nicely done," he murmured *sotto voce*. Their fingers remained interlaced in her lap and out of view.

"Thank you," she whispered back, allowing her unassailable mask to drop for a moment to reveal the vulnerability hiding beneath.

His mother the shark had affected her, it would seem. He could not avoid her any longer. The matter of her attacks—subtle and couched in politeness though they were—could not go unanswered. He decided to seek her out following the conclusion of the meal. Cleo did not deserve to be maligned. Christ knew she'd suffered enough as it was, thinking he'd betrayed her, losing their babe on her own, shackling herself to a man who posed as her savior when he was truly her damnation. And so much of it his own fault, despite what she'd said. Thornton would always own his complicity in the sorry state of their lives. He could not whitewash their past, but he could do his damnedest to protect her now.

"I believe you were on the cusp of telling us about your Wild West, Mr. Whitney," Bella reminded Jesse with an air that was far too flirtatious for Thornton's liking.

Dear God, when had bookish Bella become a coquette? She'd never even shown an interest in a man before, as far as he knew. Why, he still recalled having tea parties in the nursery with her and that ratty doll she'd always secreted under her arm until their mother had it removed to the dustbin. Bella had cried for a fortnight straight. Its name had been Miss Muffin, of all things. And now, suddenly here she was, wearing a sophisticated pale pink gown, coiffure elaborately styled and as dignified as any of the grand ladies seated around the table. He saw her for the first time as his friend must see her, a beautiful woman in her own right, shy yet blessed with a sharp mind.

He wasn't sure he liked it. In fact, he altogether hated it. But most of all, he hated the expression on Jesse's face as he regaled the table—Bella in particular—with stories of Buffalo Bill. Nor did he particularly appreciate the way Bella's entire face brightened, her blue eyes sparkling. A spear of dread shot through him.

Cleo noticed the direction of his troubled gaze and the bent of his equally turbulent thoughts. "She is a woman grown," she said in hushed tones.

"That's what I fear," he muttered, looking back to Cleo. How was it possible for her to read him so bloody well, to know his mind as well as he did?

She'd reappeared back in his life with the abruptness of a thunderbolt from the sky and a similarly shocking effect on his senses. His carefully constructed world was about to be torn asunder. Very likely, he would lose his standing in society. He would definitely lose the career he had worked so assertively to achieve. But none of that mattered just now in this moment.

What did matter was her. She meant everything to him, he realized and she always had. He'd spent seven years running from the damage she'd done his heart by throwing him over for Scarbrough, seven years devoting himself to the Liberal cause and subduing the mad passion of his youth. His political aspirations—whatever they had once been—were in tatters. After all, as a marquis he could always maintain his position in the House of Lords. Regardless, he would possess an ability to sway public policy. The die was cast. He would no longer run from Cleo, nor did he give a damn who knew how he felt for her.

ARRANGING A PRIVATE audience with his mother at a house party would have been no easy thing had it not been for the accommodating and gracious Lady Cosgrove, who was eager to assist Thornton in his purpose. She offered the circumspect use of her yellow salon and sent a maid with afternoon tea. He had an inkling that Lady C. knew what the interview was about. It seemed as if she championed his cause, though neither he nor the august lady broached the topic.

Thornton waited for his mother to take a few sips of her tea and chatter about the appalling state of Margot Chilton's garish afternoon dress and Lady Grimsby's wilted peacock feathers.

"It is difficult indeed in these times to surround one's self with worthy company at society events," his mother added. "Everybody who was ever anybody is quite going to the dogs. Why, look at the dreadful number of vulgar Americans invading our shores, clamoring for our titles. The Peerage is going to ruins, I tell you, Alex dearest, which is why it is so important for Bella to marry well.

"You won't allow your unsavory American friend to court her, I hope? He is twice her age and drinks to excess. Hollins has it on good authority that he's been making ill use of some of the household staff. A lowly unpacking maid, if you'll believe it. Hollins tells me he smokes nearly twenty cigarettes in a single day and if the conversation he offered today at luncheon was any indication, he places himself amongst gamblers, blackguards, and swindlers. America is no place for any daughter of mine. Why, it was only during their revolution not so very long ago that they beheaded the highest of their social betters. I should fear for my poor darling's life."

When she stopped for breath and a supporting sip of tea, he sighed. "Mother, you confuse the French Revolution with the American."

"Nonsense," she scoffed. "The French are forever having revolutions. The Americans had just the one."

"Quite so, but all were allowed to keep their heads in place. Unless, of course, they were lost in the heart of battle."

The dowager frowned. "I'm sure you're having me on, Alex. Have I raised you so poorly that you will condescend to your own mother, who bore you for ten grueling months?"

"Nine, I should think," he corrected out of sheer habit.

"You were a burden." She sipped at her tea. "Pray do not be a burden to me now, Alex. My heart is weak, Dr. Walmsey says so and I must avoid upset at all costs. Bad enough I should worry for Bella being taken away to a heathenish land by a loathsome American."

Weak heart his arse. Strange she'd never mentioned it before in one of her tedious epistles. "How should I be a burden on you, mother, when I support your every whim?"

She set her teacup on its saucer with a disjointed clatter. "I do not have whims, Alexander. I have needs. Have I ever burdened you unduly?"

"Yes," he answered truthfully, "though I dare say it is your due as a mother who carried me in her womb for ten grueling months. Let us be honest. I have requested this audience because it is time for a *pax* between yourself and Lady

Scarbrough."

"Do not, I beseech you, speak to me of that dreadful woman," she spat.

"You will cease all attempts to insult her through innuendo and otherwise," he ordered. "Lady Scarbrough has done nothing to provoke your wrath and does not deserve to suffer the lashings your merciless tongue can deal."

The dowager gasped. "You dare to defend her to me?"

"I care for her very deeply."

"You care for Miss Cuthbert." Her hands flailed like unsettled butterflies.

"I intend to dissolve any obligations I may have with Honoria." He did his best to remain cool and reserved, to keep the power of his emotions leashed.

"You cannot! I refuse to allow you to make such a terrible mistake."

"Mother, I am the head of this family."

Her thin mouth tightened, her steel-gray eyes snapping with indignation. She drew herself up to her full seated height with such affront that her lace cap was knocked askew. "And as such, it is your duty to keep us from shame. Your sister has yet to marry."

"It is not my intention to bring shame upon the de Vere name, but neither is it my intention to marry a woman for whom I feel no tender emotion."

His mother wrung her hands together now, her dismay evident. "What does she hold over you?"

He stiffened. "Of whom do you speak?"

"Lady Scarbrough," she gritted. "Who else? What power does that jade wield that she can make you cry off a perfect alliance?"

"This is my decision, not the countess's."

"I should never have mentioned Miss Cuthbert to her. I see that now. She has beat me at my own game," his mother said with a bitter tinge to her voice.

"There need be no games played. My decision is final. I will not marry Miss Cuthbert and you will treat Lady Scarbrough with the respect a lady of her stature deserves."

"You think she does not play a game with you?" she scoffed. "Everyone knows she's been desperate for a scandal. Hollins tells me Lady Scarbrough intends to make the earl sue her for divorce and she means to use you to do it."

Even if he believed Cleo capable of such deception, he had asked her to divorce her husband himself and she had rejected the suggestion as the impossibility it was. That was all the proof he needed of Cleo's true intentions. "To hell with what Hollins tells you. There will be no divorce," he said curtly. "Scarbrough won't give up his tight grip on Cleo's purse."

"But there will be a scandal, Alexander."

He did not deny it.

The dowager pressed a quaking hand to her heart. "Will you not have a care for your sister's reputation?"

"Bella will not be affected." He spoke with more conviction than he felt. In truth, society was fickle and loved nothing more than a good disgrace. He could not be certain that she would be received in society as well if he conducted an open *affaire* with Cleo, but he believed that the de Vere name carried significant clout and fortune behind it to allow her to continue her life as normal. He would remain a Peer of the Realm, with all the power such a position yet maintained and Bella's dowry, of course, would remain the same. He was not entirely selfish in this, but neither was he willing to live without Cleo by his side any longer.

"Dear God," his mother whispered, almost to herself, as if he were no longer in the room at all, "he means to ruin us."

FOLLOWING LUNCHEON, THE men of the company departed

for a short hunt with Lord Cosgrove while the ladies retired to the drawing room. Cleo thought she'd rather sip arsenic tea than endure several hours of banal conversation but had little choice, having already used up her allotment of megrim pleadings. She made certain to seat herself on the periphery of the gang of feathered and glittering ladies. Tia and Helen followed suit, flanking her on either side of the *Louis Quinze* sofa she occupied.

"Lovely rout of the evil Lady Thornton," Tia congratulated with a saucy grin, adjusting her violet gown with silver bead overlay. She had the regal air of a princess, twin diamond stars pinned to her bodice to complete the effect. Her blonde hair was twisted into a dashing chignon with a complicated waterfall of ringlets down her back. Tia, in typical Tia fashion, had refused to wear mourning weeds for her husband any longer than six months.

"Thank you." Cleo still did not feel as if she had been victorious in the match of wits. Indeed, she felt quite trounced. "I am not certain it was a rout, however."

"I should think Thornton is completing said rout just now," Helen added. She wore a bold red gown with a tiered skirt of ivory and a gold sash. The effect was *au militaire* and rather dashing. Her golden locks were styled in a soft coronet of braids.

A cursory examination of the occupants of the drawing room confirmed that the dowager marchioness was not among them. Lady Bella sat on her own across the room, already delving into a book and ignoring the rest of the assemblage.

"Do you think it possible?" she asked Helen, doubtful Thornton would take his dragon mother to task for her sake.

"I think it probable." Helen patted her arm reassuringly. "Dearest, do you not see how protective Thornton is of you?"

"He looked like an angry bear at luncheon," Tia concurred. "I feared he would jump across the table and stuff his trout down the dowager's gullet. Actually, I envisioned him doing just such a thing in my mind and it was immensely amusing. It would have been well-deserved."

Cleo frowned. "I thought you two didn't approve of Thornton."

"We've had a good chat about it and decided we don't disapprove," Helen said cryptically.

"By which you mean to say?"

"We wish you happy." Tia pursed her lips. "We fear for your heart. But if you must stay the course, we shall support you."

The news gratified her. She would need her sisters, always her bulwark in the past, even more now. "I haven't the slightest notion what course I will take."

Helen wore a sympathetic expression. "It's already been decided, dear. I could see it in your eyes at luncheon."

"And I could see it in your gown this morning," Tia put in with an arch air.

Cleo flushed at the reminder of her impulsive interlude with Thornton in the library. It had been very unwise and yet she would like nothing more than to repeat it as soon as possible. "Would you believe it rent on a hook?" she tried.

Tia eyed her shrewdly. "How many hooks are lingering in the Cosgrove library? I confess I have not seen any there myself."

"Nestled between the Chaucer and the Plato?" Helen suggested with a wink.

"Perhaps between his lordship's thighs," Tia whispered with a titter.

"Hush, both of you," Cleo grumbled, horridly embarrassed and afraid someone would overhear.

Just then Margot Chilton began to read the gossip papers aloud.

"Oh, do listen to this tempting *on dit*," she called loudly enough for sheep farmers to hear her in the next county. "A lady of high standing is said to be causing quite a stir at a venerable country house party. At the same fête, two gentlemen, equally notorious—one for his impeccable character and the other for his lack in that virtuous arena—came to blows and it was not over *Romeo & Juliet*." She looked up from her scandal sheets, a feline smile curving her lips. "I dare say this may well be about someone in our own company. Who do you think it could be? How thrilling to be in the moment!"

Nausea cramped Cleo's stomach into knots. A dozen pairs of eyes swung to her. Drat Margot Chilton. She held her head high, unwilling to allow them to see the effect they had on her. "Indeed," she drawled, "though I should think it rather tedious."

Tia sniffed. "I'm sure I never read the scandal rags. No one who is anyone does these days."

Margot's face flamed. Several snickers went through the assemblage. She folded the gossip sheet in her lap. "I suppose those who fear to find themselves within don't dare read it."

Lady Cosgrove interjected. "Let's do put the vulgar thing away, Miss Margot. I've more worthy entertainments in store for us whilst the men are out having their sport."

Minor relief slid through her. At least she could avoid blatant speculation. Her emotions were too fresh and raw for her to keep them at a distance. Certainly, she was most concerned with keeping Alex from scandal. His positions in society and in the Liberal Party were far different from hers as a society wife. And she could never forgive herself if she were responsible for his downfall, despite his heated protestations to her. She well knew that the words a man spoke after making love were not always to be trusted. Likely he would now regret his hasty actions. She shifted in her seat, discomfited at the thought.

Lady Cosgrove's worthy entertainments, as it happened, proved to be a series of silly parlor games that did their job with most of the ladies. Cleo, however, remained undistracted.

After an interminable hour of charades and whist, she escaped from the room. Unnoticed, or so she supposed until Lady Bella caught up with her out in the hall.

"Lady Scarbrough?" Alex's sister's voice was hesitant yet strong enough not to be ignored. "May I request an audience?"

Groaning in her mind, Cleo stopped in her tracks and faced Lady Bella. She fastened a smile on her lips and clasped her hands together. "Lady Bella. Of course you may. Where shall we sit?"

"Perhaps we ought to seek out your chamber," she suggested, unsmiling.

Oh dear. That did not bode well. But she refused to allow her concern to show. She inclined her head. "I have a small sitting area that will be of use. Let's walk together, shall we?"

Lady Bella still clutched her book and she did not speak during the entire awkward walk to the Tudor wing. For her part, Cleo could not speak past the knot of worry tangling in her stomach. And then they reached the room bearing Cleo's name, stepped inside and found Thornton waiting within, sprawled in a chair.

"Alex," both women exclaimed in unison. He appeared equally startled to see his sister swishing into Cleo's private rooms and shot up as if a chamber maid had lit a fire beneath his bottom.

Cleo acted with haste, ushering Bella inside and snapping the door closed on possible wandering servants or guests with eager ears. It wouldn't do to incite more gossip and speculation than they already foolishly had.

There was no sound save the ominous rustling of Bella's silk gown. Alex rammed his fingers through his black hair.

"Bella, Jesus Christ."

His sister flinched at his tone and his harsh language. "Pray remind yourself that you are in the company of ladies." At that, she sent Cleo a searching glance.

Her skin prickled. She was still a lady, blessed angels' sakes. Nothing had changed except her resistance had shattered. But that was the way of it in their world—the man had his pleasure and the woman paid the price. Goodness, from the expression on Lady Bella's face, Cleo mused, one would suppose she'd been caught in the act of filching Lady Cosgrove's jewels.

"Apologies to you both," Thornton muttered. "Truly, I only intended to leave a note that I didn't care to entrust to servants."

"Indeed, brother." Bella's tone was dry and Cleo realized a spitfire hid beneath her muted exterior. "This has all the makings of a sensation novel. We need only a specter moaning through the halls."

"Lady Bella," Cleo began, needing to intervene. "I expect you are no more startled than myself to find the marquis here. But I do hope we can be friends?"

Bella turned back to her, face drawn. "I do not yet know, my lady."

Cleo met Thornton's gaze. This interview was fast becoming the most unwanted she'd ever suffered. It was his fault. Was he not supposed to be the responsible, propriety-loving politician?

He sighed as if reading her thoughts. "Bella, your discretion is required."

Bella swatted his shoulder with her book. "Pooh! Act with discretion yourself if you require it, you duffer."

Thornton scowled, rubbing his arm. "Why are you angry with me?"

She sent Cleo a look that was not pleasant or even marginally friendly. "I shan't make a row in front of her."

"Lovely," Cleo grumbled to herself. They had not even begun an *affaire* in truth and already they were the butt of gossip and familial dissension.

"If you don't feel comfortable addressing Lady Scarbrough, then why are you in her chambers?" Thornton growled.

"We were meant to have a discussion," Bella answered. "Gossip has already made its way to London concerning your actions here. If you have a care for your reputation—"

"If you have a care for yourself, you'll stop speaking before you say something out of turn," he interrupted. "You are my younger sister, damn it, not my mother. And I will not have you gainsaying me, or I'll drop you and mother both and you can live with some rusty country cousin who hasn't a care for you."

His threat struck home with Lady Bella, for she paled. "Do what you must," she whispered before turning on her heel.

"Lady Bella," Cleo called after her to no avail. The door slammed closed, leaving her alone with Thornton. She pivoted back to him. "That was badly done of you. Your sister only has your best interests at heart."

"She's practically a schoolgirl," he scoffed, raking a hand through his already much-abused hair yet again. "She hasn't an inkling as to my best interests."

"Still, your words to her were harsh."

His jaw tightened. "Christ. I can't believe you would defend her when she treated you little better than if you had been swept from the gutters."

"There were scandal sheets read in the drawing room," she told him quietly. "We were mentioned in them, though not by name. It is only a matter of time before all manner of gossip erupts. Perhaps we should keep our distance for a time, until the tongues stop wagging."

"Damn it." He stalked across the chamber, heading for the door his sister had so recently tested. "You're right. I should go after her."

"Yes, do." In truth, she wished most fervently that he would remain with her, but she also understood that his duty to his family necessarily trumped any duty he may feel to her. That quickly, he was gone. He had said nothing, too, against keeping a distance between them and she worried that she could not manage a distance any greater than an arm's length. She sank down into a chair as if a great weight had been cast upon her shoulders and indeed it had.

Chapter Thirteen

"BELLA, STOP."

Naturally, being a female and his sister both, she ignored Thornton's command, bustling down the hall without a pause. Her skirt even twitched in her agitation. Hell, what had he done—what grievous sin had he committed—to deserve this punishment? Had he not just dealt with the dowager? Now he must face the dowager-in-training when all he longed for was Cleo's sweet, lush body beneath his. They hadn't even made love in a proper bed yet, Chrissakes.

"Bella," he attempted again.

She crashed into her bedchamber, oblivious to the noise and spectacle she made. He barreled through after her, patience thinning. Under ordinary circumstances, he would never disrupt Bella's privacy. But she had already taken it upon herself to disrupt his peace and meddle in his affairs where she was not wanted or needed and he meant to return the favor. First, he would give her his mind on the inappropriate attention she had been paying Jesse.

"Get out of here." She turned about in a flurry of angry green silk and launched a book at his head.

Had he not ducked quickly, it would have landed him square in the right eye.

"Get out!" she screeched.

"Good Christ, Bella, let's not make a row." He was horrified by her uncharacteristic reaction. Didn't have a clue how to respond or control her apparent rage.

"Let's not make a row?" She wrestled a book from the table beside her bed and hurled it at him. "I dare say it's too late for that, brother. You have gone from being the gem of the Liberals to the gossip on everyone's tongue. Have you no respect for yourself? Have you no control over your deeds that you must shame us all by sniffing after her skirts as if you were no better than a common hound?"

"That's quite enough, Arabella de Vere," he told her in his sternest tones. "You're making a rumpus without reason."

"Has she made you come after me?" Bella demanded to know, her cheeks flushed with rage and exertion to match her dress.

He rather didn't want to admit it, but his face must have given away the truth. His sister threw up her hands. "I despair of you. Truly, it's no better than if you were her dog."

Sister or no, Thornton had withstood all the insults and hurled objects he would from the spoiled chit. Had he ever thought her bookish and meek? Christ, what had he been thinking? She was Lucifer decked out in a lady's finery.

And she had overstepped her bounds. "That is enough out of you, miss." He stalked the length of the chamber, determined to thwart any more bric-a-brac throwing she may have in mind. "You will recall to whom you speak. I haven't an inkling what's gotten into you, but I don't like a bit of it."

"You told me there was nothing untoward between yourself and Lady Scarbrough and yet it is plain to everyone—even town gossips—that there is. I am sick with it, Alex. Already, I must endure mother's endless carping on every subject beneath the sun. Now I must also watch my brother ruin his life. All this for what?"

"For love," he said before he could hold his bloody tongue. Bella's expression could surely be no more startled than his. He wasn't the revelatory sort. "I'm in love with Lady Scarbrough. There. I've said it now."

She pressed her fingers to her lips, covering a gasp. "But

she is married."

"Oh bloody Christ," he growled. "Why can't you just go back to being a wallflower and wearing whatever dress mother tells you? I haven't the patience for this."

"Alex, think of what you're doing." She gripped his arms, her blue eyes searching his. "I only think of your best interests. Before you act with haste and indecision, think for God's sake, of what you will lose. All your life you've been consumed with politics. It's been all you ever wanted."

"Do not ask me to explain any of this, Bella." His voice was hoarse. "I cannot."

What his sister said was truth. These last few years of his life had been solely dedicated with ruthless persistence to the furthering of both his party and his own political standing. He very much believed in reform. He had long since given up the naïve notion that he alone could affect change, but he had never stopped believing that his party and his Prime Minister needed him.

Bella wanted him to choose between the life he had built for himself and the woman he wanted in his arms and in his bed for the rest of his days. Cleo had attempted to force him to recognize that just such a choice may come. He knew now it well may and sooner than he'd supposed.

"Brother, why would you do this to yourself?"

"Because to not would be the greatest mistake," he answered. "Do not think that I haven't already weighed the ramifications."

"I cannot believe it to be so."

He frowned. "You need not. But I would warn you, Bella, that you should not entertain any girlish romance between yourself and Mr. Whitney. He is your senior by many years and a man beyond your ken."

Bella's eyes flashed with angry fire. "How dare you?"

"I dare as the head of this family and as a man who knows what is best for his innocent sister who knows nothing of the hard world around her."

"You have so little knowledge of me that I wonder you think yourself a fit judge for whom I may keep company with," she sniped.

Thornton clenched his jaw and his fists, trying with great difficulty to stymie his anger and frustration. "I know enough," he bit out. "You'll stay away from him and you'll keep a civil tongue in your head. I'll not hear another word against Cleo from your mouth. Do you hear?"

Bella stared at him and he knew instinctively he'd lost whatever respect with which she may have once regarded him. "I hear well enough."

But he knew just as well as she that hearing did not mean a blessed thing. She'd gotten headstrong and he feared this was merely the beginning of a new, intrepid Bella. Damned if he wasn't cut up about it.

CLEO NEARLY JUMPED out of her skin when Thornton slipped back inside her chamber. She'd been pacing since he left in search of his sister, wringing her hands and feeling generally useless. Of course she felt awful to be causing rifts in his family. Already, she suspected that he had taken his mother to task in her name and now he'd destroyed whatever fragile bond that existed between him and Bella. The reality of what he must give up for her, the hopelessness of their future together, was bad enough without now being forced to acknowledge she was hurting his relationship with his family. She wasn't altogether certain she could bear it.

When her door clicked open, she turned to find Thornton striding inside, hair still askew, yet impossibly handsome in his irrefutable way. She knew from the hard expression on his face that it had not gone well with Bella. Her heart ached for him.

Cleo crossed the distance between them and went into his

arms. He pressed her close to his chest and she heard the heavy beating of his heart against her ear. He smelled of his own delicious scent, comforting and enticing. "It did not go as it should have done with Bella," she guessed.

Thornton sighed. "She has grown quite intractable. It's impossible to make her understand. I'm sorry for her ill treatment of you. It shouldn't have become so damned ugly."

She clung to him, savoring his strength. "It will be worse if we continue as we are."

"If?" He withdrew and gazed down at her, his expression troubled. "What is this?"

"It is only that I don't wish to be the cause of unhappiness in your life." Her voice broke on the last.

"Jesus, Cleo, you are my happiness. Can you not see that as plainly as I stand here before you?"

His beloved face had grown taut. His eyes bored into hers, searching, needing to see a response that matched his own heart. She knew that it was there, that her love for him shone on her face. She could no longer hide it from him or anyone else.

"As you are my happiness," she told him, voice soft. "It is only for that reason that I don't wish to make you miserable."

"You can only make me miserable by denying me." His mouth descended on hers in a fiercely passionate kiss.

She caught his shoulders, leaning into his solid embrace. Their breaths and tongues tangled together in a sweet dance. His hands were on her derriere beneath the *tournure* of her dress, cupping and demanding.

"I want you now," he whispered. "Do you want me?"

Although she knew she should have been shocked by his plain speaking, she could not deny she found it arousing. Her blood coursed through her veins in hot, heady pulses. She was indeed hungry for him.

"Always," she returned, taking his lower lip between her teeth and giving it a savagely playful pull.

Thornton groaned. "I'm going to take you in a bed this time, darling. I never should have presumed to take you against a bloody bookshelf the last time. It was unconscionable of me."

She caressed his aristocratic cheekbone. "My love, nothing was ever better than that moment we had in the library. I shall remember it always." She kissed him again and then looked up at him with a wicked smile curving her lips. "But even so, I should like nothing better than to make another attempt in the lovely bed just behind me."

Laughing with wicked delight, he pushed them slowly backward together, toward the bed. They kissed again, then again, then again, until he finally caught her up in his arms and tossed her onto the mattress. Cleo landed with a giggle that evaporated when Thornton joined her.

He lay beside her, his large body pressed to the length of hers and propped his head with his left hand. He splayed his right hand above her madly beating heart. Smiling, she stilled, her eyes steady on his.

"I dreamt of this," he began, his voice hoarse. "All those years ago, I dreamt of a moment when I would join you in a real bed, when you would be truly mine. It guts me that you belong to him in the eyes of the law. I would do anything to make it otherwise."

Tears stung her eyes at his confession. She well knew what the revelation cost a man like him and knew too that she wished even more fervently than him that she was not bound to another. "I am truly yours in every conceivable way. I love you, Alex. Feel it."

She clasped her hand over his, pressing it to her chest as if she could transfer all the emotions trapped within her through his skin. She wanted him to know how it was for her, how it would always be. Even if they had nothing else together beyond their time at Wilton House, she would have him know the absolute truth. She'd been foolish enough not to in her youth and she didn't care to repeat such folly for pride's stupid sake.

His palm was heavy on her heart. He lowered his head and placed an ardent kiss upon her hand. She ran her fingers through his thick black hair, smoothing it back into place in tender strokes. "I love you," she said again for good measure. "I loved you all those years ago. I wish I had not run from you. I wish I had stayed and believed—"

"It was my fault," he murmured against her skin. "I should never have abandoned you. If I could do those years over, I would."

Her fingers stopped, her heart tripping with a slight start of uncertainty. Her words had not yet been returned. "Did you love me?"

Thornton's head rose and his clear gaze fastened on her. He turned her hand upside down so that their fingers clasped. "I did then and I do now. I have never stopped." He dropped a kiss on the hollow of her throat. "I have never stopped."

His fingers tightened as he kissed a path up her neck.

"Tell me," she demanded, breathless.

He paused with his mouth hovering over hers, his eyes giving her the truest glimpse she'd ever gained of the inner man. "I love you, Cleo," he said in a firm, strong voice, so there could be no doubt later. "I love you now as ever, my darling."

"Then make me yours again."

"To be perfectly honest, ever since I spotted you in this dashing silver affair, I've been wanting to have my wicked way with you," he confessed on a grin that brought out his charming dimple and thrilled her to her toes.

She kissed him because she couldn't help herself and then leaned back to give him a saucy look of her own. "Help me off with it?"

"With pleasure."

Together, they peeled away the layers of her gown, unpinning the careful work Bridget had made that afternoon of the jet beads and the proper tucks to reveal her silver underskirt. The gown was gone in a minute. Beneath it, she had worn only stockings, a silk chemise and a naughty black corset she'd purchased on a whim but never worn. She'd anticipated this moment, it was true.

Thornton's expression gratified her. His smoldering eyes lit upon her breasts struggling to escape from the lacy corset. She was certain she looked a fair impersonation of a trollop. And she was equally certain that he approved. She knew her proper marquis had a dark undertone.

"Minx," he said, voice thick. "You've worn this for me, haven't you?"

"Absolutely. And I haven't any drawers."

To check her assertion, he skimmed a hot hand past her stockings and garters, up over her thigh to the juncture of her limbs. His nimble fingers met with moist, hungry flesh.

"Do you like it?" she asked in her most innocent tone.

He sent her an intense look. "Sweet Christ, yes."

His fingers were not content to merely try her bare skin, however. They stroked up a decadent rhythm that had her quite ready to lose her head and her breath both. Their mouths met in another series of possessing kisses. Her breasts ached. Her skin ached. Every pore in her body ached for him. She never wanted him to stop or to leave her. She thought wildly that they should lock themselves in a bedchamber for the rest of their lives and forget about the world. Forget about all else except for their miraculous love for one another. Because surely no worldly care should come between so pure an expression of love between a man and a woman. Surely nothing and no one could ever keep them from one another ever again.

"Take off your clothes," she ordered between kisses. "Take everything off."

"As you wish." He leaned above her to shuck his jacket,

waistcoat, and shirt. When he reached for the fastening on his trousers, she stopped him.

"No." She pushed him to his back on the bed and hooked her leg across his so that she straddled his lean hips. She dropped a kiss on his taut abdomen, savoring the rigid cords of his muscle, then moved lower, sinking a playful tongue into his navel. Cleo was most pleased to hear the breath hissing from his mouth. She ran her tongue lower, undoing the fastening on his trousers at the same time. When he sprang free, he was fully erect. She stopped her tongue at the base of his cock, then glanced up to look at him.

Thornton's head had fallen back, his beautiful, sullen mouth slack, his eyes glazed with passion. She had never known such a heady feeling of power, nor such a need to give pleasure to the man she loved. It was different between them. She was no longer an innocent maid, ignorant of how to touch a man. She could wield her power well.

With a satisfied jerk, she pulled his trousers down his long legs, made quick work of his shoes, and tossed all to the floor behind her. The Marquis of Thornton lay naked on her bed. It was incredible. It was terrifying. It was…right.

Cleo leaned over him once more, intent on giving him the same pleasure to which he had so recently treated her. She wrapped her hand around the base of his engorged shaft. His hips jerked. When she lowered her mouth to lick the velvety tip, he unleashed a feral moan. She took him into her mouth. Taking care to keep her teeth from scoring him, she moved up and down his length, losing herself in the rhythm. She couldn't get enough of him. Cleo tortured him until he finally seized her arms and drew her up over his body and brought her lips to his for an ardent kiss.

"Unlace my corset," she ordered, the pain of the cinching finally cutting through the hazy desire that had taken up residence in her mind.

His fingers found the ties and dismantled Bridget's formidable double knot with alarming speed and accuracy. "You're rather well schooled at divesting a lady of her undergarments," she pointed out, cupping his face in her hands.

"My prick's never been this hard," he grunted. "In my circumstances, you too could perform amazing feats of dexterity."

She laughed and dropped a lingering kiss on his lips. "You are fortunate indeed that I love you, my lord, else I may take umbrage at your shockingly depraved tongue."

"Darling, it's about to get more depraved," he promised.

Cleo shuddered. "I dare say I hope it does."

"Smart lass." He chuckled, then threw her corset over his head. It hooked on a vase of fresh English daisies and sent it crashing to the table before raining shards on the floor. Pieces skittered dully over the carpet.

"Thornton!" She felt compelled to scold. After all, their hostess was an accommodating dear. It was not done to ruin one's hostess's French vases, particularly when one could not ostensibly lay blame where it belonged, upon one's illicit lover's shoulders.

"Sweetheart?" He caught the neckline of her silk chemise and tore it in two, whipping the ragged pieces from her body and off to a similar fate to that of the corset and vase. Then the wicked man sucked a pebbled nipple into his mouth.

"Ah." She arched against him, still astride. What in the name of the holy angels had she been about to say? Oh yes. "You've broken Lady Cosgrove's vase."

His tongue flicked over the hardened bud, deliberately teasing her. He stopped, blew softly on the aching peak and looked up at her with an innocently boyish expression. "Would you like me to clean up the pieces?" He blew again for good measure.

"No," she choked. "It can wait."

"Oh? Are you certain? I could just pop 'round the back here and scoop it into a tidy pile."

"Quite all right." She grabbed one of his hands and pressed it to her abandoned breast. "Just make love to me, if you please."

"Indeed." His thumb flicked a lazy circle around her breast. "Certain, my darling? It would be no trouble."

"Wretch!" Cleo arched into him. "Cease toying with me."

He smiled up at her, his lips curving against her skin. She sank her fingers into his hair, savoring the thick waves, the feel of his hard-bodied form pressed against her. "I love you, Cleopatra Harrington."

As far as she was concerned, Harrington was the only surname she cared to claim. It had been hers so long ago when they first met. "Can we pretend tonight that I am only Cleopatra Harrington?" she asked, voice hitching.

"My darling, to me you will always be Cleopatra Harrington." He pressed an opened-mouth kiss to the tender spot of skin between her breasts. "Always my own."

And then he began a trail of soft, loving kisses down to her abdomen, where he paused once more. His large hands cradled the nip of her waist. "Thank you for carrying our child, for being strong enough for the both of us." When Thornton once again looked up to meet her gaze, there was a sheen of tears sparkling in his eyes. "I need you to forgive me for abandoning you then, because I will never forgive myself."

"I do forgive you, Alex, my love." She cupped his face in her hands tenderly. "As you must forgive yourself. We knew so little of life then. We were young and silly and I was afraid. It was my mistake as much as yours and I have made my peace. You must make yours."

"I can only make peace if you leave him, Cleo." He was once again caressing her body with his hands, skimming warm palms over her stomach, hips, breasts. Bringing her to life once more. His gaze was focused, clear and determined. "Promise me now that when I leave this house party you'll go with me."

"With you?" She searched his expression but found it impossible to decipher. To leave openly with him would be tantamount to scandal. They may as well make a joint announcement in the *Times* that they planned to cuckold Scarbrough. "Heavens, what must you be thinking to suggest such folly?"

"Not folly. I am deliberate." To illustrate the veracity of his words, he spread her legs and sank his fingers between the moist folds of her sex. Two fingers slipped deep inside her. His thumb worked the nub of her sex. "You see? Deliberate action."

Her hips jerked. "Thornton!"

A masculine smile of appreciation slid over his mouth. "You doubt me? I should hate to think you possess such appallingly little faith in me, darling."

He was stroking her, building a fire within her that threatened to consume her body. Possibly even her very soul. She'd never experienced anything more intoxicating. "I don't…doubt," she managed through clamped teeth.

Still working his evocative rhythm, he lowered his tongue to her. Cleo nearly screamed with the pent-up pleasure and mad wanting.

"It's my turn to play," he murmured, voice low and sinfully seductive. "If you don't doubt me, then you will agree."

"I agree that you are a most exasperating man," she gritted, having great difficulty exercising control of her breath or even her traitorous body at this particular juncture. His mouth was doing wicked things to her most sensitive parts and she rather liked it.

"Not good enough."

"You, sir, are impossible."

"So you've told me on numerous occasions. I'm not easily swayed from my course."

"For a man not easily swayed, you're making an awful lot of chatter," she pointed out.

Apparently, he took exception to her observation. He sucked the bud of her sex and plunged another finger inside her, stroking and stretching and bringing her to an arched-back, heaving, sobbing climax.

He gave her no time to recover. His big body was on hers, pressing her into the bed. He rubbed his erection against her swollen mound, eliciting another loud moan from her. "I'll endeavor to be more of a man of action," he whispered, holding both her breasts in his hands and slanting a possessive kiss over her lips.

She pushed her tongue into his mouth and ran her hands over the sinewy, smooth skin of his strong back. Cleo had never thought it possible to expire from sheer pleasure until this moment. Nor was she missish or given to fainting spells. But she feared both now. The feeling of Alex against her, their hearts thudding madly, tongues and breaths and legs tangling, his hardness about to enter her, all combined in a mind whirling assault. She loved this man, had always done and knew she would go anywhere, brave any scandal if he but asked it of her.

"Will you leave here with me?" He drew back, their noses brushing.

"Yes."

The moment she uttered the word, he was inside her. He took her in one deep, soul-splintering plunge. She arched her head back and his mouth feasted on her throat. In several quick pumps, she was gone again and before long, so was he. When it was over and they were both spiraling back to earth, he drew her to her side so they lay facing one another. His fingers swept unruly tendrils of hair from her face, then traced a soft path over her cheek and down to her lips.

"I shall never forget the first moment we met when you took me to task over your fat black cat," he said idly.

She swatted his chest. "Clementine was not fat, you beast. She was just rather plump in a delightfully feline way."

"You used to chatter more than a magpie."

"If it's your intention to ruin my good humor with you, you're succeeding admirably," she told him wryly.

"I'm reminiscing." He grinned and his frightfully attractive dimple made an appearance to soothe the sting. "They say there is no such thing as love at first sight, but I do believe we're proof otherwise. If I didn't love you at the first, I can't think of an earthly reason why I would have listened to so much girlish nattering."

She pulled a chest hair to get even with him for the 'girlish nattering' bit. "Are we being wise, Alex?"

"We're being as wise as we can be," he answered pragmatically.

"I've never been this happy," she confessed, almost afraid to admit it lest something should happen suddenly to ruin their carefully constructed haven. Too soon, their idyll would be at an end. And if he held her to her promise, they would leave together, making their relationship known to all the polite world. From there, things would grow more difficult.

He pulled her closer and rolled to his back so her cheek rested on his chest. His fingers began to undo her upsweep. "Nor have I."

"Do you think we will be able to keep it, this happiness between us?"

Alex dropped a kiss on her head. "I think you worry too much, Cleo. We cannot fear everything. We can only live to make ourselves happy."

"Not in this world of ours," she fretted. "It is different in our set. You know it as well as I. We live for alliances and wealth and keeping up the appearances when in truth our lives are in shambles."

"We are not everyone else." She felt him unwinding her hair and spreading the silky skeins over her shoulders and back. "We are only you and I, Alex and Cleo. That is all we must ever be, whether here in this room together or in the drawing room. If we are going to be together, we cannot hide our love as if it were damning. I won't be shamed for something that is right."

She nestled closer to him, breathing deeply of his scent. "It is right," she echoed just before she fell into a deep, careless sleep. "It is very right indeed."

Chapter Fourteen

*C*LEO AND THORNTON spent the next few nights secretly popping in and out of one another's chambers, dodging servants and guests alike. The first evening, it was a lark. Cleo and her sisters had grown up, much to their mother's dismay, with many games of spy and enemy soldier thanks to their brothers. As she ducked down a shadowy corridor, she was rather put in mind of that, merely an adult version laden with many more consequences.

On the second night they spent in secret, Thornton caught her in her bath and they made love in the warm water, splashing half the contents of the tub onto the tile floor. On the third night, he tore her night dress into pieces and tossed them over his shoulder. He also forgot to return to his bed at dawn and Bridget had entered that morning to stoke the fire. If the scarlet flush on her cheeks was any indication, the poor woman had gotten rather an eyeful of Thornton, Cleo feared. And that hastily, their secret was a secret no more. Although Bridget was a dear heart, Cleo was not altogether certain that her love of gossip wouldn't win over her loyalty to her mistress.

The day before the last of Lady C.'s house party, Cleo met Thornton for an afternoon ride. They traveled out of sight of Wilton House, into the same copse of wood they had so recently made use of. Alex dismounted, tethered his horse to a nearby oak and then helped her from her mare. After the mare was secured, he took her in his arms, burying his face in her neck, hands running over her back.

"Ah," he breathed. "If I spend one more morning having to slink away from you as if I were a bloody East End thief, I'll go mad."

"We must be circumspect," she reminded him, raising her mouth to his for a kiss.

"To hell with that. Your maid has likely told half the county she found me shagging you to death."

"Alex!"

"Darling, it's true. You must admit you were nearly swooning at that moment." The look of masculine satisfaction on his face was unmistakable. "As I recall, my head was quite under the counterpane while my hands were—"

"That's enough out of you, sir." She kissed him again to silence him. "I was utterly mortified when I heard her drop the poker to the floor."

"I thought it amusing to see how quickly she disappeared."

"You would, you reprobate."

"Reprobate now, am I?" He grinned the grin of the sinful unrepentant. "I thought you fancied scoundrels. After all, you were panting after Ravenscroft for a bit until you regained your senses."

"You're horrid." She laughed despite herself. "Julian is only my friend."

"And he damn well better stay that way," Thornton growled, cupping her breasts possessively through her riding habit and wrap. "No more talk of Julian now, if you please."

Of their own accord, her hands twined around his neck, her fingers toying with the too-long hair at the nape of his neck. How she loved this man. Her heart ached at their unbearable circumstances. "I'm worried for us, Alex. Your position in the Liberal Party could be threatened. I can't fathom the Prime Minister would allow such scandal to go unanswered."

His mouth swooped down on hers, stifling all protest. "We've been over this before, darling. Gossip is a bugbear."

"That could well be your undoing," she pressed, then kissed him before she could stop herself.

"You will be my undoing." Their tongues dueled.

"That's a bit of an understatement," she managed, breathless. "Though I dare say you shall be mine first."

"Oh?" He raised a brow and gave her a wicked grin, appearing as if he relished the notion.

"You are a naughty man, my lord." They kissed again and from that point, their conversation only traveled in a decidedly depraved fashion.

By the time they meandered back to Wilton House, Cleo's hair was in a terrible state of disrepair, the hem of her gown was torn, muddied and wet and she had dirt smears on her bodice.

"You're ruining me," she informed him without a shade of regret in her voice.

"It's my greatest hope," he said with a wink. He dropped a hasty kiss on her lips. "Until tonight."

"Until tonight," she echoed, feeling oddly bereft when he had gone. She wondered if it would always be this way between them, if she would forever feel as if half of herself was missing when he was gone from her side.

She was forced to scurry into a side entrance to avoid prying eyes again. Once in her chamber, she could breathe safely. Almost. Because Bridget was waiting for her, her costume for that evening's mask ball laid out on the bed. When she caught sight of Cleo, she frowned.

"My lady." She dipped into a stiff curtsy.

Cleo felt her face flame. "Bridget. I did not expect you so soon."

"Of course, Lady Scarbrough," she murmured, casting her eyes to the carpet. "How may I be of service to you now?"

How could she have forgotten that tonight was the night

Lady Cosgrove would stage her infamous Last Mask? On the last evening of her Shakespearean Country House Party, Lady C. always held a mask in which revelers were expected to dress as characters from Shakespeare's works.

"I suppose it's too late for a bath?" Cleo asked hesitantly.

"Too late indeed, my lady."

Cleo waltzed across the room to sit before the dressing table. She met Bridget's disapproving gaze in the looking glass. "Bridget," she started, then sighed and halted.

"Yes, my lady?"

She thought very carefully before starting anew. "I would appreciate your discretion."

Bridget's hands were already undoing her tangled chignon, but she stilled at Cleo's words. "My lady?"

Cleo cleared her throat. "I believe we have not addressed the, er, situation of the other morning."

"Oh dear me." Bridget's cheeks reflected an even brighter red than Cleo's in the mirror. "My lady, you needn't explain to me."

"Please do not speak of it to anyone," she said simply.

Bridget was silent for quite some time. She dismantled Cleo's hair, then ran a comb through the long locks. "Are you certain it's wise, my lady?"

Cleo smiled. "It is likely most unwise, dearest Bridget, but I find that it no longer matters."

"But all those years ago, when he left you with nothing more than a bye your leave?"

"It was my fault," she said honestly. "I chose Scarbrough over Thornton, thinking it the best choice. I was wrong. Surely you see that as well, Bridget?"

"It's not my place to say, my lady. I only fear for you."

"As do I." Mostly, she feared for her heart, that it would become bruised and broken beyond repair. She was still terribly uncertain as to how she and Thornton could make their unlikely relationship work outside the freeing gates of

Wilton House. "But it is what I must do, Bridget, as I love him more than I love breath in my lungs."

"My lady, I'll not speak a word of it."

"Thank you." They spoke no more of it, but it was still there, indefinable and uncertain, tingling in the air between them as Bridget skillfully curled Cleo's hair into lengthy ringlets. She had chosen to wear her hair unbound for the event in part because she knew Thornton would approve and in part because it was in keeping with her costume.

Cleo was, of course, to be dressed as a sort of modern Cleopatra, even if it meant taking liberties. Which was to say she wore impressively draped silk skirts of white, without bustle but with a great deal of ornamentation that was not perhaps altogether Egyptian.

Bridget helped her into her costume in silence, still disapproving but with less obviousness. In truth, the costume had been designed for her by Worth just for the occasion and had been extremely dear at nearly two hundred pounds. Her hair was arrayed in gold chain and scarabs of lapis and carnelian.

Her mask was too darling, a gem-encrusted affair that covered the upper half of her face and left her mouth exposed. Her curls traveled down her back and on her feet she wore, quite shockingly, no shoes. The glass in her chamber reflected a different woman entirely. A wanton. A jade. The woman she saw in the mirror well could have been the woman at the source of so much speculation. She was unafraid of consequence, marveling in her own feminine power, delighting in her sway over men. Cleo very much wished she could be the woman she saw, a woman capable of anything, it seemed.

"Oh, my lady," Bridget breathed. "It's lovely, you are. His lordship will not be able to keep a distance."

A satisfied smile curved Cleo's lips as she stared at her reflection. "That is precisely what I had hoped, Bridget."

NEARLY A THOUSAND candles lit the Wilton House ballroom that night. Cleo felt as if she had stepped into the enchanted forest. She couldn't help but notice that there was an inordinate amount of Juliets walking about, along with a fair number of Romeos. Really, did no one have a sense of adventure?

She spotted Tia and Helen instantly and joined them. "Darlings," she greeted them happily. She had been so engrossed in Alex the last few days that she had actually seen frightfully little of them. "You both look lovely!"

Tia frowned below her half mask. "How did you locate us with such alarming perspicacity? I dare say I thought myself quite incognito."

"Properly," Cleo agreed, "yet if you will but remember, you told me that you would be dressing as Desdemona."

"Never mind our sister," Helen broke in with a smile. "Tia is ever convinced there is some sort of conspiracy mucking about."

"I had forgotten I told her," Tia groused. "Really, I'm so busy these days that I cannot recall what I tell to whom. Not as much can be said for you, I should think, even given your advanced age."

"I am not so old as you would have me sound," Helen countered.

"Sisters," Cleo interrupted. "Need we argue already? The mask has yet to truly even begin and already Desdemona is at the throat of Cordelia."

"Bosh," Tia dismissed. "We're not making a row of it, Cleo. We're merely discussing. You've been so distant from us these past few days that you likely have forgotten how we deal with one another."

"I was otherwise occupied," Cleo defended herself, looking about the room, searching through glittering masks and Iagos and Romeos and King Lears in search of Thornton. She could not help herself, really. It had been all of two hours since they'd last kissed.

"The lovelorn make me sick," Tia lamented. "Do they not make you ill, Helen?"

"Virulently," Helen agreed.

"I am not lovelorn." Cleo's gaze was still skittering about for Alex. "I merely miss him."

"So very much worse than we'd supposed," Tia sighed.

"She's utterly gone," Helen confirmed.

"I love him," Cleo defended. "What have you to say of it?"

Tia shrugged. "Nothing, my dear. We only wish you happy."

"Forgive me if I don't believe you when you continually bemoan my fate."

"Don't be shrewish," Tia snapped. "Where is Ravenscroft when you need him?"

"At your service, my loves." The deep voice at Cleo's back was unmistakably the notorious earl's.

She turned to allow him entrance into their private circle. He wore an Elizabethan costume styled all in black. He was also resplendently handsome in a black velvet half mask. Cleo wondered briefly if he was harboring a *tendre* for Tia. She never would have guessed but for the way he was looking at her just now. Then again, Ravenscroft tended to examine all women like a fox eying up a choice hen in the chicken yard. Very likely, it was nothing.

"And what do you presume to be, my lord?" Cleo asked with a saucy grin. She still liked the notorious earl, even if Thornton had sworn her off him. Well, Thornton was hardly her master. She need not adhere to his every wish and whim.

Julian bowed. "Hamlet, your humble servant, my lady."

"Your highness," Tia said, grinning.

Oh dear. This promised to be troublesome. There was a dashing Julius Caesar striding in their direction with an unmistakable set to his jaw beneath his gold mask. He looked divine. His strong legs peeped out daringly from beneath a toga and his muscular forearms were bare beneath a military style cape hung at his throat with a thin gold chain. Cleo caught her lip between her teeth, thinking she'd rather enjoy being conquered.

"Your knight errant seeks to save you, Cleo," Julian intoned, dry voiced. "Let's make him stew a tad, shall we?"

Cleo wasn't altogether certain she wished to make the arrogant, frowning male bearing down on them 'stew', as the earl phrased it. After all, the earl would not have to face the serious consequences of perturbing Thornton.

But Julian was not about to give her the opportunity to refuse. He placed her arm in his and steered her into the bevy of cheerful dancers. She attempted to send an apologetic glance to Thornton over her shoulder, but she lost sight of him in the crowd.

As she turned back to her partner, Julian grinned beneath his mask and patted her hand. "He wants to tosh me."

Cleo colored. "Am I very obvious?"

"Horridly," Julian murmured, his tone unconcerned. "But don't worry, I won't let it affect my ego too much. Besides, you, my dear girl, need my assistance."

They faced one another as a lively reel struck up. She raised a brow. "May I inquire as to why?"

"You're new at this conducting an *affaire* business, while I'm an old hand." He missed a step and nearly trounced her foot. "Unfortunately, the same does not apply to my dancing skills, which are quite pathetic, really. Christ, it's difficult to dance while wearing a bloody mask."

She laughed, delighted, as usual, by his wit. "Why should you think I am conducting an *affaire*?"

"I believe we've already established the fact that you are horridly obvious, my dear."

She winced. "Of course."

They traveled through a series of spins and swapped partners, precluding further conversation until they met up once again, both laughing and out of breath.

"Do you ever fear you're getting too old for all this?"

Julian asked, his voice warm, his hand at her waist easy and familiar.

It would have been so much easier, she thought once more, to have fallen in love with him. Yet it was Alex who stole her breath, made her skin feel hot, made her corset shrink, made her ache. It was Alex who could lose so much merely by loving her in return. Alas, she had learned that life was not a fair game, nor was it an easy one.

She gave Julian a wistful smile. "Too old for dancing?"

"Zounds, yes. I think I may have amputated that poor girl's toes on the last go."

"I didn't notice any drops of blood on the floor." She was laughing again. This time, she did catch sight of Alex as she twirled yet again. He was flanked by her sisters and he was smoldering. His stare never wavered from hers. Oh my. He was not pleased.

"Thornton is probably fantasizing about skewering me about now," Julian said, gleeful.

"You enjoy his pain," she observed.

"I enjoy you," he countered, "and you need me. God, I can't take any more of this bobbing and whirling nonsense. Let's go get a drop of champagne, shall we?"

Without waiting for her to answer, he led her from the dancers and from Thornton's glittering gaze both. He led her well away from the main crowds, hailed a footman and procured two flutes.

"Here you are, my dear. Drink up while I enlighten you." He handed her a flute and winked. "I've scads of years more experience than you and by my calculations, we've only two minutes before Caesar is going to stomp into our midst."

Cleo accepted the champagne and took a sip, trying to hide her grin. Really, she liked the man too much. "Do begin, Hamlet."

"Rule number one of conducting an *affaire* is to never make one's self excessively available. Keep the blighter on his toes. Don't allow him to take you for granted." He grew serious. "And rule number two is that if he breaks your heart, I'll break his face."

She placed a gentle hand on his arm. "Julian."

"I mean what I say, Cleo. I consider you a true friend. Rare between myself and a female, but there you have it. I don't want to see you hurt."

"I won't be," she promised. "But I thank you all the same. You truly are a dear heart, you know."

He shuddered. "Don't let anyone else hear you say that for God's sake. You'll ruin me." The he cleared his throat and shook the maudlin sentiments from him. "Now, back to my rules. Rule number three…"

THORNTON WAS NOT a happy chap. He liked Cleo's sisters well enough—Tia was something of a minx and Helen was a nice sort—but damned if he'd planned on cooling his heels with them while he watched that bastard Ravenscroft attempting to seduce his woman. And make no doubt about it, that was the blighter's intention. His hands flexed at his sides with the impotent desire to thrash the grinning scoundrel.

"My lord, just what are your intentions?" Tia put the question to him then.

He glanced at her. "Intentions?"

"Yes. Clearly, the two of you cannot marry."

"Not at present," he hedged, shifting in discomfort. This was not the dialogue he wanted to be having at the moment.

"My lord, you aren't looking at me."

Of course he wasn't looking at her, the daft woman. He was trying to find Cleo before Ravenscroft dragged her from the ballroom and ravished her. He gave a small hiss of annoyance and glanced back at Tia. "Pray accept my apologies, Lady Stokey." He kept his voice dry.

"You already broke my sister's heart once before," she said, rather resembling a terrier having gotten hold of its mistress's skirts and refusing to let go.

"Lady Stokey, this conversation is fast becoming uncomfortable. Suffice it to say that I have honorable intentions."

"Honorable?" Lady Helen chimed in now. "Are you having us on, my lord?"

He sighed and raked a hand through his hair. Where the hell had Cleo gotten off to? Hell, these sisters of hers scented blood and they were determined to have the truth from him so he may as well give it over. "I have asked your sister to leave with me and she has accepted."

"Leave with you?" Tia gaped at him.

"Leave with me." He smiled politely.

"In your carriage?" Helen demanded.

"I was not planning on requiring your sister to walk the distance from here to Marleigh Manor, my lady."

"You're taking her to Marleigh Manor?"

He raised a brow. "I feel confident we are all three of us speaking in the same language. I have spoken plainly and you have heard me correctly."

"My lord, it will be utter folly to be so open," Helen protested.

"Being open is rather the point."

Tia and Helen gasped in unison. But just to be certain they understood his meaning completely, he continued. "Your sister is no longer willing to have a care for proprieties that are not nearly as important as her happiness and I have wholeheartedly offered her my support in this. I may not be able to wed her, but I'll be damned if I'm denied the opportunity to be the man who loves her."

"You are mad, sir," Tia said, fanning herself. "Utterly mad."

Sweet Christ, where was Cleo? He needed her now to fend off her wily sisters. "I expect so." He offered the sisters a bow. "And now, if you will excuse me? I have a feeling I need to rescue your sister from the earl's paws."

Alex did not hesitate but set off in the direction from whence the earl had spirited Cleo from the dancers. Apparently his costume, fanciful though it was, did not dissuade any of the other guests from his true identity. Naturally, it had taken but little creativity on his part to decide to play the part of the great statesman well before his arrival as a house guest. But given his relationship to Cleo, it made all the more sense.

He was stopped and thwarted in his hasty perambulation of the ballroom on no less than seven occasions. Even the Chilton woman tittered and threw herself into his path. On her fourth season, so he had heard, and near desperate for a title these days. It showed. He made a less than polite excuse and continued his determined routing of the earl's schemes.

At long last, he spotted the two of them having a cozy *tête-à-tête* over champagne flutes. Jealousy roiled in his gut. He could admit as much to himself if to no one else. After all they had shared, a part of him remained uncertain of Cleo. He was scared as hell that at any moment she may regain her sanity and leave him to his own lonely devices.

Ravenscroft caught sight of him and stiffened, offering him a mock bow. He inclined his head in return, determined to be no more than civil. "Ravenscroft."

"Thornton."

Cleo's lush mouth flattened below her gem-encrusted mask. He'd never seen a more desirable or beautiful rendition of the Queen of the Nile in all his days. He wanted to drag her away from the earl and everyone else in the ballroom and make slow love to her. And he wanted to tear Ravenscroft's arms from his body.

"Lady Scarbrough," he acknowledged Cleo at last, not as he would prefer to do, but as he was forced by propriety and circumstance. It struck him once more that he longed for the freedom to claim her as his own before the obnoxious bloody earl and everyone else. He wanted her by his side, as his wife.

She smiled softly, a slight upturn of her generous lips that he well recognized. It was less brilliant than her ordinary smile but more intimate. "My lord Thornton. Is my disguise so poor that you have already discovered me?"

"Was it your intent to hide?" he rejoined.

"Of course not. It is only that I am surprised. I thought my costume quite clever."

"As it is, my lady," Ravenscroft said with a dashing air.

The goddamn rogue. Alex trained his coldest glare on him. "Bugger off, won't you?"

"Aren't you soon due to be assassinated, old boy?" The earl grinned, bloody bastard.

"Not by you," he returned pointedly. "King Lear, I dare say? Clever pun."

Ravenscroft sneered. "Hamlet, actually."

He saw Cleo place a staying hand on the earl's arm and he resented that touch. "The paunch fooled me. Oh dear me, isn't that stuffing? Apologies." He was being childish, but he didn't give a damn. He wanted the bastard earl well away from his Cleo.

"In lieu of trouncing you again, I do think I shall take my leave." Ravenscroft lifted Cleo's hand to his lips for a lingering kiss and gazed into her eyes like a moonstruck puppy. "Cleo, recall what I said. Until we meet again."

With another stunted bow, he took his abrupt leave.

"Paunch?" Cleo gave him a mothering frown. "Really, Alex. That was too bad of you."

"Cleo?" he repeated, nettled by the earl's presence still. "I hardly imagined he was such a close friend to speak to you so intimately."

"I do not believe in ceremony. You know that."

"I don't like him," he growled, more peeved than ever.

"Alex, you are being an utter bear."

"I don't like him near you. Anywhere else in the world,

he's a bloody swell chap. At your elbow, I want to kill him."

"He's gone from my elbow now."

"Thank the Lord."

"Alex." She was still frowning, but damned if he didn't find it enthralling. Her eyes sparkled behind her mask.

"Cleo, darling." There was a ridiculous, lovesick grin on his mouth and he knew it but didn't give a damn. He shifted closer to her so that he could brush a surreptitious hand along the underside of her arm, much-discussed elbow to wrist. Christ, he loved touching her.

"You're staring at me in a most inappropriate manner," she said primly. "And you're quite certainly lingering at my wrist just now."

"I find the Queen of the Nile most delicious. Forgive me."

Her eyes narrowed. "You don't sound contrite."

"Because I'm not." His grin deepened and he took another step closer to her, pressing in on her skirts. He found her hand and tangled her fingers in his. She did not draw away, but clutched him as if he were her purchase.

"Lady Grimsby is watching us like a veritable hawk," she cautioned.

"Let the old crone watch."

"Alex! You are in a rare mood." Her fingers tightened.

He shrugged. "I'm Caesar."

She raised a brow above her mask. "Indeed."

"And your sisters were once again meddling." He felt compelled to inform her. "I felt as if I was facing a nervous papa. Lady Stokey demanded to know my intentions."

Cleo pressed her free hand to her mouth. "Oh dear."

"Precisely."

"And what did you tell them?"

He leaned even closer and caught the delectable scent of her, lavender and sweet. "Your sisters are hyenas. I told them the truth, that you are leaving with me and you don't give a goddamn about what Scarbrough or anyone else thinks."

"Double oh dear."

"Just so. I haven't experienced such an awkward interview since my father attempted to encourage me to sow my oats with a chamber maid."

"Surely your father never suggested you dally with the staff?" Cleo's expression read horrified, even through her mask.

Leave it to Cleo to linger upon that fact rather than the one at hand. "Sadly yes. But that is neither here nor there, my love."

"I should think it is. Are you prone to trifling with servants?"

"Cleo, sweet, I have never trifled with a bloody servant. Apparently, I'm only the sort of cad who trifles with innocent ladies of the quality, gets them with child, and then abandons them to suffer horrid marriages."

Her frown deepened. "Oh, Alex, please do not speak so. The fault is not yours but my own. We've been over this again and again."

Lady Grimsby made another, more obvious circle and Cleo broke contact from him, stepping away with a discreet cough. It gutted him that they had to hide themselves in plain sight, that they were not free to conduct themselves as two people who loved one another. He was more convinced than ever of what needed doing.

Regardless of Cleo's words to the contrary, he would always hold himself accountable for their unpardonable circumstance. Had he been constant, had he looked past his damn pride, she never would have been trapped in a loveless, bloodless union. Now he owed it to her to make restitution for what had come before between them. He would make it right, he vowed as much to himself.

Determined to enjoy the evening despite his heavy thoughts, he placed her hand in his arm. "Let's dance, love."

Her eyes sparkled. "I supposed you would never ask."

Chapter Fifteen

"I FORBID IT."

"It's ruinous!"

"Have you no care for yourself?"

"An *affaire* is to be understood, but living openly with him?"

With a sigh, Cleo looked from one indignant sister to the next. Tia was in rare dudgeon, so much so that her elaborate hair was askew and she did not bother to repair it. Her cheeks were flushed, her mask long since removed. "Cleo, you cannot be serious to be considering it."

"I have more than considered it," Cleo said softly. She appreciated their sisterly concern, but the die was cast and she was firm in her resolve. After this night, all would change. "I have accepted him."

"Darling, please rethink," Helen cajoled, coming to her side and linking arms. "When Thornton told us as much earlier, I thought him mad. How can the two of you possibly think to live with one another?"

"Ideally I would seek divorce from Scarbrough." She had decided that continuing to live a lie was unconscionable. What good was her life if she could not love Alex without fear? After so many years apart, they belonged together. "If we live together, perhaps Scarbrough will sue me for divorce." Impossible though she knew divorce was, she wanted to paint a brighter picture for her sisters. By no means would she ever want to cause them worry.

"But at what cost?" Tia demanded, throwing up her small hands and stomping her foot. "Cleo, have you forgotten the Mordaunt affair? The poor woman's name was dragged through the mud, her family had her declared mad and she hasn't been seen since."

"I am given to understand that her situation was a bit different from my own," Cleo said, voice even, determined to keep a stoic façade. "Alex and I are firm in this. But please be advised that divorce or no, we will be together. You need not support me publicly. I only ask that you continue a correspondence with me. When I am in the country and isolated from the world, I should like the comfort of a few kind words from my sisters now and again."

Helen gripped her shoulders, giving Cleo a slight shake. "Do you mean to say this is to be our goodbye?"

Sadness swept over her. She had not thought of it in those terms precisely, but she could hardly expect her sisters to join her in her fall from grace. "I suppose it may be," she admitted, hating the hitch in her voice.

"No." Tia jumped into the fray, taking Helen's elbow and pulling her aside. "Helen, we shall go with her to Marleigh Manor."

"What?" Cleo was at a loss, watching her sisters conferencing before her.

Helen beamed at Tia. "Of course we shall. I distinctly recall Lord Thornton delivering us an invitation to his country house for the next fortnight or so. Do you not, Tia?"

"Most certainly. I've scads of new dresses yet to wear in my trunks. It shall be a perfect occasion. How neighborly of Lord Thornton to entertain such old family friends."

They were doing their best to blunt the gossip, she realized, amazed at her sisters' selfless determination. Tears stung her eyes. "You need not do so on my account," she objected. "Truly, it is most unfair that you both be subjected to gossip when I have made this decision for myself. I would not expect you to attempt to save me at the cost of your own reputations."

"What cost?" Tia gave her a beatific smile. "It shall all be perfectly proper. No one can say a word against us."

"What say you, sister dear?" Helen asked.

Cleo eyed them. "I say it appears I have little choice in the matter."

"Wise girl," Tia said, stepping forward as one with Helen to envelop Cleo in an embrace.

"I ABSOLUTELY FORBID it," the dowager informed Thornton in her frostiest tone. "It's ruinous."

He sighed and pinched the bridge of his nose to stave off the onset of a bitter, painful headache. It was no secret that he disliked his mother. However, he occasionally acknowledged his duty as her son and this was one of those times. Because he knew she planned to return to Marleigh Manor with Bella on the morrow despite her prattle about the Lake District, he had deemed it prudent to inform her of his own plans. It would hardly be seemly for one to install one's mistress—even if he loved her and planned to marry her at the earliest opportunity—at the same home as one's mother and maiden sister. He had made his own decision to court scandal and it was not right that Bella should pay the price. Troublesome though she'd become, she deserved to make a good marriage and to do so, she would need to keep her name untarnished. Even so, looking at his mother now, he rather wished he'd kept mum.

"Madam, I am not seeking your approval," he said, "but rather paying you the courtesy of allowing you to make other arrangements for yourself and my sister."

"Marleigh Manor is our home," she huffed. "It has been the seat of the Marquis of Thornton since the times of Queen Elizabeth."

Her assertion was a gross exaggeration. The title had only been bestowed in the late seventeenth century by William of Orange. But never mind. He had no wish to make a row out of it with her. He'd caught her as the mask drew to an end and had requested a special meeting with her in her chamber. She had chosen not to dress and wore a simple black gown with a jet overlay, the effect being that she looked as if she had just been from a funeral.

"You will not sully my home by bringing that woman to it," she continued, her nose actually twitching in her fury.

"It is my home," he reminded the dowager. "You are more than welcome at any one of my other homes."

She stiffened, her expression taking on one of horror. It had never occurred to her that he would deny her anything. "But I am not welcome at Marleigh Manor?"

"Not at Marleigh Manor," he confirmed, keeping his voice gentle. Trying as he found his mother, he did not relish this task, nor did he savor having to bar her from any demesne. "You may go anywhere else you like."

The dowager stared at him, her sturdy frame trembling ever so slightly. Her gray eyes were cold, her mouth tightened in a stern, hard line. Before he knew what she was about, she caught up a hair brush from her dressing tray and hurled it toward him. Though it missed its mark by far, he rather understood her point.

"You are an unnatural child," she accused him. "Get out of my chamber at once."

When he hesitated, she took up a bottle of something and raised it high. "Get out!"

For the first time in his adult life, Thornton obeyed his mother.

THE DOWAGER WAS not a woman who acknowledged defeat.

Ever. So indeed, after her unappreciative son left her chamber, she called immediately for her daughter. Bella, though never her favored child, would nevertheless fill in for the purpose at hand. She had never truly loved Bella as much as her firstborn, her son and heir, and had until recently thought her a frumpy, hopeless, stick of a girl. But that was neither here nor there.

The dowager was rather beginning to think that her hopes must sail on her disappointing daughter after all. Thornton, like his father before him, was far too given to the notion of a *grande* passion. Such men could not be trusted. Horrors that she should be dependent upon him. Horrors that he should disavow her in favor of that Scarbrough slattern.

"No," she muttered to Hollins as the woman oversaw the packing of her many dresses, notions and jewels. "This will not be borne. It is an outrage, Hollins. An outrage of the first order!"

"Of course, my lady," Hollins agreed.

"Precisely." The dowager appreciated a loyal staff. Certainly she had not revealed to Hollins the reason for her ire, or their plans to depart the next morning at dawn, or even why she'd requested an emergency audience with Lady Bella. It hardly mattered. She expected her staff's support as her due, but knowledge of it always vindicated her. By the time Bella finally dragged her feet through the door, the dowager was beginning to be cheered by her ambitious plan. She was convinced she would fashion herself the savior of her son.

"Mother?" Bella eyed her with confusion, then glanced at the packing maid and Hollins bustling about the room. "Whatever do you require at this late hour?"

The dowager hastened to her side and linked arms as she had not done with another woman since her come out days. "I have a plan to save your brother," she whispered, conspiratorial style. "No one must know."

CLEO WAITED UNTIL Thornton was naked and atop her to reveal her sisters' plans to him. When she finally released the words, they left her in a long, jumbled rush that scarce passed for English. Never mind, for he caught her meaning and stilled, his body hovering hot and hard over hers. His beautiful face looked as if it had been hewn of oak, so rigid had his expression become.

"What the Christ was that you just said, darling?" His voice was breathless but urgent, with an undercurrent of something dangerous. "Because I distinctly heard the word 'sisters' in relation to my home. Surely my ears are wrong."

Her own body was thrumming with wanting him, so she tipped her hips up to brush herself against him. "You heard correctly. My sisters will be joining us."

"Jesus. Why not invite your mother and father while you're about it? Perhaps we should ask Lady Grimsby and Margot Chilton and Lady Cosgrove to join us?"

"Don't be a brute. They're my sisters."

"They're a damn nuisance."

"They only want to protect me."

He growled. "I'm not exactly Attila the bloody Hun, love."

"Let's not make a row." She wiggled against him, reveling in the sensation evoked by the peaks of her breasts brushing against his chest. "I had something more enjoyable in mind for this evening."

"As did I." He caressed her cheek, then skimmed his hand down her neck and over her chest to cup a sensitive breast in his palm. "Why must your sisters plague me so?"

"I think it may be wise to have their company. At least until we decide for certain which course we shall take."

"I don't like it." His expression was charming, boyishly stubborn.

She pulled his head down to hers for a lingering kiss. "They won't interfere, I promise, and you shall have me at your mercy."

He grinned against her lips. "If they do interfere, I'll lock them in the wine cellar. It's musty and my butler insists it's got a precocious rat population."

Cleo glossed her hands over his strong back and down to clasp his tight buttocks, guiding him into her. "You are quite a wicked man."

CLEO SLIPPED INSIDE Thornton's conveyance during the hubbub of the myriad carriages leaving for other country diversions and the rail station. Thornton let out a whoop of delight and settled her immediately upon his lap in a most scandalous fashion. Their trip to Marleigh Manor, while not terribly long in duration to begin with, passed with alarming speed for the engrossed pair. Cleo scarcely had time to recorset, rebutton, smooth hair and yes, even put her shoes back on, before the coach came to a halt.

"How do I look?" Frantic not to appear the harlot before his staff, Cleo flattened her palms over her bodice and attempted to soothe wrinkles from its stitched silk.

Thornton grinned. "Like a woman who has been well-loved."

"Beast!" She swatted him with her reticule. "I wish to make a favorable impression. Do be serious."

"I am utterly serious, my love. I'm afraid I was rather, er, ardent."

"Ardent?" Her hands fluttered, erratic butterfly style. "What do you mean to say by that? What have you done?"

He cleared this throat, looking chagrined yet pleased. "Your neck, darling."

"What of it?"

"It's a bit…ravaged."

"In what way?" She was glaring now, but she didn't give a

fig.

"I hadn't time to shave this morning, for one thing."

"I quite felt that."

It was Thornton's turn to glare. "May I remind you of the cause for it?"

She flushed, because she was thinking of the private moments to which he referred. She well recalled her mouth traveling a wickedly delicious path down his chest, taut stomach and lower. "I didn't hear a complaint."

"Christ no. But back to your request for an explanation. The lack of shaving coupled with my ardent reaction to a most debauching carriage ride…I'm afraid you have several marks on your neck and quite a bit of redness."

Only Thornton could deliver the last with such an adorable yet stiff-necked air. He had made it obvious to anyone who but looked at her that she had been making love with him in the carriage. And for his part, he did not appear particularly apologetic, his careful phrasing aside. No, she rather thought he'd done it intentionally. She would have told him so, but Cleo found she didn't mind as much as she ought. She liked being marked as his. Still, it wouldn't do for the servants to notice.

"I have pearl powder in my reticule." She fished it out with a jubilant air, then daubed it onto the affected area in liberal doses. "Does it hide the redness?"

"Absolutely."

"Are you lying?"

"Would I?"

She glared again, but the coachman threw open the door and it became too late to argue the point. Speculation belowstairs, however, would turn out to be the least of her concerns. Nothing can toss the proverbial pail of water onto besotted lovers better than the presence of not one but six unexpected and very unwanted house guests. Thornton was informed by a footman sent out at the directive of the esteemed butler, Levingood Senior, that the dowager had defied his orders and was now ensconced within, along with Lady Bella, Thornton's cousin Ford, Mr. Whitney and, worst of all, Miss Cuthbert and her lady aunt.

Cleo caught the tail of the footman's disclosure as she was handed down from the carriage and she caught the dreaded name. "Miss Cuthbert?"

Thornton's jaw was clenched, a snarl on his lips. "I'll bloody well kill her."

"Miss Cuthbert?" she repeated.

"Not Miss Cuthbert. My damn mother. This awkward little setup has her name written across it. Though how she's managed to bring the chit from the Lake District to Buckinghamshire so quickly, I'll never know."

Cleo's heart sank to her toes. How on earth was she to live beneath the same roof with his betrothed, for heaven's sake? Had he not promised her that he would throw the dreaded Miss Cuthbert over? What purpose could her presence at Marleigh Manor possibly serve? Why, it was horridly familiar for an unmarried lady and her aunt to establish themselves at a bachelor's country residence. It spoke of expectations.

She took a bracing breath and slid her arm through Thornton's, angling her lips to his ear. "Has she hopes from you yet?" Was it too much for her to wish that his words of love to her, his actions at Wilton House, had instigated a letter informing Miss Cuthbert that she was effectively thrown over? Cleo did not deem it so.

"I expect so." He was grim. "But she will not for very long."

"I should like to enter on your arm." She knew she likely hoped for too much as a married woman and as his lover, but yet she felt she had claimed him and he too had claimed her. She wanted to make clear to the Cuthbert girl that her territory had been marked.

Thornton took her hand from his arm, raising it to his

lips for a kiss. His expression was pained. "I would like nothing better. However, much as I hate to ask it of you, I think it better if you enter with your sisters just now, out of deference to Miss Cuthbert."

She stiffened. "Forgive me if I do not hold your Miss Cuthbert in my heart."

"I am aware. But she is innocent in this. Place the blame upon the dowager. I assure you that she will pay for this contretemps and dearly. Miss Cuthbert, while unwanted and unanticipated, should nevertheless be paid the utmost respect."

He was right, of course, but that did not mean she liked it. And his response begged one salient question. "Am I not due respect, then?"

"Christ, that's not what I meant, Cleo. You know better than that. You're my…"

"Your what?" she challenged him, noting his loss. He did not know what to call her and the knowledge frustrated her, perhaps without reason, but frustrated her nonetheless. He owed her nothing, after all.

He gritted his teeth. "You are my woman. But as I have already explained, Miss Cuthbert and I had an understanding. She has no knowledge of what has passed between us."

She smiled tightly. "Of course. If you'll excuse me?"

As she turned on her heel to join her sisters, he caught her elbow. "Cleo, let's not make a row of it."

She glanced back at him, wondering how he could possibly be so thickheaded. "You've made a row of it, Thornton." With that, she left him standing on his own in his drive, staring after her.

"WOULD EITHER OF you care to explain what the bloody hell you're doing in my house?" Thornton addressed his inhospitable demand to his cousin and his best friend as they lounged about in the smoking room, drinking his whiskey and smoking his damn cigars.

Ford rested in a wingback, his pose indolent, feet crossed and propped on a low marble-topped table. "What the bloody hell does it look like, cousin? We're drinking your Scottish whiskey."

He wanted to throttle the bastard. "As I can see. But you could be drinking my whiskey in town, or at any other of no less than half a dozen places. Why the devil are you here? You don't even like the country."

Ford shrugged. "I rather fancied the thought of shagging a dairy wench."

Jesse leaned against the sideboard and grinned. "Your cock's going to rot off if you don't exercise some restraint. In truth, Lady Bella suggested we accompany her and the dowager to the country."

"Bloody traitor and one to talk too," Ford objected, glaring at Jesse. "You've been sniffing round Bella's skirts like a damn dog in heat."

Jesse slammed his whiskey down onto the sideboard. "You puppy! I have not been sniffing anyone's skirts."

Thornton had heard quite enough. "Shut up, the lot of you! Ford, stay away from dairy wenches and take your sodding boots off my table. Jesse, stay away from my sister or I'll cut your bollocks off."

Ford blew a careful ring of smoke. "Who's shoved a poker of self-righteous indignation up your arse?"

Thornton plowed a hand through his hair and stalked to the sideboard to pour himself a glass of whiskey too. If he had to suffer, he may as well get good and sotted. "She's angry with me," he muttered.

Jesse raised a brow. "Your sister?"

"Not Bella. Cleo, you ass."

"What have you done to bollix it up?" Ford grinned,

clearly enjoying Thornton's pain.

"It's not what I've done." He tossed back a healthy gulp of whiskey. "It's my nuisance of a mother. She's brought Miss Cuthbert here."

Jesse gave a sympathetic wince. "That's a bit of a delicate situation."

Thornton drank some more. "Delicate does not begin to describe it. She's furious at me."

Ford raised a brow. "Miss Cuthbert? Didn't think she was the furious sort. She always seems so deuced cold."

"Not Miss Cuthbert, you dolt. Cleo."

"Hell." Understanding dawned on Jesse's face. "You brought Lady Scarbrough here and now we've all turned up, including your fiancé. Christ, what a mess."

"She's not my fiancé." He felt the need to qualify that much, if nothing else. He had never proposed to Miss Cuthbert, nor had any formal betrothal agreement been drawn up between himself and her father. He was glad for that now, for it could not be so. But he did dread the telling of this to Miss Cuthbert, particularly since she was now under his roof, obviously expecting to be treated as his betrothed while his lover was also under his roof, expecting to be treated with equal deference.

"You may want to refill your glass," Ford suggested.

"We are all of us expected to dinner tonight." He was grim. "You two may want to refill your whiskeys as well."

"Bottoms up, old boy." Ford drained his glass.

CLEO WAS INFORMED by a servant that there would be an informal gathering in the drawing room prior to dinner that evening. She'd been given a chamber near Thornton's but not close enough to garner whispers. To the outside observer, she was a guest along with her sisters, nothing more. Certainly not the woman who had been held in Thornton's arms each night, not the woman to whom he pledged his love.

She dressed for dinner with attention to detail, choosing a delicate royal blue evening dress with ochre lace overlay and hand beading. It had an underskirt of frothy blue silk that peeked beneath lace rosettes. At her neck, she fastened her favorite necklace, a diamond star. She directed Bridget to take extra care with her hair, which was ultimately styled high with diamond clips winking from within a drop of perfect curls. Even Cleo had to admit, when she surveyed the results in her mirror, that she looked very fine.

But when she walked into the drawing room flanked by her sisters, she lost every crumb of confidence within her. The dowager waited within, along with Bella and two other ladies. One, dressed in drab lavender silk and wearing a turban atop her gray hair, appeared to be a relation—perhaps a mother—acting as chaperone. The other could only be the dreaded Miss Cuthbert.

The dowager performed a stilted round of introductions and Cleo took the opportunity to study her rival. Miss Cuthbert was not at all the sort of woman she had imagined. She was tall and willowy, her waist a startling wasp silhouette that did not even appear human so small was its circumference. Her hair was an icy blonde, arranged in a rather severe chignon, her oval face pale and dotted with the slightest smattering of freckles. Her yellow dress too was plain, devoid of almost all ornamentation but a few pleats at the bodice and a line of ivory buttons. The overall effect was that she looked wan and sallow, almost as if she had been brought forth from a sick bed. Miss Cuthbert's face was pretty but not beautiful. Somehow, Cleo had expected a gorgeous, voluptuous woman had captured Thornton's interest, not the drab, tense woman before her.

"Lady Scarbrough, a pleasure to meet you." The girl dropped into a poor curtsy.

Cleo inclined her head. "And you as well, Miss Cuthbert."

Cleo, Tia and Helen settled into seats and faced a most awkward tête-à-tête. The other woman—an aunt, the dowager had said—resembled nothing so much as a terrier. When she smiled, it appeared more of a grimace.

"The dowager has been telling us that you are all directly from Lady Cosgrove's country house party. Did you find the entertainments to your liking?" she asked, aiming a particular frown at Cleo, or so it seemed.

"Quite," Tia answered, her voice cool.

"Utterly," Helen intoned.

"Most delightful," Cleo added.

Miss Cuthbert cleared her throat. "Lady Scarbrough, I believe you must have made the acquaintance of my dear friend, Miss Margot Chilton. She said as much in her many letters to me over the last fortnight." A calculating gleam lit her brown eyes.

Cleo stiffened. The girl's unspoken suggestion was clear. That she was bold enough to imply she was aware of what had transpired between Cleo and Thornton was most surprising. "Indeed? I must confess that I'm not a familiar of Miss Chilton's."

"Oh? It is strange then, for her to have remarked upon you so often." A serene smile curved Miss Cuthbert's lips.

"Not so strange," Tia interrupted, ever coming to Cleo's rescue, "for one given to gossip."

Miss Cuthbert's mouth thinned. "Perhaps you are correct, Lady Stokey."

"Miss Chilton has always been a pleasant young lady" the dowager interjected. "Why, I dare say she would not lower herself to vulgar gossiping."

"Of course not," the aunt added. "Miss Chilton is of fine family."

"Indeed." Cleo pasted a bright smile to her mouth to hide her inner laughter. "Her father, Lord Chilton, is a paragon."

Lord Chilton was an infamous drunkard. Her sarcasm was not lost on anyone except perhaps the dowager and the aunt, both of whom nodded in agreement, one warily and the other approvingly. Cleo wondered with a great sense of inner despair where on earth Thornton was. This mincing conversation was horrid.

"Where is his lordship?" Miss Cuthbert asked the dowager, seemingly reading Cleo's mind.

The dowager's face pinched in a comical fashion. "Detained by estate matters, my dear. Have no fear. I understand from Levingood Senior that he shall be with us momentarily. I am sure he did not wish to keep you waiting, Miss Cuthbert. Aren't you sure, dearest Bella?"

Thornton's sister had not spared Cleo a glance until that moment, when she locked gazes with her. "My brother adores you, Miss Cuthbert. I am certain he is doing his utmost to hurry and join us."

As if on cue, Levingood Senior opened the door and announced Thornton, Fordham, and Mr. Whitney. Thornton entered first, resplendent in all black evening clothes, but he carried himself with a looser air that she recognized. He had been drinking with the boys. Cleo did not mistake it. The coward. Detained by estate matters, indeed.

"Ladies." Thornton bowed. His cousin and friend did the same. "Shall we proceed to dinner?"

"That would be lovely," simpered Miss Cuthbert.

Cleo wanted to throttle her. Instead, she clenched her teeth and pierced Thornton with a glare. He met her gaze and looked hastily away. The rotten man. To make matters worse, Miss Cuthbert made certain she made her way to the dining room on his arm, eschewing the order of rank. Thornton did nothing to dissuade her, as of course he could not. What had seemed like a madcap getaway for the two of them had multiplied into a horribly awkward house party. She had quite lost her appetite and she would sooner pluck out her eyelashes than suffer a dinner with Miss Cuthbert fawning all over Thornton while she was powerless to stop it. Unfortunately for her, she was not offered an alternative. Pleading a headache would be too obvious and would only serve as a victory for Miss Cuthbert.

Dinner was an even more horrid affair than the drawing room had been. Lord Fordham had over-imbibed and spent a lot of time using inappropriate language and stabbing the air with his fork as he spoke. On one occasion, she was certain that he sprayed a good portion of béchamel across the table linens. The dowager insulted Americans and insinuated that Cleo was old. Miss Cuthbert attempted to engage Thornton in political discussions and exclude the rest of the table and largely succeeded. The aunt appeared to fall asleep during the fish course. Bella and Mr. Whitney occupied themselves with one another and Cleo and her sisters were an unappreciative audience to it all.

By the time Thornton slipped into her chamber later that evening, Cleo was seething. She clutched her wrapper around her and glared at him. "What do you think you are doing in here?"

He grimaced and looked chagrined. "I've come to deliver an apology."

Cleo remained unimpressed. "If you think you'll be sharing my bed tonight, you're mistaken."

Thornton sauntered toward her, a sensual, knowing expression on his face. "You know none of this is my fault, sweetheart. I certainly didn't invite Miss Cuthbert here."

"Yes, but you did listen with rapt fascination to her solution for the Lambeth street floods." She crossed her arms over her chest as if they could form a shield. "Not that I don't care about the plight of Lambeth, mind you, but she deliberately excluded everyone else from the discussion save you."

His sulky mouth tipped up into a charming grin that never failed to send heat washing through her veins. "Cleo."

But she was not ready to be swayed by him. She rather had her dudgeon up. "And forgive me if I think that raising the tenements is a horrid solution. The government needs to erect another channel for when the Thames overflows. The flooding is causing all their problems. Raising tenements will keep their homes dry, but the fevers will still strike their men, women and children."

"Cleo." He closed the space between them.

"No you don't. Not a step more. I'm not finished speaking yet."

"Cleo, what I'm trying to say is that I agree with you, love." He came closer. "Miss Cuthbert's plan is inherently flawed and I told her as much when you were engaged in conversation with your sisters. Moreover, while you think I was listening to her in rapt fascination, I was actually enjoying the most delightful fantasy in which I stripped you bare and ate cook's miniature tansy cakes off your breasts."

"The tansy cakes?"

He nodded, his grin turning wolfish. "Off your breasts. I even debated plopping one into my pocket for just such an occasion."

Drat him, he was winning her over. She had promised herself she would stand firm. "Did you tell her?" She took a step in retreat.

"Tell who? Cook? While old Mrs. Williams is fond of me, I don't think her fondness would extend to sharing my plans for her tansy cakes and your bosom. Have I told you lately that your breasts are brilliant?" He took another step toward her.

"I won't be distracted, Alex. I'm speaking of Miss Cuthbert, the woman who thinks she's your betrothed, not Mrs. Gilliam."

"Mrs. Williams."

She gritted her teeth and resisted the overwhelming urge to stomp her foot. "Williams, then."

"What was I to have told Miss Cuthbert?"

"That you shan't be marrying her, for one thing."

"Oh, that." His grin faded. "Not yet."

"Not yet?" Truly, she began to think he was obtuse. If her voice rose a trifle high and sounded very nearly hysterical, it was hardly her fault.

"Well, Christ, Cleo, when would you have had me tell her? During the soup course?" Those deep gray eyes of his turned flinty.

"Of course not, but what would you have me do? I'm your guest while she's your presumed fiancée. Do you understand how awkward this has been already for us both? In the drawing room, she all but told me Margot Chilton had written her with suspicions of us."

Thornton closed the distance between them and drew her body against his. He pressed their foreheads together. "Darling, I'm sure you're cut up for nothing."

Cleo allowed herself to soften against him. After all, obtuse duffer or not, she loved the man. Any reason to be in his arms was good enough. "Ask Tia or Helen and they shall tell you the same, Alex."

"She and I will speak on the morrow." He kissed her and it was a gentle, reassuring kiss, not borne of the frantic hunger that ordinarily arced between them. "You are the woman I love. Not Miss Cuthbert."

She sighed. "I love you too."

Their mouths met again and this time there was a fiery, carnal passion simmering beneath the surface. Heat swirled through her. Alex's hands traveled a lovely path down her back, molding the silk of her wrapper to her bare skin beneath. When his hands cupped her bottom and angled her against his arousal, she lost any sense of control. She scrabbled to remove his evening clothes, ripping at his tie and shirt.

"I thought I wouldn't be sharing your bed this evening," he whispered against her lips.

"Stubble it." Her fingers landed on the fastening of his trousers.

He obeyed.

THORNTON LEFT HER bed before dawn. She couldn't sleep after he left her, so she rang for Bridget before venturing below to the morning room for an early breakfast. With Tia and Helen still abed and Thornton off riding with Fordham and Mr. Whitney, Cleo made her way to Marleigh Manor's rather extensive—if obviously neglected—library for some peaceful time on her own. But it did not last long. Hands behind her back, she walked calmly down the wall of shelves, searching for something by Shakespeare. She'd just settled on *Romeo & Juliet* when the delicate sound of a lady's cough interrupted the silence. Almost afraid to turn, she cast a look over her shoulder and discovered that, much to her dismay, her privacy had been interrupted by Miss Cuthbert.

"Lady Scarbrough," she intoned with false brightness. "What a surprise to find you here this morning. I confess this room has always been a haunt of mine while I stay here at Marleigh Manor."

Cleo pulled the volume from the shelf and spun about to face her nemesis. "I had not realized you were such a fixture here. But fret not. I was just on my way."

"No." Miss Cuthbert held up a staying hand. As if to underscore her virginal innocence, she wore a frumpy white gown this morning and her blonde hair was twisted into a looser style that made her appear girlish. "Please stay. I had hoped to have a private word with you, my lady."

Guilt speared her, mingling with dismay. The woman before her, odious though she may be to Cleo, had no notion that her almost-betrothed had spent the evening in Cleo's bed. "Of course, Miss Cuthbert. What was it you hoped to say?"

Miss Cuthbert's small mouth tightened. "May we sit, please?"

Oh dear. She wanted to run from the room. Instead, she crossed the carpets to a chintz sofa that she knew must have been purchased by the dowager. Thornton could not abide by chintz. Miss Cuthbert seated herself with a prim air and arranged her skirts before hitting Cleo with a direct stare.

"Lady Scarbrough, I was raised to speak very plainly and I shall not hesitate to do so with you now." She tilted her head and resembled nothing so much as a sparrow. "It has been said by others that you are Lord Thornton's particular friend."

Cleo braced herself and chose her response with care. "Miss Cuthbert, you are making dangerous accusations."

"It is not I making the accusations, my lady, but a great many others who were present at the house party from which you have so recently come." Miss Cuthbert folded her hands in her lap.

"However, it is you repeating them. I do not appreciate gossip." Cleo kept her tone frosted and in control.

"If you continue on your current path, you'll only invite more of it."

She could not believe the woman's temerity. "Miss Cuthbert, you overstep."

"It is you who oversteps, Lady Scarbrough." Miss Cuthbert sat straighter, her bearing stiff with purpose. "Lord Thornton is destined to be a distinguished leader of the Liberal Party. He is single handedly responsible for the Prime Minister's victory. He is the furthermost political mind of our century. And yet, he is but a weak man, brought low by his baser emotions."

Cleo schooled her expression into one of boredom. Her heart thumped faster. "I am aware of Lord Thornton's political acumen. You need not catalog his accomplishments for me, as I'm sure they are many and I simply haven't the time." She rose. "If that is all, I must be on my way."

Miss Cuthbert rose as well. "A moment more, if you please. I catalog his accomplishments with a purpose. Don't you see that by connecting his name to yours you are ruining him?"

She attempted to skirt the adamant woman, determined to leave the room and Miss Cuthbert's troubling words behind her. "Enough, Miss Cuthbert."

Miss Cuthbert's face contorted, losing its complacency for the first time. "I love him, Lady Scarbrough. For years and years, I have loved him. For as long as I can possibly recall, I have watched him from afar, working with my father on reform, changing all of London. Changing England."

"I am not your confidante," she interrupted coolly. "Pray do not say anything more."

"I was raised to be Thornton's wife. I belong at his side. I would never bring him shame." She paused to catch her breath. "Do you think me a fool? Do you think I don't recognize why you have come here? You bring your sisters for the pretense of propriety but make no mistake about it, you have come as his mistress."

"Get out of my way, Miss Cuthbert."

Her opponent seized her arms in a grip that was surprisingly strong for such a frail-looking woman. "You will only ruin him. In these times, with men such as him, even a breath of scandal can be the kiss of death. What can you possibly think to gain? Release this hold you have over him, I beg you. You cannot think of yourself. You must think only of him."

Cleo shook her hands away. "I do not know what you speak of, nor do you. This dialogue has been most unpleasant. Do not seek me out again."

And then she walked from the room, desperate for Miss Cuthbert not to see just how much she had been shaken by the exchange.

Chapter Sixteen

THE DOWAGER WAS not a woman who believed in leaving important life decisions, like her son's marchioness, for instance, to a turn on Fortune's fickle wheel. No, indeed. She was rather the sort who instructed her maid to have an informative discussion with Miss Cuthbert's lady regarding belowstairs suspicions about her son and Lady Scarbrough. She was also the sort who wrote letters. Not particularly eloquent letters, and she spelled words in an abysmal fashion, but those factors did not curtail her *écriture* in the least.

So it was that she was not as disappointed at the lack of progress made by her protégé Miss Cuthbert during her interview with *that woman* as she may otherwise have been. For she had already spent the morning penning a lengthy, if abusive, epistle to that lady's cuckolded husband.

The dowager considered Miss Cuthbert as she sat across from her in her private apartments. The dear girl was no beauty, that was certain. Her face had an almost equine quality to it if she was to be honest. However, the girl came from a good family with excellent connections and the dowager didn't truly give a fig about her looks.

"It was good of you to come to me with your concerns, Miss Cuthbert." She paused with consequence. "Might I call you Honoria?"

Miss Cuthbert pressed a hand to her heart. "Of course, madam. I should like nothing more. Thank you for the honor."

"You will soon be a treasured member of this family." The dowager bestowed a rare smile upon her. "Think nothing of it. Now, how can I allay your fears?"

"I know I overstep my bounds in even broaching the topic. Indeed, I would not ordinarily be so bold—"

"Nonsense, Honoria. Honesty before integrity is what I always say. Or is it pride? Oh dear, I quite forget." She mulled the phrase for a moment. "'Tis of no moment. What I mean, dear girl, is that you needn't worry yourself in that particular arena. I believe the countess may soon receive a summons."

"Oh?" Miss Cuthbert's expression turned rabbit-like in her anticipation.

Goodness, the girl certainly bore a startling resemblance to creatures. But no mind. She was still the dowager's chosen marchioness for her son.

"I penned an epistle this morning and that is all you need know for the time being. My son is an honorable man, Honoria. He will do his duty to this family, to this fine country of ours, and to you."

"I am aware of his lordship's sterling qualities." Miss Cuthbert smiled. "His reforms for the London poor have changed so many lives already."

"Yes, well." The dowager gave a dismissive gesture. She was far less interested in the lower orders than she was in her son's reputation. "The poor really cannot help themselves, can they? Otherwise, I dare say they would not be poor."

"Of course, my lady."

Such a biddable girl. The dowager's smile grew. This was a daughter after her own heart. "I expect at least two grandsons, my dear."

Miss Cuthbert flushed pink. "I shall do my utmost."

"As will I."

She didn't notice Miss Cuthbert's expression of mild alarm. She was too busy crowing inwardly at her own triumph. Oh, she would turn her wayward son into a man yet.

THE DAY WAS unseasonably cold for September. This was Cleo's thought as she trudged through the wood behind Marleigh Manor. Thornton had sent her a note requesting she meet him by the lake and she had decided at the last moment—perhaps foolishly—to eschew a mount and simply go by foot. The lake was a bit farther off than she had recalled and the wind nipped her through her mantle and quite dismantled her coif beneath her dashing hat.

At long last, the trees gave way to a clearing and she spotted Thornton's tall, lean form at the lake's edge. He grinned when he saw her, striding forward to catch her up in his arms. "Darling."

She threw her arms around his neck and pressed her cheek to his chest. "Alex. I've missed you." Although it had only been hours earlier when she'd last seen him, it felt more like a week.

Cleo tipped her head back and in a breath, his mouth was fast and hungry on hers. She sank her gloved fingers into his hair and rather wished they were bare instead. When she finally broke the kiss, she asked him the shaky question dominating her mind. "Where have you been all morning?"

"Riding with Ford and Jesse." He dropped a kiss on the tip of her nose. "Christ, you've the most adorable nose. Why haven't I noticed that before?"

A smile curved her lips but she wasn't yet ready to be distracted. "I'm gratified you appreciate it." She scrunched up the nose he'd just been admiring. "Riding all morning?"

His expression turned quizzical. "You doubt me?"

"No." She gave her head a slight shake. "Of course not. I merely…I had an interview with Miss Cuthbert this morning."

He stiffened. "Cleo, there was no need for you to seek out Miss Cuthbert. I've promised you I'll tell her today."

"She sought out me." Cleo extricated herself from his embrace. "Not the other way around."

He tunneled a hand through his hair. "What did she have to say?"

"Nothing of import."

His gaze probed hers. "I don't quite like the sound of that."

"And why should that be?" She rubbed her arms, suddenly more chilled than she had been on her walk to him. Could there be more to his relationship with Miss Cuthbert than he indicated? No, she did not think it likely, but there remained a small, insecure part of her that wanted to stomp her foot and rail at him. She wanted the woman gone, wanted to be freed from her insufferable marriage so that she could be a real wife to him. She wanted to give him what Miss Cuthbert would, a wife in whom he could take pride, not a woman who would bring him scandal and shame and ruin his future.

"Are you cold?" His voice was solicitous, but there was something else in it, a tone she couldn't define.

"Yes," she whispered. "Cold and confused, Alex. What was your purpose in bringing me here? I have a husband and you have a betrothed who thinks me the world's greatest strumpet and this all seems suddenly so impossible." Tears scalded her eyes.

"Don't cry, sweeting." Thornton took her back in his arms, wrapping her snug in his embrace. His handsome face was stark in its seriousness, all harsh planes and chiseled angles. "I'm sorry if Miss Cuthbert exchanged words. And Jesus, I'm sorry for the muck I've made of everything. I planned on having you all to myself and somehow we've ended up with yet another house party watching us. I expressly informed my mother not to come here and she defied my orders." He clenched his jaw. "I'll have the lot of them gone by the morning, I swear it. Don't cry, darling."

He kissed the tears from the corners of her eyes, caught an errant drop with his thumb. His hand lingered to caress her cheek and she couldn't keep herself from leaning into his cupped palm, relishing even the smallest caress he gave her. But she could not halt the flow of tears.

"I'm scared," she confessed. "Scared I shall lose you after so long."

"No." He pressed another kiss to her forehead. "I am yours, Cleo. Yours only."

She sank her face into the crook of his neck, breathing deeply of him, seeking strength from his solid presence. "But I cannot promise you that I'll be yours."

"You are mine." His arms tightened, protective bands wrapping around her waist. "You will be mine. Don't fret on that account."

Dear God, how she loved him and how she feared she would disappoint him. Or, worse, that she would ruin him as Miss Cuthbert had accused. She needed, after her troubling meeting with the woman, to assure herself that he was being realistic about their futures.

She tilted her head back to meet his gaze. "Has no one told you that politicians are to make alliances when they marry?"

"My mother tells me as often as she can." He grinned, his eyes crinkling charmingly at the corners. "But I'm no longer a politician."

"What?"

"I've decided to pursue a different path. I've written a letter to the Prime Minister, officially stepping down from my duties to him."

"Alex, why would you do that? I thought that your work meant a great deal to you."

"It did."

"I would not have you give it up for my sake. I shall be

your mistress, or I shall go back to the country and leave you alone—"

"Hush." His mouth swooped down on hers to claim it in a deep, possessive kiss. "I won't hear of it." Before she could voice further concerns, he pulled away from her slightly, taking her hands in his and leading her toward his waiting mount. "Come, now. I have an afternoon planned for us."

As THORNTON THREW himself into the saddle behind Cleo, he sensed a stiffness in her body he knew was borne of the news he had just delivered. She worried for him. She feared for herself, that she could not escape her marriage. That her interview with Miss Cuthbert had not gone well he had no doubt. Truly, he wished the woman nothing but good health and good fortune and to get the hell out of his house. When he looked at her now, he wondered how he had ever convinced himself that a loveless, passionless union based on nothing more than a commonality in politics would be the best course.

He slid his arms around Cleo's waist and hunkered down in his seat to press his cheek to hers beneath her hat. She smelled of lavender and warm, sweet woman. Christ, but he wanted her. He didn't give a damn what he had to give up for her. Politics was a cold bedfellow indeed and he was ready to move beyond its rigid constraints. He was prepared to remove himself from the public stage and to live instead a quiet life dedicated to the purposes in which he believed. A happy life with the woman he loved, to whom he would give his very life if she but asked it of him.

"Stop worrying," he murmured to her. "We're taking a journey back to a lovely summer day long ago. We have no worldly duties calling us. No hen-witted mothers, no blackguard husbands, no misguided misses, no gossip or scandal or politics. We're young—"

"I don't think us terribly old now," she interrupted.

She relaxed against him. He grinned. "Not terribly, but you've a few more lines on your face, darling."

"Lines! You rotten cur!" She gave him a playful swat. "If we are truly going back in time, then I should think it your obligation to woo me rather than to tell me my face resembles an old crone's."

"Never an old crone, sweeting." He chuckled. "But truth be told, I do prefer you now to then."

"Truly?"

"Truly." His grin grew as he slid his right hand free of the reins so that he could cup a breast beneath her mantle. "Your bosom is a bit larger now and I quite prefer it."

"My bosom and my bottom both," she scoffed.

"I'm not complaining, love." And to demonstrate that he wasn't, his hand migrated from the lovely curve of her tempting breast to the equally lovely curve of her tempting rump beneath her voluminous dress.

"You're a wicked man."

"So I've been told. I rather think you fancy your men wicked."

It felt refreshing to bicker with her, as though they had not a care between them.

She turned in his arms so that she could meet his gaze, her mossy eyes bright with emotion. "Only you, my darling man. Only you."

"Glad to hear it." He dipped his head to kiss her soft lips again, popping up when his breath at last demanded it. She tasted as delicious as she smelled. "God, I want you." He wanted to devour her was more apt, but no need to get that specific.

"Glad to hear it," she repeated. "Have you a direction in mind for us, or is this an aimless trot we're on?"

"Impatient, are we?" Thornton kissed the delicate whorl of her ear, getting a tad irritated when the brim of her hat nearly poked his eye. "Your hat is trying to kill me," he muttered.

"You didn't answer my question."

"I recall that you had an appalling habit of talking too much. In fact, when I stumbled upon you sketching that day, you were engaged in a heated debate with yourself over the quality of your art." He thought for a moment, that day returning to him with enough power and emotion to make his gut bottom out. The sun had shone a halo in her hair. She'd managed to besmirch the front of her dress with charcoal-laden hands. And she'd been utterly beautiful.

"I was a garrulous girl." She sniffed.

He thought of something he'd been wanting to ask since their whirlwind courtship had begun at Lady Cosgrove's. "Do you still sketch?"

"For my own amusement and I'm afraid my skill has not improved much with the years," she admitted, her tone wry.

"I should like to see your sketches."

"Perhaps I shall share them with you. If you are exceedingly kind to me, that is."

A mental image of the kindness he'd prefer to bestow upon her caused him to adjust her against him for his own comfort. He nudged the horse into a faster pace. "How nice would you have me?"

Cleo cast him an arch look. "*Ça dépend.*"

"On what does it depend, *mon couer*?"

Her mouth curved seductively. "On how quickly you can take me to where we're going."

"Hold on tight." He set his heels to the mount's flanks and they cantered the rest of the way around the lake, heading deeper into the woods until they approached the old hunting lodge he'd had swept and cleaned for the occasion.

They were scarcely in the door before they were in one another's arms, mouths meeting, tongues tangling, bodies pressed breast to toe. He had meant to take his time, but the ride had whetted both their appetites and neither of them wanted to linger on platitudes now. Only skin would do.

He guided her toward the fire that still crackled low in the hearth and the quilt sprawled before it. His fingers tangled in her mantle, making short work of it and half the buttons on her gown before she had tossed away his overcoat and tore at his shirt.

He cupped her jaw, savoring the silky texture of her skin. She was so incredibly beautiful he ached to look at her. To know the woman who had haunted him these long years was now his, in his arms—the knowledge sent him reeling.

Cleo pressed a kiss into the palm of his hand, her eyes intent on him. "Do you remember what you said to me?" Her voice was breathless, hushed like the wings of a dove.

He knew without needing to ask that she spoke of that summer day he'd so often been reliving. "I told you," he said, skimming a hand down her neck to rest at the open expanse of her bodice, "that I should like to kiss you. And I dare say it's been what I've wanted to do—and more—since I first saw you."

In truth, he could scarce manage a coherent sentence beyond the roaring of blood in his ears and veins. This was more than a furtive coupling attempt in a secluded hunting lodge. Christ, he'd forgotten about the ring in his pocket.

"Kiss me," she urged.

She didn't need to give him that particular order more than once. Their lips fused again, his tongue plunging deep into the warm, wet cavern of her mouth. He wanted to be deep inside her, so deep he never had to come out again. It was frightening as hell and yet thrilling too. He wanted to lose himself in her. Forever.

But first, he needed to make it official. Thornton tore his lips away with regret, tipping his forehead against hers. "Reach into my pocket."

Her expression turned wicked. "I thought you said you were going to be nice. That sounds like a rather naughty directive to me."

He kissed her again because, well, damn him, he couldn't not. "Darling, there's no way my prick is in my pocket. It's stiff as a ramrod and about to jump out of my waistband," he drawled.

She gasped. "Alex!"

"The pocket, darling. Just put your hand…oh, hell." Her hand traveled a maddening path over his crotch. His hips jerked.

She palmed him skillfully, wringing a moan from him, before abruptly releasing him. "That was to get even with you for trying to shock me," she murmured, her voice low and soft as velvet.

He knew the moment her fingers found the small box inside his trousers. Her eyes flared in shock. "Alex? You needn't give me jewels."

Ah hell, he'd bungled it. She thought he was treating her as a mistress, keeping her content with baubles. "Not just any jewels," he hastened to correct. "Take it out."

The blue box nestled in her opened palm between them. She bit her lip, watching him.

A breath of frustration hissed from between his teeth. "Open it, love. While your hesitation is charming, my body is demanding that we take this race from a trot to a gallop."

Laughing, she delivered a swat to his chest before finally opening the lid to reveal an enormous, sparkling diamond flanked by emeralds within. She pressed a hand to her throat. "My heavens! It's the most beautiful ring I've ever seen."

"It was my grandmother's." Hands shaking a bit, he took the ring from its cushion and slid it upon her third finger, which had been happily devoid of Scarbrough's ring for some time. "Will you marry me, Cleopatra Harrington?"

She flew into his arms.

"YOU CONNIVING JADE!"

Cleo was in the midst of preparing for dinner that evening when Thornton's mother stormed in an unexpected rage into her chamber. Bridget froze in the act of dressing her hair and met her gaze in the looking glass.

The dowager thumped across the room like a ship pulling into port. Her gray matron's skirts bobbed and swished with each step. "You!" This last was directed at the unfortunate Bridget. "You are dismissed at once! I'm letting you go without a character, I'll have you know, and if you breathe a word of this to any of the other servants, I'll see you thrown into prison!"

"Madam, she is not your servant," Cleo said, striving to keep her voice cool. "You have no right to sack her. Bridget, you may go belowstairs. I shall call you when I have need of you."

"Yes, ma'am." Bridget curtsied and, with a troubled expression, quit the room.

"You are an insolent trollop." The dowager shook with passion. She closed the distance between them. "Countess, I demand that you leave this residence immediately."

Oh dear. It seemed that Thornton had divulged their future plans to his mother. "My lady, I am a guest of the marquis."

"What is on your finger?" With an ominous noise that could have been a squeak or—egads, an unladylike fart—the dowager launched herself at Cleo, grabbing at her hand and attempting to twist the ring away.

"Good heavens, my lady. Please compose yourself." Cleo tugged at her hand but to no avail.

"I'll not have the de Vere diamond given away to a slattern who only seeks to use my son for her own selfish gain. Why, it's positively American!"

"I'm afraid I don't understand." Truly, the woman's xenophobia was a wonder in its vastness. To further muddle matters, the dowager refused to relinquish her painful grasp on Cleo. With one powerful tug, she at last tore her hand away.

The marchioness harrumphed. "You need only understand this. I demand that you leave this home at once."

Cleo had no suitable response at the ready. She almost sympathized with Thornton's mother, in fact. She recognized it must be exceedingly difficult for the dowager to know that he was courting scandal and ruin for a married woman. Surely no mother would want to see her son give up his great political aspirations for a love that may never be recognized or regarded as proper. Of course, the woman need not be so brazen, rude and insulting, but she supposed it was a natural enough reaction.

"You are distraught, my lady. Perhaps it would be in our common interest to pursue this topic at a later juncture."

"I have no common interest with you. I merely want you out of this house!"

Cleo had never before confronted an enraged mother. Scarbrough's mother—before her death, of course—had always been coolly polite and most civil to Cleo. An irate mama was quite another bird. She knew she must defend herself with truth alone.

"We do indeed have a common interest, my lady," she began, watching the dowager's expression. "Your son is our common interest. I love him and so, I think, do you."

"I love him with a mother's love. You cannot possibly love him at all. You are nothing more than an opportunist seeking to align yourself with my son's rising star."

Certainly, it must seem to the dowager as if Thornton was making a dire mistake. Cleo could not argue that point, for as yet, she offered Thornton no promises of her own save love. Divorce, no matter how much she yearned for it, was never likely to be hers. Indeed, were she to pursue such an option, she would need to fight Scarbrough to attain her freedom. She would have the burden of proving cruelty, a feat that would prove near hopeless. Even if she could win divorce, Cleo herself would be open to gossip and scorn. It was not a good match for Thornton by any means. Indeed, as circumstances stood, it was not a match at all for Thornton but a scandal of the worst order.

Cleo inhaled, calming her nerves. "I love him. I love Thornton now as I have loved him always. You must know that I realize the consequences for him are grave. Accordingly, I have advised him against any attempt at making a matching with me. However, your son is quite headstrong."

The dowager's nostrils flared, her steel-gray hair glinting like a medieval suit of armor in the gas light. "Then you have not advised him strongly enough. This afternoon, he has turned away Miss Cuthbert and has informed me of his misbegotten intention to make you his wife." She scoffed and the sound was ugly. "You, who has not even liberty to wed again."

"Madam, believe of me what you will, but I would have you know that in this, every step we have taken has been your son's decision. He has asked me to be his wife when or if I am free to marry again and I have given him my word. It would be best for you if you found a way to accept my presence in his life."

The dowager's hand cracked across her face before she could anticipate it and move away. Tears stung her eyes at the woman's surprising strength.

"You will never be more than my son's whore," the dowager said dismissively. "Do not drag him down with you."

CLEO DECIDED NOT telling Alex about her discomfiting interview with the dowager was the most reasonable course of action for a woman in her position—her position being a trifle untenable within the household. Alex's initial proposal of living together openly as man and wife in all ways save name had fallen like a star from the sky. His mother refused to leave the Manor. His sister remained, as did his cousin and Mr. Whitney and Cleo's own sisters. All these happenstances conspired to make Cleo little more than a glorified house guest. She was neither wife nor mistress, both of which would have afforded more power at Marleigh Manor.

Alex, however, took great pains to make her very much at home. He saw to her smallest comfort. Each evening, a steaming lavender bath awaited her pleasure and often his. He'd even managed to find her particular Parisian *savon* and had copious amounts of it in supply. When she was cold, he ordered fur robes and extra hot bricks in her drafty bed chamber. He bought her charcoal and sketchbooks. He took her for rides to tour the estate. He even deferred to her in household matters, such as when the dowager upset the cook by questioning Mrs. Williams' ability to manage the kitchen at her advanced age. Or when the dowager delivered a scorching and unnecessary tongue lashing to the housekeeper over directing the maids in matters of dusting.

It was apparent to the staff that Cleo was in all senses Alex's mistress. This Cleo knew from Bridget, whose loyalty to her lady had proven to eclipse any passion she entertained for belowstairs gossiping. For the most, she remained unconcerned by their knowledge. After all, it was difficult if not impossible to keep any secret at all from good servants. Still, Cleo's reputation was maintained by the presence of the Manor's other guests, most notably Alex's mother.

While she lived in a murky land where the lines of propriety blurred, Cleo was not alarmed by her situation. True, there lingered a number of niggling misgivings on her conscience, including the departed Miss Cuthbert's desperate pleas and the dowager's heated setdowns. But by and large, she enjoyed an entire month with Alex at the Manor. She slept in Alex's arms and woke to his kisses.

And they became as familiar to one another in that time as an old married couple. For Cleo, it was like gaining the marriage she'd never had. Never had she experienced such sweet intimacies with Scarbrough. He had ever been impersonal and cold, not interested in her as a person with whom he shared a life. Alex was the opposite. It was as if they were starved for one another's presence. Neither could learn enough about the other.

They invented a silly game at breakfast each morning in which one of them had to reveal a secret to the other. One morning as Cleo sat snuggled in Alex's lap as they shared tea and toast in her chamber, she begged a secret of him that would begin to unravel their glorious idyll.

She sipped a bit of tea and returned the cup to its saucer with a delicate clink as she contemplated the secret she would have of him.

Alex took the opportunity to *carpe diem*, as it were and nibbled at her earlobe. "If you don't pose the question fast enough, you forfeit your right to ask," he whispered in tones that were all velvet seduction.

"Mmm." She leaned back into him, tilting her head to allow his wicked mouth to migrate to her throat. "That is not part of the rules."

"It is now." His right hand slid up to cup her breast through the thin silk of her dressing gown.

Her nipples hardened in response and heat spread between her legs. But she was stubborn and she meant to have her question. The day before, she'd been forced to answer his embarrassing query. "Stop trying to cheat, Alex. Yesterday, you made me confess I'd once put flour in my governess's knickers, for heaven's sake. Turnabout is fair play."

"My question was merely what was the nastiest trick you'd ever played on another. How was I to know of your alarming penchant for ruining the undergarments of the female staff?"

She could feel his smile against her skin.

In another half-dozen breaths, she'd be too far gone, so she offered up the first question that came to mind. "When you were a young lad, what did you dream of being one day?"

"Myself." His left hand crept to her other breast. "And I'm damn glad I grew up to be me too."

"Be serious, Alex."

"Oh, very well. Prime Minister." He opened her dressing gown and bared her breasts. "And now I'm quite done with question and answer for today."

"Prime Minister?" Her breath seemed to freeze within her lungs. She shooed his hands away from her and yanked the twain ends of her wrapper together again.

He raised an imperious brow. "What's wrong with that? It's a noble office, when held by the proper party, of course. And by proper party, I mean Liberal."

"Ever the politician." The words were said in a light tone, but as she said them, her heart gave a great pang. She needed to know more about that side of him, the man he'd spent the last seven years becoming until their mad romance had interrupted it all. "I scarcely know anything of your politics save the pamphlets on reform I read. Tell me about it."

"Christ, Cleo, this isn't the time."

"What better time than now?" She shifted in his embrace so that she was no longer plastered against him. "I feel as if there is another Thornton who I know so little. I want to know that man."

He growled. "This isn't about Miss bloody Cuthbert, is it?"

His frustration lightened her spirits, but only a bit. "Alex, don't be a bear."

"I believe I warned you about my propensity for morning bearishness."

Cleo wrinkled her nose in thought. "Is bearishness a word?"

"Likely not." He dipped his head down and gave her a thorough kiss.

When he would have deepened it, she pulled back. "I want to know more about you. For heaven's sake, we were lovers back then but I didn't even know you. I certainly hadn't an inkling as to your political endeavors. Now you want to marry me, but you won't even share your thoughts with me."

"I'm sorry, love." He kissed the tip of her nose. "What would you have me tell you?"

"Why politics? Why reform? It's not often that a Peer of the Realm concerns himself with the housing problems in poor East End districts, or in the conditions of the workhouse."

Alex shrugged, his expression turning pensive. "I honestly don't know how it all started. I think maybe it was my paternal grandmother who was always working for the London poor. After you threw me over, my life changed. I met Robin Steele, the great reformer, and where others thought him a raving pain in the arse, I saw his vision. He took me with him on trips through the streets of London. We met oyster men in St. Giles and costermongers and boardmen in Whitechapel and laborers in Covent Garden. For the first time, I started seeing those men as people with wives and children with empty bellies at home living in rat-infested flats in seedy rooks. And I knew I could try to change it. In the world of politics, nothing happens with ease or haste, but I knew my voice would be heard where their voices would not."

"You are a very special man, Alexander de Vere," she murmured, cradling his face in her palm. "So many gentlemen are content to fritter away their lives in their clubs."

"I'm not an angel, darling. I like my club as well as the next chap. It's not as if I go about reading parliamentary blue books all day." He gave her a self-derisive grin.

"You know what I mean."

"I may have taken an interest in reform, but never accomplished anything really, save publishing a handful of pamphlets no one ever read. So you see? No saving the world for Alexander de Vere. I dare say the political sphere shan't miss me much." He turned his head and dropped a moist kiss on her hand. "Nor shall I miss it."

Cleo allowed him to draw her back into his embrace, wishing she could believe him. Just to hear the passion in his voice when he spoke of going about the streets of London with Robin Steele convinced her that he was not ready to give up his position. She'd read his pamphlets and they were brilliant. No, this man was not meant to be a country gentleman. As Miss Cuthbert had so fervently said, he was destined to be a distinguished leader. And he could never again occupy a position of high office if he aligned himself with a married woman.

Alex peeled her dressing gown from her shoulders and it fell in a soft caress against her bare skin. He filled his hands with her breasts and met her gaze, his eyes blazing. "Kiss me, sweet."

She threw her arms around his neck and kissed him with all the love bursting within her. "I love you, Alex," she whispered against his mouth, praying as she said the words that her love would be strong enough to enable her to make the hard decisions facing her in the weeks ahead.

A MESSENGER RODE in the next morning at dawn and set all of Marleigh Manor into a frenzy. Precisely ten minutes after the strange man rapped at the front door, discreet tapping sounded at Thornton's bedchamber door. When the first round of tapping met with failure, a second, more prodigious series began. Cleo heard it first, stirring in Alex's arms and blinking into the semi-darkness.

"Alex." She shook his shoulder. "Darling, there's someone at the door."

"Damned impertinence," he muttered. "Ignore it and it'll go away. If it's that new footman again, I'll have his bollocks."

A throat cleared on the other end of the door. "Your lordship? I do apologize for the disruption, but there is an urgent matter."

"Nothing could be urgent enough," he grumbled. "I'll bloody well give him urgent."

"Alex, you're being a bear again." She pressed a kiss to his sulky lips. "I think it must be something of import, else your valet would not disturb you."

"My lord, it is the Prime Minister," came his valet's much-aggrieved voice from the hall.

"Good Christ." Alex shot up as if a poker straight from the hearth had come into contact with his backside. "Not here, man?"

"No." The valet popped his head in the door, light from the hall shining a slice on the floor. He kept his gaze carefully averted. "Not here, your lordship. In London. There's a man here to see you below. He says the Prime Minister has taken ill and the situation is most grave."

With an ugly curse, Thornton threw back the bed covers. "Tell him I'll be with him shortly."

"The Prime Minister is ill?" Cleo gathered the bed clothes around her for modesty's sake. "Good heavens, what could be the matter?'

His gaze was troubled as it met hers—that much she could discern even in the low light. "It can't be good if they've sent a man for me." He raked his fingers through his hair. "I hope it's not…" His voice broke. "God."

"Let me know what you learn."

"Of course." He began to throw on his hastily discarded evening clothes from the previous night.

His valet cleared his throat from the doorway. "My lord,

may I assist?"

Oh dear. This was most awkward. Ordinarily, Cleo made a prudent exit before the servants were about. If they were in her chamber, Alex did the same. However, his valet's hesitation in the hall this morning bespoke the man's knowledge of their clandestine arrangement. She scooted deeper into the cocoon of bedclothes, too embarrassed to speak.

"I'll manage," Thornton growled, buttoning his shirt.

In less than a minute, the door slammed closed behind his back. Shivering and unaccountably cold, Cleo lay in bed wondering if she should return to her own chamber or remain. The ramifications of this early morning messenger's visit assailed her as she waited. If the Prime Minister's health was compromised, where did that leave Thornton? Undoubtedly, he would be needed not only back in the city but also as a bulwark within the Liberal Party. He would not be free to pursue a relationship with her, nor could she expect it of him. It seemed the hard decisions were facing her with more speed than she had anticipated yesterday.

Unable to keep still, she rose from the bed and sought out her dressing gown. She lit the gas lights and paced the length of the chamber. Twisting her hands together in agitation, she made four passes of the room before the door clicked open once more. It was Alex, his countenance solemn.

"Alex?" Her heart trebled its beat in fear.

He reached her in three strides, grasping her arms in a bracing grip. "I'm sorry, Cleo."

"How bad is it?"

"It's desperate, I'm afraid. Gladstone's terribly ill. I've sent a message to my own doctor to attend on him. Even the queen has sent her doctors, though she despises the Prime Minister." He paused. "He's been asking for me. Apparently, he's with fever and he's in a weakened state. They don't think...they do not know whether he'll survive."

"Dear God." Understanding dawned. He was going to go to the Prime Minister. He was leaving her. Despite everything he'd said, his old life was intruding. "You'll go to him."

"I'm afraid I must." He plowed a hand through his hair. "This couldn't be happening at a worse time. Leaving you is the very last thing I want to do."

She could not accompany him. They were not husband and wife. The absolute truth of her position struck her then. She was his mistress.

Numb, Cleo nodded. "Of course you must go. You will write to me as soon as you arrive?"

"Yes." Sighing, he lowered his mouth to hers. "Wait here for me. I'll be back as soon as I can."

"Of course," she repeated.

"I love you, Cleo."

"And I love you." She gave him a tremulous smile. She knew now that it wasn't enough. Before he returned to her, she would have to leave.

He pulled away. "I must leave now. There's not a moment to be wasted."

Cleo caught his hand in hers and raised it to her lips for a kiss. "Travel with care. I shall include the Prime Minister in my prayers."

And then he was gone.

Chapter Seventeen

$\mathcal{C}$LEO DID NOT waste much time in preparing herself for what she knew in her heart she had to do. After Alex left for London, she penned a hasty letter that she asked Bridget to post for her. With a calm she didn't feel, she prepared herself for the breakfast table. She refused to show the dowager even a hint of weakness. Cleo clipped her favorite diamonds to her ears, applied some orris root fragrance to her wrists and gave herself a final inspection in the looking glass.

So much had transpired to change her forever and all in just a mere few weeks. The woman staring back at her looked older, sadder and yet somehow wiser. Her hair was the same black, eyes the same green, nose tipped up a bit at the end. Yes, she remained Cleopatra Harrington Bennington, Countess of Scarbrough, thoroughly heartbroken woman determined to carry on with head high.

She carried that knowledge with her like a breastplate into the battle awaiting her at the breakfast room. Thankfully, she came across her sisters en route, sparing her from having to take breakfast alone with the dowager, who was already settled at the head of the table in the absence of Alex. Cleo sailed into the room as if she had not a care in the world and took a seat a few places down from the dowager. Tia and Helen flanked her.

Cleo waited for the footman to serve her before speaking. "Good morning, my lady."

The dowager sniffed and continued cutting away at the

contents of her plate.

Helen slanted a knowing look in Cleo's direction. Cleo attempted a nonchalant smile, but she quite feared it more resembled a grimace. She accepted a cup of hot cocoa from the footman and sipped before making a further attempt at conversation.

"I do so love a good chocolate in the morning. Do not you, my lady?"

The only ensuing sound was that of cutlery on china.

Cleo cleared her throat and replaced her cup in its saucer with more force than required. "My lady, I thought it best to inform you of our plans. That way, you may run the household accordingly. My sisters and I will be returning to Harrington House."

Abruptly, the dowager gave an imperious nod to the unfortunate footman. Cleo noted for the first time the poor fellow wore a powdered wig and livery. Already, Alex's mother had made her mark upon the Manor. He was not a man who favored the pomp of servants arrayed in outmoded attire. The footmen wore simple livery here and no scratchy wigs. However, the dowager had already been at her best to undo that effort at liberalism.

As the footman pulled back her chair, the dowager intoned, "You may instruct Lady Scarbrough's people to prepare her carriage. We should not like to delay her a moment longer than absolutely necessary." She paused in arranging her voluminous skirts. "Please convey to Cook that the kippers were wholly unacceptable. Indeed, I could not eat them this morning. My constitution is quite delicate, you understand." Then, still ignoring Cleo and her sisters, the insufferable woman whisked herself from the room.

Helen sighed after she'd gone. "I'm sure I've never met a more unpleasant woman." She kept her voice low enough to avoid it carrying.

Tia giggled. "Did you see the footman? He looked as if he

were about to shite himself."

"Tia!" Cleo was compelled to chastise her minx of a sister. Well, she supposed it was either that or break into a fit of hysteria. Indeed, she found it wondrous—and not in a happy sense—that the world should go on so much the same when everything in it poised on the brink of ruin.

"What?" Tia blinked in feigned innocence. "Ravenscroft taught me the phrase." She broke into a grin. "But I rather like it."

"I might have known." Rapscallion though he was, Cleo found it hard to hold any anger against him.

"Why are we off to Harrington House?" Helen's voice dripped with curiosity. "Of course I've had it from my maid that Thornton's gone. It will never cease to amaze me how quickly belowstairs learns all. Sometimes, I'm convinced they know we've sneezed before we do."

"Both are true." Cleo poked at the toast on her plate, appetite gone. "Alex left for London this morning to go to the Prime Minister's sickroom."

"You can't mean to leave here just because of that odious mother of his?" It was Tia's turn for a question.

"No."

"Why then, darling?" Tia gripped her hand to stop its automaton-like movements.

Cleo attempted to form a response. She opened her mouth, moved her lips and let out an appalling blubber.

"What is it, dear?" Helen patted her opposite arm, concern lacing her tone. "Why the rush to Harrington House? You can't have had a row with Thornton?"

She shook her head, sniffing and staring at her uneaten toast.

"What then, darling?" Tia prodded. "You must tell us."

"I'm leaving him," she confessed on a rush of air that left her lungs, hollowing her out. Then she promptly burst into tears.

THORNTON LANDED IN London with an almost audible thud. The abrupt transition from country idyll to city smog and traffic—particularly bad even though much of elite London society had long since left in favor of grouse shooting and country *fetes*—was not lost on him. Nor was the sudden loss of the woman he'd come to take for granted by his side and in his bed. True, it would be over soon enough and they would be back together, the good Lord and the Prime Minister's health willing. But it was not a happy return for him.

Being without Cleo affected him badly. He missed everything about her and it had been a mere day, from the sound of her dress as she moved to the scent of lavender, her sweet voice, her touch, her kiss. This did not bode well. Christ, he was getting more maudlin than a balmy dowager who was a bit touched in the upperworks. Next he'd take up needlework and start crying over French novels. Truly, he could not afford to dwell on thoughts of her now, with his mentor teetering on the brink of death. For much of the hasty journey, he forced her from his mind. By the time he reached the city, he was very nearly composed.

His house expected him though he hadn't sent word. Apparently, one of Gladstone's men had advised the staff of his imminent arrival. He had not gone straightaway to the Prime Minister's lodgings as his instincts urged, but instead headed to his own quarters in Grosvenor Square. He had officially resigned from the cabinet and had no right to intrude upon the sickroom, despite his having been summoned. Instead, he would wait for Gladstone's secretary to fetch him.

He was greeted in warm fashion by Levingood Junior and promptly received a nearly man-sized stack of correspondence that had been held for him whilst he holidayed in the country.

"My lord ought to employ a new secretary, if I may be so bold," Levingood intoned while Thornton stared at the mountain of papers in his study.

Damn, he'd forgotten about Jones' resignation. He jammed a hand through his hair and sighed. "You may indeed be so bold, Levingood. I fear you're right. Have you anyone in mind?"

"I shall make some inquiries."

"Very good." Thornton continued to stare at the unopened letters, feeling as if a loaded train was bearing down upon him and he had been tied to the tracks. "Levingood?"

"My lord?"

"Have you word on the Prime Minister's health today?"

"None, my lord."

"Very good." Jesus, he didn't know what to say, where to begin. His whole life was in shambles, threatening to topple like a Roman ruin. "Thank you, Levingood. I shall be here if you have any further need of me."

The butler bowed and quietly took his leave. Thornton turned his mind to his papers, beginning the familiar task of opening each epistle, reading the contents and sorting them into tidy piles. Not ten minutes had passed before Levingood reentered, his expression one of nervous apology.

"My lord, I'm afraid there's a bit of a problem."

Thornton steepled his fingers. "Problem?"

"There is a gentleman here to see you."

He frowned, not wanting to be bothered with any more than he already had on his mind. "I'm not at home."

"Yes, I'm aware. But unfortunately—"

An enormous crash sounded from the entry hall. "That sounded like breaking glass, Levingood."

The butler looked troubled. "I do apologize, my lord. I'm afraid that the person will not remove himself from the residence."

More crashing ensued, along with a loud, masculine voice

and the squeal of a female servant. "Good Christ, man, who is it?" Thornton rose from his seat, ready to pummel the bastard and set him out on his bloody ear.

"The Earl of Scarbrough, or so he claims."

"Damn," he muttered, striding past his butler.

He threw open the door of his study just in time to find a rumpled, obviously drunken man chasing one of the maids and making lewd calls. The shattered remnants of several antique vases littered the floor. The poor girl skittered toward Thornton, her aggressor pursuing her in laughably awkward motions, swiping at her skirt and attempting to grab her bottom. Thornton waited for the maid to pass before putting out his leg. The duffer tripped and went down like a felled tree.

A moan sounded from the form on the floor. Thornton used the toe of his boot to roll the drunken sod over. It was indeed Scarbrough, he realized, recognizing the familiar features beneath the layer of beard and the rather unkempt, silver sprayed hair. He still wore his evening clothes from the night before and he absolutely reeked of gin and smoke.

Thornton hadn't seen him in years, but the man's problems with drink, gaming and doxies were well known throughout most circles of the ton. It was an understood thing that Scarbrough hadn't been sober in at least half a decade. He supposed he shouldn't be surprised that the earl looked more like a man from the poorhouse sent than a member of the Peerage.

"You, sir, are trespassing where you're not wanted. Unless you wish for me to call the watch, you'd best pick your miserable arse up off my floor and get the hell out of my house," he advised. Christ, but he hated the man, hated that Cleo was tied so almost inextricably to the pathetic excuse for manhood. He wanted to beat the hell out of him, in truth.

"Go ahead and call the watch because I'm going to kill you, you miserable fucker. Then they can bloody well cart me off." Scarbrough somehow managed to gain his feet. "I heard you're screwing my whore of a wife."

Sheer, animalistic rage coursed through him. "You aren't fit to speak her name."

"I've been thinking about calling her home and breeding the bitch." Scarbrough leered, weaving unsteadily on his feet. "Of course, I'll have to wait a month or so to make sure I'm not claiming your get as my own. Wouldn't want that, would we?"

"If you touch her, I'll kill you," Thornton growled, meaning every word.

"It's my right to do whatever I want with her. She's my wife, damn you."

"You don't deserve a woman as fine as Cleo."

"I may not deserve her, but I'll bloody well have her back in my bed." Scarbrough hiccupped. "Oh, don't look so sad, old chap. If you're nice, maybe I'll let you watch."

That was it. Thornton's tenuous grasp on sanity snapped. He threw back his fist and landed a crushing uppercut to Scarbrough's chin. The bastard's head snapped back but he caught himself before falling again. He launched himself at Thornton and the two scuffled like a pair of Eton lads going at it over a girl. Thornton landed a few more shots, but even sauced as he was, Scarbrough was a fair fighter and got in his share of blows as well.

Finally, they shook one another off, circling each other, puffing for breath. Thornton's fist ached like the devil. And he was quite certain his right eye was going to be black and blue on the morrow.

"I mean what I say," he began, "if you touch Cleo, I'll kill you. If your brain hasn't become too addled by the gin, you'll stay the hell away and hold your tongue." Christ, how he loathed not having any more defense against the bastard than threats. The political system he'd once so loved was proving dashed unfair and much in need of further reform.

Scarbrough let out a bitter bark of laughter. "If you think I'll let her go, you're the one who's addled. She's my purse."

There was the crux of it. Scarbrough had never wanted a wife. He'd wanted an unending supply of bank notes. Cleo had intimated that her dowry had been sizeable and with the well known Harrington wealth, he had no doubt that it had been enough to make a man lie and cheat to gain a bride. Greed conquered all in this world of theirs.

"If you divorce her, I'm prepared to pay," he gritted.

"How much?"

"Name your price."

"One hundred thousand."

"You're mad. I could have you killed for less."

"You'd lose everything. Seventy-five thousand, then."

"Fifty thousand," Thornton countered, calling his bluff.

Scarbrough grinned, insolent and arrogant to the end. "How is she?"

Thornton's jaw ticked. "Go to hell."

"I haven't had her in years. I wondered if she'd gotten any better or if she's still frigid as Wenham Lake ice."

Thornton hauled him to the door and threw it open. "Get out before I kill you myself."

"If you honestly think you'll win divorce without my cooperation, you're a bigger fool than I thought. The law is on my side and you can't prove a goddamn thing against me. I'll give you one hell of a fight. I'll drag you through the goddamn mud until all the world knows what a selfish slut she is and what a stupid prick you are."

He pitched Scarbrough through the door. "Stay the hell away from her. And never come here again."

Shaking with rage, he slammed the door at his back. He'd free Cleo of that scum if it was the last thing he did in this life. Hell, just the thought of that bastard laying claim upon her—it was enough to make him physically ill. He'd meant what he said. He would protect Cleo against him no matter the cost.

That vow made, he stalked back to his study. The servants were nowhere to be seen, but he didn't fool himself that they hadn't heard every damn word of his exchange with Scarbrough. He didn't care who knew of his feelings for Cleo any longer. In fact, after he saw to the Prime Minister, he was going to tell his mother to go to the devil and live as he saw fit.

CLEO HAD NEVER been more dejected in all her life. She and her sisters went promptly to Harrington House, where there was neither mother nor father nor brothers but rather a large proportion of servants who were not particularly grateful for their unexpected arrival. Of course, none of them had sent word ahead of their abrupt departure from Marleigh Manor and there was no reason for their people to expect a visit. But Cleo, Tia and Helen had nowhere to go following Cleo's defection save their childhood home.

Harrington House was more castle than its name implied, a drafty, tumbledown affair that had been built in the fourteenth century by the first earl with spoils from some crusade or another. There were still murder holes in the keep where defenders had once poured boiling oil and water down onto unsuspecting invaders. There were musty corners, loose stones and there was absolutely no shortage of rodents.

Cleo was not partial to Harrington House, for obvious reasons. It was cold and rather unpalatable, filled with relics from a bygone era and the prerequisite family portraits staring down from gilt frames on the walls. There was also a decidedly strange scent reminiscent of a wet hound.

The familial tradition had it that the first earl had been particularly fond of the hunt and had kept a faithful hound with him until his dying day. It was also said that the hound had never quite died, but roamed the expanse of the castle, leaving a smell in his spirit's wake. For her part, Cleo had never believed it, but she did find the odor to be altogether unpalatable, so much so that upon her initial arrival there she always carried a bottle of orris root about with her and sprayed it here and there until the hound smell dissipated in favor of a preferred floral sweetness.

There was an inordinate amount of bowing and scraping and all the covers were pulled from the furniture in the dining room and every spare inch was dusted into prompt submission. Cleo felt a mere husk of the happy woman she'd been at Marleigh Manor. Helen and Tia did their parts to cheer her, but she didn't want company. Her heart was breaking, crashing into murky depths of despair. She was not certain she could survive losing Thornton. She missed him with a desperation that didn't become her.

Several days passed, spent in her old bedchamber in a turret near the eaves. As a child, she had spent many nights nestled within its confines, often giggling with her sisters and sipping cocoa into the wee morning hours. Now she went to bed alone, spent a sleepless night without Thornton and finally fell asleep at dawn only to wake a few hours later, bereft and empty as she had ever been. It was strange, but she had to admit to herself that she was more lonesome than she had been before Thornton had come into her life although she had been essentially alone for six years or more. Scarbrough had not been a part of her world since the early days. He'd quickly become entranced by his own penchant for drink and the game and loose women. The polite world knew too well of his sins and they were many.

Tia and Helen cornered her on the fourth day at Harrington House in the breakfast room. Cleo was too nauseated to consume a bite to eat once again, but her sisters were feasting on Mrs. Simple's beloved eggs and muffins when Tia finally broke her silence on the matter.

Her blonde curls were arranged neatly at the nape of her

neck, her dress a brilliant turquoise with black netting. She looked utterly stunning—too beautiful for the mere company of sisters, certainly—and sipped her tea while pinning Cleo in an unnerving stare that gave her fair warning of the impending interrogation.

"Cleo, darling, when do you presume to tell us of your plans?" She cracked her egg smartly in its egg cup as she spoke.

"Plans?" Cleo raised a brow.

"You were madly in love with Thornton and now you have left him with nary a bye your leave. And we are together holed up in this ancestral monstrosity of ours with little hope of rescue. I confess I am quite horrified by the predicament in which you have landed us."

"You may gladly return to the city, or go to visit the rest of our family at Clowes House with Uncle." Their uncle, the Duke of Roland, owned a vast estate called Clowes in Scotland. It was a family favorite during the off season, but Cleo and her sisters had eschewed this year to attend Lady Cosgrove's country house party instead. Cleo almost wished they had gone straightaway to Clowes. But then she never would have experienced the unadulterated joy and love she'd rediscovered with Thornton. Even if she would never know it again, she had to think the small sacrifice worthwhile. So few people ever knew true love. Certainly she herself had not, before Alex had come into her world.

"Go to the family at Clowes whilst leaving you here to your misery?" Tia snorted. "I think not. Do talk some sense into our sister, Helen."

Helen placed her spoon on the table with a firm clink. "Cleo, what our sister is trying to say in her inimitable way is that we're very worried about you. You still haven't been forthcoming about your reason for leaving Thornton. We can't fathom why a woman as happy as you seemed to be would simply leave the man she loved without warning. We are your sisters, darling. You can safely tell us all without fear of it carrying."

Thank heavens they had dismissed the hovering footmen and were alone, a closed door to secure the privacy of their tête-à-tête. "I... It's complex." Tears pricked her eyes.

"So complex you cannot give it voice?" Helen tsked like a mother hen. "Cleo, you must relent."

"He is too good a man for me," she confessed in a rush. "Thornton...he could very well become the next Prime Minister. He's so honorable, so noble a man and I am a woman encumbered by a wastrel, drunkard of a husband. It's not fair for me to ask him to wait for me when I may well never be truly free."

"You seemed so set on leaving the earl." Tia scooped her egg and held a dainty portion to her lips. "What occurred to change your mind?"

"Gladstone." Cleo picked at her food with her fork, gaze trained on her plate. "When he became ill, I realized that Thornton's life is firmly entrenched in politics. He has been a respected member of the Prime Minister's Cabinet, the fixture of his election, the man of the day when it comes to reform. England needs him more than I do. I cannot in good faith require the man that I love to live in shame with me, to ruin his chances for the dreams he's entertained since boyhood.

"He told me that when he was a lad he dreamt of being Prime Minister. Now, here he is in sure position and yet his love for me will prevent him from attaining that high office. No Prime Minister of England, no matter how honored and beloved, can pass a ruined woman before the world as his wife. Even should Scarbrough entertain divorce, even should it be granted, I shall always be tainted by Scarbrough's name and reputation. And I, in turn, shall always taint Alex. I cannot countenance that. I love him too much. I will not be the reason for his downfall and resentment. Let him marry Miss Cuthbert if he must. I would have him know his true worth as a man."

"You cannot truly want him to marry Miss Cuthbert, Cleo." Tia looked at her as if she'd gone quite mad. "Miss Cuthbert is an awful, mousy, vulgar little person. She was quite rude to me and I should never know her. She's a Cit and a grasper and I don't like ladies of her ilk."

"Of course I would not wish him to marry Miss Cuthbert." Indeed, the very thought made Cleo nauseated. "I am stating fact. Miss Cuthbert would make him a far more honorable wife. He would be respected if he wed her. Should he wait and attempt to wed me, he will only face scorn and ruin. No man can marry a divorcee. It is not done. Moreover, history is clear. I will very likely never be divorced. Our laws were not fashioned for woman."

"Everything can be done in this modern world of ours." Helen pointed this out while making a rude yet somehow grand gesture with her fork. "It will be done if you choose. Scarbrough is a worthless hide of a man. Nothing can be hopeless. Send him to the gutters from whence he came and marry Thornton. You'll never be happy unless you do so. Leaving Thornton was a true mistake, Cleo."

"It was a mistake for my heart, but not for Thornton." Cleo sipped her tea in a hopeless dodge at calming herself.

"You are not so bad as that, dearest." Tia slathered marmalade on a muffin. "Good heavens, you're hardly a pariah. Indeed, you've lived a rather circumspect life whilst Scarbrough's been an utter reprobate. You cannot be as horrid a fate as you think."

Just then, the family butler intruded, addressing Cleo. "My lady, you have a visitor. He says he's expected."

"Thornton!" Helen crowed. "I knew it!"

"'Fraid not," drawled a languid voice.

"Julian, you've come." Cleo rose from her chair to greet the man who had become her unlikely friend. He looked rumpled, as if he'd been playing cards all night and had yet to get to bed. A dark stubble shadowed his jawline to emphasize the impression. She had not been certain he would heed her call, but she'd sent word to him just the same. His role in her plan was imperative. She dismissed the disapproving butler before taking the earl's hands in hers. "I am relieved."

He grinned. "I'm relieved to relieve you, in turn. May I say you're looking absolutely smashing in that frock, my love?" He bussed her cheek before stepping back to survey Helen and Tia, paused in shock over their breakfasts. "Sisters, you are lovely as usual."

Tia sniffed. "I cannot say the same for you, my lord. You look as if you've been lolling about in an opium den. Really, is that a brandy stain on your shirt?"

"I'm wounded." He cut a dapper bow. "Lady Stokey, you should know better. I'd never waste good brandy by dribbling it down my shirt."

"Good morning, Ravenscroft," Helen cut in. "I don't mean to be rude, but to what do we owe your presence here in the country?"

"Do behave, both of you. I asked him here." Cleo frowned at her maddening sisters. "He's taking me to Scarbrough's country seat." Then she promptly cast up her accounts into a potted plant.

Chapter Eighteen

A WEEK PASSED until the Prime Minister was finally well enough to truly withstand much visitation. Thornton had been to sit with him in his sick chamber every day since his arrival in London and for the first few days, Gladstone had been virtually incoherent with fever and body-racking coughs. The outlook at the onset had been bleak. Thornton's own doctor, along with the queen's, had watched over him in an endless vigil and neither of the esteemed gentlemen had offered words of promise or hope. All had been cautious in their assessments of the Grand Old Man's condition.

The delirium had been troubling—to see one so strong struck so low had been a blow to him, a reminder to grasp what was important while he could still do so. But by the conclusion of his first week in London, Gladstone's condition finally improved. The fever had gone and with it the most prominent thunderclouds on the horizon. As the sickness gave way to hopeful signs of restored health, Thornton sat down with his mentor.

Although he'd been truthful in his words to Cleo when he'd told her he'd written the Prime Minister, stepping down from his duties, he had yet to send said letter. He'd not found the confidence to post it, truth be told. For such an enduring relationship, damn if he could break the old man's faith in him down with a mere scrap of paper. No, he'd known that it needed to be face-to-face or nothing at all.

When Gladstone was well enough to take visitors in his

study, Thornton made the pilgrimage there, feeling lower than mud. The Prime Minister was, of course, happy to see him. There was the rattle of a troubling cough yet in his weakened lungs, his coloring a wan white, but beyond that, little to speak for his illness.

"Lord Thornton," greeted the hardy leader from a stuffed leather chair. "I understand you joined me in my sick room and that I owe your doctor a debt of gratitude."

When he would have stood, Thornton gestured for him to remain seated. "Please, do not trouble yourself on my account, Prime Minister. I did nothing more than any other man would have done in my place. It is only my pleasure to see you so hale and fit once more."

The Prime Minister growled. "I cannot say I'm fit, my boy, but I can say I'm a damn sight better than I was a few days ago."

"You are looking well." He lowered himself to a seat opposite Gladstone's, feeling every inch the traitor. He knew in his heart it was what he must do, but his old loyalties cried out the shame of it.

"Thank you, lad, but I have a feeling you haven't visited me to exchange pleasantries."

"No."

Silence stretched between them for a lengthy pause that could have been an hour or could have been minutes for its intensity.

"I gather," began the Prime Minister solemnly, "this is about the lovely Lady Scarbrough."

He stiffened. "You've heard, then?"

"Word travels, my lad." Gladstone hesitated. "But I would have you know that regardless of how this romance unfolds itself, there is always a place for you here. London needs you. The Liberals need you. In truth, I need you. Your role may not be as pronounced, for reasons that are as unfortunate as they are obvious. But no man deserves happiness more than you, Alexander. I would certainly never wish to stand in your way."

His throat threatened to close over with emotion. "Thank you, Prime Minister."

"No need to thank me." The stalwart leader waved away his words. "You're an important part of this Liberal leadership. Without you, Disraeli would still be manning the ship. I know what butters my bread, eh?"

It was just like the Grand Old Man, Thornton thought, to write off a gesture of supreme generosity as one of selfishness. But he knew otherwise. There were scads of others who could replace him. There were any number of leading Liberal lights in parliament who would have been only too happy to supplant him and any number of men who would be only too willing to toss him to the rubbish heap given his less than circumspect dalliance with Cleo. But not Gladstone. The Grand Old Man was making it possible for him to follow both his loves.

"I thank you most sincerely for your consideration and kindnesses." He rose, bowed and took his leave.

Now Cleo and all his dreams remained within his grasp.

CLEO AND RAVENSCROFT left together in a closed carriage for Scarbrough's country holding, despite the angry protests of her sisters. She had known in leaving Thornton that she would need to do something irrevocable, something from which there would be no returning. And so she was carefully laying the groundwork for an *affaire* with Julian. Of course, it was to be an *affaire* in name only, as he had aptly phrased it.

Julian slept most of the trip, leaving Cleo to peer out the window at the passing panorama and fret. As the carriage drew into the grand driveway and lurched over a bump, he woke with a start.

"Snoring, was I?" His lips quirked into an unapologetic grin.

"A bit loudly," she admitted, but couldn't force an answering smile to her lips.

"You're wringing your hands like a passenger aboard a sinking ship."

"Am I?" She stilled. "I hadn't noticed."

He leaned across the space between them to clasp her fingers in his. "Are you certain about this, Cleo?"

"Quite."

"You do realize the hardship for me? I can't recall when I last spent so much time alone with a woman without being in bed."

"Your sacrifice is most appreciated." Sarcasm laced her words, but she was grateful for his assistance.

He released her and turned to look out the window. "I suppose you've visitors awaiting you."

Her mind reeled. Surely Scarbrough had not brought his den of iniquity here to the countryside. It would render her plan impossible to carry out. On one ground, she was immovable. She would be seeking a divorce from her husband, no matter the cost. She would pay him off if necessary to convince him to seek it, give him every last bit of the fortune that remained within her power. To stay tied to him for the rest of her life was the worst fate her mind could fathom. She couldn't have the man she loved, but neither would she endure Scarbrough any longer.

"I sent word ahead to the servants of our arrival, but I didn't receive reply that others would be in the house as well. Why should you think that?"

"There appears to be carriage traffic about your portico, dear girl."

Cleo shifted to better see and caught a glimpse of three carriages loitering around the entrance to Scarbrough House. "Heavens, are those footmen carrying trunks inside?"

"It would seem."

"But that's impossible. I'm expecting no one. Indeed, it's quite imperative that only you and I should be in residence, else we'll never cause enough scandal to convince Scarbrough to sue for divorcement." She pressed a shaking hand to her heart.

"Precisely what is your plan?" Julian crossed his arms over his broad chest and eyed her in a considering way. "You neglected to mention we'd be creating a scandal to beat the royals."

"Pray don't pretend you're a stranger to scandal," she scoffed, turning her gaze back to the scene unfolding at the portico. Those were definitely liveried servants—Scarbrough's by the colors—and they were hefting trunk after trunk into the front door. Supervising all was a tall, gaunt man dressed all in black who looked, unless she was mistaken, very much like Cousin Herbert, the prudish baron next in line to inherit the earldom. But that made no sense at all. Why would Cousin Herbert drop in without invitation? Surely Scarbrough would not invite the man, whom he had once disparaged as a cross between a ramrod and a door knocker when it came to intelligence.

"It's not scandal that concerns me, but the wisdom of baiting your husband and your lover at the same time," he quipped. "What if they both arrive at Scarbrough House?"

Oh dear. She hadn't thought of that. She'd merely thought that for her own good, she could perhaps earn a divorce and for Thornton's own good, she could push him away from her. And all could be accomplished in one well-done scandal.

"They shan't," she told him with more conviction than she felt. "Scarbrough can't be pried away from his drinking and his lightskirts."

"You know I care for you, Cleo," Julian said, his tone quiet but honest. "But I doubt your wisdom. I've seen your happiness with Thornton, arse though he may be. I don't know why you wish to throw him over."

"I care for you as well, Julian and I'm truly grateful to you for what you are about to do. I couldn't ask it of another man."

He laughed. "Because no other man has a reputation as stained as that of a male whore's. I can be bought like a stud."

"You are a good man."

"Christ, but you'd think I'm a saint the bloody way you look at me." He hesitated. "You haven't answered my question."

She sighed. "I need to throw him over or else he'll lose everything that he holds dear. He is destined for greatness, and I would never take that opportunity from him."

"Selfless of you."

"And selfish too. I never want to be the one thing in his life that he regrets." Emotion clogged her voice and she forced her eyes back to the window to compose herself.

The carriage pulled abreast of the other conveyances being unloaded and came to a halt. The man striding toward her carriage was indeed Cousin Herbert. Which meant that something was dreadfully amiss. A grim expression haunted his gaunt face.

The carriage door swung open and Julian handed her down. Sunlight shone in harsh rays into her face. She felt suddenly dizzy. The smell of the waiting horses sickened her. Cousin Herbert stepped into her swirling line of vision and bowed.

"My lady," he intoned, "you've come sooner than anticipated. I myself have only just arrived after receiving the news."

"News?" She blinked at him, growing sicker and more confused by the moment. Had he always been so very tall? Did her dress improver need to be laced so damn tightly that she could scarce catch a breath? Good heavens, she quite feared she was going to cast up her accounts again.

"You have not heard, then?" Cousin Herbert frowned, creating a deep vee of concern on his forehead beneath the brim of an outmoded beaver hat.

"I haven't any idea what you're speaking of, Baron. Pray enlighten me."

"You have my deepest sympathy." He bowed again, looking grave. "The earl has passed on to his rewards."

Nausea roiled to a seething fury within her, competing with a terrible megrim that was beginning to make its presence known. Scarbrough had met his end? How was this possible? Why had she not heard? Good Lord, she was a widow.

She clasped a hand to her breast. "Scarbrough is dead?"

She was dimly aware of Julian's presence behind her, keeping her from crashing to the ground in a dusty heap of traveling garments. Part of her felt immense relief and the other part of her knew a great, keening sadness for the man Scarbrough could have been. That man had died long ago. And now...now, she was free.

"Could you not have delivered such upsetting news in a more civilized setting, man?" Julian barked.

"What happened to him?" she asked Cousin Herbert, clutching at his coat sleeve, needing to know.

"Hit by an omnibus," he said with a distinct tone of self-righteousness. Scarbrough and Cousin Herbert had never been friends. "Somewhere in the East End of London. The watch said he was passed out with drink when it happened. Doubt he felt a thing. They took him for a common street man initially, until they discovered his signet ring."

Cleo doubled over and lost her lunch on Cousin Herbert's boots.

WORD OF THE earl's death reached Thornton in London as

he was preparing to return to the country. With the Prime Minister on the mend, there was no longer a reason for him to tarry in the city. Scarbrough's death was the talk of town. No one could quite believe that a Peer of the Realm would be done in by an East End omnibus, but nevertheless, it was true. While he hated to admit it, the news was welcome. Now there would be no court, no scandal, no more impediments to intervene and prevent him from seeking Cleo's hand.

He fully expected to find her yet at Marleigh Manor. He'd written her twice each day during the time he spent in London, once in the morning and once before bed and he quite feared he was getting maudlin. He had never received a response, which presumably meant that his mother was confiscating his letters.

Upon his arrival back at the manor, he strode through the house, opening doors and calling her name until finally, his mother approached him in the hall. She wore her customary dove-gray gown and a lace cap covering her hair. She fluttered to him like an irate bird.

"Alexander, do cease your hollering. Why, to raise one's voice in the house is positively American. I do insist you send that intolerable Mr. Whitney on his way. He's nothing but an ambonation."

He pressed his fingers to his temples to ward off the approaching migraine. "Abomination, mother."

"I beg your pardon?" She blinked, perplexed by his terse response.

"I believe you meant to say abomination. Ambonation is not a word."

"Just so. That's what I said, Alexander. Do you not listen to a thing your mother tells you? Clearly you do not, or you wouldn't have entangled yourself with that horrid woman."

"Where is she?" he demanded, patience running thin.

A pleased smile curved his mother's lips. "She's gone."

"Hell." He jammed his hand through his hair.

"Language, Alexander."

He growled. "Where has she gone, damn it?"

The dowager shrugged. "She left with her vulgar sisters and claimed to be going to her father's seat."

Thornton had never touched his mother in anger in his life, but now he was mightily tempted to shake her. Instead, he clenched his fists. "What did you do to her?"

"Why, nothing, of course. Why should I bother myself with a grasping slattern?"

He slammed his fist into the wall above her head, sending a shower of plaster chips to the floor. "Never insult her again, madam. She is to be my wife and you'll treat her to the respect she deserves."

Although she had flinched at his outburst, she wore calm like a mantle now. "If she is to be your wife, I find it inordinately peculiar for her to be gadding about the countryside on the arm of the earl of Ravenscroft."

His gut sank. Sweet Christ, but Ravenscroft? That couldn't possibly be true. Could it? Goddamn his trip to London. It could not have come at a worse time. Knowing the dowager as he did, a tad of creative deception on her part was not out of the question. Very likely, she'd tossed poor Cleo and her sisters from the house the moment he'd gone.

"What are you speaking of, madam?"

A pleased smile tightened her lips. "I've had it from Lady Grimsby, who had it from Lady Arbuthnot, who is a neighbor of Scarbrough's, that she's gone to Scarbrough House with the Earl of Ravenscroft. They're said to be behaving scandalously, especially in light of the other earl's death. I told you she was not fit to lick your boots, Alexander."

Damn it, he would have the truth and he would have it now. There was only one way to obtain it. He spun on his heel and stalked away, leaving his mother sputtering, demanding to know where he was going.

"To Scarbrough House," he answered curtly. "Be warned

that if there is even a hint of prevarication on your part, I expect you to have your trunks packed by the time I return."

THE DAYS FOLLOWING her husband's death passed in a haze for Cleo. Ravenscroft stayed on and turned out to be quite the godsend as he helped to make funeral preparations with the increasingly odious Cousin Herbert. Cleo kept mostly to her chamber, alternately sick, sad and relieved. Tia and Helen joined her to offer her their support, given Cleo's shock to learn of Scarbrough's early demise. Tia declared his a fitting end. Helen added that no man deserved to be squashed by an omnibus more, in her humble estimation.

Cousin Herbert moved his family of eight into the estate, eagerly taking on his new role of earl. The children played tag in the halls. They broke china. They scuffed floors. They dribbled crumbs and tea on the furniture. This was another reason Cleo kept to her rooms.

Scarbrough's body arrived from London the same day she and Ravenscroft had and lay in state somewhere in the house, but she had not the courage to ask its precise location. The mirrors were draped and the servants dressed in mourning, but the entire affair had the air of a celebration and not of sadness at all. No one, it seemed, had cared for the selfish and frequently cruel earl. And no one would truly miss him.

Cleo was ashamed of herself for the great weight that lifted off her heart with his death. There had been no love lost between them. They had been strangers over the last few years of their alliance. But yet she would have fain divorced him than have him meet such an inglorious end, despite what he'd done to ruin her happiness and squander her inheritance.

The afternoon of the third day of her new life as a widow, everything changed. She still suffered from a spot of illness, her stomach nearly always unsettled—she put it down to shock. Cleo hadn't much in her stomach beyond dry toast and lukewarm tea, but she was feeling well enough to sit at her private sitting room and sift through correspondence when Tia rushed into her room in a waft of purple silk skirts.

"Darling, Thornton's come," she said in rushed tones. "He's determined to see you."

Cleo froze, a letter falling from her fingers to the floor. How eerily similar this moment was to their last breakup all those years before. She had been writing him a letter when he arrived and tipped the ink well in her upset, staining her hands. She'd been cruel to him then, her words cutting, her actions deliberate.

She met her sister's gaze, hopelessness welling up within her. "What shall I do?"

"You must see him, *certainement*." Tia crossed the room and placed bracing hands upon her shoulders. "Are you well enough, dearest?"

"Yes." She took a deep breath and closed her eyes to steel herself for the confrontation. "Bring him to me, please."

Cleo forced her guilt and panic to subside, eyes still firmly closed. When she opened them, Alex was there, standing before her. His eyes were hard, his sulky mouth pressed in a taut line. Her heart skittered and tripped over itself at the welcome sight of him. God, but she had missed him with a desperation she had no right to feel. She owed it to him to remain stoic and keep her distance, but everything within her heart screamed at her to go to him, throw herself into his arms and explain everything away.

"Alex," she said quietly, acknowledging his presence.

"Lady Scarbrough." He bowed, solemn and cold. "Please accept my sympathy."

"Pray don't act the stranger to me." Twisting her hands in agitation, she rose from her chair. Though he still towered over her, she felt as if she had regained something of her footing. "We're alone in my apartments."

"Oh?" He raised a brow. "Is not Ravenscroft hiding himself like a kicked puppy in your bedchamber?"

He had heard already. Well, it was only to be expected. She had made no secret of Julian. After all, had this not been what she intended? She'd set out to make the break easy for him, to deceive him into leaving her.

"You know he is not," she said slowly.

Thornton strode toward her, still as grim as the black mourning he wore in deference to Scarbrough. "Then explain to me what I have heard."

"I cannot when I don't know what you've heard." She searched his face for any hint of tenderness, of softness. The man she had come to know and love had dissipated, leaving another in his place.

"That you have taken Ravenscroft as your lover," he bit out. "That he is, even now, living here under this very roof." He took her arm in a rough grasp. "Can you deny it?"

"He is under this roof," she admitted. Even if it was truly better for his career that he make a suitable lady his bride, she would not lie to him completely. She found that she could not.

"What of the rest?" He shook her. "Answer me, damn you, Cleo."

She would not speak.

"Christ." He released her and spun away. "I told myself that it was a mistake, that surely you couldn't be so heartless a bitch. How could you do this to us?"

"Julian has been very kind," she forced herself to say. "I have needed a friend these last few days and you were off with the Prime Minister in the city. What was I to do?"

"Wait for me?" Thornton turned back to her, anguish evident in the harsh planes of his beautiful face. "I asked you to wait."

"I could not." Cleo's voice broke. "I'm sorry, Alex. You're better without me as an encumbrance, I assure you."

"It would seem so." He searched her eyes. "Was everything a lie to you? A game?"

"No." She shook her head, the nausea rising within her once more. "Please leave me now. Further conversation in this direction cannot prove fruitful."

"Damn it, I deserve to know why, Cleopatra."

"There is no reason why." Tears frustrated her vision. "You are who you are, Alex. I am, even newly widowed, tainted by scandal. We cannot be anything more than what we were. I shall always treasure our time together, but all good things must end."

"I was willing to give up everything for you."

"You should not have to." She threw her hands in the air in a mixture of despair and aggravation. "You have the whole world before you, all of your aspirations, the reform work you love. There is no room for a tarnished widow in all that."

"You're wrong. I made a place for you."

"Alex, it took you days to make Miss Cuthbert leave Marleigh Manor and to this day, I'm not certain that you actually threw her over."

"I ended any understanding that may have existed between our families." He was indignant, hovering over her in avenging angel style.

"I will not have you give away everything that is important to you because of me." She was yelling, but she didn't care. Her entire body shook with the exertion, the emotion coursing through her.

"You're a liar. You're too damn afraid," he sneered. "What? Does whoring yourself out for Ravenscroft make you feel better, darling?"

She slapped him. The sound of it echoed in the sudden silence of the room and pulsed in her palm. A wave of sickness assailed her. She pressed the back of her hand to her lips. "Please go."

His beloved face blurred and swirled before her and she

detected the concern in his voice just before she crumpled to a heap on the floor. Her world went black.

DESPITE HIMSELF—ALL INCLINATIONS to the contrary, urging him to run, leave her to her bloody lover—Thornton paced outside Cleo's chamber. Against propriety too, for there was a fusty little country cousin due to inherit the earldom fussing about and eying him like death. There were also the sisters hovering peregrine falcon style, ready to defend. Ravenscroft, the bastard, had pulled himself together from what was likely a gin-soaked reverie to await word as well. The damn doctor had been inside for nearly an hour already.

Thornton wanted to kill Ravenscroft. Trounce him. Break the lout's nose at the least. Instead, he paced. Christ, what was he, a mother hen? Had he no manly pride? Damn her. How could she have done this? It didn't bear contemplation and yet, somehow, the whole affair had an off feel to it. The sisters didn't seem—for all their protective instincts—terribly angry with him. And Cleo herself had been…what? Sad green eyes, wan. Ill.

The door opened and the family physician emerged, middle-aged and dour-faced, hair neatly parted and greased. His mustache twitched as he spoke. "Her ladyship needs rest," he pronounced.

"Rest?" Thornton bore down on him, prepared to grab his waistcoat and shake information from his wiry frame. "Speak, man. What ails her?"

"Ahem." The doctor cleared his throat, removed his spectacles and began a slow polishing of them. "It is not my practice to speak so openly of a patient before so many people."

"They'll go." He waved toward the assemblage in a dismissive gesture. There was more to this story than the good doctor was divulging. He could nearly smell it.

"We're her family," the sisters exclaimed in unison.

He glanced at them meaningfully. Damn it all, he had no place here and he knew it. But despite what she had done, he loved her. And he wanted word. Now.

"Ravenscroft?" Tia addressed the earl, who shrugged.

"Let the blighter interrogate the physician if he likes," the earl said, indolence personified.

Killing him would be too reasonable a solution. Truly, the man needed to be tortured. Thornton loathed him.

"Does nothing worry you, you smug son of a…" Thornton stopped himself from completing that sentiment, recalling he stood in mixed company.

"Cousin Harvey?" Tia attempted next.

"Herbert," corrected the unfortunate fellow. "Earl of Scarbrough now." With the announcement, he puffed out his puny chest.

"Not a title to wear with pride, old chap," Ravenscroft commented. "The last one was something of a rotter, I'm told."

"Now is not the time for your poor attempts at wit, Ravenscroft." Thornton rammed a hand through his already mussed hair and looked to the cousin Harry or Henry or whatnot. "Lord Scarbrough? As the head of the household, why don't you escort the ladies and the earl downstairs so they might recover from their shock? I shall escort the good doctor to the door."

If the new earl found the assortment of characters surrounding Cleo odd, or Thornton's request a trifle overstepping, he didn't show it. Deferring, as Thornton had predicted he would, to higher rank as he was accustomed, the cousin shepherded the sisters and Ravenscroft away. When they had disappeared from sight and hearing, he turned on the doctor.

"What ails her?" he demanded, aware he acted the role of

husband and that it must seem odd indeed but not giving a damn.

"Not a thing. The countess is, in fact, quite healthy. Given the stress of losing her husband, it is expected, particularly given…" He hesitated.

Thornton's gut clenched. "Given?"

"Ahem. This is a matter of some delicacy, my lord. The countess requested I keep the reason for her illness to myself."

"Is it consumption?"

"No."

Thank God. That had been his initial fear, though there had been no outward sign of the wasting disease. "Then what, sir?" He was fast losing patience.

"This is highly irregular, my lord," he sighed, wiping his spectacles again. "I gather you and the countess have a friendship?"

"Yes," he bit out, frustrated and worried.

"She is in a condition, my lord."

"Condition? Christ, that sounds serious."

"With child," the doctor amended in hushed tones. "She requests it remain unknown."

He couldn't have been more astonished had Scarbrough risen from his coffin and offered him a whiskey. "With child," he repeated, numb.

"Yes." The doctor's face softened. "I trust this news travels nowhere beyond yourself?"

"Of course not." His mouth was dry, his tongue sticking to the roof of his mouth and a tiny seed of hope sprouted somewhere within him. Irresistible, irrefutable, hope. "Thank you, sir."

Now one pertinent question loomed. Was the child his? Or did it belong to Ravenscroft?

A CHILD. GOOD heavens, Cleo had not anticipated the news Dr. Redding had delivered. It made sense, of course, and she felt the fool for not having realized as much on her own. Instead, she had caused quite an embarrassing uproar. What could she say to Cousin Herbert and Julian? To her sisters and the rest of her family? Her mother would be apt to disown her when she discovered the truth.

Everyone in her family—and truthfully, in polite society—knew she had not even seen her husband for at least a year. Which meant, of course, that everyone would also suspect the child she carried could not possibly be John's. Still, suspicion was not proof. Though she may be mocked behind her back, she could pass the child off as her husband's. She would need to do so. Besides, many society wives were rumored to father children by other men. It was almost fashionable.

The door clicked open as she contemplated the uncertainty of her future, revealing Thornton. He was alone, his hair utterly at sixes and sevens, and his mouth drawn.

"Please go," she begged, terrified she would make an even greater fool of herself by bursting into waterworks before him. "I don't care for company at the moment."

He closed the door behind his back and began a slow, deliberate stalk to her bedside. "That is rather unfortunate for you, my dear, for I'm not about to leave."

She watched him, uncertainty and dread coiling within her. Should she tell him? The last thing she wanted was to entrap him. But neither did she care to prevaricate. A child deserves a father and a father his child, she reasoned. But she still could not form the words.

"I don't want you here," she tried.

He scooted a *Louis Quinze* chair close to her bed and seated himself. His gaze pierced her with a burning stare. "Is it mine?"

The breath left her lungs in one silent whoosh. Either he

had guessed or Dr. Redding had divulged her secret against her wishes. She was not yet prepared for this confrontation. Cleo knew not what to say, where to begin, how to untangle the desperate muddle she'd made of their lives. She stared at her hand, fisted in the bed linen, and realized she still wore his ring.

"Look at me, damn it." He gripped her chin roughly and tipped her face up, forcing her to meet his gaze. "Is the babe mine?"

An admission would entrap him. She stared at him, mute and stricken. She loved him, but she would not have him in this way, when he had no choice. Never did she want to become his life's greatest regret. And so she knew in her heart what she must do next.

"I do not know," she told him, voice shaking with emotion.

"Bitch." His voice dripped scorn.

Cleo flinched as if he had struck her. "I'm sorry, Thornton. I think it best for all involved that I present this child as my husband's."

"You will forgive me if I don't agree."

She'd never heard his voice so cold and passionless. "Please, Alex. Have a care for the child, who is innocent in all this."

"Precisely. Why subject a child who is likely mine to thinking his father is a drunken philanderer who spent the last moments of his life pinned beneath an omnibus in a Bow Common street?"

"Better subject him to that than to being a bastard," she returned, her anger rising to match his own.

"I will marry you."

"And I won't have you." Not this way, she wanted to say. *Not when I have ruined everything in hopes of giving you what you deserved. Not when you think me the lowest woman on earth.*

"You loved me well enough before I went to London.

What changed?" He stood and kicked over the chair. "Is he a better lover than I, Cleo? I reckon he's had the practice, being the whore of all London."

"Don't speak that way!"

"Do you love him?" he demanded, fierce and almost a bit frightening in his dark rage.

"I do," she lied with great conviction. She grabbed up a pillow from her bed and hurled it at him. "You needn't concern yourself with us. We shall be well. I'll wed Julian if I must. You may return to your world of politics, where you belong!" To punctuate her speech, she threw yet another pillow. This time he did not duck and it hit him square in the face.

"Get out!" She was screeching now, desperate to make him go away. "I hate you!"

Tia and Helen came rushing into the chamber, their expressions pinched with worry.

Helen rushed to her side, pushing Thornton away. "Here now." She caught Cleo up in a reassuring embrace. "What's amiss, dearest?"

"I want to be alone," she whispered, aware that her emotions were spinning wildly out of control. One moment she wanted to rush to him and explain their troubles away. The next she wanted to make him hate her so much that he stayed gone forever. She loved him and yet she remained afraid to love him. She was no good for him, she knew it. She would not trap him and yet she knew that if he remained for much longer, she would do just that.

"Lord Thornton, you are distressing our sister when she least needs it," Tia said, voice stern. "I must ask you to leave. You have no business here."

"I just want the truth, Cleo," he said, sounding tired. He allowed Tia to nudge him to the door. "You owe me that much, I think."

Then he was gone and Cleo had two sisters to face.

Chapter Nineteen

THORNTON ALLOWED HIMSELF to be removed from Cleo's chamber, but only so that he could go and give Ravenscroft the thrashing he deserved. He found him in the library, dozing in a chair by the fire, and launched himself at the sleeping earl, forgetting that attacking an unaware opponent was ungentlemanly. In two punches, Ravenscroft was fully awake and swinging back at him.

"I'll be raising the child," he gritted out. "I don't give a bloody damn if she fancies you. You're a worthless shite."

Ravenscroft's fist connected with his jaw. "What child, you miserable prick? I was sleeping, I'll have you know. It isn't done to assault a man in his sleep."

"The child Cleo's carrying. The one she says may be yours." He landed a hefty blow of his own to the tosser's nose. "I don't care if you're the father. I'm marrying her and I'm raising the child."

"Oh Christ." Blood dripped from the earl's nose and his face suddenly leached of all color. "She didn't say a word about a babe."

Thornton gave him quarter, actually pitying the sod a bit. He looked as if he was about to pitch his dinner and damn if his nose wasn't nearly as straight any more. In fact, he just may have broken it.

"I'll pay you whatever you like," he said, breathing hard with exertion.

"I don't want to be paid." He pushed at Thornton. "Get

away from me, you bastard. I'm her friend. I've never been her lover. If there's a child, you're responsible, which means I should be attacking you for dishonoring a lady of my acquaintance."

"Friend?" That word stopped his world.

"Christ, yes. This was all meant to be a lark, a way of getting you to realize you loved Gladstone's cabinet more than you loved her because she couldn't rid herself of that no account husband. But then Scarbrough went and got himself flattened and you showed up and now she's going to have a child." He paused to wrestle a white linen square from his waistcoat and hold it to his scarlet-dripping nose. "I hadn't bargained for this, I assure you."

"Why would she want me to go back to the cabinet?" His heart had digested the words, but his brain was having difficulties.

"She's afraid you're giving up your silly politics for her. Says she's tarnished or some such nonsense."

"Jesus, she's not a candlestick." Thornton rubbed a hand over his aching jaw. "So you've never…"

"Not a bit of it." Ravenscroft grinned beneath the handkerchief. "Not to say I wouldn't have, had she been inclined. But no."

"Then I'm the father." Pride surged through him. He was going to be a father. There was a tiny, precious life beginning to grow inside Cleo's womb that had been the product of their love.

But she had lied to him. She had lied and despite her reasons, he could not so hastily forgive her. Since he had not been a part of her life during her first pregnancy and miscarriage, her dishonesty to him now seemed a betrayal of the first order. He was not certain he could forgive her for the hell she'd put him through over her "lark."

"You're the father, old boy." Ravenscroft rose to his feet and offered him a hand.

Not thinking, Thornton accepted it and allowed the earl to pull him to his feet. Just before he regained his footing, the bastard released him and sent him sprawling to the floor. His head smacked off the polished hardwood planks and his teeth slammed together, biting his lip.

"What the hell was that for?" He rubbed his throbbing head with one hand and his sore mouth with the other, glaring at his sometime rival.

"That was for breaking my frigging nose," Ravenscroft said, succinct. He spun on his heel and quit the room, leaving Thornton alone to contemplate this new discovery.

CLEO LOOKED FROM sister to sister, wishing she knew where to begin. Tia sat on her left and Helen perched to her right.

"Well?" Tia settled the folds of her pristine black gown. "What is the matter, darling? A feigned megrim again?"

She swallowed, contemplating her response. "No…" She faltered, took a breath…"I am with child."

Her sisters' mouths dropped open. She gave a small laugh. "I see you are as astonished as I by the prospect."

Helen squeezed her hand in a reassuring grip. "Does Thornton know?"

"He does."

"And what does he say?"

"I have not led him to believe he is the babe's father," she admitted.

Tia gasped. "You cannot be thinking rationally!"

"Very likely she is not." Helen's tone was dry. "After all, when women are *enceinte*, they are rather notoriously emotional."

"Yes, but you cannot think to marry Ravenscroft, Cleo." Tia shook her head, giving her blonde curls an artful bounce. "The man is not a father made to be."

"I'm aware of my predicament." Cleo had never been more miserable in her life. She knew not which way to turn, what path to choose that was right for her, the child and Thornton. "I don't wish to entrap him with this."

"Thornton loves you." Helen squeezed her hand again. "You should have seen him pacing about outside your chamber. He even made the rest of us leave so he could have a private word with the doctor. I've never seen him look so concerned. You won't be entrapping him, dearest."

She stared at the coverlet, noting the way its gold threads wove with the blue to create an intricate, yet almost imperceptible pattern. "I've made a muddle of everything."

"You've done your very best with the circumstances."

Tia snickered. "It's not as if you asked Scarbrough to get himself killed by an omnibus."

"Tia!" Because her scoundrel of a husband had yet to be laid to rest, Cleo found any discussion of him involving levity to be uncomfortable indeed.

"I'm glad he's gone." Her indomitable sister shrugged. "And I don't regret saying as much. He was a blighter and he misused you and the world at large is a better place without him. Your world, to be specific, will be a better place without him in it."

"You can't keep Thornton out of your life now," Helen added. "You are free to love him."

"But what of his career? He'll lose everything."

"He'll gain the woman he loves and his child. Stop fretting over circumstances beyond your control. You can't let fear drive everything, as mother will tell you."

Cleo grimaced. "Mother told me to marry Scarbrough. She thought him a better prospect than Thornton."

Helen shrugged. "She has her lapses in judgment."

"Speaking of mother," Tia interrupted, "I received word that she and the rest of the family shall arrive from their holiday in Scotland tomorrow and stay out the week. Prepare yourself for a whirlwind."

Grand. Now she would have brothers, an impish younger sister, and parents at her back in addition to Tia, Helen, and Thornton. "Please don't tell the rest of the family. Not yet. I prefer to make this decision on my own."

"You will tell Thornton," Helen said, part question, mostly dictate.

"I'll consider it," she allowed.

The door to her chamber flew open to admit an even more thoroughly mussed—and slightly bloodied and bruised—Thornton. He strode into the room as if it was his to command. "Tell your sister she is marrying me," he addressed Tia and Helen, not bothering to spare a glance for Cleo.

"They do not speak for me, my lord," Cleo was compelled to inform him.

He ignored her. "Tell her that she carries my child and I will announce it to the world unless she agrees to marry me so that my child may be born with the proper name."

It would seem that her ruse hadn't lasted long, and if his abused state was any indication, he'd gotten the truth from Ravenscroft the hard way. She frowned. Very well. Two could play at this game. She addressed her sisters. "Tell him the babe is mine just as much as his and he cannot order me as if I were no better than a parlor maid."

He clenched his jaw. "Please also inform the countess that her wishes are immaterial in the matter and I will order her about as I please." He bowed. "Oh and add that I trounced Ravenscroft once again."

Julian *had* told him. She knew then that any attempt to keep Thornton at arm's length was well and truly over.

CLEO SPENT AN all but sleepless night and woke to a house full of the Harrington clan. All told, that meant her parents,

Lord and Lady Northcote, Cleo's youngest sister Bo and her three elder brothers, Bingley, Adrian and Connor. She loved her family, truly she did, but she was not especially happy to watch the stream of carriages heralding their arrival. Their presence along with Thornton's would not render an already difficult situation any more promising.

In fact, she quite feared that, given his recent propensity for taking up the cudgels, Thornton would get into a rousing bout of fisticuffs with every one of her dear brothers. Particularly if even a whisper of Cleo's relationship with him had reached their ears. Or if Thornton announced she was *enceinte* to her family, as he had threatened. Not a bit of good could come of anything. Perhaps she could hide away in her chamber and avoid it all.

No, that wouldn't do. It was time to face everyone. She rang for Bridget, who arrived almost immediately and helped her to dress. She wore a simple black mourning gown, jet earrings and a diamond comb in her hair. Another ordinary day, except that so much faced her.

In the breakfast room, all eyes turned to her. She had not meant to create an entrance. Cousin Herbert and his menagerie were nowhere to be found, thank God, nor was Ravenscroft. Thornton was seated between Bingley and Connor, looking annoyingly well-rested and pleasant. She wanted to fling a spoonful of marmalade at his head. Instead, she allowed a footman to seat her beside her mother.

"My darling daughter." Lady Northcote gave her a gentle smile. "How are you faring?"

"Well enough, thank you." She forced a matching smile to her lips and her gaze strayed to Thornton. He watched her with a dark, inscrutable stare.

"You must forgive us for not joining you here sooner," the earl added. "We came as soon as we had word of the sad news, but we were delayed by some deuced bad roads."

"I understand." Lowering her eyes to her plate, she

scooped up a small sliver of eggs. Her stomach protested the scent. She forced herself to chew and swallow it, then reached for her tea with such desperation she upended her cup. A large, brown stain seeped into the table linen and the urge to cry welled up within her.

"Are you feeling yourself, daughter?" her mother asked quietly as footmen hurried to blot out the stain.

"Perfectly," she muttered.

"You are wan."

"I shall powder my face if you like." It wasn't kind to snap at one's mother, but she was doing so now. The woman's persistence would drive her mad.

"Powdering the face is vulgar, dear."

She took a sip of her fresh tea. "I don't think I care, mother." Cleo glanced around the table again, catching sight of her little sister. "Bo, you are looking lovely."

Bo dimpled. "Thank you, Cleo."

Cleo took another bite of eggs and knew instantly that she was about to retch. "Excuse me," she announced and hurried from the room. As it happened, she made it to a potted plant outside the breakfast room before embarrassing herself. She became aware of a presence behind her before she felt a gentle hand rubbing her back through her stays.

"Shall I fetch a glass of ice water?" Thornton's voice was very near to her ear. Perilously near.

Even with a turbulent stomach, her heart hitched at his proximity. She could smell him, feel his hot breath on her neck. And it was oh so tempting. Why was he being so kind? "Please."

He was gone but for a moment and returned with a clinking glass that cooled her sweating palms as she accepted it from him. "Thank you." She drank deeply, eyeing him over the glass's rim.

"I've been to speak with your father," he said, gently taking the glass back from her. "Easy now, love. You can't drink so quickly on an unsettled stomach."

"Why in heaven's name would you do something so foolish?"

"Cleo, I will have this child born with my name."

"You've deliberately gone against my wishes." Her anger with him renewed and burned with a brighter fire.

"As you have gone against mine." He clenched his jaw, composing himself before he continued. "Your father agrees that we will be married within the fortnight."

"Scarbrough is not yet buried."

A dark shadow passed over his face. "Do not use that man as an excuse. He wasn't a husband to you and you don't owe him the customary mourning period."

"Society won't consider it that way."

"I don't give two shites what society thinks," he gritted. "Damn it, I care about our child."

"Do you think I do not?"

"You haven't been acting the part, flitting about with Ravenscroft and lying through your perfect little teeth."

"How dare you accuse me of not wanting what's best for our babe?" Her body shook with frustration and anger.

Thornton sighed. "Cleo, let's not make a row of this now, with all your family likely pressed to the keyhole behind us."

"Am I to know what you've planned for me, then?"

"We leave for Marleigh Manor tomorrow. Your family will accompany us and my mother and sister will help you to arrange a small ceremony in the de Vere chapel."

She laughed, feeling caught between giddiness and hysteria. She didn't appreciate his high-handedness in the matter, not a bit. But that he thought for a moment the dowager might willingly help to arrange the nuptials she'd been determined to avoid…it was too rich.

"Alex, your mother despises me and your sister has made her opinion of me clear as well. You cannot be so naïve as to think they will fall in line like good soldiers."

"They haven't any choice." He was self-assured. "Let's get through this day together and then deal with what lies ahead."

There was wisdom in his words. She nodded. "Very well. Let us get through this day first."

THE NEXT MORNING a long procession of carriages left Scarbrough House, likely for the last time. Cleo took with her everything belonging to her—furniture, jewels, paintings, the remainders of her trousseau, dresses, shoes, hats, and more dress improvers than she'd realized she owned. Her departure was a contented one. As they rumbled out of the familiar, circular drive, she glanced back at the house where she had spent many days during her early marriage. It had been where she hid herself away from the cruelties and embarrassment of her loveless marriage. And yesterday, in the Bennington plot, it had been there where she said goodbye to the husband she had never truly known.

Leaving now felt right, as if a door closed on a passage in her life that was as unwanted as it was in the past. And leaving with Thornton, uncertain though she was of his feelings, felt better than right.

They rode alone in a carriage, Cleo seated opposite him. Turning away from her last glimpse of Scarbrough House, where Cousin Herbert and his brood waved from the lawns, she pretended to study her knotted hands in her lap. In truth, she studied Thornton from beneath her lashes, watching for the slightest hint of his emotions. His face remained impassive, his gaze indecipherable. He kept his eyes on the window, watching the unfurling country landscape. The unbridled passion of their last carriage ride together haunted her. She wondered if it would be possible for them to find that brief happiness again, or if she had ruined their tentative relationship.

She decided to broach the silence at last. "Have you managed to send word ahead of us?"

His gaze flicked to hers. "Yes."

"Good." She kept quiet for a moment, searching for something to say to him that wouldn't be inflammatory. "The weather is fine today."

His expression hardened. "Cleo, we aren't strangers, for Christ's sake. You needn't treat me as if we've only just been introduced at a society *fete*."

So much for her attempt at avoiding the inflammatory. "You aren't making this easy."

"Forgive me if I'm not in a lighthearted mood."

"You aren't the one with your world collapsing like a poorly constructed building. Do you think I haven't been affected by all of this?"

"Of course not."

She took a deep breath and collected herself. "I think, Alex, that if we are to move forward, I need to explain myself."

He inclined his head. "Please."

"When you were called to London, I left you because I thought it was in your best interest." She paused, losing her nerve for a moment and then began again. "Miss Cuthbert first convinced me of how selfish I was being to hold you to me when I could not lay any claim to you. Your mother, while not precisely reasonable, also helped me to see that my presence in your life would only prove ruinous. Even you told me your dream as a lad was to become Prime Minister."

"Yes, well, I also dreamt of flying to the moon as a lad." Abruptly, he reached across the space between them and pulled her onto his lap. "It's been so long since I've held you. I can't stand to be so close and not have you in my arms."

"I'm sorry for lying to you about Ravenscroft." She picked her hat off her head and tossed it to the squabs so she could look at him without it getting in the way. "I thought it would be simpler that way."

"I cannot say I forgive you yet," he murmured, his hands sliding around her to rest above where their child grew. "I need time."

"I dare say." Her hands moved of their own accord to rest atop his.

"Would you have told me if the doctor had not?"

"About the child, you mean? I don't know," she answered with absolute truth. "I didn't want to entrap you. Even now, your life can never be the same. We'll get married too soon and there shall be whispers abounding. The Prime Minister won't be able to keep you so close."

"The politics pale in comparison. How could you possibly think I would want to forsake my own flesh and blood for the Liberal Party? Or you, for that matter?"

She searched his gaze, her heart a painful throb in her chest. "I am so sorry. How can I fix this?"

"I should like to tell you I understand your reasons."

"But you cannot."

"No." He pressed a kiss to her cheek. "We've a long ride to Marleigh Manor and you need to keep your strength. Why don't you rest?"

She supposed it was down to either closing her eyes and napping or enduring more awkward and painful conversation. Her actions had proved foolish and futile in the end. She could only hope now that Alex would not hold them against her for the rest of their lives. Somehow, she had to make this right, she vowed as she allowed the carriage to lull her to sleep.

Chapter Twenty

Marleigh Manor

THE DOWAGER MARCHIONESS, in general, found that she experienced a vast amount of displeasure on a regular basis. Her subordinates continuously disappointed her. Levingood Senior, for instance, suffered from gout. Oh, he made an effort to hide his malady from her, it was certain, but there was a limp. Particularly in the mornings. Butlers—proper butlers—should never portray weakness. No, it was not done. The maids, she found, were horrors. Vulgar little imps, all quite American in perspective, one even daring to color her lips. She'd dismissed the trollop without reference.

But nothing compared to the displeasure, nay, horror, that wrought her very being at the sight of the multitude of carriages bearing down on Marleigh Manor. She spotted the deuced Harrington crest immediately. Her son, that imp, that rascal, was to blame. She knew it at once.

Levingood Senior entered in the drawing room where she was taking tea with Bella as the dust was still kicked up in the drive. He bowed, his age-spotted face blank. "Visitors, my lady. Shall I put them in the east wing?"

At the announcement, she nearly spat her treasured tea upon her new day dress. Visitors? It was unthinkable. Unconscionable. She had invited no one. Which meant one thing only.

All but tossing her cup and saucer upon the table, she rose and made her way to the window. From there, she was afforded a most excellent view of the property. The crest on the carriages beckoned. Her eyesight did not yet fail her. "Good heavens," she muttered."

"Carriages, mother?" Bella asked. "What visitors could it be?"

The dowager marchioness of Thornton never lost face before her retainers, regardless of the situation. She smiled, hoping it was gracious. "The Harrington clan, of course. Your dear brother did write ahead. My poor mind! I quite forgot myself." She turned her smile upon the butler. "Levingood, please do see the guest rooms in the east wing readied. We have a considerable amount of guests in our midst and it shan't do to be ill prepared."

For this, she vowed inwardly, she would murder her son in his sleep. Sole heir or no. Levingood bowed and disappeared from the room, as soundlessly as he had entered.

The dowager seated herself, retrieved her tea and sipped with great contemplation. "He has rather a limp, does he not?"

Bella raised a brow. "Mother?"

"Do not refer to me in such terms, pray." Would the chit never learn? The dowager nearly huffed. "*Maman*, darling. Levingood Senior. He suffers a limp. It is most inconvenient. I do fear we shall need to replace him forthwith."

Bella sipped her tea, looking quite the lady before she ruined the effect utterly with a gross display of unladylike and vulgar thought. "*Maman*, Levingood Senior has the gout. He is, otherwise, quite formidable. No butler in my experience is as well versed."

She sniffed. "You do yourself no service in such talk. I forbid you to speak to me thusly. Indeed, have I not raised you better?"

"Forgive me." Bella lowered her gaze, but the dowager did not miss the shine of insolence lingering there. "You did expect the Harrington family, then?"

"Forward girl," the dowager barked. "Do you dare question me?"

"I merely thought you would have mentioned—"

"Enough!" The dowager rose and arranged her skirts with a great show of dignity. "You are but a naïve girl. Do you honestly believe I entrust all to you? *Quelle* pride, daughter."

The deep voice of her son could be heard addressing the servants in the great hall. She steeled herself for what was to come. This arrival, after all, could only mean one horrible thing. In mere moments, the door to the drawing room swung open to reveal the marquis. His travel clothes swung about him. He yet wore a hat upon his black hair and even his face remained aloof, as if he did not know her and met her now for the first time. He acted as if she were not his mother, as if he had not sprung from her own womb.

He bowed as a footman closed the door behind him. "Mother, sister. I expect that Levingood has already informed you of the arrival of Lady Scarbrough and all her family."

"Indeed." She inclined her head, unwilling to give. This man, so cool, was of her own flesh and blood and yet he seemed so strange and foreign.

"Lady Scarbrough and I are to wed within a fortnight's time," her son continued, his tone unchanged. It was as if he spoke of nothing more than the beeswax on the floor. "I trust that you will act with courtesy and treat both Lady Scarbrough and her kin with utmost respect."

"Of course," she answered stiffly. They were, after all, peers. Even if the chit acted as a common gutter wench. "Forgive me, son, but how shall you be marrying a chit already wed to another?"

"As you know, the earl is dead, leaving me free to marry the countess. And wed we shall, mother." Her son eyed her as if she were his enemy. And it quite made her poor heart ache, it did.

"Son, this is precipitating indeed," she offered, at a loss.

"I believe you mean to say 'precipitous', mother," corrected her imperious, hateful son. "I suspect that it may be to yourself. However, there are other circumstances that render a union imperative."

"Imperative?" Her heart felt weak.

"The rooms shall be prepared for the countess and her family."

Never let it be said that she did not know her duty. The dowager raised her chin. "They are being prepared as we speak. Where shall we place the Lady Scarbrough?"

"In the east wing as well." Thornton bowed again. "It is essential that we maintain propriety."

Her smile was cold. "Then I do not understand your pressing nuptials, son."

"You are aware, of course, that the countess and her husband had been estranged?"

"Indeed."

"Then let me be perfectly frank, mother. Cleo is, quite possibly, carrying my heir."

Her heart began a dance to rival the waltz. "Possibly?" She cast a glance at her daughter, who watched the exchange, enrapt. "Bella, go to your chambers at once."

"*Maman?*"

"She may remain, mother." Her son's voice matched the iciness of his smile. "I am, after all, the head of this family. If I say she stays, she does. Bella has every right to know that Cleo and I will wed. She is of age."

"Who has created this abominable carelessness within you?" Desperation bubbled up within her. She was fast losing whatever tenuous grasp of control she'd maintained upon her family and she did not savor the sensation.

"I am the head of this family," he repeated, impassive. "When I say that Cleo is possibly carrying my heir, I mean to say that she certainly carries my child, but whether it shall be male or female remains to be seen. You will oversee the preparation of rooms for her entire family yourself. You will see that she is treated to the utmost respect. And you will never show a bit of displeasure."

"Of course," she bit out. "She is with child for certain, Alexander?"

"Yes."

The world swam before her and then it disappeared.

ONE WEEK INTO her rather ignoble return to Marleigh Manor, Cleo swore she'd go mad. The servants slipped about the house in silence, fearing, no doubt, an attack by the dowager, who could be heard shrieking from even the east wing. Yesterday, it had been the state of her eggs, then a fine sheen of dust having the nerve to settle over the late marquis's portrait, then a slouching maid.

For Cleo's part, the dowager refused to speak to her or be present in the same room as her. It was not a secret that she took all her meals in her rooms to avoid Cleo. Lady Bella cut Cleo with accusatory glares. Thornton, despite his admonition to her in the carriage for the impersonal nature of her conversation, treated her with the polite care he would show an utter stranger.

To compound matters, it rained for five days straight. When the weather finally cleared, she took the opportunity to wrap herself in a heavy shawl and make her way to the garden. She had not gone a few steps before Thornton's voice stopped her.

"Cleo, darling. Should you be about in this weather?"

With a sigh, she turned to find him striding toward her with great purpose. He was beautiful, his black hair falling over his eyes like some sort of gothic hero. In just a week, he would be hers. She tried to take comfort in that knowledge.

"Why should I not be?" She gave him her best smile,

hoping it might soften him.

"It's damn cold, for one thing." He approached her and rubbed his hands down over her arms as if to warm her. "With all the rain, it's so bloody damp I'm afraid you'll catch a lung fever."

"It's not as cold or damp as that, Alex."

"Come inside," he urged, pulling her back to the house without awaiting her response.

"No." She planted her feet on the stone walk, feeling mulish. "I won't."

He stiffened, his mouth going flat in that way it did whenever he was angered. "Have a care for the child, if not for yourself."

"I am having a care for the child. I'm wearing my warmest wrap even though I am quite warm, in truth. I have withstood all that I can of being trapped inside those walls."

He frowned. "You do not find the east wing to your liking?"

"It is quite lovely. You misunderstand me. I don't object to your home but to the stifling air within it."

"You're overheated, then?" Concern shaded his voice. "Perhaps you're with fever. I assure you I find the air perfectly temperate."

Really. She wanted to stomp her foot. Thornton was being such a man. How could he not comprehend that being trapped inside a home with one family who loathed her and another that smothered her would make her mad? If her mother brought her one more tea, she'd die of...of...tea overconsumption. Yes. That had to be possible. Did it not?

"Cleo? If you're with fever, I shall have my physician here in a trice. I won't have any unnecessary harm coming to you or the babe." He caught her elbow. "Come inside before it worsens."

She wrenched her arm from his grasp. "I do not have a fever, you duffer. Nor am I overheated. When I said I found the air stifling, I meant to say your mother can be heard throughout the house raving at the servants like a madwoman, yet she obviously abstains from my company at all meals as if I were no better than a dairy maid come to snag her son for his guineas. Your sister despises me. My family follows me everywhere—I dare say to keep a safe distance maintained between your mother and myself—and when you see me, you look at me as if you don't know me."

"Calm yourself." His tone turned irritable. "You'll harm the child."

"Now I am not allowed to experience emotions, either?" She was incredulous at his gall. "Pray, Thornton, make a list of what I may and may not do as your property."

"You're overset." He reached for her again.

"Damn right I'm overset." To emphasize her point, she kicked a flower pot that contained some sort of dead-looking herb. Pain radiated from her big toe to her ankle and up her leg. Moaning, she hopped about, wishing for once she'd gotten the best of her temper.

"Is it the babe?"

"It's my bloody toe." She was shrieking and cursing, but she found she didn't care. Quite possibly, she'd broken the dratted appendage and her husband-to-be was an utter ass.

"Stop that hobbling about." Having issued the order, he scooped her up into his arms as if she weighed no more than her hat. "I'll take you inside so I can have a look and see what you've done with your temper."

Gritting her teeth against the pain, she held her tongue and allowed herself to be carted back into the house. After all, if shaking off the shackles of being trapped inside the house had been lovely, being in Alex's arms was lovelier still. She linked her hands around his neck and admired the manly slash of his jaw. The delicious scent that was his alone teased her senses and she couldn't refrain from pressing her face to the crook of his neck and inhaling deeply. If they passed anyone, she didn't know—her face was pressed to his skin.

He cleared his throat. "Cleo, you're kissing my neck."

Dear me, so she was. His voice sounded pained, but she recognized the banked desire, knew she could claim it as her own. She suddenly forgot why she'd been infuriated by him. Her tongue darted out to taste his warm skin.

This time, he coughed. "You're, er, licking me."

"I'm doing no such thing," she lied.

The pain in her toe lessened considerably. She missed him. She missed being free to touch and kiss him as she pleased. They couldn't go on being at sixes and sevens with one another forever. Perhaps she knew how to move them beyond their impasse after all.

She had an idea. "I feel horridly ill of a sudden, Alex."

"What?" He looked down at her, questioning.

"I need to lie down."

"I'll take you to your chamber." He lengthened his stride.

"No." She made her voice become thready and weak. "It's too far."

"My chamber," he said decisively. "You can rest there."

Much better. She hid her satisfied smile against his solid chest, kept her ear to his heart, listening to its steady beats. Before long, they had made their way to his rooms. She heard him barking an order at someone to fetch her some tea and then they were alone inside, door closed. With gentle care, he deposited her on his bed, then hovered, looking worried.

"Shall I call for the doctor?"

"No." She leveraged herself into a half-sitting position against his pillows.

Grimly, he rucked up her skirts to reveal her ankles. "Which foot did you hurt?"

"The right one." Surreptitiously, she inched her gown higher, leaving a generous swath of her calves exposed as well. Thank heavens she'd worn her pretty silk stockings that morning.

Thornton unbuttoned her shoe and removed it, allowing it to drop to the floor with a thud. His large hands encompassed her small foot, tenderly moving it about. "Where does it hurt, darling?"

"A bit higher." Goodness, she was growing rather adept at prevarication. His hands crept to her ankle and warm, lazy heat slid through her.

"Your ankle?" He glanced up from his task, eyes darkening. "I thought you said you hurt your toe."

"I was mistaken." She raised her hem again.

His palms skimmed up over her calf, approaching her knee. "Where does it pain you?"

"Everywhere," she whispered, gaze fastened to him.

"God, Cleo." Thornton's hands were traveling without provocation now, gliding past her knee to the delicate skin of her thigh. His fingers caught in her garters and unfastened them. "I'm about to lose control."

"Then lose it," she dared.

He lowered his head like a supplicant and placed a kiss on her bare skin. "I don't want to hurt you or the babe."

"You can only do that by holding yourself apart from me." She reached out to him, running her fingers through his thick, beautiful hair. "I know you're doing your utmost to see to my every comfort. But without you, I find I'm quite miserable." Cleo sniffed, trying not to embarrass herself with a display of tears.

"You are not without me, love." He met her gaze. "I'm right here before you."

Of course he was before her, the dolt. Did he not understand the difference between physical and emotional presence? "You are not here. You've grown cold and I...I miss you, Alex. I need you to come back to me."

"It was you who left."

"Will you punish me forever?"

Thornton yanked his hand from her leg as if he'd been

scalded. His jaw clenched as he stood. "Were you lying about your toe?"

"No. It hurt like the devil." He had begun pacing, so she rose from the bed. "But not as much as my heart hurts."

He stilled, but kept his back to her. Cleo toed off her other shoe and followed him, wrapping her arms about him from behind. "I love you," she told him. "I have always loved you, from the first. It seems that where you're concerned I've made foolish decision after foolish decision and if you do not trust me, I cannot blame you. But know that I love you, with all my heart. I couldn't have found a better husband or a finer man than you. I do not deserve you."

He kept silent for what seemed like forever. Had she revealed too much? Did he no longer care? Before any more questions could pass through her mind, he turned in her arms. "I've been an ass."

The bald pronouncement startled her. He cupped her face in his palms and kissed her. It was deep, thorough, hungry. It was a kiss that spoke to the torment within him, the confusion, the anger, the—dare she think it—love. Her tongue played against his. He tasted like the hot chocolate he must have had with his breakfast and desire. Her fingers were in his hair again, his hands pushing her wrap from her shoulders and going for the fastenings of her bodice.

HE STILL LOVED her. Damn it, of course he did. Always had, always would. But he had wanted to hold onto his anger and use it as a weapon against her. He was afraid of everything when it came to Cleo, that he couldn't trust her, that she didn't love him enough, that he loved her too much. Christ, he did love her too much. It was as if he carried a giant splinter in his chest each moment he spent knowing she was somewhere within Marleigh Manor and yet separated from him.

He wanted to consume her, taste her every inch of sweet

skin, bury himself inside her so deep he never had to leave. Of course that wasn't possible. But his cock wanted him to at least give it a go. He heard fabric tearing, but he was so bent on ravaging her delicious mouth that he didn't stop to see the damage he'd done. It seemed he had a habit of destroying her attire.

Her hands came between them abruptly and he was dimly aware of her pushing him away. He broke the drugging kiss with reluctance, his breathing ragged and raw as he looked down at her beautiful upturned face. Truly, no woman could compare. Her pale skin was flushed with passion, her full mouth swollen from his kiss.

"What is it?" he demanded, not feeling particularly generous at the moment. He hadn't seen her naked in ages and all he could think of was how beautiful it would be to weigh her delicious breasts in his palms and suck the tips into his mouth until she was as far gone as he was.

"There's a servant at the door," she murmured. "I believe it's the tea you requested."

"To hell with the frigging tea," he yelled in the general direction of the door. "Go away and don't come back or I'll see you sacked."

"Alex!"

"I don't give a shite, Cleo. I'm starving for you."

"You certainly have not been acting it."

Ah, ever a ready tongue. That was his Cleo. Always ready with a retort, an argument. She was not a manageable female, never would be. Fortunately, he knew how to silence her. He kissed her again and pulled her bodice completely open. The chemise was short work and she happily wore no corset. His hands were filled with warm, soft flesh and his prick was stiff as hell.

"I love you." The words left him in a rush, a mad release. He couldn't run from it any longer. He kissed her neck, her collarbone, her ear. "Promise me you'll never leave me again, my darling."

"I promise." Her fingers scrabbled over his buttons, yanking them from their moorings. "I love you, Alex."

They did away with one another's clothing and fell to the bed in a frenzy. He'd wanted to savor her, to go more slowly, but it wasn't going to happen that way. He tongued her nipple, her answering moan going straight to his groin. With his knee, he nudged her legs apart. His fingers found her wet flesh. His thumb worked her sensitive nub while his fingers teased in and out of her passage, working her into a crescendo of passion.

"I can't wait," he muttered into the curve of her breast.

"Nor can I." She moaned again. "Hurry, my love."

He didn't need further encouragement. Bracing himself over her, he sheathed himself in one, sharp thrust. Her breath hissed and he felt quite certain his heart stopped. She undulated her hips beneath him, bringing him deeper, tightening around him and nearly making him climax instantly.

"Jesus." He was going to embarrass himself. A month without being in her bed and he'd turned into a bloody callow youth. "You're going to kill me, woman."

"I can't think of a better way to die."

Her smile was gorgeous, fey, alluring. He kissed it from her lips, claiming her with his mouth the same way he claimed her with his body. They began a rhythm together, straining against one another, almost violent in their mutual desire to possess one another completely. Again and again, he pumped his cock into her until he recognized the hitch in her breath, the change in her smoky green eyes, her soft, breathy moan of pleasure. She tightened around him sending him climaxing along with her.

He rolled to his side, spent, taking her with him and molding her body to his. They were mutually breathless. He felt as if he'd been thrown from a moving train and had miraculously survived the fall.

"Don't leave me ever, darling." He dropped a kiss on her flushed cheek. "I'll send my mother to the dower house and give my sister a dressing down. I can't lose you again." There was a slight, perfect curve to her soft belly now, the first sign of the changes that were about to unfold for them.

"I don't want you to pack off your family for me, though sending away the dowager is indeed a tempting offer." She sighed. "I think she shall just have to accustom herself to me as I will accustom myself to her. When the child comes, she may soften."

Thornton thought that was rather generous of her, since he'd known his mother for his entire life and the old bird had never softened a bit. Instead of pointing that out, he dropped another kiss on her cheek, nuzzling her silky skin. "Have I told you that I love you?"

"Mmm."

"And that you have the most brilliant breasts I've ever seen?" He cupped one as he asked.

"At least on two separate occasions. You're a naughty man." But there was a smile in her voice that said she didn't mind.

"It's why you love me."

She rolled over in his arms and kissed him. "One of many reasons why I love you, my darling man."

CLEO DECIDED SHE was in desperate need of a rapprochement. After reconciling with Thornton, her gray life had suddenly turned bright again. But there remained a blight—his family. She decided, unpleasant though she may find it, that she wanted to begin her marriage and her child's life in a home at peace rather than at war. Which meant she needed to seek the lioness in her den.

Two days before the wedding, she at last mustered the courage to meet the dowager in her own rooms. Well, to be specific, meet was not precisely the word. Surprised her was far more apt, because Cleo chose the precise moment that servants were taking the dowager her afternoon tea to slip into her private sitting room along with them.

Thornton's mother was seated on a sofa like a queen in repose, her gray hair in a tight upsweep, wearing her customary dove-gray gown and lace cap. Her nostrils flared as she caught sight of Cleo, but she said nothing. Cleo dipped into her most formidable curtsy as the servants delivered the tea.

While they prepared the tray, Cleo waited for the dowager to invite her to seat herself. The good lady did not, leaving Cleo to sit on an opposite chair. She waited for the servants to depart before speaking.

"My lady, I hope that you are well."

The dowager harrumphed. "I am as well as can be expected, given the circumstances."

Cleo held her tongue at the jibe. "I understand that this all must be transpiring quite abruptly to you—"

"Abrupt, of course it is abrupt!" The dowager's voice was shrill enough to break glass. "My son was on a golden path before you meddled in his life. Now you have conveniently gotten yourself with child. How nice for you. How…secure."

She would not allow the woman to spark her fury. She would not. She would remain calm. Cleo took a deep, deep breath before responding. "Your barbs are well-deserved. I acted rashly with your son, as did he with me. However, I would have you know that any indiscretion on our part was the sole product of our love for one another."

The dowager poured her own tea but did not offer any to Cleo. She sniffed. "Indeed."

"I love your son," she said with quiet strength, "and your son loves me. I realize I may not be the ideal match for him.

Certainly, he could have found a better mate than myself. But I am honored that he has chosen me as his wife."

"Has he chosen you, then? I had not realized."

"You have every right to chastise." Cleo inclined her head. "Pray do not hold my love for him against your son, or against your grandchild. You may dislike me as you please, but in a few short months, there will be a new de Vere in this family. I would have you be a part of the child's life."

"Gracious of you, Lady Scarbrough." The dowager's voice remained frigid.

Frustration shot through her. Really, must the woman be so intractable? "I am not striving for grace." She stood. "I am to be your son's wife. You are not required to like me. You are not even required to tolerate me. Let it be known, however, that I love your son more than anything in this world. And I love this child we've created together. I hope you can respect that, if not me."

As she turned to leave, the dowager halted her. "Wait."

Cleo paused and half-turned. "Yes?"

The dowager pressed her lips together. "You are not the wife I would have chosen for Alexander. Nor are you in the least suitable. In truth, I do not like you very much at all. But even I must admit that you exhibit a rare bravado—to your credit—in seeking me out."

Cleo curtsied again. "Thank you, my lady." She gritted her teeth on the words, determined to maintain her polite, cool mask.

The dowager muttered something unintelligible beneath her breath.

Cleo raised a brow. "My lady?"

She positively huffed. "I will try." She hesitated. "I shall try to find you more agreeable. Still, you have so much to learn. For starters, you must cease looking so vulgar and American in dress. I shall take you to my *modiste*."

And procure her a set of dresses in varying shades of gray?

Cleo nearly shivered in horror at the prospect. With considerable effort, she squelched any objections rising within her.

"Thank you, my lady." Hiding her smile, Cleo quit the room. It was a small acknowledgment to be sure, but it was something, a small step on the path to becoming a true part of the de Vere family. She owed that much, after all, to Alex and to the babe.

CLEO FOUND BELLA in the library, a room where the younger woman frequently spent her days. If she had to guess, Cleo would say it was to hide from the dowager. But she'd not guess it aloud.

Bella was reading a volume of Shakespeare when she entered. In truth, she was sniffling into it. Understanding instantly crept into her mind. Mr. Whitney had left prior to Cleo's return—he'd been called back to America for some urgent business, Alex said. Cleo had not mistaken the shared glances between Bella and Mr. Whitney, she was sure of it now. More to the point, the volume of Shakespeare was quite upside down in Bella's hands. But Cleo ought not to mention that aloud either.

"Lady Bella." She smiled at her sister-to-be. "Have you a moment?"

Bella raised red-rimmed eyes above the volume. "I suppose."

"Excellent." Cleo seated herself in a wingback chair. "I'm sorry to interrupt."

"No."

She adjusted her skirts. "Excuse me?"

"I meant to say that you're not sorry to interrupt me, or you would not have done so." Bella's gaze was as direct and frank as her words. "Nevertheless, I am at your mercy."

"That is not true, my dear. You are free to leave the room if you prefer no company to mine."

Bella shook her head, making her black curls dance. "I assume you've sought me out for a reason?"

Cleo shifted her skirts again. "Indeed I have." She paused, weighing her options. Although she had meant to propose a tentative friendship, seeing Thornton's sister distressed led her to believe there was something more important afoot. "Are you well, Bella?"

"Yes, of course. Why do you ask?"

"It is just that your book is upside down and your eyes are quite red and puffy." She delivered her observation with as much kindness as possible. "Is it Mr. Whitney?"

"No," Bella denied with far too much haste.

"You need not confide in me, but I do want you to know that should anything ever arise…that is to say, if you are in trouble, I will be here for you."

"You're too kind." Bella stiffened. "Mr. Whitney and I are merely friends, however."

"Very well. Then I shall keep my thoughts to myself on the matter and turn to my real reason for seeking you out."

"Do tell." Even distraught, Bella had the same biting sarcasm as Thornton.

"It is merely that, since I'm to wed your brother and the two of us will see one another regularly, I think we should be friends."

"Do you love my brother?" Bella demanded.

"Utterly." Cleo did not dither on her response. "He's arrogant, stubborn and absolutely too good for me. But I don't care."

"I suspect he feels the same for you." Bella's tone was grim, but she was no longer glaring at Cleo as if she were about to kick her pet puppy.

"Will you try to give me a chance to prove I'm not the shrew you think me?"

An enigmatic smile kicked up the corner of her mouth. "Perhaps, Lady Scarbrough."

"Then that is all I can ask of you." Cleo rose. "Please remember what I said, Bella, for I meant it. If ever you find yourself in trouble, you may depend upon me for assistance."

"Thank you." Tears welled up in Bella's eyes. "I'm fine, I assure you. Please go now."

A heaviness lifted off her chest, she left Bella to her upside down Shakespeare and her tears for the lover she'd lost. Young love. Cleo sighed. She knew it well. Strange to think of how it could, on rare occasions, endure. Happy to think of how it could endure. For with Thornton, she had rediscovered the love she'd once had and more. They were both older, wiser, more mature. Still bent on making mistakes, it was true. But it was different for them now. Better. Each day was a blessing.

"There you are, my darling." A strong arm caught her about the waist and pulled her from behind into a hard, lean body.

"Alex." She spun in his arms and rose on her tiptoes for a slow, deep kiss. "I think I have charmed your lions, at least enough so that they will not attempt to eat me for their supper."

Laughing, he kissed the tip of her nose. "If you've survived my mother and sister, anything more that comes our way will be naught but flotsam." He kissed her neck. "I adore the scent of lavender."

"Mmm." She was too busy savoring the delicious sensations coursing through her to respond in a coherent manner.

His mouth was hot and demanding, licking a deliberate, wicked path to the hollow of her throat. "Would you care to charm me next, my love?"

With a giggle, she sank her fingers into his hair and pulled him to her for another kiss. "Of course, my darling man. I thought you'd never ask." Hand in hand, they ducked through the corridor, heading toward his chamber.

Epilogue

London, five months later

CLEO'S BROW KNOTTED in concentration as she worked on the sketchbook before her. "Darling, you're moving."

"I can't help it." Thornton grinned at his wife—he was sure—like an idiot. Wife. That word still felt wonderful on his tongue and bounding about in his mind. She was his and he bloody well liked it. "You're adorable when you frown, love."

She huffed a sigh, looking even more adorable. Bridget had done her hair up in the way he loved, high on her head with a few glossy curls coming down to brush her cheeks. The roundness of her stomach could no longer be hidden beneath accommodating gowns, but she had never looked lovelier in the soft, almost Grecian drapes of the Worth gown she wore this morning.

"Alex, how am I to complete this sketch before Bump is born when you refuse to cooperate?"

They had named the baby Bump one evening while lying together in his enormous bed at Marleigh Manor. Cleo, he'd discovered, loved to chat away into the early morning hours and he found he rather looked forward to their rambling late night conversations.

He'd kissed her burgeoning belly. "I can't wait for him or her to arrive, my love."

Cleo scrunched up her adorable nose. "We cannot forever call the poor darling 'him or her'."

"What do you propose, then?" His hands smoothed a

loving trail over her soft skin and the object of their conversation chose that moment to offer protest in the form of a sharp little elbow.

"Bump," Cleo had said and they'd laughed at the absurdity together. But the name had stuck.

"Apologies to both you and Bump," he said now, setting aside the papers he'd long since given up on perusing. She'd been his for five precious months and still, going to sleep with her and waking up with her and even sharing something as insignificant as breakfast together…well, it made him nearly maudlin. He was happy. He was in love. He was a husband and a proud papa to be. Life had never been more fulfilling.

"You're being most difficult." Cleo pouted. "I shall tell Bump all about it after she is born."

Thornton rose from his chair, dropped his *serviette* onto his plate and strode to her side of the table. As a general rule, he preferred to spend as much of his waking and sleeping hours touching his wife as possible. With an ease borne of practice, he scooped her from her chair and sat down, settling her lovely derriere in his lap.

He dropped a kiss on the delicious warmth of her neck. Mmm. Lavender. "And how do you know Bump is to be a girl?"

"I prefer to alternate." She turned and met his mouth for a kiss. "It gives me a sense of fairness."

Thornton couldn't help himself. He cupped her delicate jaw and stole another kiss from her lips. "Your reasoning is beginning to sound a bit like the dowager's."

"You're an evil man." Cleo raised a hand to caress his cheek. "We have created a reluctant peace between us, your mother and I and your sister as well."

Thornton had to acknowledge that somehow, seemingly against all reason, Cleo was making remarkable inroads with his termagant of a mother and his stubborn sister. He had to admit that he was pleased. Cleo was proving herself to be a far better partner and wife than he had even anticipated. Oh, they had their minor rows, but they were…blissful. Christ, he never thought he'd use that word to describe anything, but there it was. Maudlin sentiment. Even society had embraced them both, eager to cast Scarbrough as the villain and eager to toast a rare love match. He'd been able to resume his role in Gladstone's cabinet with nary a hitch.

"I am pleased if you are pleased, darling. And I have learned well that peace is far preferable to war."

"Indeed." She kissed him lingeringly again. Her moss eyes glittered into his. "But our peace will not last long, I fear, for if Bump is anything in nature like you or I, he will have quite the personality."

"I wouldn't have it any other way."

"Oh dear." She touched his face again. "I've gotten charcoal all over your face."

"You've always been a bit of a mess, darling." Grinning, he lowered his mouth to his beloved wife's. "But I love you anyway."

"Mmm." She sank her fingers into his hair. "And I love you, Alexander de Vere."

He slid his hands down over her body to cup her precious belly. Bump delivered a sound kick to his palm. "As does Bump, it would seem."

"As does Bump," she agreed and they proceeded to spend a goodly portion of the morning making creative use of the breakfast table.

"You're a wicked man," Cleo told him breathlessly some time later.

And Thornton, honored Lord of Parliament, leading light of the Liberal Party, trusted confidante to the Prime Minister, loving husband to Cleopatra Harrington de Vere and proud father of one precocious Bump, had to concur.

THE END.

Dear Reader,

Thank you for reading *A Mad Passion*! I hope you enjoyed this first book in my Heart's Temptation series and that Cleo and Thornton's second chance at love touched your heart.

As always, please consider leaving an honest review of *A Mad Passion*. Reviews are greatly appreciated! If you'd like to keep up to date with my latest releases and series news, sign up for my newsletter here or follow me on Amazon or BookBub. Join my reader's group on Facebook for bonus content, early excerpts, giveaways, and more.

If you'd like a preview of *Rebel Love*, Book Two in the Heart's Temptation series, featuring Jesse and Bella, do read on.

Until next time,
Scarlett

Rebel Love
Heart's Temptation Book Two

Lady Bella de Vere's matchmaking mother has vowed to win her a duke and nothing less. But Bella secretly yearns for her brother's enigmatic American friend, Mr. Jesse Whitney, even if he's determined to treat her as nothing more than a younger sister.

A veteran adrift since the Civil War's end, Jesse's been through the fires of hell and back. He knows he should stay far away from his best friend's beautiful sister, but she sees past his façade to the wounded soldier within, and he's sorely tempted to take what should never be his.

Their kisses are scorching, their passion undeniable. But Jesse's bitter past refuses to relinquish its hold on him in more ways than one. Is he strong enough to fight the most important battle of all and win Bella's love forever?

Chapter One

England 1880

BECAUSE HER MOTHER had delayed their arrival at the house party over a briefly misplaced trunk, Bella missed the first day's festivities, but she didn't mind. After settling into her chamber, she ventured through the immense Tudor revival wing in search of the library. No matter where she traveled, the library was always her home. Hostesses no doubt thought her strange as it was ordinarily considered a masculine domain, but Bella didn't care. The dowager had settled in for a nap, and while she'd told her mother she would do the same, she had no intention of sleeping when there was a new collection of books to be scoured.

With the help of a kind footman, she located her quarry. The library was immense, its mahogany walls lined with books. Bella stepped inside and took a deep inhalation of the familiar, comforting scent of leather and paper. She slid her spectacles out of the hidden pocket in her gown and settled them on the bridge of her nose.

"I wonder," she mused aloud as she slowly examined the spines nearest her, "if Lady Cosgrove has any Trollope. Likely not. It wouldn't be my luck. She's probably like Mother and thinks him too fast."

"Interesting," drawled a deep, familiar, honey-slow drawl. "I wonder if you ordinarily hold conversations with yourself."

The book she'd taken off the shelf fell from her fingers to the floor with a loud thump. He was here. She spun about, gaze searching the still seemingly empty room for him. "You have me at a disadvantage, Mr. Whitney. Where in blessed angels' sakes are you?"

"Up here." There was laughter in his tone.

He was in the second level, she realized, following his voice with her eyes. She hadn't known she wasn't alone. Goodness, he must think her an utter featherhead. Of course, of all audiences and much to her embarrassment, it had to be Mr. Whitney. She had not seen him in some time, but even from so far away, she found him as wickedly compelling as ever.

"I'm quite bemused that you've been eavesdropping on my private conversation," she quipped, striving to maintain the pretense she was unaffected. She very much did not want him to think her a fool.

"Perhaps I'm the one who should be bemused." He made his way down the narrow staircase. "I was having a heated debate with myself when you walked in and interrupted it."

She snatched the spectacles from her face as he sauntered toward her, two books in his hands. "Indeed, sir? What debate was that? I confess I didn't hear a single word."

"Poetry or fiction?" He grinned as he reached her and stopped with a respectable distance between them.

Bella couldn't help but notice the way his grin produced a charming divot in his right cheek. His smile transformed his ordinary handsome charm into melting masculine beauty. After all the time she'd spent with her brother's friend over the past few years, she was still not immune to his magnetism. He possessed some indefinable quality she'd never seen in another man. It was as if beneath his polite exterior there was a wildness he barely kept contained. Maybe she was fanciful, but she'd always found him fascinating and even a trifle frightening.

"Who is the poet?" she asked, trying to keep her mind where it belonged. He had no interest in her and he never would. She would ever be his friend's younger sister and she'd accustomed herself to the unwanted role.

"Matthew Arnold." His grin deepened. "I do like your English bards."

"Arnold is a wise choice," she agreed, having harbored a secret love of poetry for years, against her mother's strict edict. "One of my favorite lines is in *Dover Beach*. It's the last stanza, I believe, where he writes, 'Ah, love, let us be true to one another! For the world, which seems to lie before us like a land of dreams, so various, so beautiful, so new, hath really neither joy, nor love, nor light.'"

She was aware his stare was suddenly intense upon her and she flushed, wondering if perhaps she'd shared too much. "I beg your pardon," she hurried to say, "I didn't mean to wax on."

"No need to beg my pardon." He winked at her, lightening the moment. "I like the sound of poetry on your lips."

For some reason, his words sent a delightful heat simmering through her veins. She had an inkling it was caused by his mentioning of her lips. "Thank you. I know the sentiment is a dark one, but I find it terribly compelling just the same."

"Life is dark." There was an underlying emotion in his voice she couldn't define.

Her life had not been, but she had a suspicion his past was indeed marred by darkness. Thornton had said his friend had fought for the Confederacy in the War Between the States. She couldn't even imagine the horrors he'd witnessed in combat. He wore the look of a gentleman well, but she wondered if beneath the polish there hid a deeply tarnished soul.

"What is the fiction title?" she asked, attempting to return their conversation to its earlier levity once more. She didn't want to pry, after all, and she feared her curiosity would get the better of her tongue soon.

"*Our Mutual Friend*." He held up the volume for her

inspection.

"Dickens." She wrinkled her nose. "I must admit I've never been partial to his writing. *Great Expectations* was a vast lot of endless sentences if you ask me."

He laughed, a rich, velvety sound. Her heart kicked into the mad gallop of a runaway mare. Goodness, he really was far too compelling for her composure's sake. Perhaps she had read one too many romantic novels. It was making her maudlin and foolish. She caught herself staring at his mouth.

"I appreciate a lady who knows her mind," he said, his tone low and intimate.

Oh blessed angels' sakes. What to say to that? *Stop staring at him like a duffer*, she ordered her wayward mind. "You're too kind, Mr. Whitney."

"I wouldn't call myself kind." His tone was wry. "I count myself a number of things, but kind isn't one of them."

Her interest was piqued. She'd always known him to be proper and considerate. A perfect gentleman. "Then perhaps you do yourself an injustice."

"If you knew the thoughts in my head, you wouldn't think so."

That intrigued her in a way she knew could be quite dangerous indeed. "What thoughts?"

His gaze dipped to her mouth. "That you're one of the loveliest women I've ever seen."

Her lungs nearly failed her. His pronouncement had a stupefying effect upon her. She wanted to say something flippant or clever but couldn't find the proper words. Instead, she opted for candor. "That's rather a kind thing to say, actually. You've bollixed it up."

"Not truly." His gaze met hers and for the first time in the years she had known him, she recognized the awareness she felt for him reflected back in his eyes. Or at least she hoped she did. "It's the thoughts I haven't said that are the problem."

"I'm sure I shouldn't ask what they are." But it didn't

mean she didn't want to know. Every part of her clamored with curiosity. Oh, how she wanted to know.

"No, you shouldn't, Lady Bella."

She found she rather liked the sound of her given name in his honeyed Virginia drawl.

"You're not playing fair," she accused quietly. "I do so hate suspense. It's why I always flip to the last page of a novel before I start reading it."

He laughed again and his dimple reappeared. "You ruin each book you read?"

She'd never confessed her peculiar habit to anyone before and she wasn't certain why she'd chosen to bestow her secret upon Jesse Whitney just then. But there was no help for it. She'd already said too much.

Bella tried to keep the telltale blush from her cheeks. It wouldn't do for him to know the effect his mere presence had on her. She wasn't fifteen anymore, fresh from the schoolroom. "I prefer to think of it as preparing myself."

Jesse took a step closer to her, still holding the books he'd been discussing. He was impossibly handsome. "Ah, I believe I understand you."

Bella fought the urge to step back in retreat. He was now too near to her to be observing the proprieties any longer and that made her rather nervous. "Indeed?"

He closed the remaining distance between them, absconding with her ability to breathe as he did so. "You seek to avoid an unhappy ending."

She faltered, as shaken by his nearness as she was by his perception. "Perhaps you're right."

"If it's a happy ending you desire, I'm afraid you're doomed to be disappointed in life, my dear." He startled her by sinking abruptly to his knees and retrieving the forgotten book she'd dropped. "Here you are."

As she accepted the volume from him, their fingers brushed. "Thank you." She struggled to appear calm, trying with all her might to remain unaffected. "You sound remarkably cynical, Mr. Whitney."

"Merely older." He winked, breaking the intensity between them. "Think of me as another brother. I'd hate to see your idealism crushed without warning."

Think of me as another brother.

Dear heavens. Another surge of embarrassment washed over her. Was she mistaken, then? Had she been reading more into his words and actions than was truly there? She'd harbored a *tendre* for him for the last four years. First, she had been too young. But now she was a lady grown, and while he was at least ten years her senior, she was far more mature than most ladies who were of an age with her. He was worldly, it was true, but he needn't treat her as if he were a kindly uncle and she a recalcitrant niece running about in skirts above her ankles.

"Once again, you're too kind," she managed past the disappointment lodged in her throat. "But as I already have a brother, I shan't need you to act as one."

"I wouldn't be so certain." He raised a brow. "I've seen the young bucks who are here looking to make matches, and as lovely as you are, I've no doubt you'll need more than one guardian to keep them in check."

She was not amused by his insistence she view him as a protector. Drat him, why couldn't he see her for the lady she'd become? She was not the same miss she'd been when he first met her, a shy girl who sat on her spectacles. "I'm more than capable of looking after myself, Mr. Whitney."

He offered her a half-bow. "Of course you are, my dear."

A strange thing happened to Bella then, to Bella who had to suffer the dowager on a daily basis, to Bella who had infinite amounts of tact and serenity. She lost her patience. "You need not placate me. I'm not a girl in the schoolroom even if you seem determined to treat me as such."

His expression changed, becoming part startled, part

admiring. "I do apologize if I've been offensive."

She remained unmoved by his apology. "It is simply that I am one-and-twenty."

Jesse's smile returned, making him appear almost boyish. "I'm well aware of your age, but you're still naïve to the ways of the world. When I was your age, I'd already been through a war."

She longed to ask him about the black cloud that was always in the room with him, but she didn't dare. "I can hardly be faulted for my country's stability."

"It seems I'm not going to end this particular battle as the victor." He held up the books. "I think I'll take the fiction and the poetry both after all." He bowed again, and this time it was formal and stiff. "Enjoy your afternoon, Lady Bella."

"Thank you, Mr. Whitney." She watched him walk away, consternation mingling with regret. That had not gone as she'd hoped.

Rebel Love is available now!

Don't miss Scarlett's other romances!
(Listed by Series)

Complete Book List
scarlettscottauthor.com/books

HISTORICAL ROMANCE

Heart's Temptation
A Mad Passion (Book One)
Rebel Love (Book Two)
Reckless Need (Book Three)
Sweet Scandal (Book Four)
Restless Rake (Book Five)
Darling Duke (Book Six)
The Night Before Scandal (Book Seven)

Wicked Husbands
Her Errant Earl (Book One)
Her Lovestruck Lord (Book Two)
Her Reformed Rake (Book Three)
Her Deceptive Duke (Book Four)
Her Missing Marquess (Book Five)

League of Dukes
Nobody's Duke (Book One)
Heartless Duke (Book Two)
Dangerous Duke (Book Three)
Shameless Duke (Book Four)
Scandalous Duke (Book Five)
Fearless Duke (Book Six)

Sins and Scoundrels

Duke of Depravity (Book One)
Prince of Persuasion (Book Two)
Marquess of Mayhem (Book Three)
Earl of Every Sin (Book Four)

The Wicked Winters
Wicked in Winter (Book One)
Wedded in Winter (Book Two)
Wanton in Winter (Book Three)
Wishes in Winter (Book 3.5) ~ Available in *A Lady's Christmas Rake*
Willful in Winter (Book Four)
Wagered in Winter (Book Five)
Wild in Winter (Book Six)
Wooed in Winter (Book Seven) ~ Available in *Lords, Ladies and Babies*

Stand-alone Novella
Lord of Pirates

CONTEMPORARY ROMANCE

Love's Second Chance
Reprieve (Book One)
Perfect Persuasion (Book Two)
Win My Love (Book Three)

Coastal Heat
Loved Up (Book One)

About the Author

USA Today and Amazon bestselling author Scarlett Scott writes steamy Victorian and Regency romance with strong, intelligent heroines and sexy alpha heroes. She lives in Pennsylvania with her Canadian husband, adorable identical twins, and one TV-loving dog.

A self-professed literary junkie and nerd, she loves reading anything, but especially romance novels, poetry, and Middle English verse. Catch up with her on her website www.scarlettscottauthor.com. Hearing from readers never fails to make her day.

Scarlett's complete book list and information about upcoming releases can be found at www.scarlettscottauthor.com.

Connect with Scarlett! You can find her here:
Join Scarlett Scott's reader's group on Facebook for early excerpts, giveaways, and a whole lot of fun!
Sign up for her newsletter here.
scarlettscottauthor.com/contact
Follow Scarlett on Amazon
Follow Scarlett on BookBub
www.instagram.com/scarlettscottauthor
www.twitter.com/scarscoromance
www.pinterest.com/scarlettscott
www.facebook.com/AuthorScarlettScott
Join the Historical Harlots on Facebook